THE RODENTIAN CHRONICLES

The Exodus

By: C.T. Fosmire

Acknowledgement

This page is to acknowledge and thank those who have helped me and motivated me to keep going and fulfil my writing career. I'd first like to acknowledge and thank my family who supported me and my decision to become a writer and author. My older brother tried to write his own book when we were children, and because of that, I decided to write my own stories as well. It never really occurred to me to write my own book or even become a published author until after high school, but it was still the foundation that started me on my writing career. My family has always been full of creative people, and I can only hope I've made them proud.

I'd also like to thank the friends I've met along the way, whom many have stood by and encouraged me to keep writing, even when I have felt like I wasn't good enough. Their encouragement and motivation pushed me to be the best writer I could be, and to never give up on my dream. And lastly, I'd also like to show acknowledgement to my editor, Kristina M. Fogle, who has played a major role in helping me launch my writing career. Without her help, it would have taken so much longer to finish my book and even begin publishing my book. We met online and quickly became friends. And when she discovered that I was writing a book series of my own, she was very excited for it. I offered to let her read my book and she fell in love from the first chapter. When I told her that I needed an editor, Kristina immediately offered her assistance. She has been a tremendous help and I am very proud to have her as my editor for this book and many more to come.

Contents

Chapter I

All was quiet in the lab. The lights were off, and everything was dark as there were no windows. The only source of light being from the double doors that led to the hallway outside, which was lit up bright at all times. The lab was a large, rectangular room, with all sorts of contraptions and gadgets, tools and appliances, all for the use of *science.* The room itself was made to fit well over a dozen humans inside, and more than two dozen if they were standing shoulder to shoulder, even with all the furniture inside. Upon entering the room, there were three long tables parallel to each other in front of the doors. They were laden with all sorts of tubes, vials and a large variety of tools assorted across them, most of which were meant to prick, poke and prod at. On the table furthest left was a large tank that was filled a quarter way with water and two platforms closer to the top, with a small bridge that was barely wide enough for a fly to stand on, connecting the two. Just a ways down the row sat another tank, though not as tall, but just as long and twice as wide, with five red lines along the bottom.

Along the left side and far end of the lab were counters lined up against the walls with a tall cabinet at the corner closest to the door and another cabinet at the end at the farthest right corner. Above the counters hung smaller cabinets and shelves filled with books, tools and other varieties held within. A little further in the lab, just past the three tables, was a rather large square table furthest from the door that was more open. On the table was a sizable maze on the left side, with blocks and other wooden shapes of all sizes just outside of it, so that the maze could be taken apart and added to, so as to shape the maze into all sorts of pathways and corridors. On the other side of the table were a set of clear containers that were meant to keep little creatures inside, with handles to move them all about the room with ease.

At the right side of the lab were racks filled with small cages, all lined all along the wall; two hundred and ten to be exact. They were lined up with numbers on the front, each one divided into two side-by-side sections. In each cage on the left side were two mice, one male and one female. The cages on the right were two rats in each cage, one male and one female as well. Most of the small rodents were sound asleep. All except for one in the small cage numbered 1-0-9, where one such little mouse, no more than a year old, tan colored fur and a white underbelly was wide awake. He was staring ahead into the empty laboratory at the only opening in his cage.

The other three walls were blocked off, with only the bars at the top and a water bottle in the left corner hanging down from them through a hole between the bars. A food tray was down at the bottom where they were given tiny pellets to eat. The hole where the tray entered was far too small to squeeze through, he would know, as he tried so many times before. The same went for the water bottle; as he would try to knock it out of place to give him room to climb out of. Unfortunately, the water bottle was connected to a pipe on top, both to keep it in place and to constantly keep the bottle full of water. The little mouse looked around at the other cages above him and then out through the front window to the rest of the lab. It was a sight he had seen for his entire life, at least from what he could remember that is. He didn't know exactly how long he had been sitting there, but he couldn't get to sleep, not with so much on his mind.

For all his life he had known nothing but these four walls, the bars above his head, this lab and the humans who worked in it. He and his fellow rodents had been subjected to the doctor's cruel experiments for as long as he can remember. These experiments mainly consisted of the doctor injecting them with something that would cause great pain to their bodies. Sometimes these alone would kill quite a few of the mice or rats, sometimes even both during the same period. Then after injecting them, the doctor would force them all into more physical experiments, such as placing them in one of those containers and putting weighted equipment on them, where they would then be forced to run for as long as they could with those weights. All while their bodies were in great pain from the serums and other experiments.

The torture didn't stop there. The humans would then place something they called a collar around their necks and force them to make the same trek, but this time they had to run on their hind legs. Every time they would land on their front paws, they would feel a shock throughout their body until they stood back on their hind legs. They would then continue to run for as long as they could. Sometimes they would just stand in one place on their hind legs until they could no longer support their weight and collapse. This is where a lot of mice and rats have died due to exhaustion and continuous shocks. Azalar had seen well over four dozen mice and three dozen rats perish to the doctor's experiments, fifty-three mice and forty-one rats to be exact. Azalar remembered every single one of them. He remembered the looks of fear and anger every one of them had before they finally died. His parents were amongst these faces.

His father died not long after he was born. He remembered the hatred he saw in his father's eyes whenever he gazed upon the humans, especially a certain one. Azalar wasn't sure if it was the serum that killed his father or the testing, but he was certain that his father didn't pass peacefully. His mother died not long after his father. She never made it past the next serum the humans injected in her. She died in great pain, but the last thing he remembered of her was the way she looked back at the cage where he was, fear and sadness in her eyes. Not for herself, but for her dear offspring. In the beginning, he remembered the fear in himself whenever the humans would approach. That fear remained for a long time, until one day everything changed.

"Azalar?" said a feminine voice from behind him, perking Azalar's ear. "Azalar, are you alright?" Azalar turned his head slightly to look upon the owner of that voice. It was Amara, his beloved mate. Her fur was as white as snow and as soft as a cloud.

Azalar had met her four months ago, when the humans placed her within his cage, scared and confused; unaware of what was happening and why she was placed in there. She was three weeks younger than Azalar, still so young and full of fear. She had been taken from an unknown place outside the lab doors, one of the very few to ever do so.

For Amara, this was a terrifying experience; being thrown into a new world and not knowing what was happening. However, for Azalar, it was love at first sight. He had seen many mice in his time in the lab, but never had he seen a mouse as beautiful as she was. It was at that moment that Azalar no longer feared for himself. Soon that fear turned to anger towards the humans, the same anger that he remembered from his father. Now he understood his father's feelings until his final moments. Why he kept fighting until the very end.

Amara was laying down in the little nest that she had made a while back. Azalar loved to lay next to her when they slept, but now his thoughts were not on sleep.

"Just a lot on my mind, my love," he replied. Amara gently stood up and made her way over to her mate, who had returned his gaze at the laboratory.

"What is it, my star?" she asked, but Azalar would not meet her gaze. "You know you can tell me."

"It's nothing, Amara," he said, trying to reassure her. Amara wasn't deterred. She moved around Azalar so that she was in front of him.

"Azalar," she said softly, but once again, Azalar avoided her eyes. Amara gently placed her paw under his chin and motioned him to meet her gaze. "Azalar, please. Tell me what's on your mind." Azalar stared into those wonderful eyes that he loved so much, and he knew that he now had no choice but to speak his mind. With his gaze downward and a heavy sigh, he finally spoke.

"I can't take this torture anymore, my fréfil," he said in a low voice.

"I can't stand the thought of seeing them tomorrow torturing us with their tools and their games." Azalar returned his gaze back to her.

"I can't bear the thought of seeing them torture you again." Amara was silent for a moment as she looked into her mate's eyes. Her heart melted at how much Azalar cared for her, but it also broke at seeing him in such anguish. She gently nuzzled her head under his in a loving way.

"I love you, my star." She pulled back to face him once more. "More than Háth knows. You mustn't burden yourself. There is nothing we can do about it. We are their prisoners, and they decide our fate." Azalar narrowed his eyes.

"I can't accept that, Amara," he very nearly shouted. "I won't accept that!" Amara gave her lover a sympathetic look but shook her head.

"I'm sorry, Azalar, but there's no point in dwelling on this." She turned away and headed back to her sleeping place. "Best to just get some sleep before tomorrow. We will need all our strength." After nuzzling into the nest, she closed her eyes and drifted off to sleep. Azalar remained where he was, continuing to stare into the lab. It was nights like these that he would remember the stories that his mother told to him when he was a pup.

"My son, have I told you the story of the outside World?" asked a feminine voice.

"No, mother," said a young mouse pup.

"It is where we come from, and it is made by the great Háth."

"Who's Háth?"

"Háth is the great God of our whole world; he created everything that we see. He gifted us a wonderful world. Then we squandered his great gift, and now we are punished for it."

"What happened, Mother?" asked the young mouse pup.

"In the beginning, there was darkness. There was no sun, and no earth; not even a single star in the sky. There was nothing. Then Háth, seeing the universe so black and empty, shed a single tear. That one tear became Light. Light that would then become the Sun. Háth had created light that would shine down upon the earth, from which He made from His pfetta."

"His droppings?" said the young mouse.

"Yes. He gathered his droppings together and created the World. Yet, even then, Háth still felt that the world was empty. So, he created the seas and the lands with endless green grass, as well as the tall,

luscious trees, long rivers that flowed endlessly across the land, and enormous mountains that stretched so high up that you couldn't see the top. Even with all these wonderful things, Háth still thought the world empty. So, he created all the living creatures of the World, known as the Children of Háth; which include us, my dear son. And for many years, all of Háth's children lived in harmony with one another. Over the years, Háth's children became too arrogant; too prideful, that they began to close their hearts to Háth. Yet, none more so than the mighty Roda."

"The Roda?" asked the young mouse. "Who are the Roda, Mother?"

"The Roda were our ancestors," Azalar's mother mouse answered. "They were giant rodents that stood tall and proud. They were among the most numerous of Háth's children. They stood many times higher than we do now. Some say that they stood almost as tall as humans."

"Wow!" Azalar said in amazement.

"The Roda were extraordinary," Azalar's mother continued. "They built such large nests that they towered over any tree and spread far across the World. And the greatest among the Roda was named Ezralar."

"Ezralar?" the young pup asked. "That sounds like my name." Azalar's mother smiled down at her young pup.

"That's right," his mother said. "You were named after the greatest of the Roda. It was because of him that the Roda grew to thrive. When the Roda were young and few and first learning to survive in the World, Ezralar, with the guidance of Háth Himself, rose up and led them to a new home, a place of endless fields of grain and bereft of fear."

"Just like in Jaina's song!" Azalar exclaimed happily with a gleam in his eye. The mother mouse chuckled at her son's behavior.

"Yes, Azalar. Just like in Jaina's song. Ezralar led his fellow Roda to build a mighty home for all. For that, he was remembered for all time as the great Theo, chief of all the Roda. With his guidance, they were able to thrive longer and farther than any one of Háth's children had before. After that, Ezralar had many children, and their children had children, and their children had children. Soon the Roda had spread far and wide, across the world. And the Roda were later known as the greatest among the Children of Háth. Yet as the years drew on, the Roda began to rely less and less on Ezralar and Háth's teachings. This led to the Roda becoming distant from Háth and becoming too prideful. That pride caused the Roda to think of themselves as superior and felt that they had no further need of Háth or his wisdom. Then, the other Children of Háth followed their lead and turned away from Him.

"This enraged Háth, for He had granted them life and paradise. So as punishment, Háth created another being that would rule over all the earth and his children: Man."

"Man?" Azalar repeated.

"Yes. Man was created to punish the Children of Háth for their arrogance. They would be Man's to do with as they pleased. They would be his food, his clothes and his tools. However, Háth was not so cruel that he would leave his children defenseless. For he granted each of his children a special gift so that they may defend themselves or even hide from Man. Some he gifted with flight; other speed, and others claws. But as the Children of Háth tried to survive against Man's cruelty, many began to turn on one another. Fighting amongst themselves, some even eating each other as a means of survival. As for us, my dear son, because we were the first to turn away from Háth, he forced us low to the ground.

"He took away our great stature and made us the lowly beings that we are today. However, even though it was a punishment for our pride, it was also a way for Háth to protect us and allow us to hide under Man's nose. We could crawl in between the cracks in their homes, eat the crumbs that they left behind. However, to punish us further, so that we may never unite again, Háth divided us into many beings. Some larger and some smaller. The most numerous were the small mice and the larger rats, who were the direct descendants of the mighty Roda. And from there, we were all forced to live under the terrible rule of Man."

"Is that why we're in these cages, Mother?" the young pup asked. "And why Father is no longer with us?"

"Yes, my son. Through their arrogance, they squandered the great gift that Háth had granted us. We must now pay the price of our ancestors. But this won't be forever. One day we will be free of this place. And we will see the green grass and blue skies again; and feel the fresh air rushing through our fur. But we must keep faith, my son; never lose faith. For Háth is a kind spirit and does love us dearly. And one day we will redeem ourselves to Háth and he will grant us a way to live in freedom; just as the mighty Roda did in ages past."

"When will that happen, Mother?" Azalar asked. "When will we get to see the endless fields of grain?" His mother paused for a moment, a small gleam in her eyes, before she smiled and nuzzled him close.

"I don't know, my son. But I do know that when the time is right, Háth will show us the way. And when that day comes, we will live in the sun once again, no longer hiding in the shadows; living in fear of the humans. And I believe it will be you who will lead us there."

"Me?" young Azalar asked.

"Yes, Azalar. I truly believe that you will lead us to freedom. Remain strong, my son. Be brave and remain faithful. If you do that, there is nothing that you can't do. And always remember, no matter what happens, I will always love you. And I will always be with you."

This was the last story that she told before she died. Azalar remembered it well. He often dreamed as a young pup of leading his people out of this harrowing place. He would even imagine himself as the great Ezralar himself. Now staring out into the lab as he was, he knew what a foolish dream it was. If he wanted to free himself and his loved ones out of this lab, he couldn't rely on dreams and stories. He closed his eyes and took a deep breath.

"I swear by Háth," Azalar whispered to himself, "I will find a way to free us." It was then that he heard a deep chuckle come from the cage next to him in the other section of the lab. A soft sound of shuffling caught Azalar's attention, and he pricked his ears up to listen closer.

"Don't get your hopes up, little mouse," said a low voice. "Háth has no place here." Azalar knew exactly who it was and quickly walked over to the far left end of his cage to get closer to the voice. He looked up at the bars and tilted his head.

"Doesn't seem much like a rat to give up so easily, Ragath." Ragath was a giant rat, the largest in the entire lab. His fur was black as darkness and had many scars over his body. He also had a strong willed temper to add to his demeanor. Ragath was amongst the oldest rats in the lab. He was also one of the strongest. All the experiments and serums had done a number on him, but they also allowed him to live much longer than many of the other rodents in the lab. How old he truly was, no one could say for certain. Not even Nikamius, who was the oldest rodent in the lab, knew how old he was. Ragath was brought into the lab one day; and at that point, he couldn't have been more than a year old. It had been two years since then, yet he still looked like he was in his prime. Azalar saw him only a few times in this place, but every time he did, he was still impressed by the massive rat. Ragath let out a small grunt.

"I have been around much longer than any mouse or rat in this hell," he said. "I have tried to escape time and time again and have failed every time. What makes you think that a worthless, little mouse like you has any chance?" Azalar didn't let his words bother him. Instead glanced back at his sleeping mate.

"Because I have someone worth fighting for," he replied. Ragath let out a low chuckle once more.

"We've all had someone worth fighting for, little mouse," he chortled. "We've all had something to drive us on. But in the end, it is all for naught. It doesn't really matter." Azalar narrowed his eyes.

"So, you have given up?"

"I didn't say that I would stop fighting," Ragath hissed. "I'm saying that there's no chance in this hell that you will ever escape with your mate. And the sooner you accept that, little mouse, the sooner you and your mate will get on with your little lives."

"This isn't much of a life, Ragath!" Azalar hissed in a hushed tone, trying not to wake Amara. "I want to have a decent life with my fréfil, but I can't have that in this place. I do not want to bring pups into this place only to be tortured for the rest of their lives."

"Then you best get on with your escape then, little mouse," Ragath mocked. "Or you be prepared to live a very short life. Because only Háth knows how much longer these humans will keep you around if you don't." Azalar then heard shuffling come from the cage next to him as Ragath moved away towards his nest.

"Just tell me one thing, Ragath," Azalar said. The shuffling stopped. "What are you fighting for?" There was a long silence as Azalar stared up at the bars above and thought that Ragath wasn't going to answer him.

"Myself, little mouse," Ragath said softly. "Myself." With that, Ragath left Azalar alone. This talk hadn't made him feel any better. In fact, it made him feel worse. It made him feel like there was no hope at all. But he shook his head of these thoughts and realized that Ragath was just trying to get into his head. Ragath hadn't given up his fight, so why should he?

Azalar turned and walked on his four legs towards his mate Amara, where he cuddled up next to her and nuzzled her close. There, he slowly drifted off to sleep, hoping that he and the rest of them would make it through tomorrow's torture.

Chapter II

Azalar's mind had been anything but peaceful. All throughout the night, he tossed and turned in the nest. His dreams were filled with the endless torture that he and his fellow mice and rats had endured for most of their lives. Sharp needles sticking into him, blades cutting into his body and tearing him apart. Being forced to run as fast as he could in these mazes and getting electrocuted whenever he made the wrong turn. Always standing above him were the humans. The same ones that have been there for as long as he could remember. Those same faces that they always had, staring down at him, not caring of the pain, and suffering that he must endure.

What was worse than having to endure that torture, was when he was put back in his cage and forced to watch so many others having to suffer it as well. Hearing the screams and cries of his fellow captives, that was the worst part. Then, he heard the screams of a familiar voice. Azalar turned in his cage to see his fréfil, Amara, tied down on a slab and a human above her, slicing her open. Every cut of the blade let out a blood curdling scream from Azalar's mate. Azalar tried to call out to her, but no sound escaped his throat. He then tried to break through the walls of his prison. Even though the walls were clear and see through, as if it was only glass, he could not break through. Repeatedly, he would smash his body against the walls, trying desperately to get to his fréfil. Over and over again until his bones cracked, and his body could no longer move, but still, he did not give up. He tried to claw at the cage walls, but it had little effect. Until, finally he could no longer hear the screams of his fréfil. He looked over to where she was, but what he saw was his mate completely torn apart, limbs and organs placed all over the slab. Her head facing in his direction, with her cold eyes staring back at him.

Pain and agony filled his heart and Azalar tried to scream, but no sound came out. Suddenly darkness swarmed all around him and Azalar found himself floating in an empty void. He turned his head this way and that, searching for Amara.

However, no matter where he looked, there was nothing there but darkness. Then, out of nowhere, a blinding flash appeared in front of him. Azalar averted his eyes from the glaring light for a brief moment, but when he looked back, he was met with a large pair of golden eyes with narrow slit pupils staring back at him from the darkness.

"Amara!" Azalar called out, jolting up from his sleep.

"I'm here, my fréfil," said a calming voice. "I'm here." Azalar looked around to see that he was still in his cage, but it was dark and there were no humans in sight. He then turned to his fréfil. Seeing that she was not harmed, he quickly nuzzled her close. Amara nuzzled back until she could feel the fur on her cheek getting wet. She pulled back to see Azalar with tears in his eyes.

"My love?" she said, her voice full of concern. "My love, are you alright?" Azalar wiped the remaining tears from his eyes with his paws.

"I'm fine, my fréfil," he said. "It was just a nightmare."

"What was it about?"

"It was nothing you need to worry about, love." Azalar tried to put it off as no big deal, but his mate wasn't buying it. Amara gave him a sad look before nuzzling closer to her mate.

"It was the same dream again," she said, a statement rather than a question. She already knew the answer when her mate frowned and said nothing.

"Azalar, you needn't have to worry about me. I'll be fine." Azalar turned his head away.

"I can't stand to see these monsters torment us any longer," he said. "To see them torment you."

"I'll be fine," Amara said again, more confidently. "Everything will be fine. It's nothing we haven't been through before, my love. We can get through this together." Azalar shook his head firmly.

"But this isn't the life we deserve!" Azalar nearly shouted. "This isn't the life I want our litter to be in." Amara smiled at her mate's spirit and determination. Soon after her smile faded and was replaced with a look of sorrow.

"I know, my fréfil," she said. "But the humans have us now. This is our life, whether we like it or not." Azalar furrowed his brows and shook his head once again and stood up, making his way to the edge of the cage.

"I can't accept that, Amara," he stated. "This will not be our lives forever." He placed his front paws on the plastic wall of the cage. Amara gazed upon her mate and made her way closer to him.

"But what can we do?" she asked. "They have power over us." Azalar didn't have the answer to that question he'd been asking himself ever since he was brought to the horrible place.

"We have to get out of here, Amara," he said just above a whisper.

"There has to be a way out of here and I'll find a way."

"Everything okay, young one?" said a male voice off to the side. Azalar's right ear perked, and he turned to the right side of his cage.

"Héffena, Nikamius," Azalar greeted. "How's Jaina?"

"Héffena, Azalar. She's still weak from yesterday's ordeal," said Nikamius. "It really took a toll on her this time. But what about you? Are you doing alright, my friend?" Azalar couldn't help but nodded his head, even though his friend couldn't see him.

"Yes, Nikamius," Azalar confirmed. "I'm fine." Nikamius was a mouse just like Azalar, except his fur was bright gray in color and was the oldest amongst all the rodents in the lab, more than three years old. He was in this lab even before Ragath was, though not nearly as angry as the black rat. In fact, Azalar had never really seen Nikamius express anger. If he did have any anger, he hid it very well, even from Azalar.

"Are you sure?" Nikamius asked. "You screamed so loud that I'm sure you woke up Juro, and he's just a couple cages over." Nikamius finished his statement with a chuckle, causing Azalar to as well.

"Yes, everything is fine, Nikamius," Azalar reconfirmed. "It was just another nightmare."

"I see," Nikamius said, "and is this dream the reason why you want to find a way out of the place?" Azalar was silent for a moment before he let out a long breath that he hadn't realized he had been holding.

"Among other things," he said softly.

"Háth must be planning something for you, Azalar," Nikamius said. "For a mouse to receive the same dream more than once must have some meaning behind it." Azalar let out a scoff.

"Yeah, to remind me of this hell that we live in. I can't even escape it in my dreams."

"Háth has a plan for all of us, young one," the older mouse replied. "It can come in the most unexpected ways. How do you feel when you have these dreams?" Azalar shook his head. The last thing he wanted was to remember his dreams. To be reminded that this hell is probably where he will remain for the rest of his life. To watch his friends and loved ones slowly vanish from his life and slow and agonizing ways.

"I feel angry," Azalar said after a long pause. "I feel scared. And I feel helpless. Like there is nothing I can do to stop this tormented existence."

"And that could be Háth speaking to you," Nikamius said. Azalar looked sharply at the corner where the older mouse was one cage up and to the right.

"How?" he said in a stern tone.

"It could be to motivate you, Azalar," said a new voice. This was coming from directly beside Azalar's cage on his right.

"Motivate me how, Bark?" Azalar asked. Bark was a brown mouse who was about the same age and size as Azalar. The two had grown up right next to each other and had formed a bond like brothers.

"Maybe to find us a way out of here," said another voice from the same cage, this time feminine.

"Thank you, Frella," Bark said. This got Azalar thinking. He never thought of his nightmares as motivation to push through. To finally escape from the doctor. To escape to a life of freedom.

"You see, Azalar?" Nikamius asked. "Even our companions believe that Háth has a plan for us."

"I'm willing to believe in anything if it gets us out of here," Bark said.

"So, do you have a plan?" Frella asked. Frella was also a brown mouse, but she was slightly smaller than the two of them. However, she had a temper that could almost rival Ragath. She arrived a month or so before Amara and had gotten close to Bark almost as quickly. True, she almost bit his head off their first night together, but the two of them had quickly become fréfil to one another. Although, Bark would occasionally say or do things that would get on her nerves on more than one occasion, Frella loved him very much. Azalar had been so deep in his thoughts that he almost missed her question to him.

"Not yet," he said. "But I promise you all, I will not rest until we are all out of here." Then suddenly, the doors flew open, startling the little mouse out of his sleep. Azalar looked up to see a young man strolling into the lab, who was quickly followed by a younger woman. The young man was tall and broad shouldered. His body was muscular and held an imposing stature over the young woman. He had long smooth black hair that reached just past his shoulders and was tied in a ponytail. His skin was fair and bright; and his eyes were bright green, yet they held a cold, dark look within them. He was wearing a black shirt under a long white coat and wore black pants. He was carrying a small silver case in his hands and was staring at it intently as he entered the room.

"It is time, Dr. Merrell," the young doctor said, his voice calm and collective, but he had a small hint of a smile on his face. "We have done finally it. The serum we've been working on for all this time is finally complete."

"Dr. Helgan?" the female assistant, Dr. Merrell, asked, a little unconvinced. "How are you so sure that this time it will be a success? The last experiments..."

"Were failures. Yes, I am aware of that fact," the doctor said with annoyance in his voice. "Those past serums didn't have the desired effect, but this time I know it will work." He placed the box on top of the desk. "But this time it will be a success. I'm sure of it." The doctor looked from the box over to the mice and rats, or more specifically, Azalar. Seeing the doctor looking his way set Azalar on edge and he backed away from the side of the cage. The doctor smiled and made his way to Azalar's cage, but not without picking up a thick, brown glove on the table.

Putting on the glove, the doctor opened Azalar's cage and reached inside and tried to grab Amara. Azalar, wanting to protect his mate, instantly jumped onto the doctor's hand making the doctor wrap his fingers around him instead. He tried to bite at the doctor's hand, but the thickness of the glove prevented him from causing any sort of damage.

The Doctor pulled Azalar from the cage, where he placed him into another containerlike box on the table that was next to the labyrinth. It was a clear square container like the door to his cage but much bigger with little holes along the bottom, too small for him to climb out of but enough to let air inside. There was also a divider in the middle that also had tiny holes along the bottom, so that the doctors could have two test subjects separate within the same container without coming in contact.

The doctor placed a lid on his enclosure before he went to the wall and pulled out Ragath, the large black rat. Just like Azalar, Ragath tried to bite at the doctor's hand as well. However, Ragath's jaw was much larger and stronger than Azalar's, he was able to cause a little pain to the doctor, giving by the wince of pain on the doctor's face whenever Ragath bit him.

"You both still have a lot of spirit," the doctor said with a smile. "Good. You're all going to need to for the future."

The doctor placed Ragath in the empty side of the glass box right next to Azalar, placing the lid down much quicker than with him. Azalar had been in this lab for his whole life, which was only about eight months, and he had seen Ragath from a distance and knew very well that Ragath was the largest rat in the whole lab. This was the first time that Azalar was this close to Ragath, and now that he was, he could see just how large Ragath was. He was at least four times his size, and Azalar was a large mouse for his age.

The doors to the lab burst open, causing Azalar to turn to see a few more humans entering the room. Dr. Helgan smiled upon seeing them enter.

"Ah! You're all here!" he said as he clasped his hands together. "Wonderful. Now we can begin." Dr. Helgan turned his back to them as he pulled the case that he had brought in closer.

"As I'm sure that you are all aware," he began, "the last few experiments held very little results. In other words, they were complete failures." The doctor began unlatching the case. "But this time will be different, my friends. This time we will see results." After unlocking the case, the doctor removed his glove and opened the lid, taking out a small vial with green liquid inside. The assistants looked at the small vial in the doctor's hand with amazement.

"Is that…" Alice began to ask.

"Serum D-1114," the doctor finished, without taking his eyes off the vial in his hands. "This is exactly what we need to make everything we've done worthwhile." He continued to examine the vial, as if it held to the secret of life itself. Then, with a sinister grin, he looked down at Ragath. Seeing the look that he was giving him, Ragath bared his teeth at him and let out an aggressive hiss. The doctor merely smirked as he turned around and grabbed a syringe off the table.

"Now," he said. "Let us begin." He then placed the needle in the vile and sucked up the liquid within. After filling up the syringe with the green liquid. The doctor replaced the glove back on his hand and moved towards Ragath and Azalar.

Both rodents readied themselves, already knowing exactly what was coming next. Dr. Helgan approached Ragath first, lifting the lid cautiously with one hand. The moment a small gap was revealed, Ragath lunged at the opening, using his powerful legs to lift himself off the floor. It was such a sudden reaction that Azalar was caught by surprise. Azalar was amazed by the sheer strength that Ragath had. His head managed to clear the opening; his claws gripped the top of the pen. Ragath was sure that this time he would finally escape. Unfortunately, just as he was about to push himself out, Dr. Helgan managed to catch Ragath mid-jump with his gloved hand. This wasn't his first attempt at escaping, and Dr. Helgan's reflexes were sharp. He gripped Ragath tight in his gloved hand, not giving him any chance of escape. The doctor smir-ked at the rat in his hand.

"Nice try," he mocked. "You almost escaped that time, but it won't be so easy, my friend. I still have need of you." He turned Ragath up, exposing his stomach. Ragath tried to scratch at the doctor's hand with his hind legs, desperately trying to get him to let go. But Helgan's grip was firm and tight, and the glove was making any attempt to pierce his skin futile. Helgan, with the syringe in his other hand, pointed the needle down at the black rat's side. However, with Ragath thrashing around as he did so, it made it very difficult to stick him. Annoyed, Dr. Helgan looked over at his assistant.

"Alice!" he called out. The assistant was startled by his voice, but quickly moved into action. Alice went to one of the drawers and pulled out a pair of gloves of her own, obviously not as thick as Dr. Helgan's. Dr. Merrell rushed back to the doctor's side and attempted to seize the raging black rat's lower body. She pulled back when one of Ragath's claws punctured her glove and cut into her hand causing her to wince. Dr. Helgan let out an annoyed sigh.

"Get ahold of yourself, Dr. Merrell!" Helgan said sternly. The assistant looked up from her now bleeding hand and nodded. She quickly reached out for Ragath again, this time she managed to grab hold of his legs with both hands. Both doctors placed Ragath down on the table, keeping their grip on him tight. Now with him completely restrained, Dr. Helgan took the syringe and pressed the point into the rat's side. Ragath let out a loud hiss as the contents of the syringe were emptied into the giant black rat. With the last of the serum gone, Helgan removed the needle and lifted the rat off the table. He watched as Ragath continued to fight and squirm in his grip.

The anger that Ragath was feeling was evident in his actions. He wanted nothing more than to rip this human apart with his own teeth and claws. He slashed and bit into the glove, but never once took his eyes off Dr. Helgan. The doctor simply stared at the rat, with that same smirk plastered on his face. As Ragath continued to fight, he started to feel drowsy. His movement began to slow until his body soon became limp. Suddenly he began to thrash around, much more violently than before. This time there was no biting or slashing at the glove. Ragath seemed to have lost all control of his body. Helgan's smile widened before making his way back to Ragath's cage. After placing the rat back in his cage and closing the door, Helgan then turned his attention to the mouse on the table.

Azalar, who had been watching the entire scene unfold in front of him, glared daggers at the doctor. Helgan took a step forward, causing Azalar to back away until he hit the other side of his enclosure. Without taking his eyes off the mouse, Dr. Helgan spoke to his assistance.

"Alice," he said, "have another needle ready."

"Yes, sir," Alice said quickly before moving to complete the task given to her. Dr. Helgan stood at the table and looked down at the mouse in the glass pen with that same exact smile. Azalar's fur stood on end at the sight. No matter how many times he saw that look in that human's face, it always made his skin crawl and his anger rise.

"Here you are, Dr." Alice said as she handed the syringe to Helgan. The doctor received the needle with his one hand, and with his gloved one, he opened the lid to the pen. Azalar knew that he wasn't strong enough to jump out of the pen like Ragath did, but that didn't stop him from attempting an escape of his own. When Dr. Helgan reached inside the container, Azalar sprang into action and attempted to jump on his hand, using it as a platform to jump out though the gap. But unfortunately, Helgan was expecting something like that and was able to grab Azalar mid-jump.

"When will you rodents ever learn?" Helgan said in a low voice. He then turned the mouse over to expose his underside. Azalar continued to fight against him, biting and scratching at the glove. He wasn't as strong or as big as Ragath, so he couldn't put up as much of a fight. Suddenly, Azalar felt a sharp pain in his belly, causing him to let out a squeal and a hiss. He glared up at the human grasping him before he looked at the syringe. Azalar watched as the level of green liquid inside began to shrink with every second, feeling every ounce of it pouring into his body.

After every drop was drained, Helgan removed the needle, still holding Azalar in his hand like he did with Ragath. Azalar stared back at the doctor, keeping his harsh glare pinned on him, but after a few seconds, Azalar's vision began to blur. He could feel his whole body beginning to tingle and slowly became unresponsive. He could still move a little, but it wasn't long until he could barely move at all.

Suddenly, seemingly out of nowhere, a sharp pain shot throughout his body, as if a bolt of lightning was traveling through every fiber of his being. His body began to shake terribly, not obeying any of his commands.

His mind was blank as he shut his eyes, focused entirely on the pain which was worse than anything he had ever felt before. Even though he couldn't think or feel anything other than the pain, he was aware that Helgan had shifted and was moving him back to his cage. He felt the human place him on the bedding of his cage, which caused him to open his eyes for a brief moment. The last thing that Azalar saw was the doctor reaching into the cage and grabbing Amara before his world went black.

Chapter III

The last few days were filled with nothing but unbearable pain and misery for all the rodents within the lab. After Helgan injected Azalar and Ragath with the D-11-14 serum, he quickly had his assistants inject the rest of the mice and rats in the lab. Azalar himself, who had grown accustomed to the pain of the doctor's daily experiments, could barely move from this new form of torture. He and Amara would drift in and out of consciousness. Whenever they were conscious, they were in far too much torment and pain to move. In fact, Azalar felt as if his own body was changing. His muscles and bones felt like they were breaking apart and tearing on their own, but he wasn't sure if that was true or not as he couldn't even move to see for himself.

What tormented Azalar the most wasn't the lightning pain coursing throughout his whole body; it was seeing his fréfil writhing in pain. Whenever he was awake, he tried to put his mind off the pain and focus completely on Amara, trying to do what he could to make her feel better in any way. He tried to do his best to be strong and comfort her, but his body made it nearly impossible. His limbs would spasm painfully out of his control, and he would lose consciousness just as quickly as he awoke. The pain in his body was too great to bear at most times. There were even times when he would welcome death if it meant an end to the torture. He couldn't even bring himself to eat or drink anything. Every now and then, he would feel another sharp pain in his side of a foreign source. Then, after a bit of time, he would feel hydrated again and his hunger would subside, but that did very little to end his misery. Not only that, but the screams and cries from his fellow captives plagued his ears, tormenting him further.

Whenever Azalar was conscious, all he could hear were the howls of agony coming from the other mice and rats. It all reminded him of his dreams, where he was powerless to help them; where he was forced to sit by and hear them in pain. All this and his frefil in misery and anguish, he cursed up at Háth. How could he allow his children to be punished in such a way? To be nothing more than playthings to the humans. Even through the pain, Azalar refused to give up. He would not let this be his fate. He shook away the thoughts of death and his last thoughts were to curse Háth once more before his vision drifted back to black.

Finally, after what seemed like an eternity, Azalar eyes opened. At first, he was unsure of what happened, but he was feeling very different. He didn't know how long he had been out this time, but he knew it must have been a good long while. The pain in his body was still there whenever he tried to move, but it was not nearly as bad as it was before. He tried to move his limbs. There was a sharp pain in them, but at least he could move them.

Azalar blinked the blurriness from his eyes and looked around his cage. He couldn't quite place it, but something was off about it. He knew it was the same cage he had always been in because of the scent, but there was definitely something different about it. His eyes then focused on his mate, who was still laying in the nest.

Fear gripping his heart, Azalar climbed to his four legs, ignoring the pain shooting through his body, and scurried over to his mate. As he crawled on all fours, he noticed that this movement didn't feel right, almost like it was unnatural to him. However, he quickly pushed that thought aside and focused on his fréfil.

Upon reaching her, he noticed her breathing was labored. To comfort her and show that he was there, he placed a paw on her back. It was then that he noticed how much more muscular she was. Just by feeling her back he could tell that her body had increased in mass. Her body was most certainly different from before.

Just as he was glossing over his mate, he also noticed something different about himself. He looked at his paw that was on Amara's back and saw that it too looked very different. Startled, he quickly removed his paw from her, lifting it in front of his face to examine it more closely. His fingers were longer than before. He looked over to his other paw to see that it looked just like the other. Instinctively, he flexed his fingers and saw that they closed differently than they used to. Before, all his fingers would close in the same direction, but now they closed into a fist. He then realized that his hands looked a lot like a human's.

"What have they done to us?"

A soft moan gained Azalar's attention as he looked down to see Amara awake and trying to stand up. Azalar quickly assisted her by placing his paws at her side.

"Are you alright, my love?" He asked his fréfil. Amara let out a small whimper as she placed her own paws on her head.

"I think so," she answered. "But my body is still aching all over. How long have we been out?"

"I haven't the faintest idea," Azalar replied. "Days I can only assume." Azalar then took notice of just how much Amara had changed. She was indeed more muscular all throughout her body. Not only that, but her arms were also a little longer and her paws looked the same as his.

Amara rubbed her eyes before turning to her mate and like Azalar, she too, noticed something different about him. She looked him up and down, examining his body as he did hers, until her eyes fell to her own paws. At first, it took her a while to understand. Realization hit her like a stone and her eyes widened in horror as she gazed upon them. She quickly looked down to inspect the rest of her body. She patted herself frantically, not believing that this was real. Her breathing became erratic as she turned to her mate.

"What happened to us?!" she said in a panic. "What did they do to us?!"

"Amara, it's okay," Azalar said softly, trying to calm her down. In truth, he was just as confused and terrified as she was. It was only a few days ago that they were ordinary mice. Now they were something else entirely. They were freaks, rejects, abominations.

"How is this okay?!" Amara practically shouted. "Nothing about this is okay!" Tears were forming in her eyes as she glared at him. Azalar knew that glare wasn't meant for him. He wanted to say something to make her feel better, but nothing came to mind. All he could do was place a hand on his mate's shoulder to try to comfort her. This seemed to work as Amara's glare softened and she nuzzled up into Azalar's chest. Azalar, with his now lengthened arms, wrapped his love in a comforting embrace. He didn't know why he did it, but somehow it felt right.

Amara seemed to agree as she leaned into the embrace. Azalar felt the fur on his chest getting wet as his mate sobbed into his chest, but paid it no mind. He slowly began stroking on Amara's back, running his fingers through her fur. Soon Amara's sobs turned to calming whimpers, but Azalar did not let go of his fréfil. Instead, he held her tighter.

"Everything is going to be different now, my love," he said. "No doubt that this is what Helgan planned.

Who knows what he intends for us now?" He pulled away from Amara, though his hold on her did not falter. Amara could see the determination in his eyes.

"But we will get through this," he continued with confidence. "As long as we are together, we can overcome this." Amara looked into her mate's eyes, believing in every word he spoke. Soon the feeling of sorrow was replaced with a new sense of comfort and faith. With her new paw, she wiped the tears from her eyes and smiled at Azalar.

"Yes," she said. "You're right. I believe you." Azalar returned the smile and nuzzled her closely. For a moment, as they held each other tightly, everything seemed to be alright. Just then, a devastating wail sounded through the air, startling the two mice.

"Jaina!" Azalar immediately recognized that voice as Nikamius'. The two mice scurried over to the front of their cage.

"Nikamius!" Azalar called out. "Nikamius, what's wrong?" There was no response to his calls at first, only cries of sorrow and pain.

"Jaina!" Nikamius cried out again. "My love!"

"Nikamius, what happened?!" Amara asked. Finally, he responded.

"She's gone!" he wailed. "My frefil is stíl!" Nikamius let out another loud cry of despair. Upon hearing the news, Azalar and Amara looked at one another in sorrow. Jaina and Nikamius were among the oldest mice to live in this hell. They had endured so much together, more than most, however they had one another to rely on for support to make it through the torture.

Jaina even helped support others in their turmoil, always being there with her voice to comfort all those who would hear her. Azalar himself felt that Jaina was a second mother to him after his own mother died. After his parents' death, she soothed his sad night with her songs of hope and love. His favorite song was the one about the star shining down upon the mice, guiding them out of the darkness and into a better future.

Come Little mouse, we must away
To find a home, a land to stay
A better place of love and cheer
A place to live, bereft of fear

But then you stop, are you afraid
The road ahead begins to fade
The sun has gone down
Darkness is all 'round

What lies ahead remains unsure
Fear and pain is what we endure
But no, little mouse, Tis not the end
Lift up your head, there is a friend

For up there in the sky
A single star is there to fly
To guide the mouse on his way
A brighter future, here to stay.

Where no mouse need to flight
To hide away in the dark of night
No more hunger, no more pain
Never ending fields of grain

Seas of green, near and far.
Here to stay, by that one little Star
Come little mouse, we must away
This is our home, we're here to stay

It was a song that always calmed him on his most dreaded nights. Whenever she would sing this song, Azalar would feel a sense of safety and comfort. Even

Amara during her first nights within Helgan's Lab were soothed by her loving and welcoming voice. Jaina was even the one who helped Amara get closer to Azalar, to rely on him for support whenever she needed it. So, to hear that Jaina was now gone, was devastating to the two young mice.

"Oh, Nikamius," Amara cried. "I'm so sorry." Nikamius didn't respond, only more cries were heard from his cage. Then they noticed another sound coursing through the air. Azalar listened carefully, trying to hear past Nikamius' cries. At first, he thought it was just Nikamius' voice carrying throughout the room. However, as he listened closely, he quickly realized that wasn't the case. Once he realized what it was, his heart sank into his stomach. Those were the sounds of the others crying in despair. Azalar was now sure that Jaina was not the only one who passed on. But in the midst of the cries and sobs, another voice came from the cage next to Azalar's.

"What happened?" Bark asked in earnest, with great concern in his voice. "What's going on?"

"Bark!" Azalar called out. "Bark, are you alright? Is Frella alright?"

"We're fine, Azalar," Frella answered. "What happened? What's going on?" There was a slight pause from the tan mouse, as Azalar was unsure of how to say it. He then took a deep breath,

"Jaina is gone," he finally responded. Azalar could hear a small gasp from Frella.

"Great Háth!" Frella exclaimed. She and Bark looked at one another in shock before looking up at the cage above them. "Oh, Nikamius. We're so sorry. Are you alright?" However, there was no response from the elder mouse, save for the tearful sobs coming from the cage above. Azalar's heart sank for his friend and was about to give comfort when Bark spoke up.

"Azalar," he said with hesitation. "What's happened to us?" Azalar knew what his friend was referring to and quickly answered.

"Helgan gave us something that has changed our bodies somehow," he said. "For what reason? I can't answer, but I know it can't be good."

"Who knows what goes on in that twisted head of his?" Bark said with venom in his tone.

"Whatever the case," Azalar continued, "we do know that the humans will have new plans for us. So, we must prepare ourselves for whatever comes."

It was at that moment that the doors to the laboratory opened. The dreaded doctor himself entered, with Alice accompanying him. As usual, Helgan had that same twisted smile on his lips as he looked at the cages.

"Now then," he said. "Let's see how many we have left." Those words left a sinking feeling in Azalar's stomach. Exactly how many of his dear friends had he lost these last few days? He was dreading to find out.

Azalar made sure to keep his eyes on both the doctor and Alice as much as possible as they looked through each cage. He felt Amara press against him as she leaned in to check as well. The two mice watched intently as Helgan and Alice looked over each cage. They would stop for a few moments before moving on to the next.

They searched through only a few before coming to a stop. Helgan stared intently at the inhabitants inside before opening it and reaching inside, pulling out a dead rat. Helgan handed the rat over to Alice, who placed it on the table behind them and wrote something down on the pad she carried. They did this with every cage they came to, stopping only to remove a dead rat and placing it on the table. With every rat Helgan removed, Azalar's heart felt heavy. So far, Helgan had removed fifty-two rats from the cages, and they were only halfway done with the rat section. Azalar was dreading every second that passed.

After a few more stops, they finally came to Ragath's cage. Azalar's heart stopped in his throat when Helgan didn't just move on. Azalar knew that there was only Ragath in that cage, as his mate died two weeks prior, so something must have happened to Ragath. Helgan continued to stare into the cage suspiciously, almost puzzled. Then the moment came when Helgan opened the cage, stared for a moment longer, and reached his gloved hand inside.

Suddenly a loud hiss sounded, louder than Azalar had ever heard before, which caused Helgan to quickly shut the cage door, with a loud thud against the door following after. Helgan leaned forwards and gave a small sinister smile at the cage.

"Good try," he exclaimed. "I knew you were up to something. A shame it didn't work this time." Helgan let out a sinister chuckle as Ragath continued to scratch at the door. Helgan leaned in towards Ragath's cage.

"I'm glad you're alive," he said with a sinister grin. "I've got big plans for you." Helgan let out another laugh as he moved on to the cages below, where he pulled out another dead rat.

Finally, he moved to the mice section, where he immediately looked into Azalar's cage first, rather than the ones above, and stared directly at Azalar.

"I'm not at all surprised you made it, subject 289." he said with a smile. "You've always been a fighter." He then raised an eyebrow as he studied the two mice for a moment.

"You both seem to have grown some." The doctor quickly looked over at the next couple of mice cages over then back again. Helgan placed his hand under his chin in a puzzled gesture. "The mice seem to have been affected by the serum on a higher level than the rats." Soon a smile began to form on the doctor's lips.

"This is excellent news." He turned to his assistant. "Let's quickly collect the dead, then we can move on." Alice gave an uneasy nod before they moved on down the rows. Azalar watched with dread as they moved to Nikamius' cage and pulled Jaina from within. Seeing her still body, his stomach turned. Amara seemed to be feeling the same way as he felt his fréfil cling on to his right arm tightly with her paws.

With each mouse they retrieved, Amara clung tighter to Azalar. He placed his own paw on top of hers to hopefully ease her mind, but he knew that was a vain attempt as his own mind was uneasy. Moments later, Helgan and Alice had finished retrieving all the dead mice from their cages, and Azalar could still hear the agony of their fréfil calling out to them. Azalar and Amare looked on at all the *stíl* bodies on the table with horror. Amara pressed her face into Azalar's chest, unable to look on any further as Azalar wrapped his arms around her. However, Azalar refused to look away. He looked at every one of those that had died these last few days, thinking about how much they suffered before they died. His blood was boiling at the thought, and he wanted nothing more than to avenge them. He looked at the Doctor with great disgust, trying everything in his power to calm himself.

"So that's a total of 71 rats and 83 mice that have not made it through the transition, Dr. Helgan," Alice said, not looking up from her clipboard. "39 males and 32 females for the rats. 43 males and 40 females for the mice." Azalar had counted every single one that had been removed from the cages as well, but hearing it out loud just made it all the more unbearable to process. They had been injected by those needles with different kinds of liquid before, and sometimes they would kill some of his fellow rodents. Yet, never in his lifetime did he witness such a slaying of this kind. It was far more than he could have expected.

Helgan stood at the table, studying all the corpses on display. He then picked up a dead rat and began looking it over in his hands. After a moment, he placed the rat down, or more correctly tossed it down, on the table and picked up a mouse and did the same thing.

"There seems to be very little changes in the bodily structures of the deceased," he said plainly, once again tossing the body on the table. "The serum must have stopped processing through their bodies once they gave out." He looked over to another mouse, this one a bit bigger and its arms were longer.

"It seems that depending on how long the subject survives through the process, the more the body changes. Very interesting." Helgan looked over at Alice, giving her a stern stare. "You're writing this down, correct?" Alice nearly flinched under his gaze and quickly nodded.

"Of course, sir," she answered.

"Good," Helgan said. He then moved past Alice and made his way towards the mouse section, stopping at cage number 1-2-8. Azalar watched as Helgan opened the cage and pulled out a young mouse that Azalar recognized as Bogger. Bogger was a dark red colored mouse who had been in this lab for nearly as long as he and Bark had been. They had been in a few of the Doctor's experiments together. He was definitely a strong willed mouse like they were.

Azalar watched as Helgan looked over the mouse, examining every part of his body. Azalar took notice of Bogger, despite being handled by the Doctor, was staring at the still bodies with a look of sadness, specifically at his fréfil, who unfortunately did not survive the serum.

"The serum has done a wonderful job with the test subjects," Dr. Helgan said pridefully. "Their bodies seemed to have grown tremendously, as compared to the rats. Their torsos have grown slightly longer, but their limbs have undergone tremendous growth. Their muscles have also grown throughout their bodies. Truly fascinating." Helgan then placed Bogger inside the glass box on the large table next to the labyrinth.

"I wonder if the other specimens will prove to be just as promising as this one," he said to no one in particular, not taking his eyes off Bogger. He then suddenly turned to Alice with a wide grin.

"Now then," Helgan said with glee as he clasped his hands together excitedly, "Go get the others together. The real testing is about to begin."

Chapter IV

Azalar was unsure of what was to come next. He wasn't expecting these new types of experiments to be the same as before. Far from it. Their bodies were much different now. Helgan had different plans for them all now. He was sure of it.

Once Helgan's other assistants entered the laboratory, they immediately tossed the bodies of their fellow rodents in a bin, as if they were nothing more than their trash. This greatly angered Azalar, seeing that even in death, these humans had no respect.

The humans then began with the usual tests and experiments like they had before. But this time, things were a lot more different for them, as Azalar would soon find out.

One of the humans, a tall, skinny male with short, light brown hair, opened his and Amara's cage and reached a gloved hand inside. Azalar hissed at the horrid hand, keeping himself between it and Amara.

Once the hand was closer, Azalar quickly lunged at it, much quicker than he anticipated, and bit down hard on the glove. This apparently caused a little pain to the human as he let out a slight hiss and retreated his hand back. This obviously angered the human as he looked down at his hand before glaring at Azalar.

"Why you little pest!" he said, reaching into the cage with more aggression and caught Azalar in a tight grasp, causing Azalar to let out a squeak in pain as well.

"Careful with them, you fool!" Helgan shouted. "I still need those specimens alive and unharmed. We've come so far already, and we can't afford to lose any more! As of right now, those creatures are worth more than your life."

"Sorry, sir," the human said as he handed Azalar to another one of Helgan's assistants before reaching back into the cage to grab Amara.

Amara was taken to the treadmill while Azalar was taken to the labyrinth. Azalar knew this part very well and hated it the most. One of the doctors placed a collar around his neck and was placed at the empty enclosure at the start of the labyrinth. Once Azalar was placed there, the entrance to the labyrinth opened and he was beckoned inside. However, as usual, Azalar refused to budge, glaring up at the human. This resulted in a shock from the collar around his neck.

Azalar jumped from the shock, but it greatly surprised him that the pain from it was not that bad. In fact, he barely felt it, however that didn't stop him from sending the humans a hate-filled glare. He recei-ved another shock, this time there was a bit of pain to it. It still didn't hurt as much, but he decided that he better not try his luck. For now, despite having a little sting to them, these little shocks were a welcome respite from the usual treatment he was used to. Send-ing them another glare, Azalar reluctantly entered the labyrinth.

As he made his way through the labyrinth, his body felt completely off. Just like how he felt in his cage, walking on all four of his legs felt wrong. However, he couldn't understand why. He had been walking on all fours for his entire life. So why were his movements feeling so unnatural?

Azalar continued to scurry through the labyrinth. As per usual, with each dead end he came across, he received a shock from the collar around his neck.

While the shocks still weren't as bad as they were before, they were still an annoyance to him. As he made his way around each corner, he also noticed something else about himself, his mind was far more focused than before. In the previous times he ventured through the maze, he would constantly forget which way he went, and would continuously hit one dead end after another, thus receiving numerous shocks. This time, however, he could remember which way he came from and which way he hadn't. Before Azalar knew it, he had made it to the end of the labyrinth in almost a fraction of the time. He still hit a few dead ends along the way, but not nearly as much as he would have previously. Azalar looked up at the humans above, seeing that they were surprised as well.

"Two minutes and twenty-three seconds," said a short, chubby male human that seemed to be balding at the top while he was holding a round object in his hand. "That's the best time that any of these rodents have ever accomplished." The other humans began to mumble about themselves for a few moments before the top of the labyrinth was lifted and a gloved hand reached in. Azalar hissed at them before they managed to grab him from behind, preventing him from biting them.

He was then taken to the front of the maze once more to run the course again. The humans removed the top, covering the entire labyrinth and sprayed everything down as they would do after every course, preventing Azalar from following his scent through the maze. After another motivational shock, Azalar ran through the maze once more, but this time it was much faster. With his new focused mind, Azalar was able to remember exactly where to go and what turn to make. Once he reached the end of the course, he heard the humans mumbling to themselves once more until Helgan approached.

"Well?" He asked impatiently. "What's the time?" The same chubby human hesitated for a moment before holding the round metal object up to Helgan.

"One minute and twenty-six seconds, sir," he said. "That's the quickest that any mouse has ever completed. Even the rats have barely made that kind of time. It's amazing! His intelligence seems to have been heightened tremendously." Helgan stared at the metal object for a moment longer before looking down at Azalar with a smirk. The fur on Azalar's back stood on its end at the look he was giving him. Helgan turned back to the other humans.

"Put specimen 364 in next," he ordered. The humans did what he said and removed Azalar from the maze and placed him inside the container on the other side of the table, where on the other side of the divider was Bogger.

Bogger was a mouse that was roughly the same size as Azalar was. Azalar had only seen him a few times but had never truly interacted with him. The poor mouse had his head down and his eyes half closed, mourning at the loss of his fréfil. Azalar's heart ached for his fellow mouse. He was sure that he'd be absolutely lost without Amara. The very thought of losing her made his stomach twist. He can hardly imagine what this poor mouse was going through. Even though he did not know this mouse well enough, Azalar scurried over to the wall that divided the two mice and placed a paw upon it. The action seemed to catch the brown mouse's attention and he turned to look Azalar's way. Azalar tried to give him a sympathetic smile, trying to give some form of comfort. Bogger stared at Azalar for a moment before returning a small, half-hearted smile himself, as if he understood what Azalar was trying to do.

Just then, the top of the container opened, and a gloved hand reached in, grabbing Bogger. Azalar watched as he was placed inside the labyrinth. Then, turned his gaze at Helgan who was watching inside the maze intently. After a few moments, the chubby human spoke up again.

"Two minutes and ten seconds, sir," he said. Helgan didn't acknowledge him as he kept his gaze on the maze.

"Again," Helgan ordered. Bogger was immediately moved to the front of the maze once more. After removing the lid and spraying it down, Bogger ran the course again. Almost as quickly as he did, he was already at the end of the maze.

"One minute and two seconds!" the chubby human exclaimed, causing the other humans to murmur amongst themselves. "That's amazing, sir!", but as usual Dr. Helgan simply stared at the mouse within the labyrinth.

"Switch up the maze," he ordered. "Change things up. Add more pieces if you have to. Make it more challenging for them." The humans immediately went to complete Helgan's instruction. They removed Bogger from the labyrinth and placed him in the container with Azalar.

While the humans were reshaping the labyrinth, Azalar looked over at Bogger, who was still gazing down at the floor. Unsure of what else to do, Azalar walked over to the dividing wall and once again placed his paw against it.

"Bogger, is it?" he asked. It was muffled, but it was apparently enough to get his attention from the other side.

"Yes," Bogger answered. He slowly made his way closer to the divider. "And you're Azalar." Said mouse gave a slight nod.

"I'm sorry for your loss, Bogger," Azalar said. He could see tears forming in his eyes when he said that, and Bogger looked away. Azalar immediately regretted saying anything, feeling like he just made Bogger feel even worse.

"Forgive me," he said. "I was only trying to-"

"It's quite alright," Bogger said quickly, looking back up at Azalar, eyes full of pain, but also anger. "You're not to blame for her death." Azalar, seeing the look in his eyes, nodded with understanding.

"What was her name?" he asked softly. Bogger's features softened as he looked back down at the floor.

"Emina," he answered softly.

"A wonderful name. I'm sure she was beautiful." Bogger smiled and nodded his head.

"She was," he replied. "The most beautiful mouse one could ever lay eyes upon. No disrespect to your fréfil." Azalar let out a small chuckle.

"That's alright, my friend. I won't take it personally." Bogger let out a chuckle as well before falling silent once more.

"I've heard a bit about you from others around my cage," Bogger said. "They say you are a mouse with great courage and conviction. I've also seen how you continuously fight against the humans. Even after all this time, you still continue to fight. How do you do it?" Azalar smiled at the other mouse.

"I simply refuse to let them win," he stated. "Nothing more to it." Bogger stared at the brown mouse for a moment before lowering his gaze to the floor.

"They have already won," Bogger stated. "Just by existing they have already won. They took my precious fréfil from me. What is there left to fight for?" Azalar's smile fell as he saw the sorrow grow on the other mouse's demeanor. He had much sympathy for his fellow rodent. Both he and others have suffered through so much in this place. He understood why Bogger and others would feel this way, however, he wasn't about to let this poor creature give up on life just yet. Azalar gave a much more serious look at Bogger.

"Life is worth fighting for," Azalar said in a firm tone. "Freedom is worth fighting for." Bogger looked up at his fellow rodent to see the fierce determination in his eyes.

"As long as there is breath in my body, I will continue to fight with every fiber of my being. They have kept us in cages all our lives; torturing us, using us for their own benefits, taking away our loved ones, only for Háth knows what's to follow next. I won't give them the satisfaction of beating me down. I will fight to live and won't rest until I find a way out of this place!" He then placed a paw on the glass, firmly keeping eye contact with Bogger. "For all of us."

Bogger was not expecting such a response from Azalar, nor was he expecting the passion in his words. He looked at the tan colored mouse on the other side of the wall, hearing his words resonating within him. This young mouse, who was probably no older than him, who had been through just as much torture as he had, if not more, had such fire in his heart that he, too, could feel the heat from his conviction stirring within. Bogger looked over to the bin where they had disposed of his mate's body. That feeling of sorrow was still in his heart, but a new feeling was arising alongside it. A new sense of determination and courage, a desire that he had not felt in all his life. A desire to break from this prison; a desire to taste the sweet elixir of freedom. Above all, he desired vengeance against the humans that had torture him and his fellow rodents for so long. And just maybe, he will be able to ease the pain in his chest, and find solace in this life without his fréfil.

Bogger looked back at Azalar, with newfound purpose in his eyes.

"Do you have a plan?" He asked. Azalar was taken aback by Bogger's change in demeanor. Just moments ago, this poor mouse was suffering from a great loss, but now he was looking back at him with a fire in his eyes that he had not seen in another mouse.

"Not yet," Azalar replied. "But I'll come up with something. We'll find a way too-" but Azalar was interrupted as the lid to their container was opened and one of the doctors reached in and grabbed hold of Azalar. Another hand reached in and grabbed Bogger as well. The two mice were taken back to the labyrinth, and both placed at the starting block.

"Now let's see which one can come out first," one of the doctors said. Azalar and Bogger looked at one another before looking towards the entrance to the labyrinth. There were two entries this time, one for each of them. They looked back at the humans above. Then, one raised his hand with the round metal object.

"Go!" he said. There was another shock from the collars, signaling the two mice to get going. This shock was greater than the ones before, but it was still bearable. Azalar and Bogger quickly entered the labyrinth, Azalar entering on the left side and Bogger on the right. Just like before, Azalar sniffed the air to find his way to the other side. As they traveled through the maze, the two mice noticed that the passages were much narrower.

The walls were just barely pressing against their sides, whereas before there was enough room for them to turn around should they need to. This proved to be difficult as when they reached a dead end, they struggled to turn around and head back; the shocks from the collar did not help either. This is where Azalar noticed something, whenever he was stuck at a dead end and had to turn back, he was forced to stand on his hind legs in order to get his body to turn. During this, he noticed that the weight on his legs felt much lighter, as if the rest of his body was weightless and it didn't feel as uncomfortable.

Then once he returned to all fours, the unnatural feeling returned once again. This really boggled the poor mouse. However, he couldn't dwell on it for long, as the shocks from the collar proved to be too much of an annoyance for him to concentrate and he just moved forward through the maze. The maze did prove to be more of a challenge to find a way through, but both mice found the exit in a timely manner. Bogger exited his side first.

"Three minutes and twelve seconds," the chubby human said. Not long after, Azalar exited his side of the labyrinth.

"Three minutes and seventeen seconds. I was honestly expecting them to take longer."

"Run it again," said another human. With that, both mice were placed back at the front of the labyrinth, which was again sprayed down to remove any trace of their scent. Once everything was ready, the human with the round metal object lifted his hand.

"Go!" he said.

The two mice ran the maze once again, both trying to remember which path they took to get to the exit. And just like earlier, Azalar had a much easier time remembering his way through. He still found it very strange how well he could remember the paths and how focused his mind was. He wasn't struggling to keep his mind straight like before. However, his thoughts were soon interrupted when he heard the humans shouting above him.

"One minute and forty-nine seconds!" the same chubby human exclaimed. "That is the best time yet! Even with the changes we added!" Azalar was astonished when he heard the time. Had Bogger really just completed the labyrinth that quickly? Azalar was sure that he was only just over halfway through the maze. Yes, he was moving quicker than he was before, but not that fast. How had he completed it so quickly?

Did he completely miss all the dead ends? Azalar had no time to think about this and pushed himself onward through the passages, only hitting one shocking dead end. Soon enough, he too exited the labyrinth.

"Two minutes and fifty-seven seconds," the chubby human confirmed. "These little guys are really getting better."

"Indeed," said a taller, slim human. "Their intelligence certainly seems to have increased tremendously." He took the clipboard in his hands and began writing something down. After he finished writing, he looked back up at his colleagues.

"Have two rats placed in here next," he ordered. "I'm sure Dr. Helgan will want results from them as well. Send these two to the treadmills." Azalar and booger were then removed from the labyrinth and placed in cages rather than the containers that they were previously in. There they saw one other mouse in another cage not far away, where Azalar noticed that Amara had been placed in.

"Amara!" Azalar cried out. Amara turned to see her beloved fréfil in the other cage.

"Azalar!" she cried as she placed her paws on the bars. Azalar did the same in a vain attempt to get closer to her. Azalar noted that Amara was leaning more on her right leg than her left.

"What happened?" he asked, motioning to her leg with his head. Amara glanced down at her leg before wincing in pain.

"They decided to take us to the weight station," she answered. "They wanted to see if we could hold more weight on our backs. Once they perceived that we could hold more than we had before, they placed even more weights on our backs. But one of the weights slipped and landed on my leg." Azalar was fuming internally upon hearing the carelessness of the humans that caused his beloved fréfil harm. However, he forced himself to remain calm, as getting angry would not be beneficial in any way.

"Are you alright, though?" he asked.

"I'm fine, my love," she replied with a reassuring smile. "Nothing a little rest won't fix."

"I doubt they'll give you the chance," Bogger interjected. "Best thing to do would be to keep as much weight off your leg as possible. Use your other legs to keep yourself balanced. And once the day is out, keep your leg elevated to let the blood flow faster to your injury." Azalar looked curiously at the mouse next to him.

"How do you know that?" he asked.

Bogger didn't answer right away, seemingly not to have heard his question, as he looked over Amara's leg once more, studying it intently. "Judging by the swollenness in your leg, I'd say it was a nine point seventy-five ounce weight that must have fallen at least a tail and a half high off the floor and landed just above your left paw. Judging by the impact of the weight, I'd say that it will take no more than three days' rest to heal, so long as you keep it elevated every chance that you get." Both Azalar and Amara just stared at the dark red mouse with astonishment. They seemed to be staring longer than they intended as Bogger started to feel uncomfortable under their gaze.

"What?" he asked. Azalar was the first to speak.

"How could you possibly know all that?" Bogger once again shrugged.

"I remember a while ago that one of the humans sprained their ankle before. They said to keep the foot rested and elevated, and it would be healed in a matter of weeks. Seeing as we are nowhere near the size of the humans, and my studying on how swollen your fréfil's leg is, I can deduce that it would take significantly less time for her leg to heal. Along with being familiar with the weights and their size and shape, I was able to calculate how the weight impacted her leg and infer what it would take for her leg to heal. So, my assumption is that it would take roughly two to three days to heal, depending on how much stress she puts on her leg while performing the humans' tests." Azalar once again simply stared at the darker mouse, unsure of how to respond.

"I'm not entirely sure what you said there, Bogger," he stated. "For a moment, you almost sounded like a human." Bogger was silent for a moment as he looked towards the floor, thinking about what Azalar had just said.

"I guess I've paid more attention to the humans' words more than I thought I did," he finally said. "I tried to learn what I could from them to prepare Emina and I for their future tortures. And perhaps the serum had more of a terrible impact than I originally thought?"

"What do you mean?" Amara asked.

"Surely you've noticed the physical changes in our bodies, correct?" Azalar and Amara instinctively looked down at their bodies. It was true that the physical changes were the first thing they noticed about themselves. "The serum they injected into us has changed our bodies to become much stronger. Judging by the weights over to the side there, I am correct in assuming that you were able to lift more than double the weight you had previously, Amara?" Amara was silent for a moment, but nodded her head.

"Yes," she answered. "Much more." Bogger nodded.

"Then by that logic," he continued, "We can also assume that the serum had an impact on our intellect to a great degree as well."

"Is that why you were able to finish the labyrinth so quickly?" Azalar asked.

"Exactly. After running through the labyrinth only once, I was able to remember exactly where to go. Surely you noticed too, right Azalar?" Azalar nodded his head quickly.

"Yes!" he exclaimed. "I noticed that I was able to focus a lot more. I could remember almost every path I took. I also noticed that the shocks on these things around our necks weren't nearly as painful as they were before."

"My point exactly," Bogger said. "The serum has made it so that we are all much stronger and more intelligent. We are now capable of doing things that we were never able to do before." An idea suddenly came to Azalar's mind.

"This could be it!" he exclaimed. The other two mice looked curiously at the tan mouse.

"What do you mean?" Amara asked. Azalar looked at his fréfil with excitement and determination.

"This could be the key to our escape. Now that we are stronger and smarter, we can come up with a plan for all of us to escape from this hell." He then looked over at Bogger. "You are obviously much smarter than I am, and you are able to learn much quicker than I can. Do you think it's possible?" Bogger looked down at the floor once again, seemingly in deep thought. He stayed like that for a good minute or sol, quietly muttering to himself. Finally, after another few moments, Bogger finally looked back up at Azalar.

"It seems possible," Bogger answered. "But we will need to find a way to open those cages. Even with our newfound strength, Háth knows it may still prove to be a challenge to get them to open."

"We can figure that out soon," Azalar replied. "But for now, I think it would be best for us to get used to these new bodies. And maybe we can get even stronger for when the time finally comes to escape."

"We must also be aware of any other possible changes in ourselves," Bogger said. "The serum may have had other side effects that we are currently unaware of. So, we must proceed with caution moving forward. We don't know what other surprises may be waiting for us." Just then, the door to Amara's cage was opened and another mouse was gently dropped in right next to her by Alice. It was a male mouse that was dark gray in color. It was Brim.

Brim was a mouse that Azalar and Amara were quite familiar with. He had a fiery spirit much like Azalar, and refused to let the humans wear him down. He would push himself further than any other mouse that Azalar had seen. Azalar held great respect for this mouse, though they had not been together for any experiments for some time. Even so, Azalar knew this mouse would push himself further than any other. His conviction rivaled that of even Ragath's.

They had first met during an experiment where they, along with several other mice were placed in a large tank filled with water. There, the humans wanted to see how long they could swim for before they all lost strength or just gave up the will to go on. Many mice drowned during that time, however, Azalar, Amara and Brim refused to give up. After several hours of nonstop swimming, Amara was soon losing strength. Azalar tried to aid his beloved mate, but he was losing strength himself. Then, Brim suddenly came to their aid and helped Azalar keep Amara's head above the water. This dark gray mouse didn't even know them, they were complete strangers to one another, yet he went out of his way to help them stay alive. With his help, they were able to keep each other afloat for another hour, before Helgan finally concluded the test. In total, they swam for over nine hours. To say that Azalar was grateful to this mouse was an understatement, and he held Brim in such high regards ever since.

Alice placed Brim on the other side of Amara's cage, she then walked away and immediately began berating another human. Brim immediately collapsed to the floor, huffing with exhaustion. Amara quickly rushed over to him, making sure to keep off her injured leg, and placed a paw on his back.

"Are you alright, Brim?" She asked, concerned. The gray mouse continued to breathe heavily for a few moments before looking up at her.

"Yeah," he said between breaths. "I'll be fine. I won't let those *mûk hrékas* beat me down that easily. But are you alright, Amara? How's your leg?"

"My leg is fine, don't worry," she said. "What happened?" Brim let out a little scoff.

"That fire-faced human decided to put more weight on my back when Alice wasn't looking, but I was more than capable of handling it. Alice didn't seem too happy when she saw him attempt to put more weights on me. She gave him quite an earful before placing me in here." He then looked over to the other cage where Azalar was in. "Glad to see you made it too." Azalar smiled at the gray mouse and nodded.

"I am too." His face then fell with concern. "Where is Della?" Brim smiled before looking down, still out of breath.

"She's fine, thank Háth," He answered. "She's still recovering from the whole ordeal from what the humans gave to us. They haven't taken her out yet, which I'm grateful for. She still needs as much rest as she can get while she can. Though I don't expect her to get much of it. Now what's this I hear about escaping?" Azalar looked over at Amara, who seemed to be just as confused as he was, before looking back.

"How did you know what we were talking about?"

"I could hear you as Alice was putting me back in here. My hearing has gotten much better since I woke up. I can hear a lot more things than I did before."

"I guess we can add that to the increasing list of skills we have developed," Bogger said. Brim looked curiously at him.

"Skills?" he asked.

"We seem to have been developing certain skills after our little transformation from the serum," Bogger answered. "We all seemed to have heightened intelligence as well as increased physical strength. But it seems that some of us have more developed skills than others. My intellect has increased significantly, while your hearing seems to be more attuned. Unintentional side effects, but valuable nonetheless."

"That's good, but that doesn't really answer my question," Brim said. "Do you guys have a plan to escape this place?"

"Not yet," said Azalar "We need to find a way to get those cages open and we need to do it at the right time. Every mouse and rat in here deserves their freedom, and I want us all to get out of here together." Hearing of this plan to escape caused Brim to have the same look of determination that Azalar had seen when they first met. Brim himself hadn't felt this excited in a long time. For most of his life, he just battled with his willpower to get through each day. Like Azalar, he refused to let the humans break him. Just surviving was his whole purpose for most of his life. Now there was a new purpose for him; not to just survive, but to live. The thought alone was invigorating for him.

"Then count me in," Brim said. "Any way I can help." Azalar nodded in acknowledgement at his fellow mouse. Just then, Azalar noticed Alice coming back towards them, still looking rather upset. Then, her face softened as she looked down at the cage with

Amara and Brim inside. She lowered her face so that she was almost eye level with them.

"Are you both alright?" she asked, her voice soft and welcoming. Amara and Brim just stared up at her. Alice smiled down at them. "I'm so sorry little guys. If it were up to me, I'd give you both a break for the whole day. Unfortunately, we both have jobs to do and Dr. Helgan doesn't take kindly to delays."

Alice Merrell was a gentle woman. She was shorter than most of the other humans with long, blonde hair wrapped in a ponytail and blueish-green eyes. She also had a sunflower pin in her hair, as well as on her lab coat with her name just underneath it. She was always kind to the mice, so much so that even Azalar found it difficult to hate her. Whenever she performed Dr. Helgan's experiments, she always handled the mice and rats as gently as possible; though that didn't really make up for the fact that she was still performing such torturous experiments.

"Talking to mice again, Merrell?" said another voice to the side. Alice's face immediately fell into a deep frown upon hearing that irritating voice. With a disgruntled sigh, she looked back at a tall, skinny man with long, dirty blonde hair with a fuzzy, half trimmed, goatee looking at her with a smug grin.

"Yes, Trevor," Alice retorted. "Because unlike you, these beautiful critters are actually intelligent and are capable of so much more than just taking up space. And I quite enjoy their company." Trevor scoffed as he shook his head.

"They're just a bunch of dumb useless rodents," Trevor exclaimed. "The only thing that they're good for is doing Dr. Helgan's experiments. And you'd rather spend your time with these rodents than with a real man?" Trevor pointed a thumb at himself to emphasize his point. Alice simply gave him a deadpan stare before turning back to the mice.

"Show me a real man and I just might," she retorted. Trevor let out a small laugh.

"That's cute," he said. "But seriously, why waste your time growing attached to these rodents? They're all going to die soon, so there's no point in actually caring for them." All four mice glared at the human Trevor for his words. Alice too shot Trevor a look of disdain.

"For your information," she said with venom in her voice, "these *rodents* are highly intelligent creatures. They are natural students who excel at learning and understanding all kinds of concepts. They can even solve challenging puzzles." Alice returned her attention to the mice in front of her.

"In fact, according to extensive research and examinations, their brains are very similar in structure to that of humans. They can understand complex problems and solve ways around them. Just like humans, they are very social creatures, living in communities out in the wild. And just like humans, they get lonely and stressed if they are left alone." Trevor let out a mocking scoff.

"They just seem like a bunch of dumb rodents to me."

"I wouldn't expect *you* to understand," she shot back. "These creatures are capable of doing amazing things with just the intelligence that they have."

"And we're hoping to increase that intelligence," Dr. Helgan said. Both Alice and Trevor stood at attention the moment they heard Helgan's voice

"Dr. Helgan!" Alice exclaimed, her voice trembling nervously. Helgan stared at the two with an emotionless look, which somehow made him more intimidating, before looking down at the mice in their cages, taking note of the injured leg on one of them.

"Mr. Berkins?" Helgan said in a low tone. Trevor stiffened at the mention of his name.

"Yes, sir?" He answered evenly, trying his best, but failing, to hide his anxiety.

"These specimens are vital to my research," Dr. Helgan said without taking his eyes off the mice. "I would greatly appreciate it if you took better care of them. Understand?" Trevor swallowed the lump in his throat before replying.

"Yes, Dr. Helgan. I'm terribly sorry," Helgan finally looked up from the mice and stared directly at Trevor. Trevor shifted uncomfortably under the doctor's gaze and wanted to avoid looking at his eyes, but he remained right where he was, unmoving. After what seemed like an eternity, Helgan took a few steps forward, standing directly in front of Trevor. Helgan continued to stare at him until Trevor, unable to bear the intense stare any longer, finally looked away from the Doctor.

"Good," Helgan said at last. "Because any further inconveniences may result in… sever consequences." Hearing that last word made Trevor's eyes widen and a cold sweat began to form on his brow. Helgan then looked down at Alice, who was also looking quite nervous.

"I don't care what grievances you have with each other," Helgan continued, his tone much lower, "but I will not tolerate it affecting my work. Your jobs are to collect as much data from the specimens as possible. I hope I've made myself clear."

"Yes, Dr. Helgan!" Both assistants said. Helgan gave them both a quick glance before nodding.

"Good. Now get back to work." With that, Helgan turned around and headed to another section of the lab. The two lab assistants stood there for just a moment longer before Alice gave Trevor one last glare. Trevor merely smirked at her as he turned to the mice in the cages.

"Let's get this over with," he said in annoyance. He reached for the cage where Azalar resided. He opened the cage and reached inside to grab Azalar. At first, Azalar hissed at him, but Trevor was quick and was able to grab hold of him. But when Trevor pulled Azalar from the cage, he squeezed too tightly. Azalar let out a squeak in pain and instinctively bit down on Trevor's hand in retaliation. Unfortunately for Trevor, he forgot to put on the leather gloves.

"Ouch!" Trevor screamed, quickly releasing his grip on Azalar and dropped the little mouse. Azalar dropped to the table, landing on all fours with no trouble.

"He's out!" a voice cried out. Suddenly, Azalar saw the other humans from all around the room running towards him. Soon Azalar found himself surrounded by multiple humans. One of them attempted to grab him, but he turned and hissed at their hands. He did the same to anyone who got too close or attempted to seize him.

"Get him before he escapes!" they shouted. In truth, Azalar wasn't planning on escaping this time. He just bit down on Trevor's hand because he was squeezing him too hard. But now Azalar found himself in an odd situation. The other mice in the cages were looking at him to see what Azalar would do next. Though he wasn't trying to escape, he also didn't want the humans grabbing him in this panicking state. So instinctively, he hissed and scratched at any human whose hand got too close.

"Don't just stand there!" Helgan shouted from the back. "Grab him!"

"Wait!" Alice called out, gaining everyone's attention. Alice pointed to Azalar. "Look!" Everyone looked at where Alice was pointing to. It took a moment, but when they all saw it, their mouths were all ajar with shock. Azalar was confused as to why they were staring at him in such a manner. Curiously, he glanced down below him. It was then that Azalar realized what was happening; he was standing on just his two legs.

Chapter V

Everyone stared in awe at the little mouse, who was now standing on just his two legs. No one had any words, for what words could be said. Never before had anyone seen such a sight before then. No one was more surprised than Alice, whose eyes were wider than anyone in the room and though she was at a loss for words, a small smile slowly grew on her face. She looked at the little mouse as if she had seen a fairy, or a little person no more than a hand tall, ready to grant her wish.

Azalar, for his part, was completely in shock at what he was currently doing. And just like the humans around him, he couldn't believe it himself. He was standing like a human, on two legs, and they weren't trembling or anything of the like; nor did they feel tired or aching. The longer he stood in place, the more it felt natural, like it was something he had been doing all his life. He went to take a step forward when a gloved hand suddenly clasped around his body. Azalar let out a squeak and looked up at the man who held him firm. It was Helgan looking down at him with a grin that would make even a giant shrink in uncomfortableness.

"It was standing like a person," Trevor said in the silence of the room, his voice indicating that he was not expecting such a result. "It was actually standing like a person. How is that possible?"

"It's because of the serum, you idiot," Dr. Helgan said as he held Azalar tightly in his gloved grip, narrowing his eyes at his subordinate. "The serum had evolved the specimens even more than I had thought it would. Not only has it increased their intelligence but a great factor, the serum has also changed their bodies to allow them to be bipedal; at least with this one." Helgan smiled once again at Azalar, bringing the now larger mouse closer to his face, but not too close.

"Yes," he said in a low voice. "Yes, this is a marvelous development. Things are progressing much quicker than I had originally thought. And soon I'll be able to continue where I left off. Yes, you will soon be capable of great things, my little ones." Helgan then placed a tiny vest, a set of leather straps that wrapped around the subject with a small latched on the back, that had been set to the side around Azalar's torso and in a clear chamber on the table where Azalar's fréfil had just been. There, Helgan placed a platform above his head, similar in shape to a round table, and hooked Azalar to the underside of the platform with the latch on his back. The platform itself was small, no more than twice the width of his body, but tall enough for him to stand under. The legs were thin, yet they stuck out at each end so that the platform would remain in place. Once everything was set in place, Helgan stepped back with a smirk.

"Let's continue the research," he said. Helgan turned to Alice. With a look of hesitancy, Alice understood what to do and took one of the weights from the table; a five ounce weight to be exact, and placed it on the platform. The platform lowered from the weight until it pressed upon Azalar's back. Azalar knew this part all too well and would often refuse to play along to the human's experiments. Since he found himself able to stand on his hind legs with no struggle, he wondered what else he was capable of. Without the need of a shock from his collar, Azalar stood up and lifted the platform with great ease. He was amazed at his newfound strength, whereas before he would have a little difficulty lifting this much. From what he heard from the humans before, his own weight was a little over two ounces. So, carrying five ounces was indeed a bit of a struggle. The most he had been able to lift was seven ounces, over three times his original body weight, but that was when he stood on all fours. Now that he was much larger and stronger, and standing on only two legs, he was positive he could lift more than that for sure. Helgan seemed to be thinking the same thing.

"Add another five ounces," he ordered. Alice did as she was told and placed another five ounces on top of Azalar. The sudden addition of weight caused Azalar to drop a little, but he immediately recovered and straightened himself up.

"It's just like the others, Dr. Helgan," Alice said. "The specimens are able to lift more than double what they were previously able to handle. The serum appears to be working wonders!" Though she said it with optimism, inside Alice was feeling quite torn. She hated seeing these creatures put through such toil. But there was nothing she could do about it. She had to do what she was told.

"Add another five!" Helgan ordered. Though with a bit of reluctance, Alice took another weight and placed it gently atop the platform above the little mouse. Once again, the sudden added weight caused Azalar to drop, but this time he was forced to drop down to one knee. The struggle was greater now and Azalar was finding it very difficult to keep himself up, but he was not going to be beaten. He then remembered Brim and his determination and strength of will. No indeed, he was not going to be beaten so easily.

Azalar managed to regain his footing and pushed his back against the platform. It raised up and Azalar was able to straighten himself upright again. However, he was finding it very difficult to keep himself steady, as he was still not accustomed to standing on his newfound legs just yet, and nearly lost his fitting again. Without thinking, Azalar placed his arms up under the platform to steady himself, which he found to ease the burden a little. During all these weight lifts, he had only ever used his back to burden the weight. With whatever strength he had in his arms, he used them to lift the platform higher above, much to his surprise. Even though it helped ease the pressure from the weights above, it was still a great struggle.

"Amazing!" cried one of the humans with excitement as he looked over to Dr Helgan. "It's using his arms to lift the weights higher. This is truly an astounding development." Helgan made no response. He simply stared at the young mouse with great interest. And he still held that unnerving smile.

"Add another!" he ordered once again. Alice, who had been watching Azalar with admiration, quickly looked over at the doctor with wide eyes.

"But, sir," she said. "That may be too much for him to handle. He's still not used to his new body." Helgan immediately turned to her with a hard glare that made Alice finch.

"I said add another!" He barked. "We are once again on the cusp of the scientific breakthrough of human history. The extension of our research takes priority over anything else. So once again, Alice, add another!"

Alice was very reluctant to follow his orders, but the cold and hardness of his watchful gaze broke any form of resistance she had, and she took another five ounce weight and gently placed it upon the little mouse.

The weight was now too much for Azalar to handle and he was forced to drop down to one knee again. His back felt like it was going to break in two from the pressure. His muscles were aching, and his chest was burning. He wanted to quit, he wanted to just drop the weights and end this terrible experience. Yet, the flames of his hatred and the pride he had refused to let him. He still refused to let these humans beat him.

So Azalar took in a deep breath, hoisted himself to and with as much strength as he could muster, he pushed up with his legs against the platform and raised it as high as he could. His arms and legs were trembling terribly, but he held the platform up for as long as he could. Try as he might, his body finally gave in. With the last of his strength depleted, Azalar dropped to the floor. The platform dropped as well. It stopped just shy of crushing him beneath its weight, thanks to the rubber stops at the end of each leg where the springs began. Thus, saving Azalar from a painful death.

The humans around him were amazed at what they had just witnessed. Despite having more than triple his body weight on top of him, the little mouse was not only able to withstand the pressure, but he was also able to push past his limits and raise the platform above his head. It was something they had never seen before. They began chatting amongst themselves, all while Helgan remained silent. Helgan, for his part, had a rather unenthusiastic look about him as he held a finger up to his lips in a thinking manner.

"Alright," he said, silencing the crowd around him. "That's enough paltry chatter. We need to continue with our work as soon as possible. Alice, grab test subject 289 and bring him along." Alice quickly glanced from Dr. Helgan to the little mouse.

Azalar was panting heavily as he lay upon the floor. His body was in terrible pain, and he wasn't sure if he could even crawl on all fours, let alone stand on his two legs again. But when he heard Helgan say his number, his body tensed, and he looked up to see

Helgan walking away towards the next experiment table. He then looked over at Alice, who was staring down at him, giving him a sympathetic look. He knew that she was a caring female human. He could see in her eyes that she hated doing these so-called *tests* to them, torturing them like this. However, when he saw Alice with Helgan, Azalar would very often see the fear in her eyes every time she looked at him.

"B-but sir," Alice began shakily. "I think it would be best to let test subject 289 rest for a little while." She immediately regretted letting the words escape her lips when Helgan almost immediately stopped in his tracks before slowly turning to Alice, his bright green eyes hard and piercing.

"Excuse me?" he said in a low voice. Alice started to panic as she could feel her heart beating a thousand miles an hour and her breath was getting heavier.

"I-I just simply mean that…" she paused while looking around the room to avoid his eyes. "The test subjects aren't used to their new bodies quite yet. It may be dangerous to exert them too much. We still don't know how their bodies will react to prolonged fatigue. If we push them too hard, they all may end up dying due to their bodies giving out. A-and we've lost quite a few test subjects to the serum already. If more of the test subjects start dying off too soon, our research could be in jeopardy, and we might be forced to start all over again and test subject 289 is one of our best specimens. If we lose him, we may lose a key component in our research."

The room fell silent as everyone stood looking between Alice and Dr. Helgan. No one had ever questioned Dr. Helgan before, let alone given him input that he never asked for. Helgan was always very strict when it came to his research and experiments. So, for Alice to speak up in such a way was completely unprecedented.

Alice's body was tense under Helgan's cold and harsh stare as it seemed like an eternity since he said anything. Her heart was pounding in her chest so much that she was sure he could hear it from where he stood. Helgan must have stood there for a good minute before he finally spoke.

"You're right," he said. Everyone was silent, as no one had any words to say.

"Sir?" was all one of the lab assistants was able to say.

"She's right," Helgan repeated with a sigh. "We've lost too many test subjects as it is. We can't afford to waste any more when we have come so close to our goals. I should have been more mindful of this, but I was so caught up in the recent achievements that it could have cost us one of our most valued specimens. Alice, please put test subject 289 back in the crate. We'll give it a one hour break." Alice smiled and, a little too quickly, unhooked Azalar from the weight platform and placed him back in the crate with Bogger.

"I do appreciate your concern, Alice," Helgan continued. "And I thank you for your input. We should not be in such haste to push progress in our research. Our experiments are vital and cannot be rushed. We should follow in Alice's lead and be more mindful in the future. Now let's get back to work." The rest of the staff within the lab turned around and went on to do their own tasks. Alice was about to do the same in setting up the weight platform for the next test subject when Dr. Helgan spoke up.

"Alice," Helgan said. Alice paused. Hearing the low tone in the Doctor's voice, she dared not glance his way. But when she heard his footsteps getting closer, she had no choice but to look up at Helgan, but his features weren't cold or glaring; they were soft and friendly, a far cry from his usual harsh gaze.

"You are a very good scientist," he said in a gentle voice. "You're very intelligent, resourceful, and you know exactly what needs to be done. You really have a keen instinct for this kind of work. I can honestly say I'm very happy and proud to have you on board." Alice could feel her cheeks getting flustered at his words and gave Helgan a small smile.

"Thank you, sir," she said softly. "I-I really appreciate that." The Doctor then took a few steps forward and gently placed a hand gently under Alice's chin, bringing her face up to look at him. Alice could feel her breath getting caught in her throat as she stared into those dark eyes, finding herself unable to look away from them.

"You truly are a very outstanding woman. And I hope you continue to be a valuable member of this team for years to come. However…" he leaned closer and whispered something in Alice's ear. A moment later, her eyes widened and all the fluster that she had in her face suddenly drained. She looked utterly horrified. Helgan turned around and walked away, still holding that same grin on his face. Alice stood unmoving for a long while, her features unchanged. When she finally moved, she looked down at the little mice before going about setting up the weight platform for the next test subject.

"Poor girl," Brim said, his tone low and melancholy. The other mice looked his way.

"What is it?" Azalar asked. "What did he say?" With a somber look, Brim turned to Azalar and spoke.

"He said, '*If you ever question me like that again… you'll be part of my next experiments.*'"

After an hour of rest, Azalar was back at it with Helgan's tests and experiments. Fortunately, there was no poking and prodding of needles this time; in fact, almost all the tests today were physical based. Still, that did ease the aches and pains that he felt throughout his body.

Now, thanks to Azalar and with the discovery that he could now stand on his hind legs, the humans ran these exercises to see how many of the rodents could stand on their hind legs as well; as they would come to find out that they all could now. The Rats proved to be very capable when it came to their new strength. Though their bodies didn't change that much as compared to the mice in terms of size, the rats still proved to be the stronger of the two species. Of course, the rats were always stronger than the mice, but with their new bodies, the mice were able to catch up to the rats by just a little bit. In total, all the rodents of Helgan's lab were much stronger than before. They could lift more, swim longer and hold much greater endurance, and Helgan was determined to see how far he could push their strength. One exercise in particular really took a toll on Azalar, just as the weightlifting did: the Sprint.

The Sprint was an exercise that required the subject to run for as long as they could on their hind legs. Before their transformation, being forced to stand on their back legs was almost unbearable. And though at first many had a great deal of trouble being able to balance themselves, standing upright was no longer painful.

Just before Azalar was next to go on the treadmill, one of the humans placed a crate with a smaller and younger mouse inside; it was Juro. Juro was a young mouse that had only been in this lab for almost three months, his fur was tan in color but with a white underbelly like him. Azalar's heart ached for the young mouse. He was known as a bit of a jokester amongst the other mice.

Even during the exercises and experiments, Juro always managed to find a joke in it. Azalar knew him better though. Juro was a very sensitive mouse, and these experiments took a great toll on the young one, but he would often disguise this pain through his jokes and harlequin banter and always tried to appear confident in front of everyone, even to the humans. Nonetheless, Azalar could always see through those eyes the pain that hid behind them.

However, there were no jokes to be had now, not for this poor little mouse. Not long ago, just a week before their transformation in fact, Juro had finally made a connection with his beloved fréfil, Milla, only to lose her just as quickly. He was far too young to experience such pain. Azalar looked over at the poor, who looked utterly defeated.

"Juro?" he said. The younger mouse looked over upon hearing his name.

"Oh. Héffena Azalar," he greeted in a dismal voice. "I'm glad to see you're okay." Hearing the monotone in the poor mouse's voice instead of the usual jest he had come to know was nearly too much for Azalar.

"Héffena, Juro," Azalar returned the greeting. "I am sorry about Milla. My heart aches at her passing." Juro closed his eyes and faced the floor.

"It's alright, Azalar. She is with Háth now, and no longer suffering in this terrible place. I can at least think of it that way, right?" Juro did his best to smile, but the most he could manage was a quick side grin before letting it fall. Azalar wasn't sure what to say to the young mouse. He had his own reservations about Háth, but he wasn't about to say such an inappropriate statement at this time, not when a dear friend of his was mourning the loss of his fréfil.

"Yes, she is," Azalar said. "She is free of the pain of this world. I'm sure she is happy by his side." Juro gave out a little chuckle.

"It's okay, Azalar," he said. "You don't need to try to comfort me. I know you don't really believe in Háth.

And that's okay." Azalar paused and frowned a little at Juro's words.

"It's not that I don't believe in him," he stated. "I just don't understand how Háth could allow so much suffering upon us. How could he allow his people? To allow us to be the playthings of humans. It just doesn't make sense to me." Juro looked at Azalar for a moment before looking back down.

"You know, I used to think that way too, so I understand how you feel. 'Why would Háth let such evil in the world?' I would say to myself. I would even often roll my eyes whenever Nikamius would say, 'Háth always has a plan for us all. And he tests us in many ways.' I never really believed him, in all honesty. It always seemed like hopeful preaching to me." He looked back up at Azalar. "But then I met Mila, and she was the best thing that ever happened to me. She was my fréfil, my love. After I met her, I truly believed that Háth was real, because he had graced me with such a beautiful creature. Then just like that, she was taken away. Even so, I can honestly say that I don't blame Háth for that. That was the fault of humans. They were the ones that took her away from me. If this is some kind of plan that Háth has in mind, or if it is some kind of test, I can't understand it."

"Whether it is Háth's plan or not, it is in our hands now. And we can't just sit by and let these humans continue to torture us and take more of our lives." Azalar thought that now would be the best time to start recruiting others to join his plan to escape. He couldn't do it by himself, and surely after what had happened to Milla, Juro would be all for it. Juro, however, didn't bother glancing his way and was silent for a moment before letting out a heavy sigh.

"Honestly, I really don't care at this point, Azalar. I really don't. Not anymore. There's just nothing left for me. At this point, I'm willing to let these humans kill me. I just want to die and be with Milla again."

Azalar frowned at the younger mouse, not taking kindly to his dark and melancholy thoughts. He understood that his heart was in great pain, and that he felt that there was indeed no hope, but if it was one thing that put a bad taste in his mouth, it was the sight of someone giving up. Not when there was a chance for something better in life.

"You think that's what Milla would have wanted from you?" he asked. "To just give up and let the humans have their way until you finally fall dead? To let her memory fade away?" Juro, who had looked back up at him from the floor, stared at him blankly.

"I can assure you, Juro, that is the last thing that Milla would want you to do. She would want you to live for her, to keep fighting, until there truly is nothing left to fight for."

"But what is there left to fight for, Azalar?" Juro asked, his eyes filling with tears of anguish, his voice filled with pain, begging Azalar for an answer. "If there is something worth fighting for, I can't see it! Please, Azalar, tell me! What is it that's worth fighting for!"

"Freedom!" Azalar exclaimed. The answer was quick and sudden that Juro was caught off guard. He stared blankly at the older mouse, unsure if he heard him correctly.

"What?" he asked above a whisper. Azalar gave Juro a serious look and moved closer to him.

"Freedom," he said with more conviction. "There is more to life than inside these walls, Juro; a place for us rodents to live and not be trapped as slaves. A place filled with green grass and tall trees, with the sun shining down on us with warmth. You remember? Like in Jaina's song? Seas of green, near and far. With never ending fields of grain. A place where we never have to live in fear or hunger. Surely that wasn't all just made up. A place like that must exist. A place far away from all the humans. A place where we can live in peace and build a life for ourselves. Where the lives of loved ones can live on in our hearts. That is something worth fighting for Juro. And I will do everything in my power to get you there. I promise you."

Juro stared silently at Azalar, lost in his words. Before, his heart was set on giving up on life. Without Milla, his world was dark and lonely, with no light in sight to give him hope. Yet, now with Azalar's words ringing in his head, there was a glimmer of hope in his heart. Juro then thought of Milla. Azalar was right. Juro knew that Milla would never accept him giving up like this. She would want him to push on, to continue living for her.

"Will you truly set us free?" Juro asked hopefully. Azalar smiled at his younger friend, glad to see the light in his eyes returning, and nodded his head.

"Yes, Juro," he said softly. "I swear this to you. I will find a way for us to escape this hell. If there is a way to get out, I will find it. No matter what it takes." Hearing the confidence in Azalar's voice brought a smile to Juro's face. He truly believed in Azalar when he said he would find a way. He had known Azalar all his life and in all that time, he had always seen Azalar push through any obstacle that the humans threw at him; and never once did he falter. So, if anyone was to find a way out of this place, it was going to be him.

"I'll hold you to that," Juro said with a laugh. "Remember; to all those that break their promise, will be awaiting a good scolding from Háth in the afterlife." He said the last statement while doing his best to mimic Nikamius's voice. Azalar smiled at seeing Juro's joking manner return to him. However, their moment of mirth was interrupted when one of the humans came over to their cages.

"Alright. Your turn little guys," the human said in a mocking tone, before placing them on the treadmill.

The Sprint, however, was just as oppressive as ever. Helgan, who had come over to watch Azalar specifically during this exercise, was determined to find out how far he could push the rodents' new bodies. He increased the speed of the treadmill as well as the voltage on the shock collars. Azalar ran for as long as he could, which unsurprisingly was for much longer than he ever could before. Soon, he could no longer continue and eventually collapsed. But what greatly surprised him, though, was looking over to see Juro still on his feet, running on his hind legs with purpose in each step. Despite his exhaustion, Azalar smiled at the younger mouse, feeling a sense of pride in young mouse. A shock from the collar signaled for him to get back up and continue running, to which Azalar begrudgingly did so. Not because of the collar or the humans told him to; Azalar was determined to keep his promise, not just to the younger mouse, but to all the rodents within this lab. His mind was set now, and he was determined to see his fellow rodents free.

Several hours later, Azalar was taken to another section of the lab and placed in a cage where many of the rodents were to get their blood tested, which was the worst part in Azalar's opinion. No matter how many times he got pricked, he never got used to the pain of it. Just before that Azalar had managed to talk to Nikamius. The poor elder mouse was still devastated over the loss of his mate. However, once Azalar told him about the plan to escape, his mood seemed to lighten, even if it was just a little bit. A small sense of newfound determination appeared to have been reawakened in him.

"Whatever you need of me, my friend," said Nikamius, "you have my word I will aid you however

I can. Háth may still have a plan for us yet. But you need to talk to the rats. They may be key to our endeavor to escape."

Now Azalar was sitting in a cage with many other mice waiting to have their blood taken. Fortunately, it was all the mice that he had hoped to see. Amara, Bark, Frella, Bogger, Nikamius, Juro, and Brim were all in the same cage with him; even Della was there. Since there were plenty of mice and rats ahead of them, and Azalar and his company were tucked away in this little corner of the lab, it was the perfect time to come up with a plan of escape. Once they were brought together, Azalar explained to Bark, Frella and Della exactly what was going on and what they were planning to do, to which they happily agreed. Azalar then turned to the others.

"We don't have much time," said Azalar. "So, we have to make this quick. Have you all gotten word to the others of the plan?"

"I've managed to convince a few to join us," Nikamius said. "They were more than eager to join our cause and escape this infernal place."

"I have talked with a few others, as well," Bogger added. "They seemed hesitant, but with a little more time and assurance, I'm sure they will come around."

"I unfortunately wasn't able to talk to anyone," Brim said dejectedly. "The humans had me in the labyrinth by myself for some time. But there are two others that I have no doubt are sure to join us. Their names are Mith and Borith. I know them well. They are strong willed mice, and I'm sure that once I tell them of our plan, they will be eager to join. But I haven't been around them in a long while, so I cannot say when the next chance I see them will come."

"That's quite alright," Azalar said. "We still have time to bring them in. But we need to come up with a plan as well, or else no one will have confidence to join us.”

“Does anyone have any idea?” Bark asked. “I’ve known Azalar for a long time and he’s always talked about leaving this place, but now we’re sitting here actually talking of escaping. Does anyone actually have a plan on how we do that?”

“First things first,” Bogger interjected. “We need to find a way to open our cages. The doors are too high for us mice to reach them; and even if we were to, we wouldn’t be able to have the leverage to pry the tops open from our positioning. Those doors have a bar on the outside that hooks underneath the lip of the walls at the top to prevent us from just pushing them open, so we would need to find something long and sturdy in order to reach that bar and free it.” Bark looked suspiciously at Bogger, not like how human this mouse sounded.

“How could you possibly know all that?” he asked. Bogger scoffed at Bark and his ignorance.

“Unlike *some* of us, many rodents have had our intelligence heightened, mine in particular has incr-eased significantly, so I am able to study things and retain memory at a much higher rate. You should give it a try some time, it may do you wonders instead of just talking with nothing significant to say.” Bark narrowed his eyes in a glare at the dark red mouse. He may not have known Bogger for very long, but he was already starting to dislike him. Frella decided to step in between the two before things got out of hand.

“Now, now boys, there’s no need for this,” she said sternly. “We’re all on the same side here, so we need to work together if we want a chance to get out of here. And Bark, there is no need to be rude, Bogger just has a better understanding of things.” Bark let out a huff before turning away.

“I suppose so,” he said begrudgingly.

"So do you have any idea where we can get our hands on something like that?" Della asked. Della was Frella's sister from the same litter, the only surviving members of their family, with Frella being older by a few seconds, something that she would often tease Della about. Her fur was a lighter shade of brown though, with a small white patch on top of her head. Bogger thought for a moment.

"It would have to be something strong enough to withstand the pressure of pulling the bar free while the holder is pressing down from the other side. Something that wouldn't easily break. Possibly metal as well."

"But how would we get something like that?" Brim asked. "It's not like the humans will just hand us one of their tools. And even if they happened to drop something, they always have their eyes on us anyway. We'd never have the opportunity to grab it, let alone hide long enough to use it."

"I have faith that we will find a way," Nikamius retorted. "Azalar has received many messages from Háth. And I know that with his blessing, we will find a way out of here,"

"I don't know if my dreams were messages from Háth, Nikamius," Azalar said. "But I do know that if my dreams are anything to go by, we cannot continue to remain here, or it will be the death of us all. And I, for one, am not willing to die in this place, nor am I willing to see any of you die as well."

"But how can you be sure that we can escape?" Juro asked. "If we do break out of our cages, how do we get outside? I don't know about any of you, but I've never been outside this room. Who knows what's out there?" Nikamius placed a gentle paw on Juro's shoulder, causing the younger mouse to look up at the elder.

"Just have faith in Azalar, young one," Nikamius said softly. "Háth has chosen him as our deliverer. As long as we stay true to each other, we will overcome any challenge. We are with you Azalar!" Azalar smiled at Nikamius. Though he still wasn't too confident in Nikamius' faith in him being the deliverer from Háth, he was determined to free his fellow rodents, by whatever means necessary.

"I agree with Nikamius," Brim stated. "Take heart, young mouse. We will make it out of here one way or another. The humans have underestimated us for too long. It's time we show them what we're really capable of." Brim's voice was filled with such confidence and determination that even Juro couldn't help but smile at his words. Della nuzzled Brim affectionately, feeling quite proud of her fréfil.

"We're going to need help though," Bogger said. "This plan requires as many minds and muscles as possible. As Nikamius had mentioned to you before, the rats would be of great value to us. With their aid, it would greatly increase our chances of success significantly."

"I'll take care of that," Azalar stated. "I'll speak to Ragath whenever I get the chance. But first we'll need a solid plan first if we hope to win him over."

"What do you have in mind?" Bark asked.

"Nothing for certain yet, but I will say this much. We'll have to be careful and stealthy. For now, let's play their little game. They already know that our intelligence has improved, but we can't let them know how much it really has. Spread the word around to anyone who will listen. I want everyone to take things slow. If we start showing the humans how much we can learn, they may grow suspicious of us and take extra precautions. Especially around Helgan. If he so much as catches a scent of what we're doing, it's over for us. So be careful!"

"Ragath is going to need more than that to join us," Frella said.

“I know, but it's the best we have so far. We still need more time to think things through. I don't want our plan falling apart before we've even begun.”

“We'll figure something out,” Amara said as she placed a paw on her mate’s arm. “If anyone can convince Ragath and the rats to join us, it is you, my love.” Azalar smiled and placed his own paw on top of hers before turning back to the other.

“This isn’t going to be easy,” Azalar started, “so I’m going to need all of your help.” The other mice around him all smiled and nodded their heads.

“Just remember that I’m holding you to your promise, Azalar,” Juro said with a laugh. Azalar smiled at the youngest mouse before patting him on the head.

“I know you will, Juro,” he said softly. “But I want you to promise me that you will never give up fighting either. We need you just as much.” Juro was hesitant for a moment. Despite his jesting manner, he was absolutely terrified of the future and what it held ahead. But hearing Azalar’s words and his promises of freedom gave a warm feeling in his heart, and he looked up at Azalar, giving him a smile and a nod.

Azalar’s smile widened as he looked at the other mice around him, all of whom were smiling at him in return. Azalar thought for a moment, feeling like he should say something else to them. But unfortunately, he never got the chance as the top of the cage opened up and a hand reached inside, grabbing the first mouse closest, which happened to be Azalar, and pulled him out. Azalar was turned around and saw the large needle slowly drawing closer to him. Azalar closed his eyes and waited for what was to come next.

Chapter VI

It was now late at night; all the humans had left a long time ago and the rodents of the lab were fast asleep. Azalar, for the first time in a long time, was far too tired to think about anything, let alone a plan to escape. After the heinous experience of the day, Azalar was for once grateful to be inside his cage.

After the blood work, Azalar was thrown back into Helgan's experiments. During those experiments, Azalar had been hard at work trying to recruit as many rodents as possible to aid in the escape, trying to see if there were any more with special skills to aid them. So far all he had talked to were fellow mice, and none of them had any skills that they were aware of, other than increased strength and intelligence. Although they didn't have any significant skills, there were plenty who were all for escaping this horrid place.

He didn't even have a chance to talk to the rats; however, Azalar didn't think that would be a problem. If he can convince Ragath to join him, the rest of the rats would surely follow, but that would have to be another time. Right now, Azalar's body was in great pain, and the pain from the needle was still fresh on his left side.

Azalar lay down in his nest with Amara nuzzled beside him, she too had endured an exhausting day, not to mention the sprain in her ankle had not helped in the experiments and exercises that she took part in. She did her best to keep her leg elevated as Bogger had suggested by piling the bedding under her leg to keep it up, but it was not as comfortable as she had hoped. Now the two lay together, trying their best to sleep the aches and pains away, but it was proving to be futile.

Their new bodies didn't help much and proved to be more troublesome to get used to as they had originally thought when it came to laying in their nest. Normally they would nuzzle themselves into little balls and curl up next to each other to sleep. However, with their longer bodies and limbs, it was not as comfortable as it had been before. No matter which way they turned, the pain in their muscles shot like lightning through their bodies, making it extremely difficult to find any sort of amenity or respite.

Until at long last, they both finally found a position they were most comfortable in, though it was not by much, but it was enough to allow them to at least not aggravate their tender muscles. They lay with their long bodies stretched out, with Amara's leg resting as comfortably as it could on a soft lump of bedding and the two cuddled up next to one another to keep warm. It was the best they could do to slowly fall into a restless sleep.

However, it was short lived when the doors to the lab slammed open, rousing everyone from their slumber. Azalar quickly sat up and turned to see a group of three humans entering the lab, all three tumbling and laughing and slurring in unintelligible words. One of them was laughing so hard that he stumbled forward and nearly slammed his head against one of the tables, the other two laughing even harder at his mishap. It took a moment for his eyes to adjust, but Azalar quickly recognized the one who stumbled as Trevor.

"You better watch yourself, Trevor," one of the humans said between laughs. "Don't go breaking anything. Or else Helgan will have himself a fit."

"Helgan can kiss my hairy ass," Trevor said after picking himself up. "Who cares what he thinks anyway? He's nothing but a huge prick." He took another drink from the bottle he was holding and staggered further into the room. As He walked, he glared at everything in the room, sneering in disgust as if everything he saw had offended him.

"This is all ridiculous," Trevor spat. "Helgan is no older than I am, yet they gave that douchebag the position as head geneticist. He only got that position because he used his family's wealth to get him there. If I had that kind of money, I wouldn't be in this stupid place. I would have had my own private beach somewhere living the good life. It's not right that I have to take orders from that arrogant creep. He thinks he's so much better than us." Trevor took one last large gulp of the contents of the bottle before tossing it into the trash bin to the side.

"To be fair, Trevor," said one of the humans, a thin, frail, yet young, looking man with long brown hair tied in a bun at the top, "Helgan was here longer than all of us. And from what I've heard, he has done quite a bit of fighting on the front lines during the war. So, it would only make some sense that they gave Helgan the position that he currently has." Trevor turned and glared at his companion.

"Are you defending that sack of piss, Evans?" he hissed. Austin raised both hands up in defense, one hand holding a similar bottle, though he didn't seem to be all that intimidated by Trevor's demeanor.

"Not at all," he said. "Just simply stating a fact. I wholeheartedly agree that he's a self-righteous, arrogant, no go charlatan. I dislike him very much; almost as much as you do." Trevor seemed to approve of this answer and turned around and wandered about the lab, seeming to be looking for something. All the while Azalar watched them closely. It had been a long while since these three came to the lab so late at night, and each time they did it was never good for them. He had a sinking suspicion of what they were up to until he caught the scent of something very sweet in the air, and a sense of dread filled his chest.

"Come on, are we going to have some fun or not?" said a short, round man with red hair. "I got the candy right here. Let's get to it already!" Trevor turned back and gave his other friend a smirk.

"Just be patient, Lebo," he replied before turning back to continue his search. "I just need to find the damn key. Alice is usually the first one in here, but she always puts it in a different spot every night, so it must be around here somewhere." He continued to search through the lab, checking under every desk and counter, even checking in between cracks and spaces between. With how much he was wobbling and swaying about the room, it was a wonder that he never knocked anything over.

Azalar's body was tense, all thought of his sore and aching body vanished as he stepped back and leaned against Amara in a protective manner with Amara curling up fearfully next to him. He just hoped that Alice had hidden the key well this time. It was taking a good while and Azalar's hopes were beginning to rise as Trevor and his two companions were seemingly getting more and more impatient, until at last Trevor finally spoke.

"Found you!" he said, pulling a key from within a book that was on one of the back counters. Azalar's hopes were dashed as he watched Trevor staggering towards one of the lower cabinets and unlocked it, pulling out a large transparent container and placing it on one of the tables. All three humans smiled.

"Here we go," Trevor said with excitement. "Now we're getting somewhere."

"Is it time yet?" Lebo asked with excitement, practically hopping up and down.

"Almost," Trevor replied. He then turned and opened one of the drawers behind him, pulling out a pair of leather gloves. With a sinister smile, he looked over at the rodent cages and drunkenly made his way over. He stopped just in front of Azalar's cage.

"Let's have some fun," Trevor said with a wicked grin. He opened Azalar's cages and slowly reached inside. His hand was swaying from side to side as it drew closer to them. Then in a quick motion, quicker than Azalar had expected, Trevor grabbed hold of Azalar and pulled him out of the cage, nearly causing the poor mouse to hit his head on the bars above. Trevor lifted Azalar until he was in front of his face.

"Let's see how Alice and Helgan feel when we have fun with their favorite pet." His words were accompanied by a foul scent that stung Azalar's nostrils and caused him to wrinkle his nose. Trevor took the little mouse towards the container, but before he placed him inside, Evans placed a shock collar around his neck. Once the collar was secured, Trevor dropped Azalar, not too gently, on one side. He then turned to Lebo.

"Go grab the giant rat!" he barked. Lebo narrowed his eyes and gave a little huff, but did as he was told, grabbing another pair of leather gloves and heading over to Ragath's cage.

Though he was nervous and hesitant, he did manage to grab hold of Ragath with both hands, but not without Ragath putting up a massive fight. Lebo ran back to Evans, who placed a shock collar on Ragath as well, and quickly dropped Ragath on the other side across from Azalar.

Azalar gazed upon the large rat in front of him. No doubt the serum had a great impact on Ragath's body. His arms and legs were longer, and his muscles were very toned and defined; much more than they were before. If Ragath wasn't a powerful rodent before, he most certainly was now. However, as Azalar studied the large black rat, he noticed that even though he was indeed the largest rat in the whole lab; still larger as compared to him, he didn't seem to be as large as he was the last time Azalar's eyes fell upon him. Could it be that Azalar had grown so much that Ragath no longer appeared to be the giant rodent that he previously was? Lebo removed his gloves and began rubbing his hands gently.

"That rotten little pest has one hell of a bite," he whimpered. "He nearly bit right through the gloves. Why can't we get those fancy gloves that Helgan has?"

"Oh, stop complaining," Trevor said. "Do you have the candy ready?" Lebo huffed again with annoyance at Trevor's attitude and took the piece of candy that was in his pocket: a large chocolate bar that was partially melted due to being inside a warm article of clothing with a large man's intense body heat emanating next to it. Lebo tore open the wrapping and broke a small piece off, dropping it in between Ragath and Azalar. The two rodents stared at the piece of candy for a moment before looking up at one another.

"I guess it's our turn this time. Isn't it, little mouse?" Ragath asked rhetorically. Azalar didn't let it show, but he was growing increasingly nervous. Once every few days for the past few weeks, Trevor and these other two humans would sneak into the lab late at night when everyone was asleep. They would then pick two rodents at random, sometimes two mice or two rats, sometimes just one mouse and one rat, and place a piece of chocolate between the two and watch them fight for it. Chocolate was very alluring to the rodents; the sweetness and flavor of the chocolate was irresistible to them. So, in many cases, just placing the chocolate in their little *arena,* as they called it, was enough to force the rodents to fight each other for it, especially the rats. If any of the rodents refused to fight, Trevor would shock them until they did. Though no one was ever killed in these fights, many received extensive injuries, which greatly impeded their performances in Helgan's experiments. Either way, Trevor got his entertainment. Azalar, seeing no way out of this, readied himself as best as he could for the coming fight.

"I suppose it is," Azalar replied.

Neither Azalar nor Ragath made a move towards each other. At first, they just stared at one another, waiting for the other to make their first move. Thinking quickly, Azalar thought that now would be as good of a time as any to talk to Ragath about his plan.

"It doesn't have to be this way, Ragath," Azalar said. "Listen to me. We can help each other. We don't have to live like this. We don't have to be their playthings anymore. The other mice and I have come together to–"

"Yes, I've heard about your little plan to escape, little mouse," Ragath interrupted in his low, harsh voice. "It is a hopeless dream! Do you really think you have what it takes to leave this place?"

"Come on already!" Trevor growled. "Fight!" But still neither rodent made a move. Fed up with the continuous stare down, Trevor took the remote to the collars and pressed it, sending a terrible shock to the two rodents. Azalar and Ragath flinched at the pain; though they had prepared themselves for it, it was still painful. But despite the pain, Azalar continued to try and reason with Ragath.

"But Ragath, if we can work together–" Another Shock came from the collars. Ragath was now growing more and more irritated.

"Enough of this!" he shouted. Ragath then lunged at Azalar, but the little mouse managed to jump out of the way just in time. Azalar turned to face the giant rat and was nearly struck in the face by his massive paw. He ducked underneath; running to the other side to keep as much distance between them as possible. He had seen Ragath fight other rats before, but none had been able to lay a scratch on him, so Azalar was sure that didn't even stand a chance in hell against the black rat.

"Ragath, please listen to me." But the black rat did not listen as he continued his assault and pounced at him. Azalar did his best to keep his distance, but his movements felt unnatural. He then remembered that he no longer needed to use all four legs to run about; he could use his newly acquired stronger legs. Azalar stood at full height and jumped out of the way of Ragath. He jumped back and forth, dodging every one of Ragath's strikes. Azalar found it to be much easier to evade Ragath than he had originally thought, as he could turn his body more quickly than he would on all fours simply by pivoting one foot onto the other. This way all he had to do was to keep Ragath from grabbing hold of his tail.

The humans above seemed to be enjoying the show, as they were all pointing, laughing, and mocking them, their foul smelling breaths emanating down upon them from their ghastly mouths.

Azalar continued to try to talk to Ragath, but every word that he attempted was quickly interrupted by Ragath's continuous onslaught. Though Ragath could stand on his back legs just as well as Azalar, he remained on all fours, refusing to stand like a human, though it would give him a greater advantage. Azalar saw now that there was no point in trying to talk to Ragath, as he did not seem to be interested in anything he had to say. There was no other choice now; he had to fight back.

Just as Ragath made another pounce for him, Azalar ducked under the black rat and hit him under the chin using his head. The blow sent Ragath staggering back and falling over. A moment later, Ragath was up again. He shook his head and was once more on the offensive. As the fight went on, Azalar proved to be much quicker than Ragath, dodging and striking at Ragath at every opening he saw, all the while the humans continued to cheer and laugh at them.

The two rodents continued to dance around each other, Azalar dodging Ragath and countering with a strike of his own, with Ragath unable to touch Azalar at all during the battle. Ragath made one more move to go for Azalar's neck, but Azalar was expecting that and countered by dodging out of the way and swiping at Ragath's mouth with his right paw. It was much stronger than he expected as the strike caused Ragath to stagger and smack his head against the wall, sending Ragath into a small daze. Just then a single drop of blood fell from Ragath's mouth.

"Oh, the mouse drew blood!" Lebo cried in glee as the other two humans laughed and cheered.

"This is going to be brutal!" Trevor laughed. They always got excited when blood was drawn, it usually meant that the fight was going to get more brutal and entertaining for them. Ragath looked down at the drop of blood on the floor before looking at Azalar with a burning fire of anger and hatred, and he lunged at the little mouse once again.

Fear gripped at Azalar's heart, but that did not stop him from keeping up the fight. Ragath swiped and bit at Azalar, but he was never able to even touch the tanned mouse. Azalar managed to keep his distance, striking only when he was able to, until he made a misstep and tripped over himself. The next thing

Azalar saw was Ragath leaping into the air and was quickly upon him, opening his mouth wide and biting down on the back of Azalar's neck just behind the collar.

Azalar squeaked in surprise and fear as he waited for the pain and the cold touch of death as the humans above cheered and roared in excitement. But despite Ragath's teeth around Azalar's neck and his claws gripping at his body, there was no pain. Azalar looked curiously at Ragath, whose eyes were so close to his. There was no malice within them, nor any anger, not towards him at least. Instead, what Azalar saw was a faint light of admiration, or at least that's as close to what he thought it could be. And the tight grip around his neck, and his teeth making no sign of puncturing his skin, told him that Ragath had no intention of finishing him off.

Azalar quickly twisted his body out of Ragath's grip, pushing off his body with his strong legs and readying himself to continue the fight. Yet, when he turned to face the rat, he saw that Ragath made no move to strike or pounce at him. Ragath just stood there on his hind legs staring at him. Azalar wasn't sure, but he thought he could see a small trace of a smile on the black rat's lips. It was then that Azalar realized what Ragath had been doing all this time: he had been testing him.

Azalar stared at Ragath for a moment before he returned the smile. The two rodents remained where they were, neither one making a move to continue the fight. This lasted a few moments. The humans above seemed confused as they looked at each other perplexed.

"What's going on?" Lebo asked unamused. "Why aren't they fighting anymore?"

"Toss in another piece of chocolate," Evans said. Lebo did as he was told and tossed another piece of chocolate in between the two. But neither rodent made a move towards the candy; instead, they simply looked at the chocolate for a moment before looking up at the humans with looks of defiance. Trevor was getting very annoyed and took out the remote and pressed it. The remote sent a powerful shock to both Ragath and Azalar, causing them both to drop down to the floor. They had prepared themselves for Trevor's coming wrath, but the shocks still were enough to bring them down.

"Come on!" Trevor cried. "Fight!" He pressed the remote again, but neither rodent made a move. They stood defiant where they were, refusing to bend to Trevor's will. Trevor let out a roar of frustration and increased the voltage on the collars.

"I said fight!" The two rodents squealed and curled in pain, but despite it all, neither made a move except to continue staring at Trevor in rebellion. This really angered Trevor as he increased the voltage on the remote again. Evans noticed his actions and grew concerned.

"Trevor, I don't think that's a good idea." Trevor shot Evan a glare.

"Shut up!" he barked; his mind too intoxicated to see reason. Trevor was not having any of it. He was not going to allow these miserable rodents to make a fool out of him. He pressed the button on the remote, but this time he kept his thumb pressed on the button with great force, almost enough to break it.

When Trevor pressed the button, the shock that came from their collars was so great that both rodents let out terrible cries of pain and agony. Never before had either felt such a pain as this, so there was no way for them to prepare for it. Only Helgan had ever used the collars to kill before, but never had the collars been used in such a way as this. Trevor kept his thumb pressed on the button as he stared at the squirming rodents beneath him, feeling a great sense of power, like their lives were now in his hands, and a sadistic smile crept on his face. Even Evans and Lebo grew uncomfortable seeing him like this.

Azalar could feel the skin under his fur burning from the collar. He desperately wanted to reach for the collar, but with the electricity coursing painfully through his body, his muscles were too stiff for him to move. Tears were forming in his eyes from the agony as each torturous second felt like an eternity, and all he could do was scream.

His mind was going crazy and all the poor mouse could think about was the agony he was in. There was no end in sight; Azalar was sure this was going to be his last night in the world. He didn't want that; he didn't want to leave his fréfil behind. He had a promise to keep. However, the pain was becoming too much for Azalar, and for the first time in Azalar's life, he silently prayed for it to end. Suddenly the doors to the lab slammed open and the pain to Azalar's neck suddenly stopped.

"What is going on here?!" cried a familiar voice. Everyone turned towards the doors to see Alice standing in the doorway, her eyes wide with shock and anger. She wasn't wearing her usual lab attire, but instead she was wearing a pink sweater and blue sweatpants and her hair was let loose down her back. Evans and Lebo quickly backed away from the box, their hands up in defense and surrender as they tried to shield themselves behind Trevor from the woman's fiery glare. Trevor, on the other hand, made no move to step away from the table, instead smiled mockingly at Alice.

"What the hell are you doing?" Alice stormed across the room with animosity in her step and drew closer to Trevor, who scoffed at her; too drunk to care about her demeanor.

"We were just having a little fun," Trevor said while laughing. However, Alice didn't seem to be in a laughing mood. She stepped forward aggressively towards them.

"What is wrong with you?!" Alice shouted. She was now directly in Trevor's face, but he did not flinch. "Forcing these poor creatures to fight each other for your entertainment? And when they don't fight for you, you torture them? You are all sick!" Trevor, not taking kindly to Alice's attitude towards him, furrowed his eyebrows and glared back at her.

"And how is this any different to what we do every day?!" he shouted. "We stick them all with needles, cut them open, and force them to do all sorts of things, and when they don't do it, we shock them. And for what? We run test after test, after test. But what is it all for?"

"That's completely different!" Alice exclaimed. "And I don't enjoy doing that either, but you know why we're doing this. Dr. Helgan is trying to find a way to save Mankind from the Scourge. We're doing these experiments so that one day we create soldiers that are capable of combating them so that we can go home; to go back to our lives. And what do you do? You three are in here, drinking, and treating these already suffering creatures as your playthings, as if you have any right to treat them that way! You are all utterly disgusting! You should all be ashamed of yourselves!" Trevor somehow found her words amusing and let out a long, mocking laugh.

"You really believe that bullshit story?" he said. "That we're here trying to 'find a way to save mankind'? Yeah right! If you ask me, that psychopathic lunatic just wants to play God. Have you seen what he does in the lower levels? Those little 'experiments' that he's made? What is the point of those as well, huh? To save humanity?" Alice didn't answer right away, for she had no answer to give. She had not traveled to the lower levels of the Laboratory, though she did hear the rumors of what Helgan had been doing down there, and none of them sounded pleasant at all.

"I'm sure Helgan has his reasons for that," Alice said, trying to sound confident; but the tone in her voice betrayed her words. Trevor gave a cruel smile.

"Of course, you would defend him," he said mockingly. "Poor, little Alice Merrell, so in love with the great Dr. Ramsey Helgan, that she will defend his honor despite how he treats her." Alice narrowed her eyes, but her cheeks were flustering terribly.

"T-that's not true at all!" Alice stuttered. "I-I just believe in what he's doing. I know that he will find a way. A-all we need to do is have faith in him." This time it was Trevor who stepped forwards, towering over Alice.

"You really think he will feel anything for you?" he said just above a whisper. "No matter how much you follow him around, no matter how much you do what he tells you, you will be nothing more than just a sad lost puppy for him to play with. He will never love you." Tears were forming in Alice's eyes.

"You don't know what you're talking about!" she shouted. Trevor laughed some more.

"It's just so pathetic, you know?" he continued. "You spend all your time following him around, being his good little lab assistant. Yet he never acknowledges you.

"Shut up!" Alice said through gritted teeth. Trevor leaned closer, his foul breath entering her nose.

"He will never love you."

"I said shut up!" Without thinking, Alice swung her hand and slapped Trevor across the face, sending him staggering back until he fell flat on his back. Everyone stood shocked at what just happened, especially Alice herself. She hated confrontation of any sort; and she had never struck anyone before, much less in anger. Yet now that she had done it, all the anger that she had quickly vanished and was replaced with fear and anxiety. Trevor sat up and rubbed his left cheek, his lips turned upward into a sneer.

"Oh," he said. "So that's how you want to play, huh?" He stood up and slowly made his way towards Alice, his fist balled up at his side. Alice took a step back, her heart beating faster with every second.

"I-I'm sorry!" she said in a panic. "Trevor, I'm sorry!"

"Not as sorry as you're going to be," he retorted in a low, threatening voice, drawing closer. Evans and Lebo made no move to step in between them, for they did not want to be at the other end of Trevor's wrath.

Better her than us, they thought to themselves. Trevor took another step closer to Alice and raised his fist. Alice raised her arms in front of her in an attempt to defend herself from what was about to come, but before anything could happen, a new voice entered the room.

"Are you all amusing yourselves in here?" came the voice from behind. All eyes turned to the doors and all their faces fell in horror, even Trevor's. There stood Helgan himself, standing tall with a black, slim fit turtleneck sweater and gray pants, his long hair falling loosely down his back with his arms behind him. He did not look pleased.

"I see we're having ourselves a party in my own lab that I was not invited to," Helgan said as he stepped into the room. Alice turned around to face him fully.

"I'm sorry, sir!" she said. "My cat got out and I was trying to catch him when I saw–" She was interrupted when Helgan raised his hand to silence her, then with the same hand waved her to the side. Alice lowered her head and did as she was silently told. Helgan then looked at the other three, Evans, Lebo and Trevor, before looking down at the mouse and rat that were lying in a clear box with shock collars and a couple pieces of chocolate between them.

Azalar, who had only slightly recovered, looked up into those cold dark eyes staring down at him. He had never seen that look in Helgan's eyes before, and it sent a cold chill running down his spine. Helgan looked back at the three men.

"So, this is what you three have been up to lately," Helgan stated rather than asked. "Using my equipment, my experience for your own amusement. I must say, I am very disappointed." Trevor narrowed his eyes at Helgan. He hated how he always talked down to him as if he were a child. He always felt humiliated around Helgan, but he wasn't going to take it any longer. Though it must be his intoxicated mind from the drinks he had, he suddenly gained a boost of confidence.

"Well, you can shove your disappointment," Trevor spat. Helgan simply raised an eyebrow.

"Excuse me?" he asked simply.

"You heard me!" Trevor barked, his confidence beginning to rise within him. "I've just about had it with your arrogance. You think you're so much better than the rest of us, yet we do all your dirty work for you. And what do we get for it? Tending to these filthy rodents day in and day out. We run your experiments for you, and we don't seem to be getting any closer to the end results. I don't even know what they are anymore, nor do I see any point to these experiments other than you wanting to play God! Well, I'm sick of it all. You can take your little research and experiments and shove it right up yours!"

There was a tense silence in the room as everyone watched on as both Trevor and Helgan stared at one another. Alice placed her hands over her heart, as if to muffle the sounds of her heart beating faster with every second; her anxiety rising in her chest and her body began to tremble, fearing what was to come next. The other two, Lebo and Evans, stood stiff where they were; afraid to make any move for fear of drawing attention to themselves. Helgan, however, despite the tensions in the air, had not moved at all; his features unreadable as he kept his eyes locked on Trevor, who stood confidently with his chest out, as if he had won a major victory. But the awkward silence and the cold stare from Helgan was slowly breaking down his confidence, but he refused to let it show. There was more silence for a few moments longer before Helgan finally spoke.

"If you're done throwing your little temper tantrum," Helgan said, "please clean up this mess and return to your quarters. All of you. We will discuss this deliberate insubordination when you're of clearer minds." Helgan then turned and made his way towards the door. Trevor, however, had finally reached his breaking point from having been talked down to like a child. His anger had now clouded his mind and he took a step forward with a balled fist.

"Don't you turn your back to me!" He shouted while swinging his fist at Helgan's head. But suddenly, Helgan turned around and caught Trevor's fist with his left hand just before he made contact. Everyone was shocked by Helgan's quick reflexes.

"You seem to be forgetting one thing, Mr. Berkins," Helgan said in a low and harsh voice. He then quickly stepped forward and, with his right hand, gripped Trevor by the throat, slowly lifting him up off the ground. Trevor grabbed Helgan's wrist around his neck with his free hand and tried to pry it off, but Helgan's grip was far too strong.

"In here," Helgan said slowly, "I am God!" He suddenly threw Trevor across the room until he slammed against the cabinets in the back. Trevor let out a gasp, the impact from the crash knocking the air from lungs clean out of him, before collapsing to the floor. Alice had let out a loud scream from what happened, but she dared not move an inch, no one in the room did. What then had just witnessed was a side of Helgan that was never thought possible. However, they saw him before, he was even more terrifying now. Helgan then turned to Evan and Lebo.

"Take him back to his room, immediately," he ordered. Lebo and Evans didn't hesitate and quickly rushed to their colleague, picking him up and taking him out of the room. Helgan then turned to Alice, giving her a gentle smile.

"If you please, Alice," He said in a much softer voice, "could you clean up this mess and return the specimens back to their cages?" With that, Helgan left the room, leaving a very unnerved Alice all alone. She was completely dumbfounded by what had occurred mere moments ago. Nonetheless, she quickly broke her trance and went about cleaning the lab and setting it back in order. She removed the collars from Azalar's and Ragath's necks and gently returned them to their respective cages. Once there, Azalar was immediately greeted by his beloved with a gentle nuzzle.

"Are you alright, my love?" Amara asked. Azalar nuzzled her in return, though he made sure to keep his.

"I'm fine, my star," he said. "Everything is fine." After a moment, Amara pulled away and looked up at her fréfil.

"What happened?" Azalar didn't answer right away, instead he looked out into the Lab where Alice was busy cleaning up after everything that happened.

"I'm not entirely sure," he said honestly. He then looked off towards the upper left corner to be specific and smiled. "But I think we may have a new ally in Ragath."

Chapter VII

Azalar dropped down on all fours, gasping for breath. He had been running at full speed for over half an hour on his hind legs with weights strapped to his back. It had been four weeks since the incident with Trevor and Helgan and since their transformation. In that time, Azalar had been hard at work trying to find a way to escape. He and the others searched for anything that could to aid them, but the humans were very careful and kept a close eye on all of them. Yet, they did not give up. The only thing that they were about to get their paws on was when one of the mice found a paperclip and was able to hide it in their cage. However, when they attempted to use the paperclip to open the door, it bent under the pressure until it eventually broke and became useless. Yet, they did not give up. Azalar reassured them that they would find a way. Until then, they all kept at it with Helgan's experiments.

Azalar had grown quite accustomed to using his rear legs during that time. He had even begun to grow used to Helgan's intense experiments since then. In fact, Azalar felt himself getting stronger with each passing day. However, Helgan would sometimes decide that he wasn't getting the desired results that he wanted and would push some of the rodents past their limits. It had been like this for a few days now, with Helgan continuously making the tests much more difficult. It was starting to become too much for them, even for Azalar. Although this wasn't always the case, especially as it was now with Alice. Azalar was very grateful that it was Alice running the tests today, since she wouldn't use the shock collars on them when Helgan wasn't around. It allowed the rodents a bit of a respite.

Trevor, however, had not been seen in all that time, not since that incident four weeks ago. It was as if he just disappeared altogether. Alice had inquired about him the next few days, but no one had seen or heard of him since. Alice, being the kindhearted soul that she was, grew concerned for him. Though she quite disliked him and found him rather irritating more often than not, she still hoped no harm had come to him. One day Alice asked Helgan about Trevor, but only got a minor response.

"He's taken some time to reflect on himself," Helgan said. "I'm fairly positive that by the end of it, he will find himself a new person." This answer seemed to satisfy Alice and she left the whole thing at that.

Lebo and Evans on the other hand were quite distant from the rest of the humans; keeping to themselves in the corner away from everyone; sometimes they wouldn't even show up to the lab on many occasions. When they did appear at the lab, they both made sure to stay as far away from the rodents as possible while still conducting the experiments and doing their jobs. Azalar found it rather peculiar, but he didn't mind in the slightest.

"I think that's enough for today," Alice said as she stopped the small device in her hand that had numbers on it, which Azalar now understood to be what the humans called a clock. Alice then removed the weights from Azalar's back before taking him off the treadmill and into another container on the table. Azalar welcomed the rest as he laid on the floor, wincing at the pain in his legs.

"Running for thirty minutes while holding 20 ounces," Alice said as she wrote down the number. "You're definitely getting stronger, little guy." Azalar could hear the sincerity in her voice and looked up at the female human to see her smiling down at him. Azalar, for his part, was still unsure on how to feel about this human. She was indeed much kinder than the others, but she was still a human who was doing Helgan's bidding, regardless of how she felt about it.

Alice leaned down closer to Azalar.

"You know," she said quietly, "I've always admired mice. How they can be so resilient. Among the smallest creatures in the world, yet can handle almost anything the world throws at them." Azalar looked away, not having the energy to really acknowledge what Alice had to say, even if it was to praise him. Alice leaned forward and rested her chin on one of her hands, still admiring Azalar.

"If only you could understand me," she said. "There's so much I would love to talk to you about." Though Azalar's body ached, he impulsively looked up at her, locking eyes with her. He felt like it was a mistake to do so, but looking in her eyes, seeing the sincerity in them, gave him a strange feeling in his stomach.

Alice had been in Helgan's lab longer than Azalar could remember, and in all that time she had always been a kind soul.

Alice had come to talk to all the rodents of the lab. Azalar always thought that she was mainly talking to herself rather than them. However, now he came to realize that she was actually talking to them as if they were her fellow humans. He found this curious and inquired about it to Nikamius some time back, but he couldn't give him a clear answer.

"It seems to give her a little comfort in some way," Nikamius said. "She rarely talks to the other humans except for Helgan. I suppose she must be feeling lonely."

At first Azalar didn't really care much for Alice's chatter. It wasn't like he could respond back that she would be able to understand. Soon he found himself with a rather peculiar feeling for this human with the way she talked to them. He couldn't quite place it, but he felt something was different about this particular human. Now he didn't mind it so much. Though she was a human, she was very kind to the rodents, so he harbored no ill will against her; but even so, he still did not trust her fully.

After a moment, Alice put on a glove and reached into the container and picked Azalar up, bringing him to another container that was next to the labyrinth.

"Last test for the day, little guy. Just need a blood sample and then we're all done," she said in a soft voice as she opened the lid and placed Azalar inside. "I'm just going to put you in here for a bit while I get the equipment ready." Azalar huffed at this. He really did hate those needles. It was always incredibly painful, no matter how many times he got pricked. But at least he knew that Alice would try to be as gentle as possible, though it did little to help.

Just at that moment, the doors to the lab opened and Dr. Helgan came into the lab, walking at a rather quick pace with a large container with little holes around the top in his arms. Alice was startled by his sudden entrance, almost dropping the needle in her hand, but soon calmed herself and stood straight to face Helgan.

"Alice!" Helgan spoke with a slight hint of eagerness in his tone, something that was quite rare of him. "I did it!" Alice was confused as she stood there silent for a moment.

"Did what, Sir?" she asked. Helgan gave her his signature smirk as he walked past her and placed the box on the table. Alice immediately took notice of the large box and looked curiously at the doctor.

"Sir, what's that?" Alice asked. Helgan chuckled at his assistant and placed a hand on the container.

"I've finally created a new species that is practically unstoppable!" The doors to the lab opened once more and two more humans walked inside, both carrying what seemed to be a much larger container that looked similar to the one that Azalar was currently residing in. The two humans placed the large square container on the center table before being shooed away by Helgan. Both Helgan and Alice walked over to the table, Helgan looking at it excitedly while Alice was looking confused.

"But sir," Alice asked. "What do you mean you created a new species?" Helgan didn't bother to glance her way as he clasped his hands together. "I have been working for weeks on a new species that has the potential to aid us in our endeavors in extraordinary ways," he answered. "With this, my research could reach new heights. And this, my dear Alice, is the ultimate test." Helgan stepped closer to the clear box and placed both hands on the top. "Today, we will see just how far our little creations have come." He turned to his assistant and she could see the pure excitement in his eyes, another quality that was incredibly rare and contrary to his calm and cold demeanor that she was used to, and she wasn't sure if it was a good kind of excitement.

"But Dr. Helgan, what is it for?" Alice asked again. That same disturbing smirk once again formed on Helgan's lips, sending a shiver down Alice's spine.

"You'll see soon enough. Now bring Test Subject 289 here and place him on one side," he ordered as he pointed at Azalar. Alice looked from the Doctor to

Azalar and back again before hesitantly doing as she was ordered. With her gloved hand, she reached in and gently removed Azalar from his container. Azalar took this moment to study this new box he was about to be placed in. From the looks of it, it looked just like the one he just came out of, but much bigger. The only difference was that there was a handle at the top where the divider was. Azalar's instincts were screaming at him that this wasn't just some test, but that his life was now in danger.

Alice opened a small sliding door upwards instead of on top of the lid like the other container. Azalar was placed inside the one section while Dr. Helgan placed the large container on the other side, making sure to connect the box to the other sliding door. After that, Helgan looked back up at his assistant, who was still giving him a questioning look.

"Now, Alice," Helgan said in a low tone. "This will be the greatest moment of our lives. Today, we will see just how far our efforts were made." Another smirk formed on his lips as he placed a hand on the box once again.

"What's in here," Dr. Helgan said with a grin, "is something that I've been working on for nearly as long as these rodents." He patted the box proudly. "A new species of insect that will be a match for any this world has to offer. I give you, the ArchBeetles!"

He then quickly lifted a small door on the side of the container that connected to the tunnel. At first, there was nothing but silence. Then, a clicking and chittering sound came from the box, and it started to grow louder. Azalar stared into the box at the other end of the cage. All he could see was darkness, but the constant clicking was evident that there was indeed something in there. After a solid minute of continuous clicking, the creature finally emerged.

Bursting from the container, a large beetle-like arthropod creature quickly emerged from the box into the light and began striking the side of the glass wall, trying to get to Azalar. The ArchBeetle was giant compared to anything that Azalar had ever seen, even compared to Ragath. It stood almost a foot tall, and its shell was a dark purple and blue color that shimmered in the light. It stood on six muscular legs, three on each side to support its massive body. It had two massive arms that had two massive pincer-like claws at each end. Its shell on its back was wide and round and functions like a suit of armor, which also formed a protective small hood, as well as a large spike, just above the head to protect the neck.

The head itself looked much too small for its body and sat forward in front of its shell, wider at the top and narrowed towards the mouth. It also had two large mandible pincers at the bottom of its head that opened wide and clicked when they closed. Its eyes were small with a dark shade of purple in color.

The ArchBeetle continued to strike aggressively at the glass with its powerful claws; creating a loud bang with every blow as it clicked and chittered ferociously at Azalar. The little mouse stood by, waiting for a possible fight. Alice stared at the giant beetle in both horror and shock.

"Sir! What on earth is that thing?!" She asked, much louder and her voice higher. Doctor Helgan stood with his hands behind his back, staring above proudly at his creation.

"This, my dear Alice, is the result of one of my hybrid experiments. I have been working on this specific species for months. It's an ingenious combination of the Hercules Beetles, Termites, and the Emperor Scorpion. The Queen is a much greater spec-imen." Alice's eyes widened at Helgan's the last statement.

"Queen?" Alice asked. Helgan nodded.

"That's correct, Alice," he confirmed. "The Queen is the most important part of the ArchBeetle colony. The ArchBeetles function in the same manner as a termite colony; These are the soldiers of the colony, whereas the workers are much smaller and more resemble their termite counterparts. These little guys will be able to wipe out anything in their path. They are even strong enough to take down any large beast. With these ArchBeetles, we can create the foundations of an army that will be unstoppable." Alice looked confused by this.

"But sir?" She said, not taking her eyes off the ArchBeetle. "Isn't that exactly why we've been running these experiments and why we've been using these test subjects? So that we can use the research we've gathered to make a serum to create soldiers strong enough to combat the Scourge?" But Helgan just waved her off.

"Yes, yes, of course," he said nonchalantly. "But these are just a precaution. In case our little test subjects prove to be invaluable." The doctor paused and looked up at the ceiling, placing a finger to his chin. Then a smile slowly creeped on his lips.

"Or..." he began, before turning back to his assistant, "if the ArchBeetles prove to be more valuable." Helgan looked down at Azalar with a small grin. Azalar didn't like the way Helgan was looking at him and he went into defensive mode; standing on his hind legs and baring his claws and bared his teeth at the doctor. Helgan chuckled at the mouse, somehow finding it very amusing. Yet Alice, seeing the way he was looking at Azalar, immediately realized what Helgan was planning and quickly spoke up.

"B-but doctor," she said, trying to keep her voice calm, "we've been testing the test subjects' physical strength for weeks. Shouldn't we see how the ArchBeetle performs first?"

"No need," Doctor Helgan said. "I've tested all I needed to. So long as I control the Queen, I control her armies. I am quite confident that I'll have the results I'm looking for." Azalar, hearing what the doctor said, readied himself for a fight. He studied the ArchBeetle carefully while it was still trying to attack him through the glass wall. He knew he was about to be in the fight of his life and tried to think about how he could possibly win this fight. However, his mind was too exhausted from the grueling hours of physical training, which had begun taking their toll on his body. His heart was beginning to beat faster in his chest, and he wasn't sure if he was going to survive this. He looked up at Helgan with a glare as he saw him place his hand on the glass and slowly began to lift.

Helgan was just about to remove the glass wall that was currently separating Azalar from the ArchBeetle completely when Alice quickly grabbed the doctor's hand, stopping him from moving it up any higher. This caused the doctor to glare at his assistant.

"But sir!" Alice said quickly and loudly, her voice filled with anxiety. "Test subject 289 has been training all day. He's not in good condition for a fight. If we put him in now, we may not get the result that you're looking for." Helgan glanced from his assistant to his hand and back again, a hard glare forming in his eyes. It wasn't a moment later until Alice realized what she had just done and quickly withdrew her hand.

"I'm sorry, sir!" Alice said, lowering her head. Helgan didn't respond to her right away, instead he paused for a moment, then looked down at Azalar, as if he was actually thinking about what she had said. He knew exactly what Alice was trying to do, but she did have a point. How was he to be sure that the Arch-Beetle was truly capable enough in a real fight if its opponent was at a disadvantage? The results would be skewed. Then, after a minute or so, he released his hand from the glass wall with a heavy sigh.

"Very well, Alice," Helgan said. "I suppose you're right. It wouldn't do well to run the test while one of the subjects is hindered due to fatigue. Please put subject 289 back in his cage." With a sigh of relief, both from Alice and Azalar, Alice quickly put on her gloves and gently reached into the container, which this time Azalar didn't fight back and was actually grateful as he let Alice gently wrap her fingers around his body. However, he never took his eyes off the ArchBeetle.

After Alice removed Azalar from the container, she made her way over to Azalar's cage, where Amara was eagerly waiting for him. As soon as Alice placed Azalar back in his cage, he was greeted by his fréfil, who immediately wrapped her arms around him and began nuzzling up to him.

"Oh, thank Háth! Are you alright?" Amara asked. Azalar smiled down at his mate as he returned the embrace.

"I'm fine, Amara," he replied. Alice smiled as she witnessed the affection that the two mice were sharing and closed the cage, until Helgan, who had a small yet sinister smirk on his lips, spoke up behind her.

"But bring me test subject 623 in cage 1-2-8," the doctor said suddenly. "He should be well rested by now." Alice practically froze like a statue when she heard his command, and her blood ran cold. Azalar, recognizing the number, quickly turned his gaze to Dr. Helgan with horror in his eyes.

"No!" he shouted. "No! Not him!" But they could not hear nor understand his words. Alice remained where she stood. Of all the subjects he could choose, why did it have to be that one? But she had no choice in the matter as she slowly, yet hesitantly, made her way over to cage number 1-2-8. Azalar ran to the edge of his cage and pressed himself against the window as he watched Alice's every move.

Alice stopped in front of the cage, where only one mouse resided within. Test subject 623, a certain little brown mouse who was still very young, barely a few months old, was trembling in his cage at the sight of her. Juro had witnessed everything that was going on, and when he heard Helgan call his number, Juro felt as if he was going to have a heart attack. Alice paused for a moment, knowing exactly what was going to happen to this poor creature. She tried to think of a good excuse not to use this little mouse for Helgan's little game, but she knew that Helgan wouldn't accept any reason she gave him. Left with no choice, Alice slowly opened the door to the cage and reached inside, quickly grabbing the little mouse, who was frozen with fear, and pulled him out. She held Juro with both hands and turned towards the doctor, who was smiling pleasantly. It was when Azalar saw Juro in Alice's hands that he began to panic frantically.

"Juro!" He called out, scratching at the plastic wall. Amara emerged from behind him to see what was happening. Once she saw Juro in Alice's hands, her eyes grew wide with fear.

"No!" She said, placing her paws to her mouth.

Juro trembled in Alice's hand as he could only look at the creature in the glass container on the table. Alice could feel the poor critter shaking and looked at the Helgan with pleading eyes, trying one last time to reason with him.

"Dr. Helgan," she said, "surely there is another way we could test the subjects. This one is still so—"

"Don't presume to think that you know more than I do, Dr. Merrell!" Helgan shouted, causing Alice to flinch. "I am perfectly aware of the fact that this test subject is still young. As I am also aware of your little infatuation with these rodents." Alice shrank back in fear as she subconsciously held Juro close to her chest, as if she was somehow trying to protect him. Helgan stepped forward until he was directly in front of Alice. He then leaned in close to her face, his eyes cold and harsh.

"Let me make this perfectly clear, Dr. Merrell," Helgan said in a low tone. "These are not your pets. You do not play with them. You do not sing to them. And you do not talk to them. They are my experiments! They are my property! And they are mine to do with as I please. In the grand scheme of things, their lives are worthless. If you continue this ridiculous behavior, there will be severe repercussions. Do you understand?" Alice was visibly shaking where she stood, her eyes closed and her lips quivering, but she nodded her head in response. Helgan seemed pleased by this.

"Good," Helgan said with a cocky smile, standing up straight. "Now, be a good girl, and put the rodent in the square please." Alice was silent for a moment as she looked down at the young mouse in her hands. Juro, who was still trembling violently in her hands, looked up at Alice with pleading eyes that only she would notice. A sharp pain stung at her heart seeing those little eyes looking up at her, unaware of his pleas. Yet, there was truly nothing she could do. As much as she hated to see these poor creatures suffer, she was afraid of Helgan more.

With a defeated sigh, and with tearful eyes, she stepped forward towards the center table. With every step, her heart grew more and more heavy, like terrible weight slowly setting itself upon it. Upon reaching the table, she placed little Juro into the box next to the ArchBeetle. Juro stood in the center of the enclosure, frantically searching his surroundings, trying to find a way out. He looked up to see Helgan standing over them. Alice then spoke up once more.

"Couldn't we at least give him something to defend himself with?" Alice asked. "Their claws aren't strong enough to break through the ArchBeetle's armor. And they have shown to be able to grip objects with their front paws as we do. Perhaps if we give him a weapon, he may understand how to use it to defend himself." Helgan glanced in her direction. He stared at her for a moment or so, seeming to ponder the idea. Finally, he nodded his head in response.

"Yes, of course. An interesting idea, Alice," Helgan said before turning to one of the drawers behind him. After rummaging for a few seconds, he pulled out a long scalpel and dropped it into the box.

Juro instantly scurried to pick up the scalpel and stood on his hind legs to face the ArchBeetle. With trembling paws, he pointed his weapon at the ArchBeetle, which had stopped striking the wall and was now staring back at the young mouse with such intensity. The hybrid beetle held its claws high, opening and closing them, ready to attack at any moment as it softly clicked and chittered at the young mouse.

Juro was panicking at this point, trying to find some way out of this. His heart was beating a million miles an hour. Fear and anxiety gripped his whole body. Trembling paws gripped the scalpel tightly, pointing the blade at the giant beetle. Out of all the things that Juro had seen in this lab, right now was the most he had ever truly been afraid. A terrible feeling of dread filled his body as he then noticed Dr. Helgan grasp the handle on the divider.

"Now the test begins." He lifted the center barrier that divided the two creatures. The moment the wall was removed, the ArchBeetle immediately went on the attack. Juro quickly rolled out of the way just in time as the creature's sharp claws slammed at the glass wall behind him. Juro quickly regained his footing and faced the ArchBeetle. The ArchBeetle opened its claws again and Juro could see the tiny razor-sharp barbs within its claws. Juro kept the blade of the scalpel pointed at the ArchBeetle as the creature clicked its pincers together in a clicking noise, almost like a battle cry. Juro could feel his paws going numb as his grip on the scalpel tightened.

The two circled each other. Occasionally they would lung at one another, but they would still keep their distance. The little mouse studied the ArchBeetle carefully, trying to find any opening he could to strike; but the ArchBeetle kept its massive claws forward and opened to keep him at bay, as well as protect itself from the sharp blade. Helgan watched the display before him, looking quite pleased with himself.

"Look at them, Alice!" he said with a smirk. "Look how they study one another. Each trying to get the upper hand. And see how Test Subject 623 is holding his weapon? I daresay, he's almost fighting as if he were a man in his primitive state. These rodents may be more intelligent than we previously thought."

Alice saw nothing joyful or educational about any of this. This was nothing but cruelty. Her heart was pounding as she watched the fighting unfold. Nonetheless, she did her best to keep a straight face. Only giving a slight nod as a response.

Meanwhile, Azalar continued to scratch and beat at his cage window relentlessly, desperately trying to break out and rescue Juro from that monster.

"Juro!" he cried out. Azalar beat and scratched at the clear plastic of the wall so furiously that the blood from his paws began to smear against the walls.

"Azalar!" Amara cried upon seeing the blood; Azalar did not stop. He continued to attack the barrier that prevented him from reaching his friend. "Azalar stop!" Amara tried to grab onto Azalar's arms in an attempt to stop him, but he simply pulled away from her and continued his assault on the wall of his cage. He didn't even feel the pain in his claws.

The two in the glass square continued to circle one another. Juro's arms were trembling fiercely and he was having a difficult time keeping the scalpel steady, as well as his breathing.

Suddenly the ArchBeetle lunged at him again, causing Juro to back away and nearly stumble. Juro steadied himself and faced the ArchBeetle just in time to block a double strike from both its claws coming down from above. The force from the impact nearly forced Juro to drop to his knees. However, he managed to hold out and pushed the ArchBeetle to the side by pivoting his weapon to the left and hitting the butt of the scalpel against its head. This caused the ArchBeetle to lose its balance and stumble over to the side. Juro took the opportunity to get around the ArchBeetle and stab the blade into its abdomen, just under its left arm. The hybrid beetle seemed to let out some sort of screech from the pain. It wasn't that deep due to its tough armor, but it was deep enough for a little green ooze to slowly leak out of the wound.

Juro attempted to pull the scalpel out, but the blade seemed to be stuck in its armor. The ArchBeetle quickly recovered and swung its arm at Juro, knocking him to the side and pulling the scalpel out. Juro quickly scrambled to his feet and held his weapon forward. The ArchBeetle picked itself up and turned to the little mouse, its arms up in front and claws open, ready to continue the fight. The two began to circle each other once more, the ArchBeetle occasionally swiping at Juro, testing the young mouse and checking for any openings. Juro did his best to keep a safe distance, but every time the ArchBeetle swiped at him, it would slowly close the distance between them, forcing Juro to take a step back each time. Just as Juro took a step to his right, the ArchBeetle swiped at him once more.

Juro braced himself, keeping his weapon pointed forward, while also taking another step back, just to hit the wall behind him. He went to take another step to his right, only to hit another wall to his side. Juro looked around and came to a horrible truth, he had just trapped himself in one of the corners of the box. There was nowhere to go now. Juro's eyes were wide with horror and began to panic as his breathing became sporadic and his limbs were trembling terribly.

The ArchBeetle continued to approach the mouse, thrusting and snapping its opened claws at Juro, clicking and chittering aggressively, each thrust of its claw getting closer to Juro. As the young mouse stared at the monster slowly approaching him, he silently prayed to Háth to come to his aid, he prayed that his divine power would intercede on his behalf and strike down this terrible creature and bring him to safety through any miracle.

As he prayed, he thought about his life, how everything in the few months of his life were filled with cruelty and torment. How each day he was plucked from his cage and made to do these terrible and painful experiments. Constantly being poked and prodded on his already weak body, the electric shocks coursing through him, and the physical turmoil they subjected him to. He had known almost nothing but misery.

The only light in his life was when his fréfil, Milla, was placed in his cage. He thanked Háth every day for blessing him with such a beautiful mouse. When Milla first arrived, she was scared just like any other mouse who first arrived in this lab. She had been in his cage for two weeks as he consoled her and comforted her after she was exposed to Helgan's cruel tortures, tel-ling her everything was going to be alright. Then, in the third week, they finally connected with one another and pledged themselves together in Háth's name as fréfils, life partners. It was the most joyous time of his life. Then just as quickly as it happened, she was taken from him.

And now, here Juro stood, with his back to a corner, with a terrible monster in front of him. It seemed that he would be joining his beloved at Háth's side soon. He'd be lying if a small part of him didn't welcome the idea, but then he thought about Azalar's plan. The plan that would allow all of them to escape this lab, to go to the outside world, far away from any humans, to live free. He also remembered his own promise to Azalar; that he would never give up fighting. He almost felt ashamed of himself for nearly giving up.

No, he wouldn't give up; he would keep fighting. He was going to keep his promise to Azalar. He had to see it through. He had to see the outside, he had to feel the breeze all over his body, to feel the sun for the first time on his fur. Most importantly, he had to escape for Milla. He had to live for her, to remember and honor her name. He just had to.

Though his body still trembled with fear, Juro gripped his weapon tightly and readied himself. This was his last chance to live. With a shout of anger, terror, and determination, Juro charged forward, the blade of the scalpel aimed directly for the ArchBeetle's head. The attack seemed to catch the hybrid insect off guard as it took a step back to avoid the blade. It swung its claw at Juro as it retreated, but Juro stepped to the side just in time to dodge the attack. The ArchBeetle swung again, but Juro was ready and parried the strike, causing the ArchBeetle to stumble forward from the momentum. Juro tried to stab at the ArchBeetle's side, but the hybrid insect was able to quickly recover and turned its body back to Juro as it swatted the blade away.

"Look at that!" Helgan exclaimed. "Subject 623 is fighting with more conviction. Simply astounding! It really wants to live!" Alice did not say a word in reply, but just kept her eyes focused on the fight between the mouse and the ArchBeetle in front of her, silently praying for the little mouse.

Azalar had not stopped his attempt of breaking through the walls of his cage. Though his paws were bloody and swollen and burned from the pain, he refused to let up, despite his mate's vain attempts to stop him from doing any more damage to himself. Azalar jumped up and grabbed the bars above, trying to shake them loose. However, the blood on his paws caused his grip to slip and he fell back on the bedding below.

"Azalar!" Amara called again, but her words fell on deaf ears as Azalar climbed back to his feet and pressed his front paws on the transparent wall, once more watching his fellow mouse fight for his life. Azalar did not seem to be alone in his endeavor, as other rodents throughout the lab began to shout and squeak for Juro, many attempting to escape their cages as well. Even Ragath was hissing and roaring as he too tried to break from his cage.

Juro had just managed to avoid another strike from the massive claw by jumping back out of reach. As soon as his feet touched the floor, he launched himself forward, his blade aiming once again at the ArchBeetle's head. The ArchBeetle raised its claws once again to strike down, but this unfortunately left itself open to Juro's attack. The little mouse ducked under the ArchBeetle's arms and thrusted his scalpel upward, just as the hybrid insect brought its arms down. The ArchBeetle wasn't fast enough, as the blade reached past its arms and struck it in its right eye. The ArchBeetle screeched in pain and recoiled back, but not before it managed to land a critical blow on Juro's back with its other claw. Juro cried out and collapsed to the floor as the ArchBeetle desperately tried to cover its wounded eye with its bulky arms.

Juro hissed in pain as he attempted to stand back up, but the burning sensation in his back was too much for him and he could only manage to half stand while leaning on the scalpel. He could feel warm liquid slowly leaking down his back and he knew that it was a deep cut. But there was no time to dwell on that now as Juro heard a loud hissing coming from the ArchBeetle. The young mouse looked back at his opponent as the ArchBeetle was seemingly withering in pain. Juro, despite the pain in his back, managed to regain his footing and stood back to full height, readying his weapon to continue the fight. The creature hadn't seemed to notice him yet as it still had its arms up to cover its now missing right eye. Juro saw this as the perfect opportunity to finish the fight and he lunged forward, determined to kill the ArchBeetle once and for all. He held his weapon forward, aiming his blade at its abdomen for the final blow.

However, just as Juro was about to reach his mark, the ArchBeetle suddenly opened its claws up and caught the scalpel behind the blade just before it reached its head. The ArchBeetle held the scalpel tightly in its claws and began to swing Juro around, trying to shake the weapon out of his grip. Juro held on to the scalpel as best as he could, but the loss of blood and the pain in his back was making it nearly impossible. Then as Juro took a step down, his foot slipped on his own blood, causing it to slide underneath him and he fell to the floor, releasing his grip on the scalpel. The ArchBeetle tossed the scalpel to the side and faced the now defenseless mouse. Juro's eyes were now wide as he realized with absolute horror what just happened, and what this now meant.

The ArchBeetle wasted no time and was on Juro immediately. It grabbed onto the little mouse with its powerful claws and pulled him in. With one final blow, the ArchBeetle bit down on Juro's neck with its mandibles. Juro screamed in pain and the ArchBeetle now began to devour the little mouse. Juro tried desperately to get away, trying to claw at his face and arms, but the ArchBeetle was too strong, and its armor was too thick. Blood spilled from his neck as Juro continued to struggle against the ArchBeetle, blood curdling screams of agony and terror escaping his mouth. Still, the ArchBeetle continued to eat, ignoring the screams from the poor mouse. Biting down on the little mouse with its powerful mandibles, tearing and eating at the same time. Soon the screams began to fade, as Juro could no longer feel the pain; his world was slowly fading away until he saw nothing but the cold comfort of the darkness. The only sound that could be heard was the sound of the ArchBeetle cont-inuing to feed on the now deceased mouse.

"Well," Helgan said simply, though he had a satisfied smile on his face. "That's that." Helgan, with his hands behind his back, turned and made his way out of the lab. "The ArchBeetle will return to its box soon after it is done eating. Once that happens, close the box immediately and bring it back to room 34." With that, Helgan left the room, leaving a mortified Alice behind. Once Dr. Helgan had left, Alice quickly covered her mouth and turned away from the grotesque scene before her. Soon after, soft sobs could be heard escaping from behind her hand.

The room was now silent as all the mice and rats had ceased their uproar and were now staring at the center of the Lab. At that moment, Azalar was feeling all kinds of emotions running through him as he stood there, watching that monster devour young Juro. So many things were running through his mind. How could this happen? Why did this happen? Why did it have to be Juro? Azalar fell to his knees, feeling utterly defeated. Though his hands were still bleeding and sore, he didn't care.

Azalar, with whatever strength he had left in him, reared his head back and let out a loud cry. It was filled with whatever emotions he could let out. He cried until his strength finally gave out and lungs could no longer sustain his grief. With no strength left in his body, Azalar curled himself into a ball in the middle of his cage. Amara crawled over to her fréfil's side, trying to comfort him as much as she could. Still, she knew that there was little for her to do. All she could do now was simply be by her mate's side. Feeling his love's presence beside him, Azalar curled up closer to his fréfil and silently wept in her arms.

Chapter VIII

Later that night, the lab was silent once again, but this time not due to the residents within that lab falling asleep. No, not one rodent had their eyes shut for slumber. They were all in mourning. Many mice cried silently during the night, even the rats mourned for the young mouse, who fought bravely today but was met with an untimely end. The air was heavy with sorrow, and it seemed that no one would be getting any sleep tonight. Yet, no one was more mournful than Azalar.

Azalar was once again up from his bedding and staring out into the lab. This time it wasn't his body that ached from today, but his heart. All his thoughts were of Juro, and how that hideous creature had brought him to a terrible death. It was the most horrible sight that Azalar had ever seen, and to hear Juro's screams of agony; it was all too much for him. He closed his eyes, but all he could see was that dreadful insect devouring him. A tear fell from his eye, and he held in a trembling breath. He had failed Juro. He failed to keep his promise to bring him to the outside; failed to give him the freedom that they had all been craving for.

Azalar held his head in his paws, digging his claws into his fur and nearly into his skin, trying his best to keep himself calm and the tears in his eyes from falling; both of which he was failing miserably at. Azalar sobbed silently, wanting nothing more than to scream and shout; to let all the anger and sadness he was feeling out. Yet, what good would that do? It wouldn't help their situation, and it wouldn't bring Juro back.

Azalar had enough. The lives that were lost prior were too much already; but the loss of Juro was the breaking point. Azalar was now more determined than ever to break out of this wretched existence. He was also feeling something that he had never felt before, yet he knew exactly what it was: the desire for revenge.

Azalar's ear twitched as he heard Amara coming up behind him.

"Azalar?" She asked in a soft voice. "Are you alright?" Azalar let out a sad laugh.

"No," he said. "No, I'm not alright. I failed him, Amara. I failed Juro."

"You didn't fail him!" Amara said as she placed her paws on Azalar's arm. "It wasn't your fault, Azalar. There was nothing you could have done."

"I could have gotten us out sooner! If I had done more for us to find a way out, Juro would still be here. He didn't deserve any of this!"

"I know, my love," Amara said. "But you couldn't have known this was going to happen." From his cage at the top right, Bark spoke up.

"She's right, Azalar," said Bark. "There was nothing you could have done."

"And even if you could have done something," Frella chimed in, "Helgan would have just thrown you in with that monster."

"It was a terrible tragedy," added Nikamius from his cage above Bark and Frella's. "No one could have predicted such a terrible event. But we must push forward Azalar, and not let Juro's death be in vain."

"But we don't have much time!" Azalar said. "For all we know, Helgan could be preparing more of those things to kill us all. Any one of us could be next."

"It is the same as it had always been, my friend," Nikamius said gently. "Any one of us could pass any day now, but that should not stop us from pushing forward. We have survived this long, and we will continue to survive until Háth has called upon us."

Azalar frowned and let out a heavy sigh. He really wasn't in the mood to hear more about Háth. Against his better judgment, Azalar partially blamed Háth for Juro's death as much as himself.

"If Háth is so powerful, then why couldn't He save Juro from that creature?" he said aloud without thinking. "Why couldn't He strike that thing down so that Juro could live?" There a small moment of silence before Azalar heard a heavy sigh from above.

"You know as well as I that it's not really our place to question the Great One or his plans, young mouse," Nikamius said softly. "Things happen for a reason, whether they be good or bad. It can be hard to understand, and I don't have all the answers, young mouse. But I do know that Háth does love and care for us. It may not always seem like it, but He truly does love and care for us. He works in mysterious ways, and He tests us in way that we cannot understand. He places obstacles in our paths so that we may overcome them ourselves. That is how we learn, my friend. Life is not always going to be easy, as you know good and well. But just as much as Háth tests us, He also blesses us with wonderful miracles and the gift of life. However, He can take it away just as quickly.

"I understand your anger, my friend. I truly do. But you must understand that Háth cannot always be there to save us at all times. You know very well that we must take our lives into our own hands, as well as keeping our faith with Him. And you could also say that Juro is safe with the Great One right now, Azalar. He is watching over you, along with all our loved ones. And they are counting on you, Azalar. Do not lose faith. We will find a way to freedom, and you will lead us there."

A deep low voice came from Azalar's left.

"That was a very nice speech, old mouse," said Ragath sarcastically. "Very heart moving. But that isn't going to help us out of here. Like I told you before, little mouse; Háth has no place here. If you want to get out, then you must fight for it on your own. No '*Great One*' is coming to rescue us. We either fight, or we die. It's as simple as that."

Azalar remained silent. His heart was too heavy with sorrow. He wanted to believe in Nikamius' words, that Juro was up there in a better place watching them, at peace with his beloved Milla, along with all the others that they had lost over the course of their lives. The pain in Azalar's heart was causing him to question things, things that he did not want to think about. Azalar let out a heavy sigh.

"You're right, Ragath," Azalar said. "Háth cannot help us here. I'm sorry, Nikamius, but prayers and faith won't do us any good. I don't know how much longer we have, but we must find a way out of this place, and we need to do it soon. I fear any day one of us may become that thing's next meal." Azalar's attention was drawn away when he felt Amara placing her paws on his shoulder. She was looking at him with sadness in her eyes.

"Azalar," she said gently. "I understand your anger and hatred for the humans. But please don't let that anger misguide you and cause you to become a mouse so full of hate." Azalar's features softened.

"I know, Amara," he said. "I will do my best."

"Just remember, Azalar," Nikamius said, "do not give up hope, and do not lose faith in Háth."

"I do have hope, Nikamius," Azalar said. "But I'm sorry to say this, Nikamius, faith won't help us right now. Action will. Can I count on you and your rats, Ragath?"

"Yes!" Ragath said confidently. "I know the perfect rat to aid us. Razor and I will do our part to ready the rats when the time comes. You can be sure of that."

"Good!" Azalar exclaimed. "Now we must find a way to open these cages. We will have to be cautious though. Maybe Bogger can find a solution-"

Suddenly at that moment, the doors to the lab opened, startling and gaining everyone's attention. At first, they thought it was Trevor again, back again to cause more mischief and harm for his own amusement. However, they were greatly surprised to see that it was not Trevor, but Alice who had walked into the room. She wore her pink sweater and blue sweatpants and trudged heavy footed into the room, hunched down and grabbing her arms as if to keep herself warm.

Alice stopped when the door behind her shut completely, and she stood there with her head down looking at the floor. She stayed like that for a long while. Azalar and Amara watched her carefully, waiting to see what she would do. It was very unusual for her to be in here after the lights were off, so they were all very curious as to her intentions. Slowly Alice lifted her eyes and looked directly at Azalar's cage. It was then that both Azalar and Amara saw sadness in her eyes. Even from this distance, Azalar could see her shoulders trembling ever so slightly.

Alice then walked over and stood in front of his cage. She looked hesitant at first, but she slowly lifted her hand and opened the cage door. She then slowly reached her hand inside. Azalar and Amara of course prepared for the worst and tensed their bodies. Then, Alice stopped and placed her hand on the bedding, her palm facing up. Azalar was of course taken aback by this and unsure about what was happening or what he should do. Was she asking him to climb in her hand?

"This is it, little mouse!" Ragath called out. "Now's your chance. The human is practically giving you an opportunity to escape! Take it!"

Ragath was right. This was probably his one and only chance to escape. With the door now open, all Azalar had to do was climb up her arm and jump out from the cage. After that he could hide somewhere in the lab and find another way to free his fellow rodents from their cages. It was almost too perfect.

Azalar smiled and readied himself and was about to lunge for Alice's hand, but then he looked up into her eyes and it gave him pause. Her eyes were full of sorrow and heartbreak, and Azalar felt a small degree of pity.

Yet, he shook these thoughts away and prepared himself once again when Amara stepped in front of him. He looked questioningly at her, but the soft look from Amara gave Azalar pause.

"What are you doing? This could be our chance?" Azalar said. Still, Amara didn't move.

"Just trust me, my love," she said. Amara then turned and slowly approached the hand. She stopped and took a moment to sniff, noticing a pleasant scent emanating from Alice's skin. Amara then slowly climbed up her hand and stood on all fours in her palm. She then turned to Azalar, who was staring dumbfounded at her.

"Amara! What are you doing?!" However, Amara didn't answer, she just simply looked at him and motioned for him to come up. Azalar had no idea what his mate was doing, let alone what she was thinking at this moment. Not even *he* knew what to think right now. He stared at his beloved, who stared back with the same words she spoke in her eyes.

Trust me.

Against his better judgment, Azalar relented and slowly, yet cautiously, climbed onto Alice's hand. Once he had fully climbed on and sat in Alice's palm, Alice slowly lifted the two mice out of their cage. Azalar took a glance behind at the other cages. Everyone was gazing at them with bewilderment. Each one of their faces was staring intently at what was happening. Ragath on the other hand looked almost disappointed, yet he too seemed to be just as curious as the rest of them.

Alice walked over to the table across the lab and slowly lowered her hand into a large clear container, the same one that Ragath and Azalar were placed in to fight, and gently placed both Azalar and Amara down inside. The two mice were incredibly curious as to what Alice would want them out here for. She was not known to be one to conduct late night experiments on them, nor did she seem to have any intent on harming them in any way. The two mice continued to watch Alice as she took a chair from one of the other tables and took a seat in front of them. She then leaned forward and rested her head in her hands.

There was silence as Alice only stared at the two mice. Azalar and Amara looked at one another for a brief moment before turning back to the human. Now that they were much closer to her, they could see just how miserable Alice truly looked. Her red puffy eyes showed that she had been crying heavily, and her unkempt hair were clear signs that she had been in great distress. Seeing Alice in such a state, even Azalar couldn't help but feel a bit sympathetic to this poor human. Alice still stared at them, and Azalar could tell that she wanted to say something, but she looked to be having a difficult time finding the words. It wasn't for a long while before Alice finally spoke.

"We've had a rough day, huh 289?" Alice asked. She then let out an exasperated laugh and shook her head. "What am I saying? Of course, it was a rough day. It's always a rough day for you little guys. Always enduring such cruel treatments each and every day. And to top it all off, you were all forced to watch your friend get killed by that monster right in front of you because Helgan wanted to test his newest creation. Like your lives don't matter!" Alice paused and lowered her eyes.

"And what did I do?" she asked, her voice so soft and low that it was barely above a whisper. "I just stood there like a helpless idiot and just let it all happen. I was unable to do anything to stop it. And that poor innocent mouse paid the price for it."

Alice's lip soon began to quiver as tears slowly formed in her eyes. Alice tried to blink them away, but they returned just as quickly. Then Alice could no longer keep her composure and she covered her face and began to whimper softly. Soon those whimpers turned to cries as her shoulders were shaking terribly. This went on for a few moments before she calmed herself enough to speak.

"I'm sorry," Alice sobbed into her hands. "I'm so sorry. None of you deserve this. Any of it! You're all beautiful creatures, and I've done nothing to help you. I've just been Helgan's little pet to help him along with his experiments. I don't even know what they're for anymore! I thought we were doing this to help mankind find a way to take back our home. But I know it's all bullshit!" Alice slammed a fist against the table, startling both Azalar and Amara from the sudden action.

"All he ever tells me is that everything will make sense! But it doesn't! None of it does! I don't even think he has a damn plan! I know now that Trevor was right. He just wants to play God!" Azalar and Amara watched as Alice let out her anger, as well as her sadness. They both looked at one another. Azalar was unsure, but Amara held sympathy in her eyes. He didn't understand why Amara was showing such compassion for this human. Just then, like a shock from an invisible collar in his head, a thought crossed his mind. What if she was just as tortured as they were in this place? From what she said, she was just as much of a prisoner in Helgan's lab as they were. Forced to conduct all these horrendous experiments against her will, the turmoil she must have been feeling inside must have been immense. He looked back at Alice with a bit of understanding. The anger in her voice subsided and she returned both hands to her face.

"And I've been helping him," she said softly, sobbing once again. "I've been such an idiot. I'm no better than he is. I should have seen it sooner. But I was just so…" Alice paused and let out an agitated groan and placed her face in her hands.

"I've just been such an idiot," she repeated. It was silent for a moment before she spoke again. "I wish I could just leave this place. Go as far away as possible and finally be free of here. But I have nowhere to go. No family. No friends. I have no one." She removed her hands and looked back at the two mice with a sad smile.

"I guess we're both trapped here, huh?" She then placed a finger on the glass wall. Azalar looked at the finger on the glass suspiciously then returned his attention back to Alice. Alice rested her head to one side and spoke again.

"Helgan really is a monster, huh? If only I had realized it sooner. I feel like such an idiot." Azalar continued to stare at the human in front of him until Amara stepped forwards and placed her paw on the glass across from Alice's finger. This seemed to amuse Alice as she couldn't help but smile at the female mouse.

"Could you ever find it in your hearts to forgive me?" she asked, not at all expecting an answer. However, just then, Amara smiled up at Alice and slowly nodded her head. It took a moment before Alice realized what the little mouse had done and quickly sat up in her seat.

"Wait," she said above a whisper. "Did you just nod your head?" Amara nodded once again, still smiling at the human. Alice let out a small gasp, placing a hand over her mouth in disbelief. Azalar's eyes widened upon witnessing what Amara just did. Amara had just broken the one rule that they had, and now Alice was aware of how intelligent they truly were. Azalar was mentally berating himself. However, his mate turned and smiled, as if telling him that everything was okay. Azalar stared at his fréfil bewildered, wondering what she could possibly be thinking. He then turned back to Alice, who had leaned in closer to the container, her eyes wide with amazement.

"Can… Can you understand me?" Azalar was hesitant and almost didn't respond. A part of him was thinking that this was a really bad idea. He looked back at Amara for reassurance, and she answered with a nod. Azalar, though still hesitant to do so, let out a heavy sigh before looking back at Alice and nodded his head as well. Alice let out another gasp as she quickly jumped back from the table, clasping both of her hands over her mouth in shock. Her eyes were so wide that Azalar was sure that they were going to pop out of her head. Suddenly a small, excited laugh escaped Alice's lips and Azalar could almost see the smile on her lips behind her hands. Alice stepped back a step, but never took her eyes off Azalar. She was now jumping up and down in place, giggling like a young girl.

"Oh my God!" she squealed. "Oh my God! I can't believe this!" She stepped closer and leaned in towards

Azalar again. "You can understand me! You can actually understand me! Can you talk, as well?" Azalar's eyes were wide with surprise at the girl's sudden excitement. He was not expecting this kind of response from a human. He thought about speaking to her, but he knew that she wouldn't understand a word he said. He shook his head side to side. This resulted in another giggle of excitement from Alice.

"But you can still understand me!" she exclaimed. "That's wonderful!" She began jumping up and down in place, covering her mouth as she squealed and giggled like a little girl. After a few moments of giddy excitement, Alice finally calmed herself down and took a deep breath before returning her attention back to Azalar and Amara.

"I'm sorry," she apologized. "I'm getting too excited. It's just that this is the most incredible thing I've ever seen. Never in my wildest dreams would I have ever imagined that I could be talking to mice, and they could actually understand me, and even talk to me. Well at least respond to me, that is. This is amazing!" She leaned down further so that she could be as eye level to Azalar as possible.

"To be able to communicate with other species has been the goal of scientists for years. It is such an experience. I don't think I'll ever be able to wrap my head around it. I have so many questions that I've always wanted to ask. So many things I want to know." She then realized that she was getting herself too worked up again and took another deep breath to calm herself.

"But that isn't important right now," she said softly. "What is important is that things are different now. You're all more than just small animals. You are all sentient beings capable of thoughts like us! Intelligent beings that deserve to be free!" Azalar perked up at her last word, his eyes wide and his ears forward. Alice noticed his reaction and leaned down just a little closer.

"Yes," she said. "You all deserve to be free. And I will help you. I promise I will get you out of here." Azalar stood on the tip of his back feet, pressing his front paws against the walls of the container. He quickly looked up at the top of the container and began jumping up and down vigorously, glancing at Alice a few times and motioning his head upwards. Alice noticed his movements and excitement and seemed to understand what he was trying to say. She frowned.

"Oh, no!" Alice said. "I can't let you out now." Azalar stopped jumping and glared at Alice, while Amara lowered her head sadly. He should have known that she was lying. Alice, seeming to know what the little mouse was thinking, lowered herself further until she was resting her chin on her arms.

"I'm sorry, little guy. I can't do that right now, Helgan has this whole facility locked up tight. If I let you out now, there'd be no way for me to get you all outside without getting caught. It's also too dangerous for you all. There are so many things in this place that will kill you if you're not careful." She gave the two mice a warm smile. "But don't you worry. I will do everything I can to get you all out of here. I promise." Azalar stared into Alice's eyes, trying to figure out if she was telling the truth or not. But the more he looked into those blue eyes, and for some odd reason, he found comfort in them and believed her. Alice then stood up and looked at the clock on the wall.

"I suppose I should be getting back." She then reached her hand into the container and let Azalar and Amara climb onto her palm, where Alice then took them back to their cage. Once the door was shut, Alice gave the two mice one last smile.

"But don't worry," she said, "I'll be back as soon as I can." She placed her finger on the window of the cage. Azalar and Amara looked at one another. Amara smiled before she walked over to the window and placed her paw on the spot where Alice's finger was. She turned back to Azalar and gave a nod of encouragement. Azalar was hesitant at first, but after a moment he too placed a paw on the window. The smile on Alice's face widened greatly and her eyes glistened with joy. She let out a delighted giggle and turned around and was practically skipping out of the lab. She stopped one more time to glance back at Azalar and Amara to give them one last smile.

"This is so amazing!" Alice cried out before finally leaving the room. The two mice, along with all the other rodents in the lab who had witnessed all that had transpired in front of them remained silent as they watched as the doors to the lab closed behind Alice. This had been a strange turn of events that no rodent could have possibly predicted, and Azalar, who was at the center of it all, still wasn't sure how to process it all.

"That was… interesting," Frella said, breaking the silence from the cage next to theirs.

"Do you think we can trust her?" Bark asked. Neither Azalar nor Amara responded right away as he stared at the doors that Alice walked out of.

"I'm not sure," he finally said. "The last thing I want to do is to trust a human."

"But?" Frella asked, beckoning him to continue.

"But her eyes were nothing but genuine," he answered honestly. "Nothing about them told me that she was lying." Azalar remembered how her eyes were shining bright with joy and amazement when she saw that they could understand her. Like a little pup seeing the world for the first time. He still wasn't sure how to feel about it all.

"Whatever the case," he continued, "we have no other choice but to trust her."

"I think we should," Amara said, gaining Azalar's attention. "Her words were indeed genuine. I could tell that she was telling the truth about everything." Amara looked towards the doors where Alice had left as well.

"She is just a scared pup, afraid to stand up for herself out of fear of Helgan. He must have some kind of hold on her that we don't know about or understand. But I have a very good feeling about her." Azalar looked towards the lab doors.

"I hope you're right," he said softly.

Chapter IX

Azalar could say this for certain, he was not expecting what came next. The very next night, after the usual exercises and experiments, Alice came into the laboratory after hours when the other humans were asleep. However, this time she was carrying a large stack of books with her. She set the books down on the table and turned to the rodents, as if she was addressing students in a classroom.

"Okay, this may seem unprecedented," Alice said, "but I really want to see how far all your intelligence goes." She then walked over and took Azalar and Amara from their cage. She placed them on the table next to her books, but she did not place them inside any container. This greatly confused the two mice as they looked up at her curiously. Alice noticed their behavior and smiled at them.

"No, I won't be putting you in any cages or boxes tonight, 289," she said. "You're not just animals anymore. You're all so much more than that now and you don't deserve to be treated as such." Azalar and Amara looked around the room. It felt so strange to not be confined to such a small space. Yet, now here they were, with no walls to keep them trapped. It was a wonderful feeling.

Azalar suddenly thought about running and hiding like he originally planned the night prior. Now he had the chance and the temptation to take it was growing with every second. However, he then thought of how

Alice vented to him and Amara last night; how devastated at the loss of Juro and how trapped she felt here by Helgan. He realized how similar they were. If he were to follow through with his plan, it would only be worse for Alice. With a feeling of guilt in his chest, Azalar gazed back up at Alice, who leaned down until she was almost eye level with them.

"And I also want you all to trust me. I know that you have a great mistrust for humans after everything you all have been through, but I truly want to help all of you. I hope you can believe me." Her voice was so sincere, and her eyes gave no sign of deception. It was difficult for him to admit, but he did trust her. Azalar turned to his mate, who was smiling happily and seemed to be thinking the exact same thing. Azalar returned the smile and the two mice looked up at Alice and nodded their heads. Alice gave a smile from ear to ear before she turned back to the books on the table.

"I'm assuming that none of you know how to read, right?" she asked. Azalar and Amara shook their heads from side to side. "I thought not. I suppose we'll start with something simple then." She took out a small book and placed it open in front of the Azalar and Amara. The two mice looked at the book, then looked back at Alice with puzzling stares. Alice seemed to understand what they were trying to say and let out a small giggle.

"I know this may seem pointless, but there is a good reason for it," she said. "If you are all able to read and write, it will be a lot easier to plan your escape." Azalar's eyes widened, and he pursed his head up.

"The whole facility is like one giant maze," Alice continued. "Escaping the lab won't be easy if you don't know where to go. And if you're not careful, you could find yourself somewhere that you don't want to be. And the best way to do that is to read a map. I can get one for you, but it would be pointless if you couldn't understand it, right?" Azalar was reluctant to learn human literature, but after listening to what Alice said, Azalar couldn't disagree with that logic. If there was any chance of escape, then they needed all the help they could get, no matter where it came from. Azalar nodded his head again.

"Excellent!" Alice exclaimed, clasping her hands together. "Let's get started right away! But first..." Alice quickly turned and walked over to the other cages. The rodents all looked up at her curiously.

"I think this class needs a few extra students," she said confidently with her hands on her hips. The moment she said those words, many mice jumped up and down excitedly, wanting to have a taste of freedom as well. Alice slowly brought more rodents out from their cages and placed them on the table with Azalar and Amara. Just as they did, the rodents felt euphoric about their freedom from their confinements. Some of these rodents were so excited that they tried to venture off, perhaps planning escapes of their own. Azalar stopped them, however, and gave them all warning glares, which brought them all back in line.

Bogger and Nikamius were among these, as well as Bark, Frella, Brim and Della. Bogger appeared to be very excited about learning from the human books. With his great intelligence, Bogger easily passed all of Helgan's intellectual tests. However, because he didn't want the humans catching on, he had to tone down his performances, which got increasingly boring for him. So, with Alice wanting to teach them how to read, Bogger was very keen to learn something new, to see how far his intellect really went. Nikamius was very happy with what was happening, not just from being out of his cage and free to walk about, he was pleased to see that they had a new ally in Alice. He looked over at Azalar and with a pleasant smile.

"Háth works in mysterious ways," he said simply. Azalar rolled his eyes, though a smile grew on his lips, and turned back to the crowd around him. Azalar never thought that he'd ever seen a sight like this, seeing so many of his people out of their cages. It was invigorating. Most of those that were here were mice, as many of the rats did not want to take part in anything that had to do with humans, finding it to be useless and insulting, with many hissing at Alice as she walked by. Still, there were some rats, though not many, who wanted to learn, or rather just wanted an excuse to be out of the cages. With her class now all gathered together, Alice picked up a book and turned to the first page.

"Now then," said Alice, "Class is in session!"

This went on for three weeks. Alice would come in every night after everyone had left, just as excited as the day before, and would continue the lessons. She would even give them extra lessons during her shifts in the labs. She taught them all about the alphabet, vowels, and vocabularies and how to use them to form words and sentences. It was not an easy process, since there was a bit of a language barrier, but many of the rodents were beginning to understand little by little.

Bogger and Nikamius looked to be getting the hang of it all quite well, as did many of the other mice, as well as the few rats that took part in the lessons. Azalar was not so fortunate in this regard. Many of the words that Alice taught seemed very complicated and he found them very difficult to understand. The subject of spelling didn't seem to be much better for him for much the same reason. However, as the weeks went on, and with much aid from both Alice and Amara, who appeared to have more of an understanding of the subject then he had, he was able to get the bare minimum down. Soon he was able to read and write a quite a few sentences by himself.

Ragath was still as stubborn as he ever was. Nonetheless, by the end of the second week, after seeing the mice as well as a few rats out and about for so long, he finally relented. One day, when Alice passed by his cage, Ragath tapped on the window to gain her attention. When Ragath motioned his head for her to let him out, Alice was overjoyed; especially when he allowed her to carry him out of his cage without hissing or acting aggressive towards her. This in turn prompted the other rats to join in the lessons as well. Alice's 'class' had grown by a lot after that; so much so that there was barely any room for all of them on the table, but Alice was able to make it work by teaching her classes in shifts. Fifty mice and fifty rats for one night and another fifty mice and fifty rats on another. This was mainly to help her focus on teaching and seeing the progress of each mouse and rat. Though that didn't mean that the rest of the rodents weren't able to pay attention from their cages, especially the mice.

By the time the fourth week came around, Azalar, along with the vast majority of the mice and rats, had at least a basic understanding of the human literature. He was now able to read almost every book that Alice brought without too much difficulty. Alice found it incredible how quickly they were able to learn; much faster than she had originally thought. Now she thought it was time to move on to the next lesson: writing.

However, this proved to be a little challenging at first since there weren't many things small enough for a mouse or rat to write with properly. She tried to have them use pencils or pens in the beginning, but their handwriting was sloppy and unreadable. Then Alice came up with the idea to use the lead inside the mechanical pencils that she had in her room. Though they were quite fragile and broke very often, they were the perfect size of the rodents to fit in their little hands. Their hands were dirty from holding nothing but the lead, but then Bogger had the idea to use tissues to wrap around the lead, which in turn made them a little easier to handle.

After finding the perfect tool, Alice had all the rodents practice writing each letter of the alphabet for the whole week. This came as no trouble for Azalar, as well as many of the other rodents. After learning the words and letters, writing them down was much easier. In fact, after working so hard to understand the human literature language, this was the easiest part of the whole curriculum. After just over a week, Azalar's handwriting improved greatly and he found himself understanding the words more clearly. Alice noticed his improvements as well.

"You're really getting the hang of this, 289," Alice said. Azalar stopped what he was doing and looked up at Alice. She had continued to use the numbers that Helgan had given them during their whole lessons, and he found it to be rather bothersome. Alice noticed his frown and looked confused.

"Is everything okay, 289?" she asked. Azalar frowned some more and shook his head vigorously. He took his piece of lead and began to write down a few letters that he thought best fit together. Alice leaned in closer to get a better look at what he was writing.

"*A. Z. A. L. A. R.*," Alice read slowly aloud. She looked down at Azalar with a questioning look. "Azalar? What's an Azalar?" Said tanned colored mouse smiled and pointed a finger to himself. Alice saw his movements and immediately recognized what he was saying.

"Wait? Is that your name? Azalar?" Azalar nodded his head and Alice let out an excited squeal. "Oh, my goodness! You have your own names! That's amazing! I never would have thought that mice could come up with their own names. Does each of you have your own name? What are they? Oh, this is so exciting!" Alice was talking so fast with so many questions that Azalar couldn't keep up. Though he had to admit, it was quite enjoyable to hear a human say his name rather than call him by his number. After a few moments, Alice finally calmed herself down.

"I'm sorry," she apologized. "This is the second time that you all have surprised me. It may only just be your name, but I now know more about you than I ever hoped to learn. Thank you so much, 289. Oops! I mean…" Alice leaned down until she was eye level with Azalar.

"Thank you so much, Azalar." Azalar smiled up at Alice, who then turned her attention to Amara. "Do you have a name as well?" Amara nodded happily and began to write down her name.

"Amara. That's such a beautiful name!" She looked at the rest of the rodents on the table.

"Do the rest of you have names? I would love to know them all!"

Many of the other rodents couldn't quite figure out how to spell their names. This is where Bogger came in best; he knew everyone's names and knew exactly which letters would be best to spell them. However, since there were so many names to remember, Bogger figured out a way for Alice to remember them all by writing down each mouse and rat's number and writing their names down next to them. This proved to be a big help for Alice, and she was able to remember the names of most of the rodents within the lab.

This seemed to be the end of Alice's lesson, as now the rodents were now the ones giving Alice a few lessons in return, or more specifically Azalar, Bogger and Nikamius; though it seemed as though Bogger was the main one giving lessons. He taught her everything he could think of when it came to the rodents. He even taught her a few words in their own language. Alice was so excited and happy to be learning so much about what she called their *culture*. This word was unfamiliar to Azalar, but Bogger and Nikamius seemed to understand it just fine.

"Culture is the arts, customs, social institutions and other manifestations of intellectual achievements of a particular nation, people, or other social groups," Bogger stated. "I guess you can say that we fall under that category as well to a certain degree. We have our own language and customs, so to speak; and we also have our own beliefs, or religion, as it were." Azalar found this statement to be particularly interesting but decided to think on it at a later time.

One day, on another particular day when Alice was in the lab by herself, Alice was showing Azalar a special book of wildlife while the other rodents were getting their exercises done. Azalar had finished earlier than the others and Alice wanted to show him the dangers of the outside. She said that if they were going to escape, then they had to learn about some of the wildlife that inhabited the outside world. She flipped through the pages, explaining to Azalar of the animals on each page. Currently she was on the subject of predators, specifically birds of prey.

"This one is called a Barn Owl," Alice said. "It is another species of bird of Prey. There are many types of owls in the world. Some are as small as you are, but they are still just as dangerous; and some are much larger. But these Barn owls are the most common. So, if you all travel at night, keep your eyes up and open. Owls are known as the silent killers because they make very little sound as they fly. So be careful when you're out there."

She taught them about all sorts of animals that were extremely dangerous, especially to rodents, and the best ways to avoid them and protect themselves from them. There were so many different kinds of creatures that he had never heard of in this book alone that Azalar wasn't sure if he would remember them all, let alone all the ones outside. She told them previously that if they were to travel, it was best to do it during the day when most predators were asleep. If they stopped for any period of time, always make sure to find shelter from both the predators as well as the weather. Bogger had learned from one of Alice's books on how to start fires to keep warm as well as keep predators away. Though Azalar didn't know how effective that last part would be due to their small stature, Alice seemed to have the answer to that question.

"And above all else," Alice said, her voice becoming more serious, "always stay together! That is the most important thing I could tell you. There is strength in numbers. So, if you all stay together, you can protect each other, and you'll have a much greater chance of survival." She flipped to the next page and the image gave Azalar a start.

There, seemingly staring back at him from within the pages, were two large yellow eyes with narrow slit pupils. Attached to the eyes was a round face, small nose with long whiskers with pointed ears at the top of the head. Azalar stared at those eyes, and he was instantly reminded of his dreams, of all his friends and loved ones being tortured and killed by Helgan as he was forced to watch, then a pair of golden eyes shining and staring at him. It had been a long while since he had that terrible dream, but the horrible images have never left his mind. Azalar jumped from where he was and pointed at the page. Alice looked at the page then back at the little mouse.

"Oh! That is called a cat," Alice said. "They are one of a species known as felines, which come in all shapes and sizes, but all of them can be very deadly to mice. I actually have a cat in my room." Azalar quickly looked up at Alice with widened eyes upon hearing this. Alice noticed his reaction and let out a soft giggle.

"Oh, don't worry," she said in a reassuring voice. "He's nothing to worry about. In fact, he is quite gentle when it comes to others. Even when I let him out, he never goes too far and has never harmed anyone. He loves attention too. Although Helgan doesn't like it when I do.

"But even still, you should always be cautious of other cats. They are actually one of the most common predators of both mice *and* rats, the same goes with owls, hawks, dogs and even snakes. Each one is just as dangerous as the rest if you're not careful and that's why I say to always stick together. There's no greater strength than that of a strong group of friends. Rely on one another, and you can survive anything." Alice then left to tend to the other rodents in the lab; as well as to attend to her tasks so that she would have something to write down for Helgan, leaving Azalar alone to look over the wildlife book in front of him. He stared at those eyes that were very similar to the ones that had plagued his dreams a while ago.

Azalea then looked out to the lab, where Alice and all his fellow rodents were still going about with their lessons.

Azalar thought about how these last few weeks had been, and how they were far more amiable than Azalar could have predicted. At first, he thought the whole ordeal unnerving, and completely unprecedented, and even at times altogether unnecessary. However, as the days went on, Azalar found himself with a peculiar feeling of enjoyment. Even during the times when he struggled with learning the human literature, he still found it more preferable than their daily routines of tests and experiments.

During all the time that Alice was teaching her lessons, Helgan rarely visited the lab, which made things a lot easier for the rodents. He would stop in every so often, but rarely did he stay for more than ten minutes before heading out again. Alice had told them that he was far too focused on his newest creation, the ArchBeetles, to bother with the rodents anymore; though he made sure to have the other lab assistants keep track of all their progress. However, the lab assistants grew quite inattentive in their tasks, which allowed the rodents of the lab to have a bit of respite. Sometimes it would be Alice in the lab by herself, which was how she preferred anyway.

But now she used this time to give extra lessons, with the occasional running of tests and experiments, just so she could write something down to give Helgan, and to allow the rodents a bit of exercise as well. Alice told them that exercise was very important; and that if they were going to escape, they needed to keep their strength up.

Azalar looked to Alice, who was currently with Nikamius, Bark, Frella and Amara, reading a note that Nikamius had written for her; possibly sharing some more information of their culture at her request. Azalar stared at the smiling human, and in his heart, he felt a sense of admiration towards her, but also a sliver of guilt. She had been so kindhearted and gentle to him and his fellow rodents for as long as he could remember. Though she had indeed been so compassionate towards them, he had been very distrusting of her.

But now, as she laughed and conversed with his fellow rodents, he held nothing but respect for her. If it wasn't for Alice, they would still just be a part of Helgan's experiments; still trying to figure out a way to escape on their own. But now they were more than that. So much more. They were their own beings that had the capability and means to live their own lives. And it was all thanks to that human. Azalar smiled at Alice.

He couldn't be more thankful to her.

It was early in the morning, and Azalar woke up from what seemed like the most pleasant sleep he had in a long time. He couldn't remember what his dream was, or if he had one at all, but it was pleasant sleep, nonetheless. Azalar looked down at his beloved fréfil, watching as her chest gently rose up and down with a soft smile on her lips. Azalar chuckled to himself.

She must be having a nice dream, he thought.

Azalar stretched his body out before walking over to the front of his catch where he let out a rather loud yawn.

"Héffena, Azalar," said Nikamius from above.

"Héffena, Nikamius," replied Azalar. "How did you sleep?"

"Like a little pup," Nikamius said with a laugh. "Though, I'm sorry to say that I still woke up as an old mouse. It has been a long time since I've had a sleep like that." Azalar chuckled as well.

"I know the feeling," he said. "It has been a long time. I can't even remember the last time I slept so well."

"Well, I'm glad you guys were able to get some decent sleep," said Bark suddenly from his cage. "Frella kept kicking me in her sleep. She says that she was chasing a huge piece of grain that just walked up and ran away."

"I said I was sorry!" said Frella. "And it did run away. It just grew legs and ran away from me. And you know me. I wasn't going to lose to a little seed." This earned a laugh from Azalar and Nikamius.

"Seems everyone had a delightful night," Nikamius said. He then let out a small chuckle. "Well, most of us that is."

"Well, I was at first. It was an amazing dream until I was rudely interpreted from my own wonderful dream." Bark had a slight teasing in his tone, earning him a little swat from his mate's tail. "Ow!" Azalar gave a small chuckle.

"Careful, Bark," Azalar teased. "Or Frella might have sudden urges to chase more grains in the middle of the night again." Azalar had to admit, it was a refreshing change of pace. His spirits were surprisingly higher than normal, and his nights weren't filled with as much terror and stress. He supposed that Alice played a large role in that regard. Ever since Alice found out that the rodents of the lab could understand her, and her teaching them how to read and write, Azalar felt a great weight had been lifted off his shoulders.

"Glad to hear you're all having a good time," Ragath said in his usual low voice, not at all amused. Azalar gave a slight chuckle.

"We're just having a little fun, Ragath," Azalar said. "No harm in that. This may actually be the first time in our lives where we can actually have a heartfelt laugh."

"Good to know," Ragath said sarcastically. "But heartfelt fun isn't going to get us out of here. We need a plan, and we need it now."

"Yes, Ragath, I agree," Azalar said with a hint of annoyance. He then looked up at the bars that hung over his head. "But first we need to find a way out of these cages. And after that, we need to find a way out of this room. And that's just the easy part. We still don't know where to go from there or what's even out there. So, we're going to need to plan this out carefully."

Just then, the doors suddenly flew open, giving the rodents in the lab a start. Alice hurried inside and shut the doors quickly; her breath heavy and raspy. She was much earlier than expected, and she wasn't wearing her usual lab attire. She looked through the little windows on the door before she turned to Azalar's cage. Azalar could see her eyes were wide and full of fear. Azalar's instincts were screaming at him that something was terribly wrong. Alice rushed over to his cage as she reached inside her pocket.

"Azalar!" She said, her voice full of panic. "Azalar! Amara! You all have to leave! Tonight!"

"What?" Azalar squeaked, even though she could not hear nor understand him. Amara quickly rushed over to Azalar's side.

"Helgan's going to kill you all!" Alice exclaimed. "He's going to feed you all to the ArchBeetles!" The moment Alice mentioned that name, the rodent went into an uproar. Panic swept throughout the room, as the mice and rats became frantic, trying desperately to get out of their cages. Azalar and Amara, however, remained right where they were, too bewildered to move in the slightest, the memory of the ArchBeetle devouring Juro was still fresh in their minds. Azalar could feel his heart racing in his chest as he felt Amara cling to his arms tightly. She was practically digging her claws into his fur, almost piercing the skin underneath. But he ignored the pain as he stared up at Alice, waiting for her to say more.

"I overheard him in his office," Alice continued. "He's planning on unleashing the ArchBeetles on you all in what he calls his *Final Test*! I don't know when and I don't know how. It could be as early as tomorrow, for all I know. But you all have to leave tonight! Even if he doesn't conduct his *test* tomorrow, you still need to leave tonight because they'll be cleaning your cages tomorrow morning."

Alice then pulled from her pocket a thin box, from which she pulled out a long sewing needle and dropped it inside Azalar's cage. Azalar quickly picked up the needle and looked back up at Alice.

"Hide this in your bedding. Make sure that none of the other assistants see this. Tonight, wait a few hours after everyone has left. After midnight would probably be best. After that, take this needle and pry the cage open. I'm sorry I couldn't find anything better; this was all I could find on hand." She then reached into her other pocket, pulling out a small, folded paper and placing it inside his cage.

"That's the map to the whole facility. I've mapped out the best route for you all to take. Study it as much as you can and hide it in case you need it again. Or even give it to Bogger once you're out of your cages. Hopefully you'll find the exit without running into any danger. Be sure to leave before tomorrow morning so that they don't find these. If they do, then it's all over. You won't be able to get out and I won't be able to help you again. So please get out as soon as you can."

There was a slight noise from outside, startling Alice. Her eyes went wide as she looked at the doors, as if she expected to see someone standing outside. She then looked back to Azalar. Azalar could see the terror in her eyes, but there was something else in them as well: sadness.

"Here." Alice quickly removed something from her ear and dropped it inside Azalar's cage. Azalar picked it up and studied it closely. It was a circular piece of metal with a tiny dark blue gemstone in the middle. Azalar stared at the object and was confused before looking up at Alice, who smiled as tears were forming in her eyes. "So that you have something to remember me by."

Alice took a step back and stared at each cage in the lab, getting a good final look at every mouse and rat that she had grown to care for all these weeks. She then smiled sadly.

"I've had so much fun getting to know each and every one of you," Alice said, her voice soft and full of pain. "I've learned so much from you all; your names, your language, your very identities! It has been a wonderful journey. I only wish we could have spent more time together. Thank you all so much. For everything!" Alice turned to a certain large black rat with a smile.

"Yes, even you Ragath!" Her smile was wide and genuine. Ragath stared at the young human woman, taken aback by her gentle words. She had always been kind to him, even when he would show aggression towards her. But never once did she fail to send a gentle smile his way. Alice then turned and headed for the doors. And just before she left, she turned one last time to look at the rodents, or more specifically at Azalar and Amara. The two mice stared back at Alice, and from where they were, they could see a single tear fall from her eyes. Even though there was still fear in her eyes, as well as sadness, there was also just a sliver of joy in them. Alice gave the two mice one last smile.

"Màfalín," she said softly before promptly leaving the room, disappearing behind the shutting doors. With that, Alice was gone, leaving a room full of anxious rodents behind to dwell on her warnings. Many rodents began to scream and cry in panic.

"What are we going to do?"

"The ArchBeetles are going to get us!"

"We're all going to die!"

"Everyone, calm down!" Nikamius called out. "We are not going to die and the ArchBeetles are not going get us. You all heard Alice; we still have time to prepare. She gave Azalar a map and a way to break free of these cages. We still have a chance!" Amara looked to her fréfil, who was still staring at the palace where Alice had left.

"Azalar?" she asked with concern.

"This is it!" Ragath said. "This is what we've been waiting for right? Azalar, open the cages now."

"No!" said Azalar. "We have to follow Alice's instructions. If we try to escape now, we're sure to be caught. We have to wait at midnight like Alice said. That is our only chance."

"So, you expect us to just sit here and wait for death?" Ragath argued.

"No! I'm asking you all to follow the humans' tests and experiments one last time until they leave. We have to be careful now and act as if everything is normal. If the humans notice anything different in our behavior, they may grow suspicious. And that could potentially ruin everything. So, I ask everyone to be a little more patient."

Several murmurs could be heard throughout the room, with many voicing their distress and worries; some shouting their objections, and that they should escape right now. Azalar was growing concerned that the others were becoming too anxious to listen to him, fearing that their chances of escape were slowly closing. If he couldn't get them to calm down before the humans arrived, then any hope of freedom would be lost forever. Suddenly Bark's voice boomed throughout the lab.

"Hey!" Bark shouted, his voice louder than anyone ever heard before, gaining the attention of every rodent in the room. "What's the matter with all of you? Why are you all doubting now? I've known Azalar all my life, as have many of you here. He has always been a strong mouse and has always looked out for all of us. I trust Azalar with my life, so why don't any of you?" There was no response from anyone for a long while. Bark spoke again.

"Juro believed in Azalar," Bark continued. "He believed that Azalar would get us out of here. And look at what Azalar's done so far. He has done the impossible. We've all seen it with our own eyes. He befriended a human and convinced her to help us escape. And because of him, we now have that chance. Come on, everyone! This is what we've been preparing all these weeks for. If Azalar says that we should follow Alice's instructions, then I say we follow Juro's lead and put our faith in Azalar."

A deafening silence fell upon the room. Azalar thought for a moment that Bark's words would have no impact on them. But regardless of whether it did or not, Azalar was very grateful for his friend's kind words and encouragement.

"Thank you, Bark," Azalar said.

"Just speaking the truth, my friend," Bark replied. "I've never doubted you before, and I'm not about to start now."

"That was a wonderful speech, Bark," Frella said, nuzzling closer to her beloved fréfil. "I never thought you had something like that in you."

"What can I say? I'm a mouse of words." This gained a few chuckles from Azalar and Frella. Just then, Ragath spoke up.

"Very well," Ragath said. "I shall trust you for now, Azalar. Don't let me down."

"You have my support, Azalar," Frella said.

"And you have mine as well," said Nikamius.

"I'll gladly stand by your side, Azalar!" Brim called out from his cage. Other voices slowly began to rise and shout their agreement. Soon every rodent in the lab was cheering their support to Azalar. The mood in the lab quickly changed as Azalar sat in his cage listening to the rodents of the lab all shouting and cheering for him. He couldn't help but smile as he felt as if a small weight had been lifted from Azalar's shoulders. He then felt Amara's presence as she sat next to her beloved fréfil and took one of his paws.

"I will always be by your side, my love," she said. Azalar smiled at his fréfil before taking both her paws in his.

"Thank you, my star," he said softly. "I promise to give us a better life," Amara returned the smile and nodded her head.

"I know you will."

At that moment, the doors to the lab opened once again, causing all the rodents to quiet down. The other humans then entered the lab like they always did and went straight to work to complete their usual tasks before running the day's tests and experiments. As the humans prepared for the day, Azalar couldn't get the last thing that Alice said out of his mind. Azalar had a terrible feeling deep inside him that this would be the last time he would see the human Alice ever again.

Màfalín. Goodbye.

Chapter X

The time had finally come. The humans had all left for the night, leaving the lab dark and empty, the same as it was the same as every night at the lab. But this time, the air was different. Tonight, the rodents of Helgan's laboratory would finally be free. Azalar held the large sharp needle tightly in his grasp. He had been preparing himself for this moment all day. And now that it had finally come, he felt a tremendous amount of pressure weighing on his chest.

He also thought of Alice throughout the whole day. He was worried for her. Azalar also noticed that the humans were increasingly anxious throughout the day; barely paying attention to the rodents at all. It was as if their minds were somewhere else; somewhere terrifying. It was especially evident when Helgan came into the room only once, and the humans were practically frozen in place every time he was near them. Only when Helgan finally left did the tension in the room drop, but only just a little. In all that time, all Azalar and the other rodents could do was think about Alice's final warning.

Now that the humans had left, Azalar held the needle close to him. His heart was beating a million miles an hour and his paws were shaking tremendously. His grip on the needle was so tight that his paws were starting to feel numb. There was great fear and anxiety in him right now, so many things could go wrong in so many ways. If he did this, then he'd be responsible for so many lives. He wasn't sure if he was ready for that.

However, if he didn't do this, they'd find the needle when the humans cleaned out their cages tomorrow morning. Then they'd have to endure this life of never ending torture.

Azalar looked behind him at Amara, who seemed to be just as nervous as he was. Still, the moment he looked into her eyes, she smiled at him and all that fear he had begun to disappear. No, he had to do this. For his fréfil. For his friends. For their future. A newfound sense of courage filled his heart as he steeled his nerves, willing his paws to stop shaking. He stepped forward to the front of the cage.

"Azalar?" Bark called out in a whisper. Azalar took a deep breath. His friends were waiting. It was now time.

"Is everyone ready?" he called out.

"We're ready," answered Bark and Frella.

"Ready when you are, my friend," Nikamius said.

Azalar took another deep breath, readying himself, and gripped the needle tightly in his paws before placing it in his mouth and jumped up to the bars above. Azalar pulled himself up with little effort until he was able to place his head between the bars. He placed his back paws against the front wall of the cage in an attempt to steady himself, but his feet kept slipping on the smooth surface. Finally, after several attempts, Azalar was able to keep his back paws firmly in place by digging his claws into the plastic wall of the cage. Making sure he was secure, Azalar then removed the needle from his mouth and then, just like Bogger instructed him earlier, he placed the tip of the needle between the small bar that hooked under a small lip in the rim of the cage that held it firmly closed; though not without great difficulty, as he had to reach and lean forward in order to get the tip in under the lip of the cage and over the bar that gripped it.

Azalar steadied himself once again, trying his best to keep both himelf from falling, and losing grip on the needle. Anxiety coursed through Azalar's body. If he were to slip now and drop the needle, then any attempt to escape would be impossible, and all hope would be lost. Just then, before he began to pull, Az-alar's back paws slipped, nearly causing him to fall. However, he suddenly felt the paws of his fréfil, Amara, grab hold of his back paws and pushed him upwards, aiding in keeping him steady. Azalar thanked his beloved mate and pulled himself upward again. Azalar still held a firm grip on the needle and after making sure that the tip was once again secured tightly in place between the bar and the rim of the cage, he pulled with all his strength.

At first, the latch only moved a little, but Azalar wasn't getting good enough leverage to free it in his current position. Azalar told Amara to let go of his back paws so that he could place them on the cage wall, which he pushed hard against as he pulled the needle back. Just then, there was a sudden snap and Azalar was thrown back, falling on Amara.

"Are you alright, Azalar?" Nikamius called out.

"We're fine," Azalar and Amara answered. The two mice picked themselves up and Azalar noticed that he no longer had the needle in his paw. But that didn't matter, for when he looked up at the top of the cage, the door was opened.

Azalar looked over to his mate in disbelief before approaching the front of the cage. He couldn't believe it at first, but the Cage was truly open. He jumped up and climbed the wall, peeking over the edge.

"We did it!" cried Azalar. "We're out!" Cheers could be heard all around as Azalar climbed out of the cage; but Azalar quickly shut it down.

"Quiet!" he called out. "We're not all out yet! We need to be careful and remain quiet." He then turned around and reached down for Amara's paw. Just before she could grab hold of Azalar's paw, there was a loud noise coming from outside the lab doors, gaining their attention. Suddenly there was a figure that appeared in one of the windows. Panicking, and unsure of what else to do; and refusing to go back into the cage, Azalar dropped down from one cage to another until he had reached the floor, where there was a large gap between the floor and the cages above. Azalar hid under one of the cages just as a human walked into the laboratory. It was Lebo.

A foul smell entered the room and met Azalar's nostrils, the same foul scent from when he, Trevor and Evan tried to have him and Ragath fight for a piece of chocolate, causing Azalar to cringe from the horrible smell. Azalar watched as Lebo staggered into the room, nearly tripping over himself as he did so. He had a glass bottle in his hand, from which he took a large drink from before letting out a loud burp. He wasn't wearing his usual lab coat, but simply a green shirt that barely covered his round belly and brown pants. His hair was disheveled, and his eyes were red and puffy. He suddenly turned his head and glared at the cages.

"You!" he said, pointing at the cages. Lebo stormed over, standing right next to where Azalar was hiding. "You dirty little rodents caused this! You did this to him!" He took another large sip from the bottle.

"If it weren't for you miserable little cretins, my life would be fine right now. Yes, I would still be working for that egotistical, imbecilic, sociopath who calls himself a scientist, Helgan. But at least we'd still have Trevor here with us; and I wouldn't feel so alone." Lebo took another sip, but this time not so large as the last. When he was done, there were tears quickly forming in his eyes. "Trevor was my best friend. He was the only one who stood up for me around here. He took me in, and both he and Evans made me feel like I belonged somewhere. But now that he's gone, Evans barely speaks to me; and my life has been nothing but feeling alone. And it's all because of you creatures!"

Azalar looked confused at his words. Did this mean that Trevor really did disappear? That would certainly explain why the other humans were so on edge after he never showed up. But then he thought about Alice, and how the humans were acting today. Had something happened to her? His heart sank at the thought. Alice hadn't thought much about it before, but he realized now that he truly did care for the human woman. Lebo moved down the line, glaring at every rat and mouse he saw.

"Helgan has been obsessed with you little rodents for years. Always making you his top priority for some stupid reason. I don't even know what he wants with you all." Lebo then stopped, his feet directly in front of where Azalar was hiding. Lebo wasn't wearing the usual shoes that the other humans did when they entered the lab; he was wearing some other form of footwear that exposed his whole foot, save for a few straps that wrapped around his toes. The smell emanating from his feet was repulsive, and nearly caused Azalar to gag. Azalar held in his breath and peeked out from his hiding place at Lebo, who was staring at a particular cage in front of him. It was at that moment that he realized that Lebo was now glaring at his own cage and at his beloved Amara inside. Lebo took another sip from his bottle before a sinister grin formed on his lips.

"But now that he has his new little pets to play with," he said in a low tone, "he doesn't need you so much anymore." Lebo tossed the now empty bottle aside, glass shattering as it landed on the floor. He then opened the cage, not realizing that it was already opened, and reached inside the cage. Amara tried to back away as far as she could, but she was petrified with fear. Lebo quickly grabbed hold of Amara and pulled her from the cage. He then turned around and headed to one of the far cabinets, opened them and pulled out a metal slab with wires protruding from one side before turning to the table in front of the cages.

Once there, Lebo placed the slab down and practically slammed Amara on it, causing her to squeak in pain and fear. Lebo then proceeded to tie each of Amara's limbs to the slab with the wires. Once she was fully secured down, Lebo went back and opened a drawer, where he then retrieved a long scalpel with a long blade at the end and made his way back to Amara, turning his back to the cages. Amara looked up at the intoxicated human, who was glaring down at her with a wide and sinister smile.

Azalar's eyes widened in horror as he realized what was about to happen. It was his dreams all over again, but this time they were happening right in front of him. From his hiding place, Azalar started to panic, unsure of what to do. He tried to look for the needle, hoping that it might have fallen on the floor, but he couldn't see where it had gone.

"If it's an experiment that Helgan wants," Lebo said menacingly. "It's an experiment that he'll get. Now let's see what all these experiments have done to your insides." He then held the scalpel up and began to slowly descend the blade down towards Amara's chest. Tears formed in Amara's eyes, and she let out a horrible scream.

Hearing his fréfil's scream removed all fear from Azalar and sent him into a rage. Refusing to wait a moment longer, Azalar rushed from under the cages across the room and bit down on Lebo's exposed Achilles' heels. Lebo cried out in pain and jerked his foot up. He looked down to see Azalar right at his feet.

"Why you little!" he cried and attempted to stomp down on Azalar. But Azalar was too quick for him, especially due to Lebo being too intoxicated, and would every so often take the opportunity to nip at his toes. However, his senses were too dulled from the alcohol for him to feel much of anything, other than the blind rage he felt throughout his body. Thus, no matter how many times Azalar bit and nipped at his feet, Lebo only grew angrier.

Azalar just narrowly avoided getting crushed under Lebo's foot when he jumped back and touched something sharp with his foot. Azalar looked back to see a long piece of glass that had been broken from the bottle that Lebo had tossed. He picked the shard up, ignoring the sharp pain in his hands, and went on the offensive. Lebo continued to try to stomp on Azalar, from which Azalar would easily dodge and stab and slash at his toes, drawing blood every time. This made Lebo's anger only grow, and he began using his scalpel to stab down at Azalar, but once again his intoxication only served to slow him down.

Azalar continued to hold off against Lebo's drunken rampage. His fellow mice and rats were squeaking and cheering him on. Never before had either mouse or rat stood up against a human in such a way, so to see Azalar now facing off with one before their very eyes was truly a sight to behold. Even Ragath found himself amazed with such conviction. However, it was all short lived as Azalar had slipped on a drop of Lebo's blood, causing him to trip and slide; thus, giving Lebo just the right moment to kick Azalar away, sending him sliding across the floor until he slammed against the lower cabinets on the far side of the lab.

The impact wasn't enough to hurt Azalar too badly, but it was enough to stun him a little and put him in a daze. He shook his head to clear himself and narrowly avoided Lebo's foot coming down on him. Azalar decided to take a different approach and jumped on Lebo's leg, where he then began to climb up his clothes. Lebo tried swatting him off, but Azalar had a firm grip on the fabric and was able to move away from his hand. Then, one of Azalar's claws got caught on a thin strand of fiber and stopped him in his tracks. Azalar tried to pull it free, but it was too late as Lebo was able to grab hold of him and pulled him off.

"I got you now, you little vermin!" Lebo shouted as he held Azalar tightly. Azalar glared up at the fat human and was about to bite down on his hand when he suddenly found a blade tip at his throat. "You thought you could get the better of me? Well, you thought wrong!" Lebo pressed the blade of the scalpel closer to Azalar's neck, very close to puncturing skin. A wicked giggle escaped from Lebo's throat.

"You have no idea how much I'm going to enjoy this. I'm going to make it slow, and I'm going to make it hurt. I promise you that. And when I'm done with you, I'm going to move on to your friend on the table. And all of your little friends will know exactly what will come every night from here on out." Lebo let out a victorious cackle when suddenly that cackle turned into a shriek of pain. He staggered back, only to slip on the blood on the floor, forcing him to release his grip on Azalar and the scalpel. Lebo tried to steady himself but was unable to regain his footing. He tried to reach for anything to stop himself from falling, only managing to grab onto the drawer he opened previously, scattering the contents of the drawer all over the floor as he fell, slamming his head against the lower cabinets.

Azalar had fallen to the floor with a thud. Although there was a sharp pain throughout his body from the fall, he was otherwise uninjured. He picked himself up and noticed a black figure standing not too far away.

His vision was a bit blurry, and he first thought it was Ragath, but as his vision cleared, he realized it wasn't. It was Razor, another black rat who was the second largest rat in the whole laboratory, and he was holding the needle, which was covered in blood at the tip.

Razor's real name was Roro, but he earned the name Razor from when Trevor and his friends would force many rodents to fight one another, from which he won many due to his razor sharp teeth. He also had a ferocious attitude to add to that. The only one that Razor could not defeat was Ragath himself; and the two held a great deal of respect for one another.

"Razor?" Azalar asked. "How did you get out?" Razor looked over to the tan colored mouse and scoffed and held up the needle.

"Your little needle thing fell into my cage after you opened yours," Razor answered. "I used it to open my own cage. Luckily for you, I managed to get mine open in time, otherwise you and your mate would have been cut to bits by now and would have completely ruined the rest of our chances of escape. Typical of a little mouse." Azalar didn't appreciate the little comment at the end of his statement but decided to ignore it.

"Well, thank you, nonetheless, Razor," Azalar said gratefully. There was then a low groan and both Azalar and Razor turned to see Lebo rubbing the back of his head as he tried to pick himself up. Azalar was preparing for another fight when Razor tossed him the needle.

"Leave this to a real fighter, mouse," Razor said. With that, Razor charged forward, picking up the scalpel from the floor as he did so. Lebo noticed the black rat scurrying across the floor towards him with the scalpel in his paws, blade pointed at him. It was then that Lebo realized that this was now a dangerous situation, and all of Lebo's anger and animosity vanished and was replaced with fear. From his position on the floor, he started kicking at the black rat, trying desperately to keep him away. It did very little, however, as Razor dodged his kicks easily and was able to jump onto his stomach. Lebo tried to swat him away with his arms, but Razor simply used his new weapon to slice and cut at his arms. Lebo screamed in both pain and fear and tried to cover himself to prevent Razor from getting closer to his face. Undeterred, Razor stabbed at one of Lebo's arms, causing him to jerk his arm back in pain. With an opening, Razor squeezed between his arm and with as much strength as he could muster, Razor thrust the blade of the scalpel deep into Lebo's neck.

Lebo's eyes widened as blood slowly began seeping from the wound. Razor, with a smirk and a scoff, quickly sliced the lesion open more, causing more blood to pour out like a waterfall. Razor slashed at Lebo's throat again and again before giving one final thrust with his blade under his chin; pressing the long blade deep within. Lebo tried to cover his hands over the gash, but it did very little to keep the blood from draining out of his now opened throat. He tried to scream, but no sound escaped other than the terrible coughs and gurgles from his own blood cutting off his air supply.

Lebo looked up at the black rat on his chest, who simply looked down on the fat human. A large pool of blood slowly expanded on the floor, and he could feel the warmth slowly leaving his body as his vision began to blur. And just before the long embrace of darkness took hold of Lebo, he thought he could see a small trace of a smile on the rat's lips. The life in Lebo's eyes finally faded and his arms fell limp to his sides. Razor smiled victoriously at the now dead human before him. He then wiped his blade on the human's clothes before hopping down.

Azalar stood aghast as he witnessed all that had transpired before him. He knew that Razor had a sort of brutish temperament, but never had he seen such ferocity from either rat or mouse, not even from Ragath. It was almost terrifying. Razor then approached Azalar, giving the mouse a curious look.

"Well?" Razor asked. He then pointed the scalpel upwards towards the table. "Are you going to free your little fréfil?" Azalar looked up at the table above, where he could hear the soft terrified sobs of his beloved mate.

"Hold on, Amara! I'm coming!" Azalar called out. He then rushed back to the cages to free the others, feeling absolutely foolish for briefly forgetting about his fréfil, and how terrified she must be. He went about freeing as many of his fellow rodents as quickly as he could. It was much easier to open the cages from the outside, but it was still difficult nonetheless and he was able to open a few cages within a few moments.

A few minutes later, Azalar had freed many other mice and rats from their cages. While many rodents went about freeing their fellow rodents from their cages, others aided Azalar by forming a small pyramid by a nearby chair, where a few other rodents lifted Azalar up until he was able to grab hold of the table and pull himself up onto the table. Once Azalar had reached the top, he hastily freed his beloved mate from the metal slab, who immediately embraced in a tight hug as she trembled terribly in his arms.

"It's alright, my love. I'm here," Azalar whispered softly to calm his mate down. It seemed to work as Amara's trembling and sobs soon softened. After a moment more, Azalar pulled Amara up off the table and they carefully descended down to the floor with the aid of their fellow rodents. Once they reached the bottom, they were quickly approached by Bark, Frella, and Nikamius.

"Amara, are you alright?" Frella asked as she and her sister quickly embraced their dear friend.

"I'm fine, Frella," Amara said, returning the embrace as Bark came and stood next to Azalar, where he patted him on the back and expressed his amazement at what Azalar had done.

"I didn't do much," Azalar said while averting his eyes. "Razor was the one who finished him off."

"Yes, but you were the first among us who stood up to him," Nikamius said. "When your beloved was in most dire need, you risked your own life and faced off against the giant. The first rodent to ever stand up against a human, let alone a mouse. Háth and Ezralar himself would be proud. I believe there will be songs written of your bravery." Azalar smiled as Amara pressed herself against her mate and nuzzled him closely.

"It certainly was brave," Amara said lovingly. Azalar smiled as well and nuzzled his fréfil in return. "Although he did take his time untying me from the slab." This got a small chuckle out of everyone, until they were interrupted by a deep voice.

"I don't see what's so exciting to celebrate over," Ragath said as he wandered over to the group, accompanied by a band of rats, Razor being among them. "Azalar may have been the first to face off against the human, but it was a rat who finished the job. So, if there are to be songs about anyone, it should be of Razor and his courage."

"While we do appreciate his contribution," Bark said, "It was Azalar that delivered the first blow that set the stage for all of this."

"And if I had not escaped when I did, he and his beloved fréfil would have been cut to pieces and tossed in the bin like the others. He's only lucky that the needle he lost had fallen into my cage, otherwise we would all have been ArchBeetle food tomorrow, just as that little Juro friend of yours was." The mention of Juro's name brought a burning sensation in Bark's chest and he glared dangerously at Razor.

"What did you say about Juro?" Bark shouted as he took a step closer to Razor, his anger starting to get the better of him.

"That's enough!" Azalar said, stepping in between the mouse and rat. "He's right, Bark. If it wasn't for Razor, I wouldn't be alive right now and our chances of escape would have been impossible." Azalar then turned to the rats and lifted his paw out to Razor.

"We wouldn't be here if it wasn't for you Razor. You have my eternal gratitude." Razor stared at the extended paw in front of him and looked up at the mouse skeptical. He then turned to Ragath, who gave him a simple nod. Razor returned his attention back to Azalar and, although very reluctant, extended his own paw to Azalar's and took it in his own, though not without giving a disgruntled sigh before he did so. With that, the rats walked past the mice to where Lebo had fallen, where many other rats had laid claim to most sharp tools that Lebo had spilled, hoping to make weapons out of them. Just then, the mice heard another voice call out.

"Azalar!" Azalar, Amara, Bark, Frella, and Nikamius turned to see Brim and Della, along with two other mice, walking towards them; one orange in color, and the other a slight silver, who had managed to fetch themselves a couple of scalpels and sharp tools as well, one tool having a slight hook at the end.

"This is Mith, and the other one there is Borith. They are the mice I told you about before." The orange mouse, Mith, stepped forward and bowed his head slightly.

"Héffena, Azalar. It is an honor to meet you in person," Mith said. "Borith and I have heard amazing things about you and have seen you at a distance accomplish so much, especially during Helgan's horrible experiments. You are truly an inspiration. And the way you fought off Lebo like that, words cannot express how remarkable-"

"Easy there, Mith. Don't lose your head just yet," said Borith, the silver mouse, who then turned to Azalar, and he too gave a slight bow of his head. "Héffena. But he is right. It is an honor to finally meet you face to face, Azalar. Whatever you need, we will do our best to provide." Azalar smiled and bowed his head in return.

"Héffena. And thank you to you both. Brim has told me a little about you both, and I have no doubt that you two will be of great aid to us all. First, we need to free the others from their cages. Once we do that, we need to find a way to open those doors. Has Bogger been released yet?" Bark looked up towards the cages and pointed to Bogger, who was just climbing down to the floor.

"There he is," Bark said just as Bogger had arrived where they stood. He was holding a folded piece of paper in his paws.

"You had left this in your cage, Azalar," Bogger said, holding out the folded paper. "Alice's map. This is paramount to our escape." Azalar nodded his head understandingly.

"I'm sorry, Bogger, but things were moving too quickly, and Amara was in danger."

"Yes, indeed," Bogger said. "It was very fortunate of us that Lebo was too far into a stupor to notice anything amiss. But in the future, we must take greater care and caution. Luck may not be on our side next time. Oh, and I also picked this up from your cage as well." Bogger lifted his paw to reveal an object, the blue gemstone earpiece from Alice, and handed it to Amara.

"Oh, thank you, Bogger!" Amara cried, clutching the gemstone close to her chest.

"You are quite welcome, my dear," he said with a bow of his head. "It wouldn't be proper if we left a memento from our dear Alice behind, since she had so graciously left it behind for us. Now then, let us begin planning on a way out."

"Any idea on where we should go?" asked Bark. Bogger was about to unfold the paper when Nikamius stopped him.

"We should include Ragath in the plans as well," The elder mouse said. "He is a vital ally, and we will need him and his rats to aid us."

"I agree," Azalar said, before turning to where Ragath and the other rats were collecting whatever weapons they could. Azalar called Ragath over, though he came with a disgruntled disposition after not finding any suitable weapon for himself.

"What is it, little mouse?" Ragath said in a low tone.

"We were just about to go over our next move on how to get out of here. And we thought you should be a part of it." Ragath raised a brow at Azalar, but nodded his head, nonetheless.

"Very well. Let's get on with this then. The sooner we get out of here, the better." Azalar turned to Bogger and nodded for him to proceed. Bogger then opened the folded paper up and set it on the floor for everyone to see. The map revealed a large network of hallways and corridors with many different rooms lining each side. The mice stared at the map in wonder at how vast the world outside this laboratory truly was.

"It's almost like the labyrinth that Helgan always had us doing," said Frella.

"Yes. But fortunately, we have a cheat sheet this time," said Bogger, as he pointed to the arrows on the map. "These arrows that Alice drew on the map tell us exactly which way to go. If we can get to this hallway at the far end of the facility, we will find a room categorized as *'shower room'*. Then, according to the instructions that Alice has written, this is where we will find our exit."

"That doesn't sound too complicated," said Bark, looking at the others with a confident smile.

"Maybe," said Azalar, looking at the map with a serious expression on his face. "But we still have to make it to this *'shower room'* without getting caught."

"But first we need to get out of this room," said Ragath, looking up at the doors to the lab. "Any idea on how we do that?" The other rodents looked up at the doors as well.

"Well, the doors open inward right?" asked Borith. "Maybe we could find something to wedge between the doors and pry them open?"

"We'd still need to find a way to the handles to even open the doors," Brim answered. "If we climb on one another, we could form a small tower high enough to reach the doorknobs."

"That wouldn't work," said Bogger, gaining everyone's attention.

"Why not?" asked Azalar. "Surely it will be no problem for us. We were able to climb on one another for me to reach Amara on the table."

"Yes, but you are all forgetting one key factor in all of this."

"And what is that?" Ragath asked, getting quite annoyed by the brown little mouse. Bogger pointed towards the top of the lab doors, where there was a little red light shining facing down at an angle towards the front of the doors.

"I've noticed for the last few days that just before the humans exit the room, that little red light turns green before they open the doors. I don't know how, but I think that light opens the door. And just the other day, when one of the humans approached the doors from the side, not in view of that light, the light never turned green and the doors didn't open, it wasn't until he took a step back that the light turned green. With that in mind, we can indicate that the doors will not open until that light turns green."

"So how do we get it to turn green then?" Ragath asked impatiently. Bogger looked down at the floor in thought. Everyone waited for Bogger to come up with a plan, and after waiting a long while in silence, Bogger finally spoke up.

"I have no idea," he said. "That light is obviously designed to register humans coming out, not for mice or rats. I don't think that there is anything we could do that would open that door. Maybe if i had more time to observe how it work-"

"Well, we don't have time!" Ragath shouted. "We only have a few hours left before the humans come back and find us." Azalar frowned and placed a paw under his chin.

"There has to be a way out of here," Azalar muttered aloud as he crossed his arms and frowned while staring at the floor.

"There is no other way out! We went through all this trouble of getting out of those cages, and we're still just as trapped as we were before. What was even the point in all this if we can't even get out of this room? That stupid human girl. I knew that we shouldn't have trusted that human girl." Azalar quickly looked up at the large black rat.

"You can't honestly blame Alice for all this," Azalar said sternly. Ragath glared down at the tan colored mouse.

"Who else should I blame? She should have known that we couldn't get out of here on our own. Getting us out of those cages only to keep us trapped in this room. This was probably just another cruel test of the humans, and she was meant to lower our guard. I told you, little mouse, that humans cannot be trusted. Yet you were foolish enough to believe in one just because she was *kind* to us. Face it! She tricked us."

Azalar turned away, refusing to believe that Alice would betray them like that. There was no way. Alice had gone out of her way to teach them how to survive on their own, giving them a chance to fight for their freedom. Why would Alice do so much for them, only to go back on it now? Was it a way to earn Helgan's favor? Or was it really all just some cruel trick for another one of their experiments like Ragath said? Azalar's head was spinning with all these thoughts, and he wasn't sure what to think. Then, he remembered the last thing that Alice had said to them, as well as the look in her eyes. There was no deception in those eyes. Alice had meant every word that she said to them, and her eyes did not betray her. Azalar narrowed his eyes and turned back to Ragath.

"No!" Azalar very nearly shouted. "I refuse to believe that Alice would betray us like this. She had done so much for us. She risked everything for us. And I have faith in her, just as she had faith in us. There must be a way out of here, and we are going to find it. Somehow."

"Then what do you suggest then, little mouse?" Ragath challenged. Azalar was silent for a moment before looking back up at the giant black rat.

"I honestly don't know, Ragath. But Alice gave us this chance for a reason. She had faith in us. And I have faith in her. There has to be a way of escape. I'm sure of it. We just need to find it." Ragath gave Azalar a sneer, still not convinced in the slightest. However, after a moment, seeing the defiance and determination in the young mouse's eyes, Ragath's demeanor softened.

"Very well. I'll humor you with this little belief that you have. But be warned; you had better be right about this, little mouse. Or I swear by Háth, the last thing I do in this world before they feed us to the ArchBeetles will be to tear out your throat." Azalar simply stared back at Ragath, but soon gave the giant rat a small smile.

"Fair enough. Save the ArchBeetles the trouble." Azalar then felt Amara cling to one of his arms and held him tightly.

"Let's hope it doesn't come to that," said Nikamius. "For either case."

"Now that that *charming* conversation is out of the way, does anyone have any idea on how to get out of this dreadful place?" asked Bark.

"We will soon," Nikamius said. "We just need to be patient. I'm sure that if we stay strong and keep our hearts full of faith, an answer will come to us eventually."

It was at that moment that the lights from the hallway, the only source of light in the whole lab, suddenly went out, leaving everything in complete darkness. Many of the rodents squeaked and cried in alarm, startled by the sudden lack of vision. Then there was a bright red light blinking on and off from the ceiling; along with a terribly loud high pitched buzzing noise that rang out.

"What is that horrible noise?" cried Frella as she desperately tried to cover her ears. Many of the other rodents began to panic, unsure of what was happening. Azalar himself didn't understand what was going on and looked around frantically as he held his fréfil close.

"Look!" cried Bogger, pointing to the red light once again, but this time the red light was off.

"What does that mean?" asked Della.

"It means we might have a way out of here!" exclaimed Ragath as he ran past the mice towards the lab doors. "Razor! Over here!" Razor quickly followed Ragath, along with a few other rats, to where Ragath was. Once there, Ragath turned to Azalar and the others.

"Climb up there and get this door open!" Ragath called out. Azalar and the other mice, along with all the other rodents in the lab, rushed towards the doors. However, just as they arrived and were about to begin climbing on one another, the doors suddenly swung open, almost hitting Azalar and a few other rodents. Azalar and the other rodents looked up, and there, standing in the middle of the doorway was Evans, whose eyes were wide with panic.

"Lebo! Are you finished throwing your temper tantrum yet? We have to get out of here now! There's been a breach in the upper-" He stopped when he noticed the large gathering of rodents in front of him, all staring at him. It was then that he noticed at the far end of the lab was Lebo, lying on the floor in a pool of his own blood with his throat split open. Evans was petrified by the sight before him, the panic and fear in his eyes intensifying. He then looked down at the rodents below him, many of which had sharp tools in their hands, with many pointing those sharp tools at him. Evans slowly raised his hands up and took a couple steps back. He then suddenly broke off into a sprint down the hall. The door slowly started to shut behind him.

"Don't let the door shut!" cried Azalar as he dashed forward and threw himself against the door to keep it from closing. Bark, Brim, Bogger, Mith, Borith, Nikamius, and even Ragath and Razor, as well as a few other mice and rats were quick to join him, and together they were all to keep the door from shutting; or at the very least slow it down as their bottom paws were gradually sliding against the smooth tile floor.

"Everyone out now!" Azalar ordered. Without a moment's hesitation, the other rodents of the lab immediately rushed out the doors. Azalar and the others were doing their best to keep the doors open, but their bottom paws held no traction, yet they still held them open. Then, just as the last rodent ran past them, Azalar and the others jumped out of the way and the doors finally shut. However, unlike the last time those doors closed, the rodents were now on the other side of them.

Though the alarms roared above their heads, the rodents stood silent in the hallway, with many flabbergasted that they were now free from the lab and one step closer to total freedom. However, there was no time to relish in this accomplishment, they still had a long way to go.

"Everyone! Let's move!" cried Azalar as he dashed through the crowd of rodents, pointing his needle forward. He was quickly followed by Amara, Bark, Frella, Bogger, Brim, Della, Nikamius, Mith, Borith, Ragath, Razor and the rest of the throng of rodents. Bogger rushed forward at the front of the crowd with Alice's map in paw, where he would guide Azalar on which hall to take, and which ones to avoid. But as they traversed through the hallways, there was another sound that was barely covered by the blaring alarms. The further they went, the more they could hear the distinct sound of shouting and screaming up ahead. Something terrible was happening here, that much they knew. So Azalar beckoned his fellow rodents onward, hoping and desperate to avoid whatever was causing this calamity.

"Turn right at this corner!" Bogger hollered. It was then that they rounded the corner that they came across a horrid sight. There in front of them was a dead human, and his body torn open and blood everywhere. It was a more gruesome sight than when Razor had sliced open Lebo's throat. Azalar stood horrified at what was in front of them, but what terrified him more was the scent that emanated off the corpse. Along with the smell of blood, there was the scent of another creature, and it didn't smell friendly in the slightest. Not wanting to stay a moment longer, Azalar motioned to Bogger.

"Where to now?" Azalar asked. Bogger looked at the map and pointed forward, past the corpse. With great reluctance, but left with no choice, Azalar led the throng of rodents and pressed onward.

The rodents continued through the maze that was Helgan's facility and it was complete chaos every which way they went. Azalar could hear the screams from the humans all around as he and his fellow company of rodents made their way through the facility, making sure to stay close to the walls and away from any possible danger. The red lights blazing, and loud screeching sirens echoed throughout the halls. The further the rodents went; the more chaotic things were. Just as Azalar continued to lead his fellow rodents through the halls, a human woman with short brown hair came around a corner, where she then spotted the rodents. They prepared themselves for a fight when she let out a horrid scream.

"There's more of them!" She cried as she proceeded to run in the other direction. "More of them got out!" The rodents paid no mind to her words, as they were just thankful that there was no need to fight. They all continued through the facility until Azalar stopped everyone at one corner of a hallway intersection with three different directions to go. Azalar looked to Bogger as he was reading over Alice's map.

"Which way do we go?" Azalar asked. Bogger was silent, squinting his eyes as he looked over the map.

"It's very difficult to read in this light," Bogger answered. "But if I'm reading this right, if we go down the right corridor and keep straight, it will bring us to another intersection, where we will need to take a left and straight onward."

"Okay then. Let's get going!" Azalar said. But before they could move, there came a blood curdling scream from down the hall that Bogger had pointed down. Suddenly a male human appeared from around a corner, covered in blood, stumbling and falling to the floor. He then turned on his back, facing the way he came with a look of pure terror as he tried to crawl away. Not a moment later, a loud screech came from behind the corner and a large, fat creature appeared and pounced on the human, quickly followed by two more. Their skin was a brownish red color, and they all had a patch of black fur at the top of their heads that ran down the center of their backs. Their noses were flat, yet they had large nostrils. Their bottom jaws were large, and they had tusks poking out from the bottom of their mouths. They were nothing like Azalar had ever seen before, even in Alice's books.

They couldn't have been more than half the size of a human, but their ferocity was frightening. The creatures beat him with their massive arms, clawing and biting at the poor human as he screamed in agony, trying desperately to get away. Then one of the beasts, one with much larger tusks than the others, grabbed hold of the man's head and bit down on him, silencing his terrified screams. Azalar averted his eyes as the other rodents gasped and murmured in repulsion at the horrible sight before them. Azalar turned again to Bogger.

"We can't go that way. Is there any other way we can go?" he asked. Bogger quickly glanced over the map before pointing ahead.

"If we head down that corridor there, we can go around. It will take us longer, but it will take us back on track and we can avoid those creatures." With that, Azalar and Bogger urged their fellow rodent onward, careful not to draw the attention of those horrid beasts.

The journey was not as easy as they had thought though, as the corridors they scurried through were far more chaotic than the ones they had left behind. Humans were scrambling in sheer panic and terror throughout the halls, many covered in blood. But there were far more beings than just humans that rampaged through the halls. There were many beasts and birds, many that Azalar could recognize, but there were many that he had never seen before; none that he could distinguish from Alice's books. Nonetheless, they all looked dangerous. Fortunately, they had not attracted any of their attention, despite the rodents having a rather large number amongst them; but who knows how long that fortune would hold out.

As the band of rodents raced through the halls, something off to the side caught Ragath's eye when they passed by one of the rooms. Through an open door, across a dark room by a large desk, something glistened on the floor by one of the legs. Ragath entered the room cautiously. The room was dark, but the light from the hall was enough to allow Ragath to see clearly. He drew closer to the shining object on the floor until he rounded the corner of the desk and came into full view. Whatever it was, it looked long and sharp and came to a point.

Ragath picked up the weapon and inspected it further. It was a long piece of metal with a sharp blade on one side and smaller handle, with two smaller metal parts projecting outwards just below the blade where the handle meets. It reminded Ragath of the knives that the humans used in the lab, but the blade was much longer, and the handle was shorter, but the entire design was interesting and different. with an interestingly designed silver hilt and a human skull on the crossguard. The skull itself was black in color with two blood red eyes. But for a weapon, it looked too small to fit in a human's hand, but it was almost as long as Ragath was tall, so for Ragath it was quite large. It looked like a weapon that he could use.

The handle was long enough so he could grip it with both paws side by side. Ragath swung the weapon around a few times to get a better feel of it. It was a little heavy, but it felt good the way he held it in his paws. Ragath smiled with satisfaction. Yes, this was perfect for him. With that, he took the weapon and left the room. He just managed to catch sight of the last rodent disappearing behind the corner before quickly following suit, holding his new sword close to him.

"Turn this way!" cried Bogger, leading the rodents down another hallway. The throng of rodents followed Azalar and Bogger every way they turned amongst the carnage of the facility, desperately trying not to attract the attention of any possible threats that they might come across. This proved to be a great challenge due to the high numbers of rodents in their group. Every time they came to a corner or intersection, Azalar would scout ahead to make sure the coast was clear before moving everyone forward. This slowed their progress significantly, but somehow, they had managed to remain inconspicuous, at least for the time being.

Azalar stopped at one last corner, where the corridor ended with different a hall to the right and to the left. Azalar surveyed for a moment or so to make sure everything was clear before turning to Bogger.

"Just to the right you said, correct?" Azalar asked. Bogger glanced down at the map.

"Yes," Bogger replied. "We must go down the left hallway, where we will find our exit inside a door on the right side near the very end. After that, we should find our way of escape that Alice told us about inside." Azalar looked down the hallway to the left. It was a long corridor, but he could indeed see a large black door near the end though it was a great distance away. He then looked down the right side hallway, so far it was clear.

"Alright! Let's move!" Azalar called out as he led the large company of rodents down the left corridor, scurrying as fast as their legs could carry them. On top of the constant running and adrenaline, Azalar's heart raced with excitement and anticipation; freedom was almost within reach. They were halfway down the corridor now, when suddenly there came a loud crash from behind at the far end of the other hall. Everyone stopped and turned to see what had caused it, including Azalar, though he could not see what it was through the crowd. Ragath, however, who was still a good distance away at the very back of the crowd, looked back as the crash sounded. Just then, a large metal bin was then tossed across the hall against the wall and three monsters appeared from around the corner, the very same beastly creatures that the rodents saw attack the human before. The beasts sniffed the air and looked around when they spotted the rodents down the hall. They then let out ghastly roars before charging towards them. Ragath's eyes widened as the beasts charged towards them.

"Run!" Ragath called to the front. Panic ensued and the rodents began to scream and holler as they all ran towards the black door, with many pushing and shoving to get by one another, with some even shoving Amara to the floor. Azalar pushed through the crowd to get to his fréfil and shielded her from the panicking rodents. They were quickly aided by Bark, Frella, Brim, Della, Bogger and Nikamius and they helped Amara off the floor and quickly made their way towards the black door, where there was a large crowd of rodents trying to push it open. Fortunately, with the number of rodents pushing against the door, they were able to open it without too much difficulty. Once opened the rodents rushed through, pushing and shoving past one another.

Azalar, Amara, Bark, Frella, Brim, Della, Bogger and Nikamius entered through the door, where they met with Borith and Mith, who were trying their best to keep the door open as long as they could for them. The door wasn't as heavy as the one in the lab, but it was still enough of a struggle to keep it open. Once they were inside, Azalar left Amara's side and quickly rushed back to aid Mith and Borith in keeping the door open. He was quickly followed by Brim and Bark, as well as a few other mice; Mint, Lonro, and Talbin, who stopped and lent their aid. Together they pushed against the door for the rest of the rodents to get inside, with a few other rodents stopping to aid them. Many rodents continued to panic as they pushed through the door, very nearly pushing Azalar and others over. Just as the last of the rodents cleared the doorway, the mice began to shut the door behind them. However, Azalar peeked around the door and looked out to make sure there was no one left. To his horror, he saw that Ragath was still out there, and those monsters were right behind him, and they were quickly gaining ground.

"Come on!" Azalar cried out to Ragath, holding out his paw to him. Ragath raced down the hall as quickly as he could, holding his new sword closely, not daring to look back. He could hear the loud thumping behind him, and he could almost feel their breath on his back. He could feel the floor tremble with every step they took, which urged him to run faster. Against his better judgment, Ragath took a brief glance behind him. It was a terrible mistake, as all he could see right behind him was the figure of the monstrous beasts behind him and the hand with long claws reaching out for the black rat. Ragath, for the first time in his life, felt fear inside him. He looked forward once again and saw the little tan colored mouse reaching his paw out to him.

Ragath reached out his own paw as he drew closer to the door. And at the very last second, Azalar grabbed hold of Ragath's paw and quickly pulled him in just as those beasts reached the door, slipping and falling over themselves due to the slick tile floor. With Ragath safely inside, the rodents shut the door behind them. However, just as the door shut, there was a loud bang against the door, sending a few mice flying back from the force of the impact. The remaining rodents held firm and pressed themselves against the door to keep it shut. Azalar and Ragath quickly rushed to aid them, and they were soon joined by Razor and five more rats, such as Ruthin, Mino, Ritti, Res, and Lan, all of which were rats with gray fur that knew Ragath personally and made up his personal squad.

"Nikamius, get everyone back!" Azalar called out. Nikamius did as he was asked and ushered the other rodent further inside. The terrible banging and hideous roars from those beasts coming from the other side of the door caused great fear amongst the mice and rats.

"What are we going to do?" many cried out.

"They're going to get in!" others said.

"Everyone, remain calm!" said Nikamius as he tried to calm the panic from the crowd. Amara, Frella and Della watched as Azalar and the others did all they could to keep those monsters from getting inside. It was during this time that Bogger was searching around the room. This was where Alice wanted them to go, he just had to find what she wanted them to find. The '*shower room*', as it was called according to the map, started as a small halfway that opened up into a large room It was a very large and empty room, almost bigger than the laboratory that they spent their entire lives in, with small little sections divided by walls that lined across both sides of the room, as well as little metal funnel shaped objects that protruded from the walls within each divided section high above. He searched around some more, moving to the far end of the shower room, but from what he could see, it was nothing more than an empty room.

However, just as Bogger reached the end of the room, he noticed something in one of the stalls; each stall had a small metal drain in the floor, but with the one stall that he was looking at, the metal drain stuck out more than the others. With no time to lose, Bogger quickly rushed into the stall to examine further, and found that the drain was indeed loose. He pulled the metal piece that covered the drain and tossed it aside and stared down into the dark abyss below. This had to be the way that Alice wanted them to find. Bogger then stepped out of the stall and called out to the others.

"Nikamius!" Bogger called out. Nikamius heard his name and pushed through the crowd to get to the back, where he saw Bogger waving to him. "Over here!" Nikamius quickly turned and made his way towards Bogger. Many other rodents turned and saw Nikamius making his way down the chamber and over to Bogger. Thinking that they may have somehow found a way out, they followed the elder mouse to where Bogger was, where the dark red mouse showed them the large hole in the floor.

"Everyone down here!" Bogger shouted. "This is where we need to go."

"But how do we know where it leads?" a mouse called out.

"We don't have much of a choice, my friends!" Nikamius replied. "It's either down here, or back there!" He pointed back towards the doors, where those horrid monsters continued to bang on the door. Fear gripped the hearts of the rodents as they were unsure of what to do. It was then that a young male brown rat stepped forward from the crowd, along with two other young rats who accompanied him.

"We'll go," the brown rat said. He then turned back to the other. "Be sure to stay close to me and stay together." But just before he jumped down, Nikamius stopped him.

"What is your name?" Nikamius asked.

"Reemus," the young brown rat answered. Nikamius smiled at him.

"Thank you, young rat. And may Háth watch over you," he said and stepped aside. With that, the brown rat nodded and jumped down the dark hole, soon followed by a pair of rats, one brown and white and the other a dark tan color. They were then followed by a mouse, then another rat, and so on. One by one, the rodents hopped down into the drain. Though they were in a rush to escape, they were careful not to get in each other's way for fear of blocking the entrance and getting themselves stuck, which would have then rendered them all unable to escape. So far, everything was going quickly and smoothly, despite the panic and fear that they were all feeling.

Amara, Frella and Della noticed that most of the rodents were gathering towards the back of the room. They were just about to follow when Amara stopped herself. She turned back to where her beloved mate and the others were holding back those dreaded monsters. She couldn't just leave them like that by themselves. She had to do something. Amara searched around for something, anything that she could use to help. Just then, Amara noticed something at the far corner of the room, just behind a large circular bin. Frella and Della stopped when they noticed that Amara wasn't beside them. They looked back to see Amara staring at the corner of the room. They returned to her side and glanced in the direction she was looking at. They too saw it and an idea began to form in their heads.

The three beasts outside continued to bang aggressively on the door, trying to force it open. Azalar, Ragath, Bark, Brim, Mith, Borith, Razor, along with the five other rats and the three other mice, were all mustering as much strength as they could to keep them from getting in. Still, with every blow from those beasts, the door opened wider and wider, and the rodents were quickly losing strength. It was only a matter of time before they broke through. Azalar looked back to see the rest of the rodents had gathered at the far end of the room where they disappeared behind the wall of the stall at the end.

They must have found the exit, he thought to himself.

Azalar was relieved by this. They were that much closer to freedom. However, that would have to wait as they had to deal with the current crisis at hand. With one last bang, the door was pushed open further and a large reddish-brown arm reached inside, trying to swipe at the rodents behind the door. The rodents tried to push the door closed, but the beasts were much stronger and were slowly opening the door wider. They were almost inside and Azalar had to do something, or else none of them were getting out of here alive. He then had a thought: if the rest of the rodents were able to escape from this dreaded place, then Azalar would gladly sacrifice himself if it meant that could happen.

"All of you get out of here!" Azalar called to the others. "I'll hold them off for as long as I can while the rest of you escape! Go now!" But no one made a move. They all remained exactly where they were, pressing their bodies against the door to keep those monsters out.

"I said get going!" Azalar shouted. But again, they did not move.

"We're not leaving you behind!" Bark retorted. "We started this together and we will finish this together!"

"Don't be fools!" Azalar hollered. "You don't stand a chance! All of you get out of here while you still have the chance."

"That's not going to happen, Azalar!" said Brim. "If you think that we are just going to abandon you, then you really don't know us at all!"

"I'm not asking you to abandon me!" Azalar said. "I'm asking you to go and look after the others."

"And what are we supposed to tell Amara?" Bark asked. "That we left you behind while you foolishly decided to sacrifice yourself for us? I don't think she would like that at all." Azalar narrowed his eyes at his longtime friend.

"She will understand–"

"Just save your breath, little mouse!" Ragath interjected. "Even if we did just leave, there's no way you can hold them off by yourself and they'd devour you in a second."

"And you're not the only one who has something to fight for!" exclaimed Brim. "We're staying, Azalar, whether you like it or not. We're all in this together!" Azalar looked at all the rodents beside him, who all gave nods of agreement, and a great deal of pride welding in his chest. Though he wished they did as he asked, he was happy to know that they were willing to fight and die alongside him.

"Alright then," Azalar said. "Together!"

Razor, however, gave Ragath a little side glance. The idea of fighting for a mouse was appalling to him. If he had it his way, he would leave the little mouse to his fate. But Ragath was his chief. If Ragath decided to stay and fight with the little tan colored mouse, then Razor would do the same, despite the fact that he didn't like it one bit. If he was going to die, it was not going to be for Azalar, but for the pride of being a rat and fighting alongside Ragath.

"Everyone!" Azalar called out. "On the count of 'three', we jump back, and we face them head on! Everyone ready?" He received multiple voices of confirmation on the plan.

"Alright then! On three! One! Two…"

"Azalar!" a voice cried out. Azalar looked back to see Amara, Frella and Della sliding what looked to be a long, triangular shaped object across the floor at full speed towards them. "Get out of the way!" she called out to him. Azalar jumped out of the way just in time for Amara, Frella and Della to shove the triangular object under the door, wedging it in place. The other rodents stepped back from the door now that it was secured. However, Della was too close to the edge, and just as the beast, with its arms caught between the door and the frame, swung its massive arms, and caught hold of Della. The poor mouse cried in terror and pain as the beast squeezed her tightly in its grasp.

"Della!" cried Brim as he watched in horror as his beloved fréfil was lifted off the floor. The beast then tried to squeeze its large head through the crack of the door and raised Della towards its massive, opened mouth. Seeing those terrible tusks draw closer, Della screamed even louder. Azalar didn't hesitate and dashed forward with his needle in paw. He sprinted as fast as he could and leaped onto Razor, then used that momentum to jump higher into the air where he then raised his needle above his head and stabbed it deep into that beastly hand. The monster let out a painful roar and released its grip on Della's body.

Della fell and landed safely in the arms of her beloved mate, who was fortunately waiting below to catch her, and was quickly carried away. Azalar, who was still hanging on to his needle, braced himself on the monster's hand. The beast tried to swing Azalar off and the tan colored mouse nearly lost his grip. Azalar had to let go soon or he could possibly be crushed against the wall or thrown off and seriously injured or killed. With little choice left, Azalar quickly raced his back paws against the monstrous hand and pulled the needle out, where he fell to the floor with a bounce and a thud.

"Azalar!" cried Amara as she rushed to his side. Azalar looked up at her with a reassuring smile.

"I'm okay," Azalar said as he quickly picked himself up, though in truth he was in a good deal of pain, but he refused to show it. He glanced back at the door where the beasts were now banging on the door more ferociously than before. With every bang, the door was slowly opening inch by inch. "But that won't hold them for long."

"Azalar!" called another voice. All the rodents turned to see Bogger and Nikamius waving over to them. Most of the rodents had already gone, only Azalar and the rodents remained.

"Everyone, move now!" Azalar hollered. The company of rodents all hurried towards them as quickly as they could across the room. Once they reached them, Nikamius and Bogger showed Azalar where the others had escaped.

"Down here!" said Bogger. "This is our escape!" The others looked skeptical, until they heard the loud bang on the shower room door once again. Ragath immediately stepped forward. He looked down into the darkness below before glancing over to Azalar.

"You better be right about this," he said in his trademark low tone before holding his sword tightly in his arms and dropping down into the drain. Razor followed after, who was then followed by the other rats. Once the rats had all descended down the drain, Brim was the next to step forward, but not before turning to his beloved Della.

"I'll go first," Brim said gently. "Be careful coming down, okay?" Della smiled before nuzzling her fréfil.

"I will. But you need to be careful first." Brim smiled in return before turning and jumping down the dark hole. Della soon followed a moment after. Bark stepped forward next and turned to Azalar.

"See you on the other side," he said with a nod and quickly jumped down the drain. Frella followed next, then Mith, then Borith, and then the rest of the other mice until it was only Azalar, Amara, Bogger and Nikamius. It was then the elder mouse's turn to descend.

"Be careful, Nikamius," said Azalar. Nikamius chuckled at the younger mouse.

"I may be an old mouse, young one, but I've still got a few more springs left in me." With that, the elder mouse descended downward. Just then a much louder bang was heard by the door. Azalar quickly rushed to see what had happened. To his horror, the three terrible beasts had burst through the door and were now entering the room. They sniffed the air, searching for the little rodents, until one of them caught sight of Azalar. It let out a loud roar and charged forward. With wide eyes, Azalar turned to the other two mice.

"Get down now!" he shouted! Bogger didn't hesitate and jumped down the drain. Amara, however, was hesitant and looked back at Azalar, who quickly rushed to her side.

"Azalar," she began in a fearful voice, but Azalar stopped her.

"I'll be right behind you, my star. Now go!" he said in a reassuring voice. Amara turned and, though still hesitant and anxious, jumped down and disappeared into the darkness below. Azalar clutched his needle close to him, turned back one last time at the terrible beasts behind him, before following his fellow rodents down the dark hole, just as a monstrous hand slammed down right where Azalar had been just a moment before.

Azalar slid down the metal pipes until he rolled to the bottom. He then sat up and searched his surroundings. It was cold and damp, and all Azalar could see was darkness. He slowly began walked forward.

"Amara!" he called out.

"Over here, Azalar!" Amara called back. Azalar stood up and pressed forward, feeling his way through the pipes as his eyes began to adjust, but there still wasn't much to see. He could hear the voices of his fellow rodents further down the pipe, but he wasn't sure just how far away they were. Then there was a sudden drop and Azalar fell down into another pipe. It was a bit of a fall, maybe a moment or two, before his feet hit water, which broke his fall, preventing major injury, though the impact was enough to cause him a bit of pain when he landed. He then picked himself up when he heard a voice.

"Azalar?" Amara spoke. Azalar reached forward into the darkness until he felt the touch of a familiar paw on his own.

"Amara? Is that you?"

"I'm here, my love," Amara answered.

"Everyone is here as well," said Bark a little further away. Azalar peered into the darkness until his eyes began to adjust. From there he could see the familiar shapes of his fellow rodents all around him. The pipe was much larger than the one he was previously in, but it was far more foul smelling. Though the smell was terrible, Azalar let out a sigh of relief.

"Alright!" he called out. "Let's get moving. We still have a long way to go." Azalar, with his fréfil beside him, quickly pushed his way to the front of the crowd and led his fellow rodents through the dark and putrid tunnels. He only hoped that they would find the exit soon.

Evans ran through the halls of Helgan's facility, trying to find a safe place to hide. Yet, everywhere he went, there was chaos and death at every turn. He suddenly found himself running down a hall until it came to an end, save for only a door to the left side. But Evans was reluctant to go through it. It took him a moment, but Evans knew exactly where he was now. That door led to the lower parts of the facility, where it was absolutely forbidden to enter. Evans had heard rumors of what went on down there, and all of them were terrible.

There was a loud crash and a horrible scream from behind, and Evans made the decision to take his chances down there, rather than get torn apart up here. With a deep breath, pulled on the door, both relieved, and concerned to find it unlocked. He opened the door and disappeared into the darkness behind it. He felt around for a light switch when the lights suddenly switched on all on their own and Evans noticed the stairway in front of him. Though he was quite hesitant, he nevertheless made his way down the long, winding stairs until he came to set doors at the very bottom. With shaking hands, he pushed open the doors to find a long corridor with doors that lined up on each side. As he entered, his heart was pounding in his chest. He knew he was not supposed to be down here. Even so, it was better than being in the upper levels, where all sorts of pandemonium was occurring.

Evans slowly tiptoed through the hallway, as if he didn't want to disturb anything or anyone that could be lurking down there, specifically Helgan himself. Curiosity was growing inside him as each door was widely spaced apart from one another and were all numbered. But there were no windows to peek through, so whatever laid behind those doors would probably remain a mystery, at least for now.

He was three quarters down the hall, when he heard a noise come from up ahead behind the very last door, which was slightly ajar. Though anxiety filled his entire body, Evans had always been curious about the lower chambers of Helgan's facility. Slowly, Evans made his way down the corridor towards the door. Upon reaching the door, he pushed the slightly ajar door and entered. The room was dark at first, but once he took a few steps inside, the lights suddenly lit up, revealing an enormous laboratory. Inside the laboratory, there were many massive machines and giant vats all around the room. The technology in this lab was something that Evans had never seen before; far more advanced and superior to anything in the whole facility. Evans explored more of the lab, amazed at the machines that were scattered throughout the room; machines that even he didn't know what they could possibly be used for, and he considered himself a highly intelligent and educated man. Yet even though he was amazed by all these things, there was a very eerie feeling about it all. Something didn't feel right about this place.

Evans continued wandering through the lab, fascinated with everything that he was seeing, that is until he reached the very back of the room. There he saw little green vats, similar to the ones at the front, and there were hundreds of them. Though many had been smashed to bits, there were few that remained with tiny things inside them. Evans stepped closer to get a better look. From what he could gather from the beings inside, it looked almost like a huge black insect, but much larger, and looked far more menacing than any insect that he had ever seen. But there was something off about it. Evans leaned closer to the glass, staring intently at the creature inside. He stared into those cold black eyes, when suddenly it lunged at him as it let out a high-pitched screech.

Evans jumped back with a start nearly tripping over himself. He looked back at the creature as it continued to twitch and screech inside the vat and took a deep breath. Suddenly there was a loud noise, followed by a bright light off to his right. He turned to see another set of doors. Evans slowly moved towards them and gently pushed them open. However, the moment he opened those doors, something small and dark dashed passed his feet, giving him another start. He didn't get a good glance at it, but whatever that tiny thing was, it disappeared into the laboratory. Evans shook his head vigorously, getting rather agitated by all these sudden surprises, before exiting the lab and finding himself inside another long corridor, though the lights were much dimmer, with some even flickering on and off, with more doors on either side spaced further apart.

Feeling a small sense of Deja vu, Evans slowly and cautiously entered the hallway. He stepped very lightly through the corridor, taking each step with care and did his best not to make any noise. The lights in the hall continued to flicker on and off from above, making it difficult at times for Evans to see where his feet were, which caused him to stumble once or twice. He finally reached the end of the hall, where there was a small bright blue light shining through one of the door windows. Evans peeked through the window and looked inside. The glass was cracked and dirty, so it was rather difficult to see through. From what he could see, it seemed to be another kind of laboratory; but for what, Evans didn't know.

As he continued to peek into, he noticed what looked like a large computer with a massive screen at the other side of the room. Evans squinted his eyes to see what was on the screen. He couldn't tell for certain, but he thought he could make out a human and some animal shapes on the screen, but as for the words next to the shapes, he had no clue what they said. It was then that he noticed something on the floor in front of the computer. It looked like a person. Evans adjusted his glasses and peered closer to the glass. It was definitely a person on the floor covered in blood, but Evans couldn't quite see who it was.

Suddenly there was a loud crash, quickly followed by a deep bellowing moan, that echoed throughout the room, startling Evans. He didn't know what it was, but it did not sound human. Fearful of what it may be, Evans quickly backed away from the door and ran back down the hall to search for a place to hide. He tried for the first two doors to his left and right, but they were both locked like the ones before. He moved to the next two further down, but they too were locked tight. There was a second noise up ahead, this time it sounded closer and heavier. Left with no choice, Evans ran back down the hall until he came to a door. He pulled at the handle, and it opened with ease. Evans quickly dashed inside and shut the door behind him. He then found himself in complete darkness, save only the faint light that outlined the door.

There was a moment of silence, then he heard what sounded like footsteps walking down the hall towards him. Evans slowly backed away from the door, hoping to avoid being detected. The footsteps grew closer and closer, until they stopped right in front of the door. There was silence once again, with the only sound being Evans' shaking breath and his heart pounding in his ears. Evans didn't say a word and took another few steps back until he bumped into what he presumed to be a desk. Suddenly Evans could hear the faint sound of chittering and clicking sound coming from behind. Evans was startled and instinctively turned around, but he couldn't see a thing in the darkness. The chittering was growing louder now. Evans took out his little penlight from his pocket and quickly switched it on. Evans shined the light into the room. What he saw nearly made him drop his light.

The room that Evans had assumed was just another office room was actually an enormous exhibit-like enclosure, and in the center of the room was a massive round tower with dozens of holes scattered all around it. The tower itself was surrounded by smaller towers of various sizes, all with the same holes as the center tower. The desk that Evans had backed into was one of these towers. The chittering was much louder than before, and it was coming from one of the holes in the tower next to Evans. Evans stared at the mouth of the hole where the chittering was coming from, when something large, purple and very angry emerged.

It was an ArchBeetle.

It hissed at Evans and raised its claws at him ready to strike. More chittering and clicking could be heard coming from all around the room and more ArchBeetles began to surface from the towers. Soon the whole room was filled with hundreds of ArchBeetles, and they were all moving in towards Evans. Evans stood petrified for a moment before he was able to regain control of himself and let out a horrified scream. He quickly ran back to the door. He was horrified, however, to find that it was locked.

"Help! Someone open the door!" Evans shouted, trying desperately to get out. Evans continued to pull on the door, but it wouldn't budge. "Please! Anyone! Let me out!" There was no answer. Suddenly there was a click, and when Evans turned the knob, the door opened. Evans quickly rushed out the door and tried to shut it behind him, but the ArchBeetles were right behind him and began to pour through the open door. Evans ran down the hall as fast as he could, when he made the mistake of looking behind and tripping over himself. He tried to pick himself up, but the Arch-Beetles were already upon him. Some bit and pinched at his ankles while others moved further up his body. Evans screamed in pain and tried to crawl away when he noticed a dark figure walking through the exit doors. He couldn't make out their features, but he was hopeful that whoever they were would save him.

"Please! Help me!" he cried, reaching out to the figure ahead. The dark figure stopped just as the doors were closing before slowly turning its head. The last thing that Evans saw before the doors shut were a pair of deep red eyes staring back at him. The last thing that could be heard was the horrible screams that echoed throughout the laboratory.

Chapter XI

The large band of rodents were running as fast as they could through the darkness of the sewers, staying as close to the walls as they could. They ventured further and further into the black tunnels, unable to see clearly where they were going. They kept close to one another, never straying far from those ahead of them. Every twist and turn they followed, looking for any sign of escape. The foul stench of the tunnels and the dark waters beside them made it increasingly difficult to catch their breath, but still they pushed onward. They were running for nearly half an hour now, and they were growing tired. Nikamius noticed this from the few mice closest to him and called out to the front.

"Azalar!" Nikamius called ahead, but Azalar didn't respond. "Azalar, we need to rest!" The brown mouse finally looks behind him. Even in this darkness, he could see behind that, although the rats were able to keep up effortlessly and could probably go on for a good while longer, his fellow mice were beginning to grow weary and fatigue. He knew that this was not the place to respite in, but if he did not find an exit soon, he would soon have little choice. Fortune seemed to smile upon him, however, as a tiny sliver of light could be seen further up the tunnel.

"There!" He called out. Seeing the light ahead gave the rodents enough cause and motivation to push forward just a bit more. They came to the light, which shone through a small crack in the wall. The gap was deep and narrow but could be seen through to the other side. Though the means of escape was within sight, there was a small degree of hesitation from the company. What danger lay beyond the crack and into the world was uncertain. Azalar sniffed the air, trying to detect any sign of danger ahead. The air was still foul and wet, but he did not detect anything suspicious and dangerous, though he was still skeptical and was averse to going through. Ragath had pushed his way through the crowd, spoke up with confidence.

"I'll go first," he said and crawled down into the small passage, his weapon pointed forward in case of any unwelcoming surprises. It was narrow and cramped, but Ragath had little trouble squeezing though. Upon exiting the crack, Ragath looked around cautiously, it was still dark, but there was indeed a source of light from above. A single ray of light shone from the ceiling as a dimly lit light bulb that would flicker every so often. There were two other lights on the ceiling, but they were so dim that they barely gave off any light whatsoever. Ragath looked at his surroundings at what appeared to be another tunnel, but this one was far larger and much more spacious than the one he emerged from. Ragath carefully looked around, taking notice of a pair of large metal beams running parallel to each other, with a few wooden planks beneath it in front of him running along the tunnel.

Ragath sniffed the air and investigated his surroundings further. The air was stuffy and stale, but there seemed to be no sign of any threats at the current moment. There were piles of rocks and debris scattered throughout the tunnel as well. With his weapon ready, he wandered over to the nearest rock pile and quickly climbed to the top to get a better vantage point.

He reached the top and surveyed the area around him, perking his ears up for the slightest noise, with the only sound being the occasional ominous sound of a drop of water hitting an unseen pool deep within the distant tunnels. He glanced left and right, searching for any sort of danger. The tunnels stretched far on either side, with the metal beams and wooden planks following both sides until they were swallowed by the darkness beyond. No matter which way he looked, it was as if he was staring down the throat of a massive beast. Yet so far, despite the dreariness of either side on the tunnel, there appeared to be no sign of immediate danger. Ragath turned back towards the crack, where Azalar stood just outside waiting. Ragath gave a nod, signaling that all was clear, and Azalar slowly motioned the others to come out.

"Okay, everyone, stay quiet and stay together," Azalar said to the others. Slowly the rodents made their way out of the crack and into the dim light of the much larger tunnel.

"Which way do we go?" one of the mice called out. Everyone turned to Azalar, who had been thinking the same question. After a brief moment he turned back to the crowd and answered.

"I'm not sure just yet," Azalar answered. "We need to gather our bearings first before we go wandering aimlessly into the darkness again.

"I think we should go that way," Nikamius said, pointing down the right side of the tunnel. "The air doesn't smell as foul as it does down the other direction. If we are to leave these wretched tunnels, I'd say that way is our best chance."

"Alright then," Azalar said. "Let's rest here for a while, then we will go on then. I know everyone is tired and hungry, but we must move on from this place and find a way out. Or at the very least find a more suitable place to rest. Hopefully we can find some food and clean water soon."

After about an hour of respite, Azalar gathered the rodents together to make their way down the tunnel.

"Everyone, stay together!" Azalar called out to everyone. "It's going to be dark, and I don't want anyone falling behind or getting lost. Link tails if you need to but be sure to keep close and watch your step."

The throng of rodents, though still tired from their harrowing escape from the lab, were eager to get out of the dark gloom of this dreaded tunnel. They all clung together as the last light from the crack in the ceiling faded away and they were consumed by darkness once again. They all trekked for a long time through the dark, with Azalar and Nikamius leading from the front, with Amara, Bark and Frella following them close behind. Behind them were Bogger, Brim, and Della, who clung to her mate closely for comfort. In the center were the remaining hundreds of mice and rats gathered tightly together in between the metal beams, with Mith and Borith tasked with guarding each side of the rodent throng from the top of the metal beams, each accompanied by three other mouse bucks to make sure no one wandered off or got separated. These squads included Mint; a brown mouse, Lonro, an older gray mouse, and Talbin, a bright gray and white mouse, on Mith's side, and other mice such as Fin, Miltig and Horthim on Borith's, all of which were beige colored mice.

Ragath and Razor, along with a few other rat bucks, with whatever weapons they had managed to scavenge from the laboratory, guarding the rear in case anyone fell behind; or in case there were unexpected surprises that may be following them.

For a long time, they journeyed silently through the tunnels. The path was dark and bleak, but the rodents didn't seem to be having as much trouble finding their way around. The silence of the eerie dark, with only the sound of their paws and the dripping of water echoing through the tunnels, was making them very uneasy, but nobody dared to speak a word to break the silence. The only voices that could be heard were Azalar and Nikamius, with the occasional voice of Bogger chiming in, discussing on how best to proceed forward.

Azalar would often ask Brim if he could hear anything up ahead, but the patting of hundreds of feet and the constant dripping water echoing through the tunnels distorted his hearing and he couldn't make anything out too clearly. However, Brim failed to mention that amongst the patter of the company's feet, he thought he could hear movement coming from all around them, as if something in the darkness was moving with them. They seemed to move when they did and stopped what the company stopped. Brim, still unfamiliar with all the new sounds of the world, brushed it off as merely echoes, but still felt an uneasy feeling in his stomach.

The road twisted and turned, and sometimes they would climb over piles of rubble that had blocked their paths. Every so often the path seemed to take them upwards, where the air grew stifling and foul smelling at times, though not as foul as it had been during their time in the sewers, before descending down for a long while to cooler temperatures and would become level once more. At times the tunnels were void of any light, making their journey that much more difficult to traverse. Though they were nocturnal creatures by nature and could still see in the dark, even without light; they had spent their entire lives trapped in a bright laboratory and had never truly experienced such darkness. Yet they traveled onward, careful to watch their step and to avoid any deep cracks and pits they may appear underfoot. Other times there were lights that shined or flickered from the sides of the tunnel or from the ceiling, but they were far in between. Though it allowed them to see further ahead and quicken their pace; but there were still obstacles that they would encounter that would cross their path and slow them down.

One such obstacle was a large cave-in that blocked off most of the path, forcing them to climb over the massive wall of debris. Another obstacle that they came across was a massive sinkhole that stretched from one side of the tunnel to the other, which had caused most of the planks and beams to fall into the pit. It was far too wide to jump across and much deep to climb down. Fortunately, there was a single beam that hadn't fallen in and the rodents were able to slowly, but safely, cross the pit.

Ragath and the other rats kept their guard up while covering the rear. They may be far away from any humans, but that did not mean that there weren't other things in the world that couldn't harm them, and Ragath didn't like to be caught off guard. He kept his sharp ears open for any suspicious sound that echoed through the tunnels. He thought on more than one occasion that he heard feet pattering on the wet ground behind them, but every time he looked back, there was nothing there. Ragath had an unnerving feeling that they were being watched, and that thought alone made the fur on his back stand on end. Even if it was just his imagination and paranoia, Ragath was not going to brush anything off and kept a lookout for anything, gripping his sword tightly in his paws.

"Are you sure about sticking with these mice, Ragath?" Razor whispered. "I think it would be better to take our chances and leave them behind the first chance we get." Ragath shook his head at this.

"No," he said. "Our best chances of survival are to stick together. We don't know what's out there and we need numbers if we are going to make it through this." Razor shook his head and sighed.

"I don't know about this," Razor said. "We rats are superior in every way. Strength. Speed. Everything!

Why do we need these mice with us? They'll only hold us back."

"Be that as it may, Razor. We still need to work together with the mice. Azalar hasn't led us astray so far and they may prove to be useful. But if he proves to be incompetent, and the mice do indeed cause us hindrance, then we won't hesitate to leave them behind." Razor looked away with a heavy sigh.

"Very well," he said lowly. "I hope you know what you're doing." Ragath looked up ahead towards the front of the rodent band, where a certain tanned colored mouse was leading the group.

"So do I," Ragath whispered to himself.

As the throng of rodents continued their journey, the tunnels began to widen and there were more of these metal beams and planks started appearing, running parallel alongside the first set that the rodents traveled upon. Although the tunnels were widening, their paths became more obstructed as the ground became more dense with the fallen debris that littered the floor. It took more effort to climb over the steep piles as the band of rodents grew more weary. Through the beams of dim light coming from the lights above that did work every so often, Azalar could make out different shapes scattered within the tunnel amongst the rubble: giant metal rectangular structures that sat upon large wheels. Yet most of these shapes didn't look as they would have been designed that way; distorted and broken, with pieces that implied that they were once part of the structure, while others looked to be crushed or smashed together. The rodents wondered curiously as to what these strange structures could be, or what their purposes were. Still, none paid them much mind for too long and simply wished to be out of this dreary place already.

Azalar soon took notice that the band of rodents were beginning to fall behind due to fatigue and weariness, and both he and Nikamius, as well as Bogger, knew that they had to find a spot to rest, and it had to be soon. The rodents were growing wearier with each passing minute, but there had not been any decent place to set up camp that would be both dry and flat, as well as provide enough protection for the entire group. Their choices appeared to be very limited, and they would have to make a choice soon to either keep pushing forwards or sacrifice the means of protection and simply find the next best spot available to rest. Azalar thought about resting inside one the large rectangular metal structures, but most of them looked to be very rusted and unsafe to reside in. Many of them looked as if they would collapse on themselves at any moment. He decided against it and moved forward down the tunnels.

However, after an hour of travel, they came to a crossroads where the tunnel split into two different directions. The tunnel on the left was completely dark and seemed to go downhill, whereas the tunnel on the right still had few lights flickering in the darkness; though they were dim and there was great distance between each source of light. The large throng of rodents stopped short of the crossroads as Azalar stared puzzlingly between the two paths.

"Any idea which way we should go?" Bark asked. Azalar remained silent for a few moments as he looked from one tunnel to the other. The tunnel to the right was indeed more welcoming, but it turned right into more darkness far off in the distance, whereas the tunnel to the left that went downward, though it was dark and mysterious, could potentially lead them to their exit from this dreadful place. But despite that thought, Azalar felt a ominous sense of danger coming from down that path. He looked over to Nikamius.

"What do you think, Nikamius?" Azalar asked. Nikamius was also silent as he stared intently down the left side tunnel with a deep frown,

"I think we should take the right," Nikamius said. "There is a terrible smell coming from that way. As if the smell of death itself took residence down there." Now that Nikamius had mentioned it, a foul smell entered Azalar's nose, causing the mouse to cringe slightly.

"I think it would be best to avoid that path at all cost," said Nikamius. "And hopeful the journey doesn't force us to return to this point." Azalar nodded his head in agreement, silently thankful that the decision to travel down that way was avoided. But as he led the rodents towards the right tunnel, Azalar felt the sudden urge to take one last glance down the dark tunnel. He couldn't quite place it, but Azalar felt as if there was something down there, staring back at them from the blackness, and it did not feel friendly.

They had traveled for a few more hours, and as they did, the tunnels seemed to become more broken and crowded with fallen rocks and debris; and the air had become more stifling and staler, but that was the least of their troubles. Just as they rounded a turn, they came to a massive roadblock. The entire tunnel had collapsed in a massive cave-in. However, unlike the previous cave-ins from before, this cave-in was much larger and reached all the way to the top of the tunnel. There seemed to be no way over or around it; at least from what they could see. Azalar stared at the rock wall that blocked their path with a frown when Bark approached.

"So, what now?" he asked. Azalar was silent as he just stared at the cave-in in front of them. With a heavy sigh he turned back to his companion.

"There is nothing for us to do now," he answered. "We will just have to rest here for a while." He turned to Mith and Borith. "Spread the word and let the others know that we will be stopping here until we can find a way around. Then once you have done that, come back to me so that we can plan what to do next." Mith and Borith nodded their heads and went to complete the task given to them. Once they were gone Azalar turned to Brim.

"Any idea on how we get past this?" Brim looked up at the rock wall and studied it for a long while before returning his attention back to Azalar.

"As far as I can tell, there doesn't seem to be any way we can climb over. Maybe if we scout the area for a while, there should be a few cracks that we can squeeze through; though that may take a long time."

"Time with which we do not have," Azalar stated. "With each passing moment, we continue to grow more weary and more hungry. We'll rest here for now, but I want you to gather a few other bucks to help you scout for a way through. And if he is willing, ask Ragath if he can spare a few rats to help you in your search."

"I think I may have a solution," Bogger interjected, gaining everyone's attention.

"What is it?" Azalar asked.

"I saw what looked to be a door along the wall a good while back," Bogger said. "From what I gathered, it seems to be a side entrance for maintenance of these tunnels to keep them functioning, though I doubt it has been used for a long while."

"Really?" Azalar asked. "I didn't notice any door."

"I noticed it too," Brim said. "It was hidden behind one of those massive metal things. Perhaps if we were to open it, it should lead us around the cave-in; or better yet, out of these tunnels entirely." Azalar thought about this for a long moment. This plan would require turning back the way they came, which would mean more time and energy that they can't replenish without food. Their options seem very limited, and neither was very appealing.

"We'll search for a way through here first," Azalar said. "But if we don't find any, then we'll try for that door.

"I would greatly advise against it," Ragath said as he approached the group of mice.

"What do you mean?" Azalar asked curiously. Ragath gave a frown.

"I noticed that door as well, but I don't think we should go there. I don't know why, but once I saw it, I immediately got a bad feeling from it. I don't think we should go that way if we can find another. I fear death awaits us if we were to go through that door." There was a tense pause.

"Are you sure about this?" Nikamius asked. Ragath nodded, then looked back to Azalar.

"I strongly suggest we either find a way around or through this blockage."

"And what if we don't find a way through?" Brim asked. "What then? Do we go back the way we came? Back to where we started in the first place?" Ragath, for the first time, did not have an answer, and turned his head with a deep frown. It was then that Nikamius spoke up.

"Let us just rest here for the time being," Nikamius said. "We're all weary and stressed from the long journey. We will begin our search in a few hours when we have calmer and clearer heads. But if we can't find a way through, then we will come together to make a decision on what to do next."

"Very well," Ragath growled in his low voice before turning to Azalar. "But I warn you now, little mouse, if we go down through that door, we may not reach the other side." With that, Ragath turned and headed back towards his fellow rats at the back of the group. Azalar watched as the large black rat disappeared into the crowd, his words still filling his mind. He then felt a grip on his left paw and turned to see Amara smiling up at him encouragingly. Azalar returned the smile and nuzzled his mate before turning to the rest of the rodents, telling them that they would be resting here for the time being. Many looked thankful to finally have a chance to rest their aching legs, while others looked at their surroundings with skepticism and apprehension. This wasn't the most ideal spot to rest, but there were little choices they had in the matter.

The large band of rodents took shelter underneath a great metal box-like structure that didn't look to be on the verge of collapse anytime soon, though it still looked rather uncertain. The rodents huddled together in small groups to keep each other warm, as well as provide some sense of security. It had been several hours and most of the rodents had fallen asleep, all except for Azalar, who sat a little further away from the rest of the rodents next to a large metal wheel, with Amara nuzzled up next to him. He had decided to forgo a little sleep and keep watch while the others rested, staring back down the tunnel where they came.

As he stared, an uneasy feeling in him slowly began to grow. Azalar couldn't quite understand why, but he felt that something was terribly wrong. A small part of him thought that it was just his imagination, that his tired and worn mind from the long journey, along with Ragath's words of warning, were causing him to become a little paranoid. He tried to shake off these feelings and thoughts and rested his head atop Amara's, slowly allowing his heaving eyes to close for some much needed sleep. But then he heard a sound. *Tap-tap. Tap-tap. Tap-tap.*

Azalar's eyes widened with a start, and he jolted his head up, causing Amara to stir in her sleep. It was faint, but he was sure that he heard the sound of little paws tapping against stone. Azalar was alert now, and he peered out into the darkness beyond the few dim lights close by, but there was nothing there, only the silence.

Nothing more was heard for several minutes, and Azalar came to think that maybe his tired mind had imagined the sound. Yet, he was wide awake now and sleep would not be coming anytime soon. Azalar attempted to calm himself and lean back against Amara and tried vainly to get some sleep; but then it came again. *Tap-tap, tap-tap, tap-tap.* Azalar sat up again, more alert than before. His movements were so sudden that it had disturbed Amara from her slumber.

"What is it?" Amara asked groggily as she rubbed her eyes tiredly before looking up at Azalar; but he quietly hushed her and placed a finger to his lips.

"Listen," he whispered in a low tone. Amara perked her eyes up, now fully awake and alert. They listened intently for several minutes, but nothing came; the air was still and silent.

"I heard something out there," Azalar finally said. Amara's eyes grew wide, and her blood ran cold as she looked in the direction Azalar was looking.

"What is it?" she asked again, her voice much lower than before.

"I'm not sure," Azalar answered, "but I think something is out there. I think whatever it is may have followed us from the other tunnel. We have to wake the others and get moving." Then the sound came again, gaining both their attention. *Tap-tap, tap-tap.* The noise stopped abruptly just as it came, it was then followed by a louder *clunk* of a small stone falling to the floor echoing through the tunnel. The two mice remained silent and unmoving for a few moments, watching the darkness, almost expecting some dreaded thing to emerge.

"We have to move, now!" Azalar said. "But don't tell the others what just happened. I don't want to cause a panic."

Azalar and Amara then proceeded to awaken the rest of the rodents as quickly as they could without giving any sign of alarm as best as they could. The only rodents that Azalar told about the events that had occurred during their sleep were Bark, Brim, Bogger, Nikamius and Ragath. And the moment he did, Ragath's face fell.

"So, something *was* following us," Ragath muttered aloud. The others all turned their attention to the giant black rat.

"What exactly do you mean 'following us'?" asked Bogger.

"I thought I heard something behind us as we were traveling," Ragath answered. "I wasn't sure at first; I simply thought it was the echo of our paws tapping against the floor. But now that Azalar heard the same thing a few moments ago, there is no doubt in my mind now!"

"I thought I heard the same thing too," said Brim. "I didn't think to bring it up because, just as Ragath did, I thought it was just the echo too, but I couldn't hear it well enough with the sound of everyone moving along overtaking it." There was a brief pause amongst the rodents. Fear and anxiety were growing within them with every passing second.

"This is very ill news," Nikamius said. "If it is indeed the case that we are not alone in these tunnels, and something is following us, then our journey has become all the more dangerous. We have to find a way through without delay."

"I agree," Azalar said. "We'll gather a few teams together to scout out the debris. Hopefully we can find a way through. But if we can't, then we may have no choice but to go back and through that door you all mentioned."

"You want us to turn around?" Ragath asked. "Back down the tunnel where Háth knows what may be waiting?"

"We may not have much of a choice," Azalar retorted. "I don't like the idea either, but if we can't climb or crawl through that rock wall, then we will have to go back. But only for a little ways until we reach that door. I'm sorry, Ragath. I know you warned us about going that way, but it may be our only option. Whatever it was that made that sound wanted to stay hidden, and it may have ill intent. Though it probably won't come for us while we're in a large group, but it may not be alone. And I don't want to be here long before it gathers its friends and comes back." Ragath gave a low growl before glancing back down the tunnel for a moment and turned back to Azalar.

"Very well, little mouse," Ragath said. "If there is no other way then I will agree to go with you through that door. But know this: if anything, terrible happens to my rats, I will be holding you responsible." Azalar frowned but gave the giant black rat a slight nod of understanding.

"Very well," Azalar said. Azalar then turned to Brim, Bark and Bogger. "Gather as many bucks as you can that are capable of scouting the area quickly. Brim, have Mith and Borith do the same and they can lead a few parties as well. But try to be as quiet as you can. We don't know what else may be lurking down here. Ragath, if you could gather a few bucks from the rats as well, that would be a great help." Ragath merely snorted before turning around towards his rats.

For nearly an hour, many mice and rats worked tirelessly to find any way they could pass through the caved-in tunnel. With each passing minute, Azalar's hopes for finding a safe path began to diminish. He was also aware that none of them had anything to eat since the night they escaped. So, no doubt that many of the rodents had little to no energy. Just then, Brim, along with Mith and Borith, approached Azalar and he was climbing down a large rock after searching through a small crevasse that ultimately led to nowhere.

"Anything?" Azalar asked. Brim frowned and shook his head.

"There is no way through," Brim answered. "The rocks are too steep to climb and too packed together. Whatever cracks we could find did not go too far in before they came to an end." Azalar shook his head and gave a heavy sign.

"I was afraid of this," Azalar said. "Ragath is not going to like this."

"He doesn't seem to like much of anything," said Mith. At the mention of his name, as though he heard it himself, Ragath appeared with Razor from a thin cranny at the far side of the tunnel near the wall and began to approach the band of mice, a solemn look upon his face. He looked at each of the mice before him, and his frown grew deeper. By the look on his face, they could clearly see that he had no luck as well.

"Don't say it," Ragath said.

"I am sorry, Ragath," Azalar said. "We tried our best, but there is no way through." Ragath gave a low grumble in response before hopping down the rock he was standing on and towards the rest of the rodents with Razor close behind. After that, Azalar gathered the rest of the rodents and told them what would be happening, and what they should expect.

"As I'm sure you are all aware, we cannot get through this way!" Azalar stated, his voice echoing throughout the tunnel. "We have searched all we can, but there is no way through. So, we will have to turn back another way." There were a few murmurs and whispers of concerned from both mice and rats here and there.

"Where are we going to go?" shouted a mouse buck from the crowd.

"We will not be going back far," Azalar said. "A few of us saw a door a ways back that may lead us to a way out. But it is a good distance back the way we came. There is also another matter I must inform you all about. We may not be alone in these tunnels."

The crowd suddenly became very alarmed, with many looking around the tunnels frantically, as if expecting to see a thing hiding behind a stone peering at them with menacing eyes while others looked at Azalar, waiting anxiously for him to continue. Some even spoke up in concern.

"What do you mean we may not be alone?" cried a mouse doe voice. "Are there others down here with us?"

"We don't know!" Nikamius spoke up. "All we know is that Azalar and Amara heard something as we slept that was cause for concern. But we must not panic! We have faith that Azalar will lead us through this."

"That's right!" Bark said, voicing his support. "Remember; Azalar was the one that got us out of Helgan's lab. I'm sure he will get us out of here." Azalar, while appreciating his friends' praises, felt that his friends were putting too much faith in him. He was just one small mouse after all.

"I will do what I can," said Azalar after a short pause. "But I need your aid as well. I do not know what lies ahead of us, but we must not let our fears take hold. So long as we all stay and work together, we can overcome anything that comes our way. And I promise you all that I will do whatever it takes to keep you all safe. Are you with me?" There was a tense silence from the crowd, all with looks of worry and dismay;

but soon, slowly, the mice all began to nod their heads, with some voicing their approval. The rats, on the other hand, remained silent and unmoving for a moment before turning to Ragath, seemingly asking for his approval. Azalar noticed their apprehension and waited patiently for their response. Ragath stared at the little mouse and Azalar waited for his answer. After another short pause, Ragath nodded. Azalar, feeling as if a weight had been lifted, smiled. "Alright then, let's head back."

Azalar led the rodents back down the tunnel the way they came. He told them to stay close together, and for any mice or rats that had a weapon should be on the outside of the group to defend against anything that might be lurking about. Azalar gripped his needle tightly in his paws and held the point forward, cautiously looking around for any movements.

It was a long, slow, and anxious journey, but after well over an hour they finally came to the door that bogger had mentioned. It was a massive metal door that was hidden behind a large metal structure that looked to be tipped over with its wheels to the side. From its position, it would have easily been missed coming from one side of the tunnel. But now that the rodents were coming from the other side, it was in clear view for them to see. When they came upon the door, they found that it was a door similar to the ones at Helgan's lab, though this one looked much heavier.

"So how do we open it?" asked Bark. Bogger stepped forward and examined the door more thoroughly. He placed his ear on the door and gave it a couple knocks.

"I don't think this is going to be as easy as we had originally thought," Bogger said. "This door seems more solid than the ones we've encountered before."

"Couldn't we just form a tower like we were going to do back at the lab?" asked Mith. "Surely we should have no trouble reaching that handle up there if we climb on top of one another.”

“I don’t think it will be that simple,” said Nikamius. “We’d still have to pull it open, and that would prove difficult for us with a pile of rodents standing in front of the door.”

“Great,” said Ragath with a huff. “Right back to where we started. Anymore bright ideas, little mouse?” Azalar, however, said nothing in response and just stared at the large door silently for a few minutes; thinking long and hard about what to do next. He was very perplexed about their current situation as this door was their only solution to finding a way out. Azalar tried to think of multiple solutions that they could try, but none of them seemed logical in practice.

Away from the rest of the crowd, a trio of young rats, who overheard the dilemma that they currently faced, one of them, Reemus, had pulled a couple companions away and separated from the rest of the group and began searching for anything that could be helpful.

“Are you sure this is a good idea, Reemus?” asked a male rat with brown fur with white colored patches named Ramy. “I don’t think Ragath or Razor will be very happy with us wandering off like this.”

“Yes,” said Reemus. “Azalar has led us all this way. It is our duty to aid him whenever possible.”

“So, what are we looking for exactly, Reemus?” asked a female rat with dark tan colored fur named Litha.

“I don't know just yet. Anything that could help Azalar get that door open.”

“Why are we doing this for a mouse, anyways?” asked Ramy. “We're rats. Shouldn't we be more loyal to Ragath instead of a mouse?” Reemus shot Ramy a look.

"He's not just a mouse, Ramy!" Reemus exclaimed. "He's a lot more than that." Litha frowned as she stepped closer to Reemus, placing a paw on his shoulder.

"Does this have anything to do with your dreams, Reemus?" she asked in a soft voice. Reemus glanced back at his friend but did not answer. Instead, he returned his attention forward to continue searching for anything that could possibly help Azalar open that door. It was then that he noticed something hanging from under one of the nearby metal structures. Reemus quickly scurried over, and upon inspecting what it was, a smile formed on his lips.

"I think this could work!"

Back with Azalar, it had been several minutes since they had arrived at the door, and he was still pondering on a solution to getting the door open. Even Bogger was uncertain of how to go about it. Yet they couldn't give up now, not with the potential danger lurking around them. Though they seemed to have little options left.

"There must be a way," Azalar muttered aloud. Amara, seeing her beloved fréfil so perplexed, stepped closer to him and wrapped her arms around one of his.

"You'll think of something, Azalar," she said gently. "It will come to you eventually." Azalar smiled and placed his paw upon his fréfil's.

"I appreciate that, Amara. But I think we're going to be stuck here for a while. Even Bogger is having trouble finding a solution. So, unless we can find another way, we seem to be stuck here."

"Azalar!" cried a voice. Everyone turned to where the voice came from to see a brown rat, the same brown rat that volunteered to go down the drain first, standing not too far away near one of the metal structures. He was pointing at something underneath one of the wheels. "Do you think we could use these?" Azalar and the others hurried over to where he was and saw a few sets of large black wires running up under the metal structure. Azalar turned to the brown rat and smiled.

"This is perfect!" Azalar exclaimed before turning to Bogger. "We can use these wires to pull the door open!" Bogger examined the wires for a brief moment as he thought it over in his head. He then smiled and gave Azalar a nod.

"The wires are a little thick, but if we could cut them long enough, they should indeed be the perfect tools we need to get the job done." Azalar turned to the brown rat.

"This is an excellent find! Good work to the three of you. What are your names, my friends?" The brown rat bowed his head slightly.

"Reemus, sir." The young rat then gestured to his two companions. "And these are my good friends Ramy and Litha."

"These three are actually the very same rats that volunteered to lead the others down the hole back in the shower room," said Nikamius in a proud voice. "He has a great deal of courage inside him. And that courage motivated the other to follow him down below darkness."

"Really?" Azalar said with a smile and turned back to the trio of rats. "That's quite admirable of you. It's great to know that we have some courageous rodents that we can depend on whenever needed." Reemus gave another slight bow of his head.

"Thank you, sir." Azalar raised an eyebrow and shook his head with a sheepish chuckle, unsure of how to react to being given such respect from another rodent. Azalar waved his hand dismissively at Reemus. "There's no need for that, Reemus. Azalar will do just fine." Reemus lifted his head and smiled at the smaller tan mouse.

"Of course, Azalar." Reemus and the other two rats gave another slight bow, earning another small chuckle from Azalar. Razor sneered and snorted at the trio rats' actions before leaning over to whisper in Ragath's ear.

"Rats bowing to a mouse," he whispered. "Such deplorable behavior." Ragath didn't answer and simply gave a small grunt in response, though deep down, part of him couldn't help but agree with Razor.

Azalar turned to face the rest of the crowd. "Okay, everyone! Let's get to work!"

Sometime later, many rodents had chewed through the wires and brought them to the door, where they had formed a small pyramid just high enough to wrap one cord around one end of the door handle and another three around the other end. The first cord was designated to pull the handle down to unlatch the door while the other cords would pull it open. It was tricky to get the cords in the right positions, but eventually they were able to fasten them in place. Azalar was on one of the wires that would pull the door open, along with dozens of other rodents, including Brim, Nikamius, Ragath, Razor, Reemus, and Borith, while six other rodents, including Bark, Bogger and Mith, held the cord that would pull on the handle. Once everything was in order, the rodents took their positions and waited for the order. Azalar glanced at everyone around him, making sure that everything was ready before giving Bogger a nod. Bogger returned the nod and spoke to everyone.

"Alright! When I give the word, our side pulls. The moment that handle is down, the other side will pull! Ready?" There were many nods of confirmation. "Pull!" Bogger and the others pulled on the cord, bringing the handle down completely. As soon as the handle was down, the other rodents pulled on their cords with all their strength. The door was shut tight and would not move an inch. The rodents pulled harder, and soon even more rodents joined in to pull. Then, slowly, the door began to grind open. Seeing the door opening, Bogger, Bark, Mith, and the other three rodents quickly dashed towards the opening and began prying it open further. The rest of the crowd began to encourage the rodents onward, such as Amara, Della and Frella. After another moment of struggle, the door was finally opened wide enough, and some rodents began to cheer, which were quickly silenced by others.

With the door now opened, the rodents slowly began entering into the darkness of what appeared to be a hallway. Azalar was the first to enter, followed by Amara, who was then followed by the rest of the throng. Azalar paused when he was a good ways in and started sniffing the air.

"The air smells a bit fresher than outside," Azalar said. "I think we might be going in the right direction. Everyone, stay together. It's going to get very dark." Azalar took Amara's paw and slowly led the rest of the rodents down the hall. Their eyes slowly adjusted to the darkness, and they were soon able to see where they were going; if only just a little. The rodents traveled in the same way as they did before; Azalar leading from the front with Nikamius and Bogger with Brim, Mith and Borith at their sides and Ragath and Razor and a few armed rats covering the rear. The hallways were littered with litter and debris. Sometimes their paths were blocked by a pile of rubble from the walls on either side that had been destroyed by some unknown force leaving gaping holes within them, but they were easily traversable.

They traveled for many yards through the dark halls, turning this way and that, sometimes coming to a crossroads with multiple corridors going in each direction. Azalar would take the time to sniff the air to find their way, but the air was still and stagnant and so it was difficult to determine which way to go. The idea of sending a few rodents out to scout out which way to go did come to mind, but he quickly thought against it, as he thought it better to stick together rather than split apart. So, he decided to take the chance and led the throng down the hall leading straight.

Ragath was feeling more uneasy than before as he followed behind the rest of the throng. Now that they were sure that they weren't alone in these tunnels, he was constantly looking over his shoulders and keeping an ear out for anything that may be deemed a threat. Though he hated being at the rear, it was where he much preferred so that he and his fellow rats could be most alert for any ambush that may possibly occur, though he did wish that the group at the head would move faster.

After some time, the hall took a left turn where there were many rooms on either side of the hall, some with their doors slightly ajar. Some rodents took small peeks inside, but the smell that came from them quickly caused them to reconsider. They continued down the hall until they came to another intersection. Azalar was unsure of which way to take until Bark spoke up.

"There's a light up ahead," said Bark, pointing down the hall. There was indeed a light down the corridor, but it was dim and faint and barely visible as it shone a deep shade of red on the wall as the hall turned to the right, but it was there.

"What do you think, Azalar?" Nikamius asked.

"We don't have much of a choice. If there is any chance of a way out, it's that way. Worst case, it may be a place for us to rest." Thanks to that glowing sign, it was much easier to traverse through the scraps of debris that scattered the floor. It took a little longer than they thought, but as they rounded the corner of the hall, they could finally see the bright red light shining in the distance hanging high on the ceiling in bright red letters that read:

EXIT

The path was much brighter now, and the rodents had no trouble finding their way, but there was something up ahead, down beneath the light that Azalar nor any other rodent could quite make out. They made their way down the hall until they came to a door blocking their path. Upon further inspection, they found that it had no handles at all. They tried to push it open, but it would only move so far before hitting something solid on the other side.

"Something must be blocking it from the other side," said Mith.

"I think we gathered as much," said Borith with a bit of sarcasm in his voice. Azalar took a few steps back, looking up at the door.

"There must be a way through," he said aloud.

"Should we try heading back?" asked Bark. Azalar stared at the door for a few more moments, thinking of any way they could possibly get through. After a moment longer, he let out a heavy sigh.

"We might have to," Azalar replied. "I don't see any other way through."

"Azalar!" a voice cried from the back of the crowd. Azalar and the others turned headed towards the back of the throng of rodents. There they saw Ragath, Razor and a group of rats were waiting for him further down the hall by a slightly opened door inward. Ragath was pointing inside the room.

"There's a hole in the wall inside this room," Ragath said. Azalar went and peeked around the doorframe into the dark room. At first, he saw nothing, but when he leaned in further into the room, he saw it. There, at the far end of the room to his right, at the very base of the wall was a tiny little hole. And how he saw this was because there was a very dim light shining through the hole.

Azalar entered the room and made his way towards the hole, with the rest of the rodents following close behind. When he reached the hole, it was just large enough for them to fit through one at a time. He leaned down to inspect further. The hole was on the same side as the door just outside the room, but it stretched further by at least a meter or so, where he could see the faint glow of a light source from the other side. Azalar looked back to the other rodents.

"I'll go in first," he said.

"Surely I, as well as Mith and Borith should go first, Azalar," said Brim. "It would be better for us to scout ahead before the rest follow."

"That's quite alright, Brim," Azalar replied. "I'll be fine. If I find anything dangerous, I'll run straight back here without hesitation." With that, Azalar held his needle forward and entered through the hole. It was more cramped than he had originally thought, but by simply leaning down, he had no trouble traveling through the narrow passage. Once he had reached the other side, he was amazed at what he saw.

Before them was a wide, massive hall that looked as if it was carved from the stone walls around them, with tall, thick pillars that stretched high to the ceiling. All throughout the hall were wooden pallets stacked high in tall piles. Some of these piles were toppled over and some seemed to be tossed haphazardly across the floor, with broken and shattered pieces of wood scattered all over.

At the far end of the hall, there was a bright yellow light hanging from the ceiling, though its light flickered every so often and did not fully reach where Azalar stood. However, it was enough for him to see most of the massive chamber. Azalar stared in amazement at the sheer size of the enormous hall. Never before had he seen such space, even with it being as cluttered as it was. His eyes then fell upon a large pile of wood and debris that had been blocking the door. After double checking that the coast was clear, he signaled to the others that it was safe to come through.

Sometime later, after every rodent had entered safely through the small passage and everyone was accounted for, Azalar led the rodents down the massive hall towards the light at the very end. As they walked, they all looked around in amazement just as Azalar did. The wonder, for Azalar's part at least, had eventually faded and he was more focused on surveying the area for potential dangers. As they traveled across, Azalar saw more doors on each side, all blocked off by piles of wood, stone, and other debris. Azalar found this to be a little curious and brought this up to Nikamius.

"I noticed them too," Nikamius replied. "Every door that we've passed was the same. It seems as though someone was trying to keep something out." Something about his words sent Azalar even more on edge than he already was. There was definitely something strange going on down here.

Suddenly Azalar heard a new sound in the distance and perked his ears up to listen more carefully. Azalar couldn't quite tell what it was, but the more he listened, the more he could hear what sounded like a great roaring, rumbling, and gurgling up ahead. He had everyone stop so that he could hear more clearly.

"Do you hear that?" Azalar asked. Nikamius perked his ear up as well. He too could hear the roaring ahead.

"I do," Nikamius answered. "It sounds massive, whatever it is. And it doesn't sound too pleasant."

"Perhaps we should avoid it," Bark said, overhearing Azalar and Nikamius.

"We don't have much of a choice," Nikamius replied. "The path only goes forward, and there have been no other paths that I nor Azalar have found that could lead us around. Unless you have found something that we haven't, Bark." Bark shook his head and remained silent as Azalar climbed on top of a nearby pile of wooden pallets and listened intently.

"It doesn't sound alive," Azalar said. "I don't hear any sort of breathing coming from it. It sounds constant, like a long continuous roar, yet it also sounds like a thousand giant feet stomping and rumbling together all at once." Bogger climbed up behind Azalar and listened closely.

"I think you would be correct, Azalar," Bogger said. "It doesn't sound like anything living. But I can't make out exactly what it is. But if my hunch is correct, I think I may know what that is."

"What is it?" Azalar asked. Bogger didn't answer right away and remained silent as he continued to listen. By this point, Bark, Brim and Nikamius have also climbed up beside them.

"Yes," Bogger said. "Yes, I do believe that is what it is."

"What?" Bark asked, growing a tad impatient. Bogger turned to the others with a confident smile.

"I do believe that is water," he answered. The others looked at one another confused.

"Water?" Azalar asked.

"Or more correctly, a waterfall."

"But how can water make that kind of noise?" asked Bark.

"From what I've read in Alice's books, when large amounts of water flow down a singular path, it is called a river. And rivers tend to make lots of gurgling and splashing sounds as they move. But they make loud rumbling sounds when a large quantity of water falls over a steep ledge and plunges into a pool below. That is called a waterfall. And if I'm correct, that is what lies ahead. And from the sound of it, it doesn't seem to be too large of a waterfall."

"But how is a waterfall underground?" asked Brim curiously. Bogger shrugged his shoulders.

"Probably due to a multitude of reasons. Groundwater that collects beneath the surface over the years or some underground reservoir that the humans built. Who could say for certain? But there is no doubt that is what is up ahead."

"Well, there's one thing that is for certain," Azalar interjected, "Our path lies in that direction. Let us hope that it won't be another obstacle for us to cross." With that, Azalar jumped from the wood pile and led the throng of rodents back on their journey.

After a long while of walking, they had finally come to the end of the cavernous hall where they came to a massive archway with the light hanging down from the ceiling just below the top of the arch. The arch seemed to have been carved from the stone wall itself and came to a sharp point at the top. Just beyond the archway was a wide foyer. The right side was simply just the stone wall, but to the left was a rather large window. At the edge of the foyer was a bridge, with two small beams hovering over the floor that were connected to each side of the foyer.

The bridge wasn't nearly as cluttered as the rest of the hall, but with still a few piles of debris scattered all about the bridge. The bridge had thick metal railings on each side, but beyond those railings was nothing but darkness. Azalar could only tell that there was a river down there because of the slightest bit of reflection glittering in the water from the yellow light above. Azalar couldn't see what was beyond the bridge as it was too dark, but he figured that this was as far as they would travel tonight.

There was a great deal of space between the bridge and the archway. It was wide and spacious, and however it looked a little damp the closer it got to the bridge. However, the area just outside the archway was nice and dry. It looked to be the best spot to set up camp. If they were to construct a wall in front of the archway from all the wooden pallets throughout the hall, it would provide a decent amount of protection and a safe space to rest. Azalar then gathered the rodents in a large group by the archway just under the light.

"We will be resting here for the time being!" Azalar called to the crowd of mice and rats. "Get settled in, then we'll gather whatever wood we can find and build ourselves a wall around the camp. We'll pile what wood can't be used for the wall in the center here! We will be lighting a fire to keep ourselves warm." Azalar then turned to Nikamius, Bogger, Bark and Brim.

"We'll need to set up watches throughout the night. Brim, talk to Ragath and see if he and a few rats would be willing to take up first watch along with a few mice. I will be taking the first watch as well, and I would feel much better if he were up with me." Brim nodded and was about to head out when Mith and Borith emerged from the crowd and approached the group.

"Azalar," Mith said, "We have a slight problem." Azalar turned to face the pair of mice.

"Yes? What is it?" Azalar asked.

"We need to do something about food," said Borith. "We've been traveling through these dreaded tunnels for ages, and we haven't had anything to eat since last night. Some of the others are having difficulty keeping up." Nikamius was next to speak up.

"It will be hard luck to find any sort of food in this place," Nikamius said. "It looks like there hasn't been any life down here in a long time. But I did see a few tiny insect critters running about on our way here, every so often, as I'm sure many others have. It may not be much, but if we could find enough of these insects, they may sustain us for a while and regain our strength; even if it's just a little." Frella and Della did not seem to be too keen on that idea in the slightest.

"Eating bugs?" Della questioned. "Are you sure that's a good idea?"

"It's actually some of the best food for us," Bogger interjected. "According to what I've read about our ancestors, insects were very common in our diets. They are very nutritious and very high in protein. And with the humidity in here, there's bound to be plenty of insects for us to hunt." Frella visibly cringed at the thought of eating bugs.

"It may not be the most ideal of food choices," Nikamius said. "But it is far greater to have a full belly of an unsavory meal than an empty one. Besides, we don't need to eat them raw. Once we get a fire started, it should be more pleasant to eat once it's cooked up." Frella still had an uncomfortable frown on her lips.

"That doesn't make me feel any better," she said. But she then let out a defeated sigh. "But I suppose if it's the best we can do, I'm willing to give it a try. But you're going to eat it first, Bark! You hear me?" Bark let out a hearty laugh at his fréfil; he wasn't the type to back down from anything, and the thought of eating a new kind of food was quite intriguing to him. Everyone shared in a quick laugh as well, but then Amara noticed that Della still looked apprehensive about it. So, she gently took each of her paws, gaining the female mouse's attention, and gave Della a warm and reassuring smile.

"It will be alright," Amara said encouragingly. "Bogger and Nikamius have read quite a few of Alice's books, so I'm very confident that those two know what they're talking about."

"It isn't that." Della's voice was soft and hesitant. "It's just that… the ArchBeetle." The mere mention of the horrid monsters brought an uneasy silence about them, and each one of them was reminded of what it did to Juro.

"The ArchBeetle?" Azalar asked.

"Yes," Della said, trying to keep herself from getting emotional. "The very thought of eating bugs brings a sickness to my stomach, and I'm reminded of how that terrible creature killed Juro. How that thing just ripped him apart and ate him. It was horrible. I'm sorry, I don't think I could do it." Della was visibly distraught at the memory of the ArchBeetle, and her shoulders began to tremble.

"It's alright, my love," Brim said. "We understand how you feel. The memory of what happened that day is still fresh in all of our minds. You're not alone in feeling this way. We will all be here to help you through this. But, Della, I can see how weary you've become. You need to eat something so that you can keep your strength up. It won't do you any good if you don't eat something soon. And don't worry, my love, I'll be right by your side."

Della looked away though, still reluctant about eating something that reminded them of that awful ArchBeetle. But feeling her fréfil's arms around her gave her a bit of encouragement, and she finally nodded her head.

"Alright," she said. "I-I'll do my best." Brim gave her a tight squeeze and nuzzled her cheek.

"That's my fréfil," he said.

"Alright then," said Azalar. "Let's set up camp first, then we can do what we can for food." Just then a voice spoke up.

"Azalar!" Azalar and the others turned to see a dark tan colored female rat quickly her way towards the group. Azalar remembered that she was one of the two rats that were next to Reemus from before.

"I remember you," Azalar said upon her arrival. "Your name is Litha, correct?" Litha smiled and bowed her head. Azalar noted that she was a little small for a rat.

"Yes, sir. Reemus wanted me to find you. He said that he and Ramy may have found something that you might find interesting." Azalar nodded his head and told Litha to lead the way. She then led them through the crowd towards the left hand side of the archway. Once they had cleared the crowd, they could see Reemus, who was a good distance away with another rat named Ramy, standing next to a large wooden door. Azalar and the others quickly made their way over to him.

"What is it, Reemus?" Azalar asked. Reemus pointed to the bottom of the door, where there was a small hole at the left corner.

"We found this entrance to the room behind this door," Reemus answered. "We thought it best to inform you of what we found before we entered inside," Reemus said. Azalar stepped closer to the hole for further inspection. It was strange, but he thought that this hole was very similar to the hole that they came through when they first entered through. Nearly identical in size and shape. Azalar found this very suspicious and held his needle tightly in his paws. He looked back at everyone around him.

"I'll go first," he said. "You all follow close behind." But before he could take another step, another voice sounded close by.

"What's going on here?" said Ragath as both he and Razor approached. Ragath had seen Azalar and the other mice making their way over to the group of rats standing by a door. Curious as to what was going on, he motioned to Razor, and they made his way over to the group. Reemus gestured to the hole in the door.

"We just found this," Reemus answered. "I thought it best to let Azalar know before proceeding further."

"Ragath narrowed his eyes at the brown rat. He found it contemptuous that these rats thought to consult the little mouse rather than with him first. He stepped forward and nearly pushed Azalar out of the way, not wanting a little mouse to show him up.

"I'll enter first," Ragath stated. "Razor, you follow behind me. The rest of you can follow if you want." Ragath then leaned down and entered the room, closely followed by Razor. Azalar glanced back at the others, who all looked just as confused as he did, before shrugging his shoulders and following Ragath and Razor inside the dark room.

Azalar emerged through the door, followed by Brim, Bark, Bogger, Nikamius, Amara, Frella, Della, Mith, Borith, Reemus, Litha and Ramy. After they all entered the room, and after their eyes adjusted to the darkness, they quickly began surveying the room. For the most part it was empty. However, there was a large stack of boxes by one corner of the room, where Ragath and Razor were standing by a large pile of bo-xes. Ragath was leaning down, trying to decipher the wording on one of the boxes on the floor.

"K-ka. Ka," Ragath whispered slowly as he tried to read the words. "Kan-da-la?"

"It's pronounced '*candle*'," said Bogger as he stood beside Ragath and leaned down to read the words. "You probably would have known that if you had bothered to join us for reading lessons." Ragath glared at the dark red colored mouse and gave a scoff.

"Don't get smart with me, mouse," Ragath hissed. "As if I'd learn that foul human language that you all seem to be fond of."

"It would probably help you out in the future," Bogger countered with a smirk. "Especially since you found us exactly what can help us get through these dark passages. These candles are what give the humans light for long periods of time. I have to admit to you, Ragath. This is an excellent find." Ragath's features softened at receiving a bit of praise, though he was still a bit bitter at the mouse's comments about his lack of ability to read. Bogger climbed onto the box and attempted to open the top. However, he was unable to get the tape off. He looked down at the large black rat.

"May I inquire as to requesting your aid in perforating this perdurable package?" Ragath looked to Razor for a brief moment before turning back to Bogger with a furrowed brow.

"What?" Ragath asked. Bogger rolled his eyes before letting out a heavy sigh.

"Can you help me open this box?" Ragath huffed before tossing his sword up and climbing on top of the box.

"Why didn't you just say that?"

"He likes to hear himself talk," Bark commented with a chuckle, earning a slight glare from the dark red mouse. Ragath pointed the blade of his sword down and lifted it high above his head before thrusting it down into the tape that covered the lid of the box. With its sharp blade, Ragath guided his sword down from top to bottom, allowing Bogger to open the box, revealing neatly stacked long white sticks. Bogger's smile widened as he lifted one of the white sticks out of the box. It was heavier than he expected, and it stood taller than he did, but he was able to pick it up, nonetheless.

"Excellent!" Bogger exclaimed. "Now we will have plenty of light to guide our way. All we need now is a way to light them. Though we'll most likely have to find a way to ignite a fire ourselves."

"Any idea on how to do that?" asked Brim.

"I have a few. But they might not be so easy. One way we could try is to take two pieces of wood…" As Bogger began rambling about the many ways to start a fire, Bark had wandered off looking for a much easier way to light a fire. He looked all around the room, but it was quite empty, save for the boxes that they found. Then, Bark noticed a small human desk at the far end of the room against the wall on the right hand side. He thought that if there was anything that could make a fire, there would be the best place to find something. He quickly made his way over to the desk, but the moment he rounded the corner, Bark let out a terrified scream. All the rodents in the room were startled and quickly rushed over to Bark, who was laying on his back with wide eyes and a heavy breath.

"What happened?!" Azalar asked. Bark didn't respond right away, but he lifted his arm and pointed behind the desk. They all looked in the direction he was pointing. Azalar glanced at both Brim and Ragath before they all readied their weapons. Azalar told the other to stay back and slowly approached the corner of the desk. They paused right at the edge for a brief moment. Azalar took a deep breath and prepared himself. They all then jumped from the corner and raised their weapons for a fight. But none came. Instead, they stared in shock at the horrid sight in front of them.

There, sitting against the wall, was the remains of a human skeleton. Its clothes were all tattered and torn, and some of its bones seemed to be missing. The rodents looked on with grimace as Bogger and Nikamius came around the corner.

"Oh, now that's quite a sight." said Nikamius. Bogger nodded in agreement. Bogger stepped closer to one of the skeleton's feet and examined the bones.

"It goes without saying that he's been dead for a long time," he said.

"Oh really? You think so?" exclaimed Bark sarcastically as he picked himself off the floor. "Creepy thing nearly gave me a heart attack."

"A shame that it didn't succeed," Bogger commented with a smirk, not even bothering to look back at the dark brown mouse, who was no doubt giving him a hard glare. It was then that Bogger noticed something lying next to one of the skeleton's hands. Bogger quickly scurried over and picked up what seemed to be a book, no larger than he was. It was old and dirty, and when he opened it up, the pages were even more so.

"Interesting," Bogger said aloud.

"What is it?" asked Azalar, stepping closer to the dark red mouse. Bogger didn't answer as he tried to read the contents of the book, but he could make nothing out in this darkness.

"It's a book of some sorts," he finally answered. "I'd be very much interested in taking a look at this later."

"Why would you want to look at something that belonged to a dead human?" asked Razor with a low tone. Bogger turned back at the black rat and smiled.

"Knowledge is key, my friend," Bogger replied. "It can unlock many secrets."

"Well in any case, I think we should leave," said Azalar. "We obviously won't be finding anything else of use here. And I don't want to be around this thing any longer than we have to. So, let's grab those candles and get out of here. Hopefully we can find a way to make a fire some other way." Azalar then turned and headed towards the box of candles with the others following close behind. Bogger, however, stayed where he was for a moment longer. He looked from the book in his paws to the skeletal remains one last time before turning back to join the others.

When Azalar and the others returned from the side room, the rest of the rodents had gone about to complete the task of setting up camp, as well as gathering large quantities of wood for both the wall and the fire. Once enough wood had been gathered, Azalar and Brim formed separate teams to begin building the walls. Bogger went to work straight away on getting a fire started; but unfortunately, nothing he did worked. He tried rubbing two tiny twigs together, taking a couple rocks and hitting them against each other to create a spark. Yet, no matter how hard he hit, neither he nor any other rodent had the strength great enough to get a spark. So many other methods were used, but none of them worked. The wood would not catch fire. Bogger was growing increasingly frustrated, but his pride refused to let him give up. As Bogger continued to work on the fire and the rest of the mice and rats were hard at work setting up camp, Bark was just aways from the rest of them, scavenging through the wood, debris, and trash for anything that could be useful.

Just then, Bark caught sight of something small scurrying across the ground on the right hand side and crawled under some debris, a few pieces of wood and a tall yet thin metal pole, leaning against the wall by a little corner of a pillar next to the archway.

"What was that?" he asked aloud. Bark wandered over to where whatever that was had taken cover, curious as to what it could be. Brim noticed Bark walking away.

"What are you doing there, Bark?" Brim called out to him, but Bark was too preoccupied to answer. He lowered himself and peered behind the wooden pile. He could see something black moving in the back. It was dark and he couldn't tell what it was, but it looked long and had many tiny legs. He leaned closer to get a better look at whatever it was under the debris, when it suddenly lunged at him and quickly crawled between his legs.

Bark jumped back with a start, bumping into a small pole leaning against the wall. Bark fell back as the little creature scurried away towards the rest of the group. Azalar, hearing Bark squeal in surprise, looked to see something crawling towards him. Azalar took his needle and quickly stabbed the critter through its back. The critter was still moving in place, but Azalar's needle kept it firmly in place. Bogger quickly came over to examine what the creature was.

"It's just a cockroach," Bogger said, looking at Bark with an annoyed frown. "All that noise over a cockroach?" Bark stood up and frowned at Bogger in return.

"It was dark, and it came after me," Bark said defensively. "How was I supposed to know what it was?"

"Well, at least we found something to eat," Azalar said.

"And if there's one, there's bound to be more," said Nikamius. "We should search the area for more of these cockroaches. We may be able to find enough to feed all of–" Suddenly there was a small grinding noise coming from the wall where Bark had been. Everyone turned to see that the pole that Bark had hit was slowly sliding backwards down the wall until it hit a long beam of wood, which then began leaning forward towards the rodents.

Everyone backed away from the falling beam, but the top of the beam caught on to a piece of wire close to the ceiling. The beam pulled on the wire, which then pulled onto the red light and quickly raised it up until it hit the ceiling. The impact caused the light to come loose and plunged to the ground below. The rodents scattered at the light came crashing down and shattered into pieces. The crash caused a loud *bang* that echoed throughout the tunnels. After everything had settled down and was silent, everyone looked to Bark, who was looking rather sheepish.

"Sorry," he said as he laughed nervously. Everyone frowned at Bark, but none looked more annoyed than Bogger.

"Nice going!" Bogger nearly shouted. "Not only did you destroy our only source of light, but you probably just announced to whatever may be in these tunnels to our presence."

"Hey! I said I was sorry!" the dark mouse retorted defensively. Azalar quickly stepped between the two mice.

"That's enough. Nothing to be done about it now," Azalar said. "What's done is done and everyone is safe, that's what's important. Let's just try to be more careful from now on, alright? Now let's get back to work. We still need to finish setting up camp." With that, Azalar and the others went back to work completing their tasks, all the while two black rats were watching them from a little ways away.

"I told you that these mice were going to bring us down," Razor whispered to Ragath. The giant black rat looked at the group of mice and let out a heavy sigh.

"You may be right, Razor," Ragath admitted. "But we can't do anything about it now. Once we're out of these tunnels we can talk more about leaving these mice behind. But for now, we sit back and bide our time." Just then, Brim approached the two rats.

"Ragath, Azalar requests that you and a few other rats take the first watch, seeing as you are the among the few that possess weapons. Azalar and I will be taking the first watch as well, and we'd feel more reassured if you were with us."

Ragath was silent for a brief moment, seemingly in thought, before turning back to Brim with a nod, much to Razor's dismay.

"Alright then," Ragath answered. "I will gather five other rats to keep watch. But I want Azalar with me."

"Excellent!" Brim said. "I'm sure Azalar will have no problem with that. I will gather an additional seven mice and we'll set up a perimeter. I think ten along the wall and five under the arch before the bridge will be sufficient."

"Very well," said Ragath. "But how will we be rotating shifts? We can't exactly tell time down here."

"I will discuss that with Azalar. I'm sure Bogger will figure something out. But in the meantime, let's gather those who will be on watch first. And since there aren't enough weapons to go around, I think it would be best if those on first shift will hand their weapons over to the next."

"No one is touching my sword but me!" Ragath asserted, gripping his weapon protectively in his paws. Brim smiled and held up his paws.

"I wouldn't expect anything else, Ragath," he said with a chuckle. "We'll have to find a few extra weapons for the others. But we do appreciate the help Ragath. I'll let you know what the plan is after we've set up camp." With that, Brim left the two rats to gather volunteers for the first watch. With the mouse gone, Razor turned to Ragath with a frown.

"Why did you volunteer us for watch?" he asked. "Why have us rats lose sleep over protecting these weak mice? I say we leave them while they're sleeping. If these little mice want to play guard duty, then let them. We don't need them. We should just move on and head off on our own now." The large black rat narrowed his eyes at Razor.

"Like it or not, we still need them," Ragath answered in annoyance. "We don't have many options. We don't know what's out there and we need all the aid we can get if we're going to survive. And we are going to be traveling with them for a while still. So, it's best to play nice for now until the time is right to leave." Razor turned away and looked at the mice around them. He despised having to work with such inferior little beasts. Razor was silent, but after a short while before he turned back to Razor, though the frown had not left his face.

"As you wish," Razor said. "You're in charge and we'll do as you say." Ragath nodded his head with a smirk.

"Good. And after my watch is over, you will be taking my place. So, get plenty of rest while you can." Razor furrowed his brows further, but he did not say a word.

The rodents had been hard at work setting up camp and had scavenged through the piles of debris and rubble, some had even ventured a short ways onto the bridge to collect anything that may be of use. After a while, they had managed to collect a large amount of timber and had it all piled in the middle of their camp. They had also scavenged a decent pile of metal as well, with most of which were nails and sharp oddments that could possibly serve as weapons. On top of all that, they had also managed to hunt down quite a few decent sized bugs that had been hiding amongst the scraps and debris, all killed and neatly piled together. It wasn't much, but it should be enough to sustain them, at least until tomorrow.

Now that camp was set up and everything Bogger stared at the pile in deep thought.

"Now that we got all the wood together," Bark said from the side, "how do we get a fire started?" Bogger didn't answer right away as he was still in thought.

"Maybe we could rub some wood against each other?" Mith asked. "I read in one of Alice's books that you can start a fire by rubbing two sticks together."

"That wouldn't work at all," Bogger said, shaking his head. "It would take too long. And we would need larger sticks than we are able to carry. And even if we did try that, we'd need to apply enough pressure and friction in order to even get it to smolder, let alone ignite a flame. Which, due to our size, would be impossible."

"So, what do you suggest then?" asked Azalar.

"I'm thinking. I'm thinking," Bogger said. He began to pace back and forth with his arms crossed, a deep furrow on his brows. Just then Bark called out to the others.

"Hey Bogger," he called, gaining everyone's attention. Everyone turned to see Bark standing by the broken light on the ground. "You think we can use this?" The others hurried over to where Bark stood by the light. Bogger gave Bark a deadpan expression.

"How is a broken light going to help us start a fire?" he asked. Bark stepped closer to the light where part of the glass was missing and placed his paw inside.

"It's pretty warm inside," Bark said. "And when I looked inside, there was still a bit of light in there. You think we could use that?" Bogger and Azalar looked at one another before Bogger stepped closer to the light and stuck his own paw inside. There was indeed heat coming from within. He looked inside the light and saw within the broken glass a tiny sliver of wire that was still glowing orange; it was faint, but it was still glowing. An idea struck him, and he looked over to Bark with a smile.

"Well, I have to admit it, Bark," Bogger said. "Even though you are a clumsy mouse, your antics may have just provided us with the means of starting a fire." Bogger then turned to the others.

"Quick! Someone grab me something sharp and a piece of lumber!" He then removed the remaining glass from the light just as a mouse appeared hastily with a long piece of splintered wood and another mouse came with a thin scrap of metal and handed it to Bogger. The dark red mouse took the scrap metal and examined it.

"Good," he said. Bogger took the wood and placed one end on the ground and the other against his right shoulder. He then took the scrap metal and attempted to scrape the wood with the sharp end downward; however, when he tried to scrape down, the metal would get caught in the wood and wouldn't budge. He tried to push down harder, but it still would not move.

"I'm not strong enough," he whispered, irritated. He looked over to the rats. "Ragath! I request your assistance please!" A brief moment later, Ragath appeared next to the gathered mice.

"What is it?" he asked impatiently.

"We need to shave off tiny fibers from this wood for the fire, but I'm afraid I'm not strong enough for the task. I'm asking for your help because you are the strongest one among us." Ragath turned to Azalar with a smirk.

"Seems to me that you mice would be lost without us rats," he said smugly. Azalar didn't respond and simply rolled his eyes as Ragath took the metal and wood from Bogger. Bogger instructed him where to place the wood and scrap metal and how to scrap the timber for fiber. Bogger then turned to a couple of mice off to the side.

"You two grab one of the empty cans and make three large holes around the bottom with those nails. Hurry!" The two mice quickly rushed to complete their task as Bogger returned his attention back to Ragath.

Thanks to the large black rat's strength, the task came quite easy, and he was able to shave off enough fibers. Bogger collected the fibers and made a small tinder pile in his paws before hastily moving to the fallen light once more.

"Get a small pile of kindling close by!" he ordered. Bogger raised his paw though the glow from the wire had begun to fade a little. He cupped the tinder to the glowing wire and began to blow. There was still heat; he just hoped it would be enough to catch.

Bogger gently blew into the tinder, which caused the wire to glow a little hotter; but it wasn't enough. Everyone was crowded around Bogger, anxiously waiting for something to happen. Bogger blew again, but again nothing happened. Bogger wasn't about to give up just yet and kept blowing into the tinder. Just then, a tiny sliver of smoke began to rise. Bogger's eyes widened, but he did not stop. He blew a little harder this time and more smoke began to rise and the tinder in his paws grew hotter. Bogger gave one last breath when the tinder in his hands finally caught fire.

Bogger smiled gleefully and quickly, but carefully, brought the fire to the kindling pile that had been prepared next to him and gently began placing tiny strands of fiber and kindling over it. Soon the fire began to grow and was now burning bright and hot.

"Quickly! Get the can!" Bogger called. A couple mice brought over the can that they had made holes in; where they then placed a few pieces of broken wood through the top of the can and the little bundles of tinder and kindling through the holes at the bottom, where Bogger then took the fire and quickly lit the wood in the can on fire.

Within just a minute, the wood caught fire and began to grow larger, and the air grew warmer. Everyone stared in awe at Bogger's work as his smile widened further and he turned to the crowd around him.

"My fellow rodents!" Bogger called out. "We now have fire!"

Chapter XII

After Bogger was able to make the fire, the rodents had quickly gotten to work setting up camp. For their campsite, Azalar had the rodents collect as much of the wood from the pallets, both broken or not, as they could manage, and they laid them in a massive square just in front of the archway. The rodents took apart the unbroken pallets by prying them apart with the metal nails, which resulted in a lot of snapping and broken planks.

They then placed the long unbroken pieces on the floor and arranged them in a large square around them and placed the broken planks atop to heighten the walls to make makeshift fortifications, leaving only one gap in the walls at the front while leaving the back of the camp towards the bridge open. There were a few planks laid out at a few sections of the walls to allow the rodents to climb up and walk along the walls. The walls themselves stood just over a foot tall in height. At each corner was a large lit candle to provide those on the wall with a little light, with two more candles on each side of the opening.

The nails that were taken from the planks and pallets were separated between the rusted nails and the cleanest one, with the most rusted or unusable being discarded away and the cleanest ones being placed in small piles around the walls. Azalar thought they would make good weapons for the rodents to defend themselves with should the need ever arise.

Within the campsite, several cans with lit fires were scattered about, with the rodents who were not on watch surrounding each can for warmth and light. At the center of the camp was a candle with its top lit up. From what the writing said on the box that they found the candles in; each candle could remain lit for up to twelve hours. For every inch of wax that was melted indicated one hour had passed. So Azalar developed this as a way to signal when to change shifts for the next watch. How they could be sure was to measure the height of the wax with a stick that Bogger had made that was roughly the same height as the candle. Bogger had marked the stick with the approximate number of inches that would show how much the candle had melted over time, letting them know when it was time to change shifts.

After deciding who would be taking each watch, the rodents all settled down for the time being, while those who were chosen for the first watch took up their posts. It had been almost an hour after everyone had settled in and most had already fallen asleep, very weary from the long and eerie journey in the dark tunnels. Some were still wide awake; some awaiting their turn on the watch, others too anxious to find sleep.

Azalar stood on the ramparts of the makeshift wall, watching the darkness that had surrounded them. He couldn't quite place it, but he had a sinking feeling that as he stared out into the darkness, there was something in there staring back at him. A set of footsteps was then heard from Azalar's right and he turned to see Brim approaching him.

"Is there something wrong?" Azalar asked. Brim shook his head.

"Nothing to report as of yet," Brim answered. "I just came to inform you that our shift is almost over, and that a mouse named Til will be along to take your place."

"Thank you," Azalar said with a nod. A few minutes later, a dark brown mouse with bits of gray in his fur came to replace Azalar's shift on the wall and Azalar climbed down and made his way towards the center of the camp, where Amara, Bark, Frella, Brim, Della, Borith, Mith, Nikamius, Bogger were sitting by the large candle. The company of mice were sitting in a circle around a fire lit can with several different kinds of bugs roasting over the fire on three different spits. What Azalar found curious was that Ragath was sitting alongside them as well.

"I'm surprised to see you here," said Azalar to Ragath. Said black rat scoffed and looked away.

"Nikamius said I should be here for this. For whatever reason that is," he retorted while nodding his head towards Bogger and the book.

"I would agree with that," Azalar responded with a nod and a smile and took a seat next to Amara, who nuzzled up close to him. Ragath snorted but said nothing else and stared at the fire in the middle of the group. Bark, who was eating a cockroach with Frella, tore off a piece of the insect and handed it to Azalar. Azalar took a bite of it, only to squint and cringe at the terrible taste in his mouth. Bark cuckold at his friend's reaction.

"Tastes good, doesn't it?" Bark asked. Azalar swallowed, doing his best to keep it from coming back up.

"Delicious," he said sarcastically. The others around the fire all chuckled at his response. It was then that Azalar noticed Reemus and his two fellow rat companions walking by after finishing their watch.

"Reemus! Ramy! Litha!" he called out to them. The trio of young rats turned his way and Azalar beckoned them over. "Come join us."

The trio stood confused for a moment before glancing at one another, as if asking if Azalar was really asking them to join his group. Reemus, with a smile, quickly headed over to Azalar's camp, quickly followed by Ramy and Litha. Brim and Bark moved aside to give the trio room to sit.

"Have you three eaten yet?" asked Azalar. Reemus shook his head.

"No, we didn't, sir. We just finished our watch and haven't had the chance to." Azalar nodded before standing up, grabbing a cockroach from off the fire and tossing it to the trio. They looked at the insect with reluctance.

"It looks better than it tastes," said Brim. The trio were still hesitant to try, but the grumbling in their empty stomachs let them know that they had to eat something. So, with great reluctance, they each took a bite of the cockroach. The moment they did, they each squirmed and quivered, Litha nearly spitting it out right there. This earned a laugh from everyone else, even Ragath gave a small chuckle.

"Though it still tastes pretty bad," Brim laughed. The whole group was now full of mirth and for the first time in their lives, there was a sense of merriment in their hearts. At this time, Azalar turned his attention to Bogger, who had his full attention fixated on the contents of the large book.

"Have you had any luck figuring out what that book says?" Azalar asked. Bogger glanced up from the page he was reading at Azalar before quickly returning his attention back down. He ran his fingers across the pages.

"From what I can tell," he said, "It seems to be a record of that human's life. "A journal of some sort; with little notes here and there, as if he was telling the story of his life for someone to read it someday."

"What does it say?" Frella asked. Bogger didn't answer right away, instead he continued to flip carefully through the pages of the old journal. After a few moments Bogger spoke up.

"There's quite a lot in here, with some passages worn away and some pages stained. It will be a bit difficult to interpret what he's saying, but I will do the best that I can." He flipped back to the first passage on the first page, clearing his throat as he prepared to read aloud.

"The beginning is a little hard to decipher, as it seems to be written sloppily, almost as if it was their first time writing, but there is still some intelligible wording here, so I'll give it a go. Alright. It starts with, '*November 4th, 2022. I don't know why I'm even writing this. My mother got this for me for my birthday. She told me that it would help me with my… anxiety… if I could write down my feelings. I don't know if it will work or not, but here goes nothing. My name is Mathew Stone. I am eight years old, and I was born in a city called Boston in a country called the United States of… America.*' I don't believe I'm familiar with that place. I might have missed it in Alice's books. Let me think. Ah yes, I remember now. It was the name of a large region of Earth."

"Earth?" asked Bark.

"That's the name the humans call the outside world," Azalar answered.

"Yes, if you had been paying attention to what Alice had taught us. Or even picked up a book for more than five minutes," Bogger said with a small hint of irritation at being interrupted before returning to the journal. "Where was I? Ah, yes! '*I live with my mom and dad in a little house by the river. I don't have many friends, only this one girl named Christie. She's the same age as me and is my best friend. We do everything together. She understands me more than anyone. She moved away last month, and I've been sad ever since, but I know I'll see her again. We promised we would. Why did she have to move away? It's not fair! Why did she have to leave me behind? Why*</i>

couldn't she take me with her? It's not fair!'" Bogger turned the next few pages, looking them over quickly with a frown.

"The next few pages are difficult to decipher. They seemed to be rushed and clumsy, with a few of what I believe to be misspellings here and there. But from what I gathered, there is a lot of emotion and anger in his words, he was clearly in some sort of distress. This one seems readable. It says: '*February 8th, 2023. I guess writing down my feelings does help a little. I don't feel so angry anymore. And my mother says it helps to keep a record of my progress.*' Interesting, writing things down to keep a record of it. I'll have to keep that in mind for our journey as well. Now let's see. '*I have also learned to keep my anxiety under control as well, which has helped me a lot at… school*'?"

"What's a school?" Bark asked curiously.

"From what I read in Alice's books; it is a large gathering of fish. But what would a human child be doing around a school of fish in the middle of the water?"

"Perhaps he is learning to catch his own food?" Brim suggested with a shrug. Bogger didn't respond and continued to read from the journal. A moment or so later, Bogger let out a soft chuckle.

"He writes down in the next passage that a school is a place of learning for young children." This earned a chuckle from the elder mouse.

"What a peculiar and clever young child," Nika-mius said. "Writing it down as if he were explaining it to the journal itself. Sometimes even humans can surprise you."

"Is there any point to all this?" Ragath asked impatiently. "Why are we reading about some human child's life?"

"It may give us a clue as to what we may deal with once we find a way out of here," Bogger said. "How the humans behave and how they may react to us. It's better to get all the information that we can, while we can."

"It doesn't matter," Ragath retorted. "They are humans; and therefore, they are our enemies. We shouldn't be wasting our time trying to learn from them. They would sooner kill us the moment they set eyes on us."

"I agree with Bogger," said Azalar. "It is best to learn as much as we can for the betterment of our survival. I would rather know more about the humans than they do of us. Please continue, Bogger." Bogger turned to the next few pages of the journal.

"These pages are too worn and stained. I cannot read them properly. He seems to be explaining something called '*summer break*', but I don't know what that means and there isn't enough information to explain more, at least from what words I can read. He then goes on to say that he and his family attended an '*amusement park*', or something like that." He stopped on a page and there was a pause. "That's interesting. The last decipherable text was when he entered this place called a... '*middle school*', with the last date reading September 8th of 2026. There seems to have been a bit of time passing between that date and the next. The current passage reads: '*October 25th, 2029. It has been a long time since I've written in this Journal. A lot has happened, and I had completely forgotten about this; but I've just found this journal under my bed and I'm actually excited to start writing in it again. I've just started high school now and things are crazier than ever, but I'm excited about the future ahead. I've started on my...*' the rest of the passage is covered with a large dark stain that seeps into the next few pages. Some of the others are smeared, bent, and damaged. It is difficult to read them in this light." Bogger turned the page and began looking it over. He paused and looked puzzlingly at the page.

"Well, now this is indeed interesting," he said.

"What is it?" Azalar asked.

"His next passage tells of some terrible events happening around him. Listen to this. '*March 14th, 2032. It was horrible. They came out of nowhere. Massive ships suddenly appeared in the skies above every city around the world. At first, we didn't know what they were or why they were here, but we soon found out. They began dropping terrible explosives everywhere. Cities were wiped out overnight. We were defenseless. They wanted our planet, and they wanted to kill all life on Earth to get it. Before the News shut down, many came to call these beings the Scourge.*'"

"The Scourge?" Azalar said. "I remember Alice saying something about the Scourge."

"I remember that as well," said Nikamius. "She said that Helgan was trying to find a way to help mankind fight against the Scourge."

"And that's what he's been using us for," said Brim. "At least that's what his excuse was."

"So, the humans were attacked," said Bark. "By these things called the Scourge. But what are they?"

"I'm not sure," Bogger answered. "So far there is nothing to tell of them. But the passage doesn't end there," Bogger said. "Listen. '*There was nowhere for us to go. There was chaos everywhere.*' A few of the lines are blurred but I can make out a few words like '-*panicking-*' and '-*bodies everywhere. Death is everywhere.*' Then it continues on with: '*We had to run. We had to hide.*' There are more blurs and stains, but then the passage ends with '-*found a military base where they took us in and gave us food and shelter. We had to work in order to get food, but it was nice to feel safe again.*'

"'*June 17th, 2032. We are still safe in the base, but life is hard. However, I do think there is hope. After the invasion first began, the nations of the world united to fight against them. People from all over the world were called to fight. My father was one of them, but because I was the only child of my parents, I was not allowed to join the army with him. It has been four months since then. I never saw my father again.*'"

A twinge of pain was felt in Azalar's chest when he heard that last sentence, and his thoughts immediately turned to his own father and the last time he ever saw him. In a sense, Azalar could relate to this human, even if it was just a little. Amara, sensing her mate in distress, placed a paw on Azalar's and nuzzled close to him, which Azalar greatly appreciated.

"'*October 10th, 2032,*'" Bogger continued to read. "'*It has been five months since my last entry, and things have not gotten better. The Scourge have begun launching their ground invasions across the globe. The battles, from what I heard, have been absolutely brutal, with thousands of casualties every day. Those that survived the battles told terrible stories of the Scourge and from how they were described, the Scourge were just as terrifying as we had thought they were. Maybe even more so. I had hoped that we may win this war, but now I'm not so sure. This may be our downfall.*'" Bogger paused as he read the next passage of the following page. He then looked up at Bark with a smirk.

"Seems you may get your answer after all, Bark," Bogger said, then looked back down at the journal. "'*January 28th, 2033. About a month ago, the soldiers came back from battle, but they didn't come back alone. They brought back with them a few cages and inside the cages were the Scourge. I managed to get a glance at them, and from what I saw they were horrible. They were massive, green insect-like crea-*

tures with massive heads with seven eyes and massive pincers for their mouths. They had four arms as long as their slender bodies and thin legs that bent backwards. If I had to make a comparison, they looked like giant monstrous versions of grasshoppers. The soldiers brought them back into the base, where they are now currently studying them.'" Bogger paused again, but this time his eyes widened, and his mood became unsettled. "'*There is a man leading the scientists. With any luck, he may find their weaknesses. From what I've hear, he's a very brilliant man. His name is Dr. Helgan.*'"

"Helgan?" Azalar very nearly shouted, but stopped himself quickly as he was sure that name would cause a panic amongst the other rodents.

"Helgan was there? What else does it say?" Bark asked just above a whisper. Bogger kept his eyes glued to the next few pages of the journal.

"The words are too smeared and are barely readable, but so far there seems to be no more mention of Helgan. But there may be something further on. Ah, yes! Here we go. '*August 4th, 2033. We have finally beaten them back! We're winning this war! Thanks to Helgan and his team, we've discovered the weaknesses of the Scourge and are driving them back. We may finally see the sun again.*' The passages become blurred some more but there seems to be something about '*-disrupting the hivemind-*', I don't know what that means. The next passage takes place a long while after the last.

"'*June 10th, 2034. We did it! The Scourge have been defeated! We drove them out! The last of their ships had left and any Scourge remaining have been destroyed. We've won!*' The next few pages are very wrinkled, worn and torn; they are impossible to read in this light." He kept turning through the book until he could find the next readable passage.

"Here we are. Let's see. It's still worn out, but there are few parts still readable." Bogger paused for a moment looking over the pages. "The tone seems to have taken a dark turn. From what I gather, it says something about '-*plants dying*-' and '-*water drying up*-'. The last line of the passage reads: '*the Earth is dying.*'" Bogger turned to the next page.

"A great deal of time appears to have passed before Mathew writes in the journal again. Listen: '*September 17th, 2040. The Earth is dying. It can no longer sustain life. It has been six years since the Scourge's defeat, but the battles must have been too much for the planet to handle. Thousands of people are dying every day. I don't know how much time we have left, but I hope there is still a chance for us.*'"

"'The earth is dying'?" Frella asked. "What does that even mean?"

"Were the humans planning to leave the Earth?" asked Bark. Bogger did respond as he continued to look over the pages.

"I don't know," Bogger said. "There isn't much else written here that gives further details. Wait a moment, here is something. It's faint but I think I can read it. It says: '*May 8th, 2041. The world leaders have deemed that Earth is no longer safe for humanity. They have announced that they have begun building massive Arks to take us, and whatever remaining life off the planet. They said that they found another planet for us. Hopefully we can find a new home.*'"

"So, the humans were planning to leave earth," said Azalar.

"Then there might not be many of them left out there," said Brim. "But what are these '*Arks*'?"

"I do believe that they are some form of transportation the humans have made to take them off world," Nikamius said. "Like how the Scourge arrived in what were called '*ships*', if I remember correctly.

But that doesn't make any sense, though. If the humans were going to leave earth, why would they leave Helgan behind then? He seemed like someone of high value since he was the one who was able to come up with a way to defeat the Scourge."

"There is still more to the story," Bogger interjected. "Listen. '*October 30th, 2042. They have begun to load the Arks. There are a total of twenty Arks built to carry us off this planet. I was a part of the construction of the Arks, so my mother and I were guaranteed spots on the Ark for launch. But the Arks can only fit 200,000 people. Many will be left behind. I am sorry for them.*' There are several passages that are blurred, but there seems to be something about a '-*Revolution-*'? And '-*a terrible battle outside the Arks-*' and '-*thousands dead-*'

"'*November 5th, 2042. The Scourge came back! We were about ready to launch the Arks when their ships suddenly appeared in the sky, just like before. They began attacking the Arks as they launched. We tried to fight back. Many Arks were lost. The Scourge chased us until we left the atmosphere before they turned back. They had been planning this. They did something to the Earth and were waiting for us at our weakest. So, they could take our planet for themselves. Those monsters. They took our home away from us. They'll pay for this!*'"

"So, they did leave Earth?" asked Borith. "But then surely, they must have come back, right? I mean, the humans are here now. So, they would have had to come back at some point. Right?"

"I'm not sure," Bogger answered, still staring at the pages. "There doesn't seem to be any straight answer here." Bogger shuffled through the next few pages. "There is very little to make of these in this light. All I can make out are the dates such as: '*Day 5*', '*Day 30*', '*Day 80*' and so on. These go on for a long way, with only small passages explaining very little. There are many passages that are very far between; some going as far as hundreds of days between the next passage. I don't understand why he is using days instead of the proper dates as he was before. Maybe they are using some different way to track time. But with the pages being so blurred and damaged, I can only guess at this point." Bogger flipped the page.

"The next passage takes place a long time after the last. It says: '*Day 4387. At least that is what the Ark's calendar says. Who truly knows at this point. It has been a long time since we left earth. I can barely remember what the grass looked like before the war with the Scourge. The mountains. The oceans. All nothing more than distant memories. The President says that we are close to finding a new home. But he's been saying that for years now. I wonder if anything he says is true. We may be doomed to wander the endless darkness of space forever.*'

"'*Day 4439. It's been a horrible day. My mother… passed away today. She went to bed last night, but she never woke up. It wasn't unexpected. She had been sick for a long while now. Still, it hurts. I'm going to miss her very much.*' Poor human. I can only assume that he means his mother died during their travels. How tragic." Bogger turned to the next page and silently read the words. Suddenly his eyes widened as he looked over the contents of the page.

"Well, now here's something interesting," he said. Bogger looked up at the rest of the rodents around him. "It seems that they never returned to Earth."

"What do you mean?" Azalar asked. "They would have had to. How else could they still be here?"

"The answer lies on this very page. Listen. '*Day 4470. The President has just announced it. He said that we've found a new planet! He said that it's exactly like Earth. Green grass, clean air, and clear water. A planet that can hold life. Have we really found a new home? We've been wandering the stars for so long that I almost don't want to believe it. It's almost too good to be true. If it is, hopefully we can have a new life there.'"*

"So, they found a new planet?" asked Brim. "Does that mean that we're not on earth after all?"

"If that's true, then that means no one returned to Earth," said Brim. he placed a paw on his forehead and sighed heavily. "This is making less and less sense."

"Is there anything else?" asked Azalar. "Something that can give us more answers?"

"I'm not sure," Bogger said. "The next few passages are smudged; I can't make out many words. But the ones I can say '*-the Arks has slowed down-*' and '*landing soon-*'. There isn't much else I can read. But there does seem to be a name written here, though it is difficult to read. I believe it says: 'we've finally *made it to Hera.*'"

"Hera," repeated Azalar. "That must be the name they've given this new planet."

"But if that's true," said Amara. "Then that means we're not on earth at all." The other rodents looked towards Amara.

"What do you mean?" Frella asked.

"Think about it," Amara said. "This journal came from the man in that room. If he is here on this '*Hera*' planet and not on Earth, then that must mean that we're not on Earth too."

"She's right," said Bogger. "It's the only explanation that makes any sense. Which means that everything we learned from Alice's books is wrong. And that also means that what we expect to encounter in this world will be far different."

"But then how did we get here?" Ragath asked. "This journal doesn't mention us at all." Bogger looked back down at the journal.

"Let me see here. '*Day 1, year 1. We have finally landed on Hera and have begun building ourselves a home.*' No, that's not it. Let's see. No, nothing on this page either. There must be something in here somewhere." Bogger turned a few more pages, but most of them had no valuable information or were too damaged and worn to read. He then turned to the ninth page before he finally spotted something of interest. "Wait! Here is something! '*Day 87, year 7. Another Ark just landed today. We thought there were only nine Arks left from the original twenty. But apparently one other made it out. This one was much larger though. Much larger. But it wasn't filled with people though. It was filled with animals. But what surprised me more was who came out of the Ark. It was Helgan. As I found out later that day, This Ark had been placed in charge of preserving all the wildlife of Earth, and Helgan had somehow managed to gather almost every animal species there was that was on earth, or at least that's what it seems. But the strange thing about it all, was that he didn't seem to age a day. Apparently, as a friend of mine revealed to me, we had been traveling through the stars for over twelve years. And we have lived on this planet for over seven years. Yet he still looks as young as the day I first saw him. Maybe even younger. There's something off about that man.*'"

"He doesn't know the half of it," Bark said with a snicker. Bogger ignored his comment and continued reading through the pages.

"There doesn't seem to be much more useful information here for the moment. The next few pages tell of the humans' continuous efforts to build new cities and towns, the struggles of their winters, and then something about '*protests*' or something of the sort; I'm not familiar. Very little else is mentioned that I can make out, and there is quite a bit of time that has passed between each entry. Let's see. Wait a moment.

I believe I found something. '*Day 236, year 15, I saw that man again today, Dr. Helgan. He came by my jobsite, where we were almost finished with the construction of a new apartment building. He said that he was looking to hire us to help build his new Laboratory up on the hill outside of the city. Don't know why he wants it so far away from the city, but I didn't bother to ask further. The money he was offering was too good to pass up. So, we took the job without hesitation. But I still got an off feeling about him. He still looked the same as he ever did. In fact, if I didn't know any better, I'd say he hadn't aged at all. I don't know what it is, but that something is not right with him. I'm just going to keep my distance from him until the job is done.*'

'"*Day 276, year 15. We arrived at the construction site for Helgan's new Laboratory. Apparently, they were already in the process of building, with several other teams working there prior to us arriving. Seems Helgan wants this place built as soon as possible. Doesn't matter to me though, we signed a contract, and the money was good anyway. But I've been very curious about this lab though. What could he be planning to do all the way out here? I know I shouldn't think much of it, but there's something nagging at the back of my head about all this. Oh well. I'll just keep my head down.*'

'"*Day 123, year 16. Construction is moving quicker than we thought it would. Several more teams had arrived at the site, and we're just about done putting up all the walls and windows. All that's left is the interior.*'

'"*Day 157, year 16. Something strange is going on here. Helgan refuses to allow anyone down into the lower levels of his lab, save for only two teams. Two dozen men went down there, but none have come back up. Not even when our shifts have ended. I'm usually one of the last to leave the site, and I still have not seen them emerge from down there. It has been over a month since we last saw them. And Helgan makes absolutely sure no one goes down there. No one asks about it either. The last time someone did, it was one of my coworkers. Helgan smiled and said nothing more. But the smile he gave wasn't a gentle one. There was something terrible within that smile. It has been over a week since that happened, and no one dared to ask about it again. I don't know what is going on here, but I don't like it one bit.'*

"'*Day 189, year 16. We've finally finished the construction of Helgan's Lab. And no sooner than we have, Helgan began moving his equipment inside, along with teams of his lab assistants. There were all sorts of tools and machines. Many I had never seen before. I wonder what he's planning to do in there.*'"

Bogger let out a heavy sigh once more. "The next four pages are too blurred, stained and torn. And there isn't anything of great use from what words I can gather. Let me see. It appears that Helgan dismissed them, and Mathew '*-got a new job in the… underground ware-house-*'."

"I guess that's how he ended up down here," said Borith.

"Yes. Not a very reassuring sign for us," said Brim. "Is there anything else?" Bogger continued to read through the pages as best as he could.

"I'm not seeing anything of relevance at the moment. There are still many pages that are very damaged, and this journal is already very difficult to read." He turned to the next page; we're the next entry wasn't so heavily blurred. He paused and silently looked over the words. Then his eyes widened. "Here! I have something. I can't make out much, but here's what I can read. '*-just saw another cart of equipment heading to Helgan's lab. I think I saw some mice in* *there too, as well as some rats I believe. Many of them were white as snow.'"* At this, many of the rodents looked over at Amara, who perked her ears up as she clung to her fréfil. Bogger continued. *"'I knew they were being taken to his lab too. This is the fourth cart with these small critters that arrived. What could he possibly want them for up there? When I asked around, I was told that Helgan seemed to have a peculiar interest in them. What kind of mad scientist stuff is he planning to do? I'm not sure I want to know.'"*

"Well, that answered a lot of our questions," said Bark.

"But many more remain," said Azalar, who was looking down at the floor; his eyes furrowed. Yes, he now had a lot of his questions answered. But one burning question remained. He looked back up at Bogger with a serious look. "Does the book explain what he wanted from us? Or why Helgan put us through all this hell?"

"Didn't Alice say something about finding a way to take back Earth from the Scourge?" asked Amara.

"She did," said Brim. "At least I'm sure that is what she was led to believe. I highly doubt that was his real intention."

"So, then what was the purpose of his experiments then?" asked Frella.

"I remember some of the humans saying that it was because he wanted to play… What was the word Alice used again? God?" asked Bark. "What does that mean anyway?"

"It's the human word that we use for Háth," Nikamius answered. "If I am assuming correctly, it means that, like Háth, Helgan is trying to create things in his own image, as if he were Háth himself. A blasphemous way of thinking."

"I don't think Helgan, or the humans much cared for what is blasphemous or not," said Ragath. "They're all filled with greed and have lust for power. Helgan just had a stronger drive than the rest.”

“But Alice wasn't like that,” said Amara. “She was a kind soul who wanted to help us and even aided us in our escape.” Ragath looked away and scoffed.

“She may have been the one exception.” He said nothing else after that. Azalar turned back to Bogger.

“Is there anything else that we can learn from the journal?” he asked. Bogger looked through the pages once more, trying his best to decipher the contents of the journal as much as he could.

“I'm afraid that there isn't much else,” he answered honestly. “None that I can interpret that can help us, at least. There are many pages that tell of some ‘*struggle*’. And the phrase ‘*his puppet*’ is repeated many times. But I don’t know what that means. Wait! Here there seems to be something happening. Listen to this. ‘*Day 134, year 37. There is panic on the upside. We can hear it from down here. Loud booms have been going off for hours. I don't know what they are. We can feel the tunnels shaking. It almost sounds like a war is going on above us. Have they finally reached a breaking point? Has he finally done it? Has he finally gotten what he wanted? I don’t know. But we should be safe down here.*’”

“What does that mean?” asked Brim. “Who has gotten what they wanted? Was it Helgan?”

“I don't know,” Bogger answered. “The pages don't mention him at all from what I can understand. But there must have been some form of conflict between the humans. Something to do with this ‘*puppet*’ that has been mentioned; I’m sure of it.” Bogger turned the next page and read the next passages silently; but his mood became dark as his face slowly fell to a frown the more he read.

“The next few passages take a grim turn. There are no dates to them, as far as I can tell, so it will be hard to tell when one entry ends, and another begins. The first one reads: '*I'm trapped down here! The tunnels and the bridge have collapsed. There's no way out! I'm all alone here. The others ran away during the chaos, and I was left behind. I don't know what to do! I have food and water, but I don't know how long they'll last. It's dark in here. I don't want to be alone.*'"

"Poor fellow," said Nikamius. "He was left all alone in the darkness, abandoned by his friends. Such a terrible fate for anyone."

"The passage doesn't end there," Bogger said. "There is still plenty more to read. The next passage reads: '*I don't know how long I've been here. There's no way to tell time. My light is about to die. I've found some candles and brought them here. I need to find a way out. I won't die in this place.*' The next page is not marked as well, but it says: '*The candles last twelve hours each, so I now have some way to tell time down here. It has been four days since I've been trapped here, at least according to the candles I've used. My food rations are running low though. I need to think of a way out of here. And soon.*'" Bogger turned to the next page. He frowned a little, trying to read the words.

"The next few pages are damaged heavily again; I will try to read what I can. But the next visible lines read: '*-tried to build a bridge across the gap.*' and then, '*-but can't hold my weight. I'll try to think of something. I won't give up.*'" He turned to the next page and read the words silently until he let out a slight chuckle.

"You're not going to like this one Ragath, but the next passage reads: 'Day Seven. *Those damn rats! They keep stealing my food. I'm getting so sick of these little*' what is this word? '*Shits*'? I'm not familiar with that word. Must be some vulgar term that the humans use." There was a low growl from Ragath, not at all finding it amusing. Bogger continued reading. "*"I don't know how much longer I can take this. I don't have much food left, and I'm almost out of water. I can't wait for help anymore. I'm going to search for a way out tomorrow.*

"The next passage is too blurred, but it starts with: '*Day Nine.*' and '*-walking down for two days. So far, there's no way out.*' and then later, '*-the rats keep following me-*' and '*-taken shelter in a train cart.*' and then '*-go on forever. I don't know if I'll ever get out.*'

"The next passages are very hastily written. And it seems as though his hand was trembling as he wrote. '*Day eleven. There's no way out! Everywhere I've turned is blocked off. The tunnels are collapsing. The rats. The rats won't let me leave. They're blocking every way out. They're getting closer. They're not afraid of me anymore. One of them tried to bite me. I didn't get a good look at them, but there was something very wrong with them. Their skin was gray and mangy, and their eyes were blood red. But what was most strange was that some of them… were able to stand on two legs*'?" Bogger glanced up from the page to the others around him, who also looked at him with great curiosity. Bogger went back to reading. "*"I don't know what happened to them down here. But I don't have time to think. I'm running out of food and candles. I have to go back. It's the only safe place left. I need to think of a way out. This can't be the end!*"" Bogger turned to the final pages of the journal, where only one passage remained.

"This is the final page," he stated. He then took a moment to read over the first few words, and his brow furrowed, and a deep frown formed on his lips. "I'm afraid it doesn't end well. It says: '*I'm trapped in here. I went down the left tunnel, hoping that I might have missed something. I found their nest. I disturbed them. And now they've followed me back here. I can't escape them. They're everywhere. They're not rats at all. They're monsters. I've tried to block them out. But nothing works. I can't sleep. I have no food. No water. There's nothing left. They're in the walls. I can hear them! It's like they're right above me.'* The final line just under the passage says: '*I don't want to die.*'" Bogger slowly closed the book.

Chapter XIII

The air was suddenly silent and filled with dread as the surrounding rodents stared horrified at Bogger and the book.

"I guess it was fortunate of us that we did not go down the left tunnel," said Nikamius. There was another small moment of tense silence.

"This proves it then," said Bark, staring into the fire. "We are not alone down here."

"We have to get out!" exclaimed Borith, though not too loudly for the rest of the camp to hear, yet his voice was still full of anxiety. "We need to get out of here now!"

"Now, now, let's all remain calm," said Nikamius in a calming tone. "There's no cause for panic just yet."

"Haven't you been listening, Nikamius?" asked Borith. He then pointed to the darkness on the bridge beyond the archway. "The bridge is destroyed! There's no way out of this place. We're just as trapped here as that human was. And look what happened to him!"

"Keep your voices down before you cause a panic!" said Azalar, noticing some of the curious glance coming their way from the commotion. "We don't know that for certain. For all we know, there could very well be a way out of here that Mathew hadn't found yet." Borith was about to speak again when Bogger cut him off.

"Are you forgetting that we're much smaller than the humans?" he said. "What may seem impossible for them may not be so for us. We are much smaller, which means that we can squeeze into tight spaces. So, there are plenty of possible paths for us to take that a human cannot."

"On top of that we haven't seen hide or hair of whatever those things are," said Brim. "For all we know they could have died off a long time ago. They might not have even been the things we've heard in the tunnels, but probably some other unfortunate creature." There was a tense silence as nobody was willing to either confirm or deny this theory. It wasn't until a moment later when someone spoke up.

"What are those things anyway?" asked Della softly, as if afraid to even ask the question.

"If I may?" said Reemus. Everyone turned their attention towards the brow rat. "I remember before my father died, he told me stories that were passed down from his father about what happened in the lab. I don't know exactly how long it was, but many years ago, Helgan was conducting his tortures on mice and rats alike. Then, one day Helgan came into the lab with this strange liquid that he injected into them. From what my father told me, most of them died because of it. All except for a few rats. And it changed him."

"I believe I remember my father telling me that same story as well!" exclaimed Nikamius. "Helgan injected them with a serum. But unlike the serum that he injected into us; this serum made those rats far more aggressive. It was as if their minds had all gone *forn*. Many began calling them the Fornóc; the mad ones."

"Exactly," said Reemus. "It was said that these rats were so mad that they would attack anyone and everything in sight. Nothing could allay them. They were so full of anger that the humans could no longer go near them. So Helgan had the humans take them away somewhere where they could no longer harm others. But then something happened. No one knows what exactly happened, but the story goes that there was some kind of accident at the lab and the Fornóc were able to escape. No one knew where they had gone, but they all seemingly disappeared."

"And you think that's what killed that human in there are those same rats that escaped so long ago? The Fornóc?" asked Azalar. Reemus shrugged his shoulders.

"I can't say for certain," Reemus answered honestly. "But if I had to guess, it could be them. From what I heard from the stories, these rats bear almost the same description as what is said in that book. Like how their hair would start falling out, and how some of them could walk on their two legs. And their eyes." Reemus stared at the fire within the can. "Their eyes, my father said, were as red as fire full of rage. A fire that would burn, destroy and devour all in its path. If those things are down here with us. Then may Háth help us all." The air was silent for a long while.

"Alright then! We need to prepare for the worst." Azalar turned to the trio of young rats. "Reemus! You, Ramy and Litha will tell those on watch to keep vigilant for any sign of anything strange. If they see anything, tell them to immediately report back to us! And spread the word that no one is to go off alone. I don't want any of those things catching us off guard."

"Yes, Azalar!" said Reemus. The rat trio nodded then quickly stood up and set out to do as they were told. Azalar then turned to Brim.

"Brim, I want you, Mith and Borith to go around and gather as many weapons as you can and distribute them amongst all the bucks. I want us to be ready in case they come for us. And Bogger, we also need to build something for the front of the camp. Right now, there's nothing there. Do you think you can come up

with something that we can build to keep them out?”
Bogger turned towards the front of the camp at the gap
between the two walls.

“It would be a waste of time and effort to build a
proper set of opening doors,” Bogger answered. “I
suppose the best we can do would be to build a simple
barricade. But what I think we should do is build a
platform to cross the bridge.”

“But don't you remember?” asked Bark. “The human already tried that, and it didn’t work.”

“But you're forgetting that we are several times
smaller than a human. We could build a simple
platform and our weight wouldn’t put much strain on
the wood like it would for a human. But we will need
plenty of supplies.”

“Then that is what we'll do!” exclaimed Azalar.
“We will send three or four more teams out to collect
the wood for both the barricade and the bridge, and
possibly more weapons. Bark, do you think you can
handle gathering a few bucks together to do that?”

“You can count on me!” Bark replied with a
thumbs up. Azalar gave him a smile.

“Thank you, Bark. Ragath, if you could gather your
rats to…” Azalar turned to Ragath, whom he had
noticed was particularly quiet as he stared at the sword
in his lap.

“Ragath, are you listening?” Azalar asked. The
giant black rat didn't respond as he continued to stare
at his sword, running his fingers over the blade. His
face was in his usual serious frown, but there was something in his eyes that had Azalar concerned. Azalar
called his name again, this time getting the rat's
attention with a start.

“What is it?” Ragath nearly hissed. Azalar gave the
giant black rat a slight frown.

“Ragath, is everything okay?” he asked. Ragath
furrowed his eyes and glared at the tan mouse.

"Nothing you need to concern yourself with, little mouse," the black rat hissed. "Now what is it you want?" Azalar resisted the urge to press further but stopped himself, knowing that it wouldn't end well.

"Brim, Mith and Borith will be collecting weapons together to distribute amongst us, while Bark will be assembling a few teams to go out and bring back more supplies to build a barricade and possibly a bridge to cross over the water. But we need to gather every buck we can and form a defense in case the Fornóc do come. We need you to do the same with your rats." Ragath stood up and placed his sword on his shoulder.

"Very well," Ragath answered. "But my rats will get the first pick of whatever weapons we find." Brim frowned at the large black rat.

"Hold on, that's not-" "Fine," Azalar interjected. Brim and the other mice looked at Azalar questioningly. Azalar ignored them and continued. "They will collect the weapons and your rats will get to choose first. But in return, the rats will help the mice with the defenses. Deal?" Ragath stood tall and stared down at Azalar.

"Fine," Ragath agreed. "I suppose we are in this together, after all. Aren't we."

"Then I believe we should begin after a good night's rest," said Nikamius. Azalar turned to the elder rat with a frown.

"But we don't have time," the tan mouse said. "If the Fornóc are out there, they could very well attack us at any moment. We need to prepare for that."

"And it will do none of us any good if we're all too tired to defend ourselves," Nikamius retorted. "We've been traveling for a long while without any decent rest. We are unlikely to get anything done if we all drop from exhaustion. I think it would be beneficial for all of us if we all rest first so that we have clearer minds for what is to come."

"I have to agree with Nikamius on this," said Bogger. "A night's rest would allow us to form proper plans and strategies. And with the amount of work, we will be doing tomorrow, we are going to need all the strength we can get." Azalar wanted to protest, wanting to prepare for any possible Fornóc attack. He hated feeling so vulnerable, and he hated waiting for things to happen.

But he knew that they were right. Azalar looked around at the rodents around him. Many were sitting tired and wearily by their fires, with many more sound asleep. He, himself, was lacking much needed sleep as well, and he could feel the fatigue growing in his body with every second. Though reluctant, he nodded in agreement.

"Alright," Azalar said with a heavy sigh. "We rest for now. But we start work as soon as we've all gotten the rest we need." Ragath let out a disgruntled grunt before turning and walking away. The group of mice watched on as the black rat wandered across the camp until he came to a group of rats where Razor was sitting.

"I don't understand," asked Brim, turning to Azalar. "Why are we allowing the rats such privilege?" Azalar let out a deep breath before pinching the bridge of his nose, suddenly feeling a headache coming on.

"Because, whether we like it or not, we need Ragath and his rats. Without them, we don't have much chance of survival. If we don't find a way to compromise, the rats are just as likely to run off and abandon us as they are to help us."

"But that Reemus pup and his friends don't seem too eager to leave your side anytime soon," joked Bark. Azalar rolled his eyes.

"That may be the case for a few. But most of the rats look to Ragath and respect him. If Ragath decided to leave, they would follow him with no hesitation."

"And why should we care if they leave?" asked Brim.

"Because we need each other to survive," said Nikamius. "We need them just as much as they need us. Whether they want to realize it or not. Our strength is in our numbers. The rats may be stronger, but we mice are faster on our feet. Using those strengths would do better if we used them together. And Ragath may be stubborn, but he is not a fool. He knows this. Either way, I agree that it is best that we not press him on this. Something is clearly troubling Ragath, as you may have noticed, and it won't do well for us to dismay him further. So, for now, let us all get some much needed rest. We have a lot of work to do tomorrow." With that Nikamius and the other mice laid their heads down and, despite the fear of the dreaded Fornóc watching them from the darkness, attempted to get some sleep, with Brim and Bark nuzzling close to their fréfils.

Azalar, however, placed another few more pieces of wood onto the fire and sat down next to Amara. Though his aching body and heavy eyes begged for sleep, his mind was filled with fear and uncertainty. He thought about the Fornóc and the threat that they posed. He also thought about his fellow rodents and what they had all been through. They had finally escaped from Helgan's land and had come so far. Yet, just when they felt that freedom was close, here they were; trapped in the darkness with these ghastly creatures possibly lurking about. It felt as though they were never going to be safe. Azalar let out a heavy sigh before he was nearly startled when he felt a soft paw placed on his back.

"Azalar?" asked Amara. Azalar turned to see his beloved fréfil staring at him with a loving smile, though her eyes were full of concern. "Please don't trouble yourself, my love. Everything is going to be alright. We will get through this." Azalar smiled at his beloved mate, but her words did little to stem the dark thoughts growing in his mind. He turned his attention back to the fire.

"I'm just worried, Amara," Azalar whispered to her. "I'm worried that we might not ever find a safe place. That no matter where we go, there will always be something out there to harm us. We escaped from the hell that was Helgan's lab, only to find ourselves in darkness with the Fornóc possibly stalking us. It's just one obstacle after another." Azalar breathed in a weary sigh.

"All I want now is for us to find a home. I promised myself that I would find us a home. But the pressures of leading us are starting to weigh on me." He looked back at his fréfil. "Do you think I'm doing the right thing?" Amara smiled once again and placed a paw on her fréfil's cheek.

"I believe you are doing all that you can," she said sincerely. "Whether that is the right thing or not is impossible to say. But what I do know is that if it wasn't for you, we would all still be trapped in those cages back in Helgan's lab." Azalar looked away with a frown.

"And if you remember correctly, it was Razor who killed that human back there. I just got myself caught and nearly killed." Amara placed a paw under his chin and turned his head to face her, the smile never leaving her face.

"No one ever said you had to do all of this alone, Azalar. It's okay to rely on others, as you have been doing all this time if you haven't noticed. But don't let yourself feel doubt now. I have faith in you, my love. And I always will. Try having more faith in yourself." She nuzzled her head against his before pulling away and lying down. "Now try to get some sleep. Everything will be alright."

Azalar watched his fréfil as she closed her eyes and drifted off to sleep. He watched her chest as it slowly raised up and down and his thoughts returned to the lab for a brief moment, and he smiled. No matter how hard the day was or how cruel the humans were, Amara always had a way of calming him down. Furthermore, watching her sleeping form always made him relaxed and at peace. It also made him more determined to protect her. Although there was still worry and doubt on his mind, her words did indeed make him feel a little bit better.

Azalar then looked down at the needle at his side, the needle that Alice had given him. He picked up the needle and held it in front of him. As he gazed upon the long piece of sharp metal with a thin loop at the bottom, he thought of Alice and all that she had done for the rodents. She spent weeks teaching them to read and write, as well as prepare them for this journey. And the sacrifice she made for them.

Alice believed in Azalar, and so did his mate. These thoughts caused a small smile to form on his lips. He then looked down at Amara, who had Alice's blue gemstone close by. Amara had made sure to keep it in her grasp the whole journey and seeing Amara clutching it in her paws right now, brought a warm feeling in his heart.

"Thank you, Alice," Azalar whispered to himself. With a small yawn, Azalar slowly laid himself down and allowed himself to relax just enough for him to close his eyes and drift off to sleep.

No more than a few hours later up on the camp wall, a pair of rats were on watch duty and were facing out into the darkness of the massive hall. They were told to be extra vigilant in their watch, and to immediately report anything out of the ordinary. However, these orders came from that tan colored mouse. Roth, a very lightly gray colored rat, let out a scoff and shook his head.

"Taking orders from a mouse," he said to himself in a low voice. "The idea of a mouse giving orders to us rats. Completely ridiculous and insulting. I don't know why Ragath allows that little pest to tell us what to do."

"Who knows?" said Rutu, a rat with brown fur that was dark at the back and lightened towards the belly. "Maybe Ragath is just letting the mouse do all the work at finding a way out of this place. Then once we're out, he takes charge." Roth smirked at the idea.

"A pleasant thought," Roth replied. "And perhaps after that, the rats will be the ones in control while these little mice serve us. As it should be. We rats are stronger and smarter in every way. Why shouldn't it be us in control?" Rutu let out a small chuckle.

"Wouldn't that be a sight?" he said before sitting down, making himself as comfortable as he could. Roth then turned his attention back to the gloom.

"It sure is creepy out there though," he said. "Don't you get the feeling that something out there is watching us?" Rutu shrugged, not paying it much mind.

"Nah. I'm sure it's just your imagination. We've been wandering through these tunnels for a long time, and we haven't seen hide or hair of anything to be afraid of." Roth glanced at his companion for a moment before turning back to the hall.

"I don't know. What if there is something out there? You don't think it could be the Fornóc, right?" Rutu let out a scoff.

"You don't really believe that old pup's tale, do you? The Mad Ones lurking around in the darkness, waiting to pop out and grab you?" Roth didn't respond, except with a slight frown.

"Maybe," Roth answered honestly. "I just don't like this. Staring out into the blackness, just waiting for something to happen. But maybe Azalar really did hear-”

“Weren’t you the one just complaining about that same mouse giving you orders?” Rutu shot at his companion. “I’m telling you there is nothing out there for us to worry about.” Rutu glanced at the brown rat for a moment, then looked back out into the hall with a sigh.

“Maybe you’re right,” Roth said, though a part of him wasn’t too sure. Just then the brown rat stood up from his post and began to climb down the other side of the defenses. Roth noticed this and quickly spoke up.

“Where are you going, Rutu?” the gray rat called out to his companion.

“*Zet pfetta*, Roth” Rutu answered back with a smirk. “Nature calls, you know?” Roth shook his head and sighed. He didn’t like that his fellow rat was about to wander off out there, but it would be the preferable option than for him to drop his pellets near the campsite; Ragath wouldn’t like that at all.

“Alright. But make it quick and return to your post quickly. Or Ragath will have both of our tails.” Rutu nodded and headed down the wooden palisade and disappeared into the shadows of the hall. Roth’s eyes followed Rutu until he could no longer see him. The moment Rutu disappeared; Roth's face fell into a frown of concern. He didn't want to say it out loud, but he had a terrible feeling about something.

Rutu wandered into the darkness for a few moments, looking for a place that was private enough to do his business, but would still be close enough to have “the camp in sight. He settled on a little spot behind a stack of broken wood not too far away. He placed his weapon, a long scalpel from the lab that was handed to him for his watch, on the wood pile and proceeded to do his business. However, it wasn’t until he was just about to start that he realized how alone he was. in the gloom that surrounded him, and the complete silence of the hall, he slowly began to feel uneasy. Being alone as he was, he suddenly felt very small; much smaller than he had ever felt in his life. His fur stood on ends and his heart began to race. And soon all the courage he had before slowly left him, and paranoia took its place. He suddenly found it increasingly difficult to do what he originally came for as he listened intently to the cavernous hall.

Every little noise that he heard off in the distance, from the soft dripping of some far off water, to the scurrying of tiny nearby insects, set him on edge. His imagination soon began to get the best of him, and he thought he could see shadows moving about in the blackness. He imagined the soft pattering of paws tapping against the floor all around him. He tried to tell himself that it was all in his head, and that Azalar's little story of hearing paws footsteps in the dark was just getting to him now that he was all alone. Yet, no matter how much he told himself this, he had the terrible sense that he wasn't quite so alone; almost as if there was something close by, and it had very ill intent.

Rutu looked frantically from one side to another, hoping and praying that it was all just his imagination. After a long while of hearing and seeing nothing, he finally started to calm down just enough to finish dropping, when he suddenly heard a sound that filled him with dread. *Tap-tap. Tap-tap. Tap-tap.*

It was as clear as if it were right next to him and whatever confidence he had left was now gone. He tried to stand up fully, but his body was petrified with fear. His heart was pounding loudly in his chest, and his breath was trembling. *Tap-tap. Tap-tap.* It was getting closer, but Rutu's body still refused to move. He looked around for his weapon until he saw it on the wood pile not too far away.

Finally regaining control of his body, Rutu slowly reached for his weapon, his trembling hands gripping the handle. With his weapon back in hand, Rutu's courage and confidence rose just a little, but he wanted to get back to camp as quickly as possible. Rutu poked his head from around the wood pile looking to his left. The camp was in clear sight, with the candles lit around the walls. Rutu was about to make a run for it when the terrible sense of dread returned. Rutu turned to his right where he was met with a pair of wide yellow eyes.

A sudden horrified scream echoed through the hall. Azalar awoke with a start and sprang upwards, instantly grabbing his needle weapon beside him and dashed towards the front of the camp. The rest of the camp had been awoken by the horrible scream and they were all in a panic wondering who or what caused that scream. Azalar had just reached the front of the camp, where Ragath and Razor had already arrived moments prior. "What happened?" cried Razor.

"There was a scream coming from beyond the wall!" cried a dark blue mouse buck named Fiz from the top of the wall.

"Who was it that screamed?" asked Azalar. Bark, Brim, Mith and Borith arrived only a moment later.

"We don't know!" cried another mouse with bright dove colored fur named Torno. "We're doing a head-count as we speak." Ragath looked at the rodents that lined the wall, and he noticed that one rat was not at their post.

"Where's Rutu?" he asked in a low voice.

"He went out beyond the wall!" said a voice. Ragath and Azalar turned to see Roth running their way.

"The stupid rat left his post?" cried Razor in frustration.

"Why would Rutu leave the campsite?" asked Azalar. Upon arriving, Roth glared at the little mouse.

"I don't answer to you, little-" he didn't finish as Ragath was already directly in front of him, his eyes hard and his teeth bare as he looked down at the light gray rat.

"Answer the question!" Ragath said in a low hiss. The action caught both Roth, Razor and even Azalar by surprise. Though he had much anger in him, Ragath rarely lost his composure and lashed out in anger. The only exceptions were with the humans back at the lab. Roth's eyes were wide, his body stiffened with fear.

"He left a few moments ago to *zet pfetta*," Roth said quickly. He then pointed to the direction Rutu went in. "He left that way!" Ragath looked to Azalar and the two rodents, along with Razor, Bark, Brim, Mith and Borith and many other mice and rats, rushed out of the camp walls and into the hall. They scattered and searched all around, but the gloom of the hall made it difficult to see anything and the light from the candles of the camp made it difficult for their eyes to adjust. They called out to Rutu, but there was no response. Bogger and Nikamius then rushed out of the camp with lit candles, but each candle was cut halfway for easy carry. This made things a lot easier to see and they were able to search deeper into the hall. Azalar separated from the rest of the group and had just rounded a corner of a pile of wood, and that's when he saw a rat huddled down in a small ball on the floor. It was Rutu and he was shaking horribly.

"I found him!" Azalar called out. The others quickly rushed over to where Azalar was, where they saw Rutu shaking on the ground, his eyes wide with terror.

"Rutu?" Nikamius said calmly, kneeling down and slowly placed a gentle paw on the rat's back. But the moment he did, Rutu cried and jumped away as if his paw had burned him. "Rutu, it's us! You're safe. What happened?" But Rutu didn't look his way, nor did he respond right away. Instead, he stared out into the darkness, his breath heavily and shaking. After a few moments, Rutu raised a trembling paw and pointed towards the dark hall.

"Out there!" Rutu said softly. "Those eyes! There's something out there!"

"What eyes?" asked Nikamius. "What is out there? Speak!" Slowly, Rutu turned his head to Nikamius, and the elder rat could now truly see the terror in his eyes. Rutu tried to speak, but he had great difficulty and all that came out were small stutters. Finally, after a moment or so, Rutu was finally able to speak.

"The Fornóc," he said. Nikamius immediately looked to Azalar, who had the same look of worry on his face. What they had been dreading had been realized. The Fornóc were here, and they were close. Ragath stepped forward and approached Rutu, his eyes full of anger as he grabbed Rutu by his fur and lifted him off the floor.

"You fool!" Ragath hollered. "What were you thinking? Wandering off alone like that? How could you be so reckless?" Rutu was startled and had difficulty finding his words.

"I'm sorry, Ragath! I-I…"

"Ragath! That's enough!" cried Nikamius. Ragath turned to the elder mouse with a glare. But Nikamius did not back down. "The poor buck has already been through enough. Let him be." Ragath bared his teeth and gave a low growl. But then he noticed that every mouse and rat was staring at him in alarm; even Razor stood wide-eyed at the giant rat's outburst. Ragath then looked back at the quivering rat in his paws, cowering like a small pup. And with a disgruntled sigh, he softened his demeanor, if only just a little, and released his grip on his fur and stepped back. Rutu collapsed to the floor, his body still trembling. Nikamius rushed to his side.

"You are alright, my friend," Nikamius said. "Everything is alright now." Rutu slowly began to calm down, his breathing became steady, and his body slowly ceased trembling. However, when Rutu looked up and saw a shadow scurry across the floor from left to right just out of the light from the candles. The look of horror returned in his eyes, and he let out another terrible scream that gave everyone a start. Rutu pointed behind Ragath.

"There!" Rutu cried. "The Fornóc!" Everyone turned in the direction he was pointing to, Bogger raising his candle higher to give more light. And there, just at the edge of the light, something small sped away.

"Over there!" cried Bark. Azalar turned to a pair of mice next to him.

"Take Rutu back to camp!" he ordered. "Then have everyone gather whatever weapons they can find and be ready for a possible attack!"

"Yes, Azalar!" The two mice said. Azalar then turned to the rest of the band of rodents.

"Capture that thing! Don't let it escape!"

"Is that wise?" asked Nikamius. "We don't know what's out there."

"We need to know what we're dealing with!" replied Azalar. He then sped off to give chase, quickly followed by the rest of the band. Ragath stayed for a moment before turning to Razor.

"Get back to the camp and prepare for a possible attack!" He ordered. Razor nodded before turning around and ran back to the walls as Ragath hurried to catch up with the others. Azalar and the rest of the band chased the dark figure through the hall as it dashed from cover to cover, trying desperately to lose its pursuers. Azalar nearly lost sight of it on a few occasions, but thanks to Bogger and his candle, they were able to keep the chase. Just then, the dark figure ducked behind a massive pile of stone, wood and debris. Azalar was merely moments behind it and rounded the corner and found the creature trapped on all sides with wood and stone piled high on two sides and the massive stone wall that marked the edge of the hall. The dark figure was trying to climb one of the massive stone blocks, but it was far too high for it to reach. Suddenly it turned and faced Azalar, but instead of bracing itself for a fight, it immediately scurried to the far corner and curled itself into a small ball.

Azalar stared at the thing in front of him. It was much smaller than he expected a Fornóc to be. Azalar wasn't sure, but he thought he could hear soft sobbing coming from it. At that moment the rest of the band had arrived and with Bogger's and Nikamius' lights they could now see exactly what they had been chasing. And they were shocked at what they saw. There, curled up in a small ball in the corner, trembling and sobbing, was a small young chipmunk.

"Please!" said the young chipmunk, her voice small and frail. "Please don't hurt me!" All the rodents looked confusingly at one another.

"That's not a Fornóc," said Bark.

"No, it is not," replied Nikamius. "Azalar, seeing the poor creature cowering before them, slowly lowered his weapon and placed it on the floor. He took a single step towards the chipmunk, but she cowered away from him.

"Please don't hurt me!" the chipmunk cried again. Azalar stopped where he was and raised his paws up to show that he meant no harm.

"It's alright little one," Azalar said softly. "No one is going to hurt you." He was about to take another step closer, when suddenly there came a deep cry from above, startling them all. Just then, another figure leaped from the top of the stone blocks on the left hand side and landed between Azalar and the chipmunk, causing Azalar jumped back in surprise. Standing in front of him, with a hard look of anger and defiance, was a gray mole. But this mole was standing on its hind legs and its arms were longer and muscular. Its eyes were black and hard as it glared dangerously at the tan mouse. It bared its claws out in front of him and appeared ready to fight. Azalar noted that one of its claws on its right paw was broken, still swollen and red with dried blood.

"Sûtkal!" he cried. "Kash nor crësha!" The mole seemed to be speaking a language that Azalar could not understand. But, nonetheless, Azalar kept his paws in a show that he meant them no harm.

"Whoa there!" he said. "We're not going to hurt anyone! We thought you were someone else." The mole showed no sign of calming down, however. In fact, he only looked even more ready to fight. Brim, Mith, Borith and Ragath noticed this and immediately stepped forward with their weapons ready. Nikamius quickly rushed out and stood next to Azalar to stop them.

"Everyone, stop! Let's all calm down!" he cried out. Nikamius then turned to the mole with a gentle smile and lowered his voice to a softer tone. "It's alright, my friend. We are not here to fight." The mole turned his head slightly, but never took his eyes off of Azalar or the other rodents.

"Elia! Anûl dú míyàn?" he called back in his own language.

"Énì. Suíl nof miyàn," said the young chipmunk in the same language. She slowly stood up and looked at Azalar. Azalar lowered himself slightly and gave the young chipmunk a small smile.

"What is your name, young one?" he asked. The young chipmunk was for a moment, looking towards the floors with nervous eyes before looking back up at Azalar.

"I'm Elia," she answered timidly and then gestured to the mole beside her. "And this is Kilma. I'm sorry. We didn't mean to intrude. We saw the lights and we were hoping to find a safe place to hide." A small frown formed on Azalar's lips.

"Hide?" Azalar asked. "Hide from what? And where did you all come from?" It was then that Azalar took notice that both the chipmunk and the mole were standing on their hind legs, just like they were. He raised an eyebrow curiously. "Did you come from Helgan's lab as well?" The moment Azalar said the name, the young chipmunk flinched, and the mole's eyes narrowed into a hard glare. Though visibly shaken, the young chipmunk nodded her head.

"Yes," she said, her voice low and trembling. "We just escaped from that horrible place. There were more of us, but we got separated. And we've been wandering these tunnels for a long time." Ragath stepped forward and glaring at the duo.

"There are more of you? How many more?" demanded Ragath. The young chipmunk flinched back, while the mole raised his claws and returned the glare.

"I don't know!" the chipmunk cried, almost on the verge of tears as she stared up at the giant black rat. "I-I think around a hundred or so. But Kilma and I got separated during all the chaos. I-I don't know where they are."

"Ragath! Calm down! There's no need to interrogate her on that now," said Azalar. However, there was a burning question lingering in Azalar's mind and he returned his gaze to the young chipmunk.

"And was it you that had been following us in the tunnels?" asked Azalar. The chipmunk's eyes widened at the question, but she soon lowered her eyes to the floor.

"Yes," she admitted. "We saw you back in that chamber when you escaped from those three giant monsters. We figured that you must have found a way out. So, we waited for them to leave, and we followed you down the hole. And we've been following you ever since." The young chipmunk bowed her head. "I'm sorry! I know we shouldn't have followed you. We should have approached you first, but we were afraid of how you would react to us. Please forgive us." The chipmunk looked up and expected to see anger in his eyes. But when she lifted her head, there was no anger at all; in fact, there appeared to be relief as Azalar let out a sigh.

"Well, that is a relief to hear," Azalar said." Azalar smiled at the young chipmunk.

"I'm Azalar. I can't tell you what a relief it is to know that it was only you two we've been hearing all this time." The young chipmunk frowned and raised an eyebrow slightly.

"I'm sorry?" Elia asked. "What do you mean?" Azalar gave a small chuckle.

"It's just a relief to know that it was only the two of you all this time," he said.

"Rutu will be pleased to know that it was just a chipmunk and a mole that startled him in the darkness and not the Fornóc," said Nikamius.

"Umm," said Elia hesitantly, causing Azalar and Nikamius to look her way. "Kilma and I weren't the ones that frightened your friend." Azalar's face immediately fell into a frown.

"What?" he asked. Elia suddenly felt a little nervous by his change in demeanor.

"Kilma was out looking for food in the other direction, away from your people, and I was all alone. That's when I heard a terrible scream. I didn't know what to do, so I panicked and ran off to find Kilma. But I had no idea where I was going. And that's when I came across all of you."

"So, it wasn't you that startled Rutu?" Azalar asked. Elia slowly shook her head. Azalar had an unsettling feeling. "But what about in the collapsed tunnels where we were resting? Was that you sneaking around in the dark?" Once again, Elia slowly shook her head. But this time her eyes were wider.

"No," she answered. "We were hiding in one of those giant metal things. But then I woke up to something walking past us. They didn't notice us, but they were close. Then they ran past us again, going back down the tunnel. And when I tried to peek out at what it was, all I saw were terrible red eyes." The band of rodents each looked at one another with an unsettling demeanor.

"Was this the last you saw of them?" asked Nikamius hastily. Elia shook her head.

"No, I'm afraid not. Just before you entered this great chamber, we heard a noise coming from down the hall behind us. The scattering of many paws followed close behind, but always kept their distance. Then when you entered through that hole in that wall, we could hear them getting closer. It felt like they were right behind us. We stayed behind the wall so that we wouldn't be spotted. Then when you were out of sight, we entered the hall, but we still lingered back by the hole just in case.

"That's when a terribly loud crashing noise came and echoed throughout the halls. But it wasn't the crashing sound that scared us. It was the shrieks that came from the room that we just left. It was horrible. They sounded mad. I looked back at the hole and saw those same horrid eyes again. But this time there were more of them. Kilma and I immediately ran away as fast as we could and tried to find a place to hide. Whatever those things are, they're out there. And they're coming."

A sense of dread and horror overcame the rodents after hearing Elia's tale. Fear began to grip them as many of them huddled together, looking from side to side and this way and that, searching for, but also hoping not to see, those horrible eyes in the darkness. Even Ragath was on edge, which was very rare. The large black rat held his sword out and pointed it in every direction he turned so that he could be prepared for anything that might jump out at him. Azalar, for his part, was nearly petrified where he stood. His blood ran cold, and he felt his fur stand on ends. There was no doubt in Azalar's mind now that the Fornóc were there, somewhere in that giant hall, and they were close.

Suddenly there came a noise off in the distance. A low rumble, then the sound of many feet scurrying across the stone floor. It came from nearly all sides, and they seemed to be getting closer by the second. Realizing what was happening, Azalar's adrenaline peaked, and he quickly turned to the other behind him.

"We need to get back to camp, now!" Azalar cried as he quickly spun around and picked up his needle weapon off the floor before he and the other rodents quickly turned and sped back to camp as quickly as they could.

"What about us?" cried Elia from behind. The band of rodents stopped and turned back to the young chipmunk, who was clinging close to Kilma as he held her protectively in his large arms.

"You both will come back with us," Nikamius said. Elia and Kilma looked at one another in surprise.

"You want to bring these strangers into our camp?" asked Ragath. "You can't be serious?"

"I never thought I'd say it, but I'm afraid I must agree with Ragath," said Brim awkwardly. "We know nothing about these two. They could be a danger to us." Azalar looked back at the young chipmunk and the mole. While the mole did appear intimidating and looked capable of causing a bit of trouble if he wanted to, the young chipmunk looked absolutely terrified. With little time to think, Azalar made his decision.

"We're taking them back with us," Azalar said.

"Azalar, are you sure about this?" asked Bark.

"Yes. We can't leave these creatures out here to die. We're bringing them back with us. And that's the end of it!" Azalar then turned back to the mole and the chipmunk and extended his paw out. "Come with us. You'll be safe." The mole and the chipmunk pair looked at one another for a brief moment and began to speak in their foreign language. Kilma didn't look so sure about the idea, but when Elia nodded her head and a few more words, his features softened, and he gave a defeated sigh. Elia then turned back to Azalar. Though hesitant, she slowly stepped forward and accepted his paw.

A few minutes later, Azalar and the others had arrived back at the camp with their two new guests. When they arrived, they saw that the walls and the entrance to the camp were all packed with rodents. While Azalar and the others were out, Razor had done what he was told and prepared the camp in full defense mode, as ever rat and mouse were at the walls with whatever weapons they could find. Razor had a large group of armed rats at the front. Amara, Frella and Della were there as well. The moment Azalar and the others were in sight, Amara rushed out from the camp entrance and embraced her fréfil.

"Are you alright?" Amara asked. Azalar could hear the worry and relief in her voice and smiled reassuringly as he returned the embrace.

"Yes," he answered. "We just met some unexpected guests." Azalar stepped aside to reveal Elia and Kilma. Amara was taken aback by the two in front of her.

"Oh, my!" she said as she placed a paw over her mouth.

"But we have no time for introductions," said Azalar, suddenly becoming very serious. "We need to prepare everyone. We are not alone down here." Amara's eyes widened at the tone of her fréfil's voice, and a cold shiver of fear ran down her back. Azalar then took Amara by the paw and made their way back to the camp. Razor, however, stopped them just outside the entrance.

"What in Háth's name is this?" Razor said with a scowl, gesturing to the two newcomers behind Azalar. "We're welcoming strangers now?"

"This is Elia and Kilma," said Azalar quickly. "They will be staying with us for the time being."

"And why are we bringing them in here?" Razor demanded, his furrowed in a harsh glare. "We're just going to be welcoming in every little creature we find down here, are we?" Azalar's fell into a frown.

"Razor, we don't have time for this!" Azalar retorted. "The Fornóc are out there! We need to prepare the camp for a possible attack. Hearing that name, the rodents began to stir with concern and whisper amongst themselves. Razor however did not move and stared down at the mouse.

"The Fornóc are just an old pup's tale!" Razor hissed, refusing to believe such a ridiculous story. "They don't exist!"

"Razor, this is no joke!" cried Azalar. "Whether it is them or not, there is something out there! We need to gather everyone we can and fortify the camp."

"You do not give orders to us, mouse!" Razor shouted.

"This isn't about who is giving orders! It's about working together to keep our people safe!" Razor scoffed.

"And that's why you're bringing in complete strangers into our camp?" he said with a smug look. Is that keeping our people safe?" Azalar was growing tired and impatient with this argument. But he knew that no matter what answer he gave him, it would never be enough to satisfy Razor.

"We weren't going to just leave them out there alone, Razor," Azalar said honestly. "We have to look out for all those in need." Razor let out a sarcastic laugh before turning to Ragath.

"Ragath, you can't be serious. We're not seriously going to accept these *ikhrórin* inside. They are not even of our kind! And now this little mouse expects us to take orders from him?" But Ragath gave no direct response at that moment as he simply stared at the floor with a deadpan expression. A moment later, he looked up at Razor, his eyes dark and serious.

"Do as he says," Ragath ordered. Razor's eyes widened for a moment, then his face fell into a frown.

"Ragath-"

"I said do as he says!" Ragath hollered, not letting him finish. "Get as many rats as you can together and go get more wood to fortify the walls. Now!" There was silence through the camp as tension filled the air. Every rodent looked on at the two largest of the rats staring each other down.

"Yes, Ragath," Razor said with a sneer. He then turned to the rodents of the camp and hollered as loud as he could. "You hear him! Get your sorry *nàhras* moving!" The whole camp suddenly went into action as everyone scattered about to get things done. Azalar turned to Bark, Brim, Mith and Borith and told them to go through with the plan they had before and gather the teams. They then sped off to complete their tasks while

Nikamius took Elia and Kilma inside the camp. Azalar turned to see Ragath just as he was walking past him, his head down and his eyes towards the floor as he held his sword close to his side. Azalar continued to watch the large rat until he disappeared within the walls and the crowd.

"Azalar?" asked Amara. Azalar turned to see his beloved mate staring at him with concern. He smiled to give her comfort.

"Everything will be alright, my love," Azalar said. He then retook one of Amara's paws and led her inside the camp. But in truth, Azalar wasn't so sure. Not only was he concerned about the growing threat of whatever lies within these horrid tunnels, he was also concerned about the large black rat, unsure of what to make of his recent outbursts. Something was definitely bothering Ragath, Azalar knew that much. But that would have to wait. There was a lot that needed to be done before the Fornóc, or whatever was out there, arrived. Azalar had a sinking feeling in his stomach that there wasn't much time left.

Chapter XIV

It had been around two hours and the camp was now more fortified than before. The walls were higher, nearly twice their original height; and a huge barricade had been built at the front of the camp, with splinters of wood and rusty nails and metal poking outwards towards the gloom of the hall. More rodents had been placed on watch, almost double in size; and with the new weapons that had been scavenged; whatever nails and pieces of sharp metal that could be fashioned into makeshift weapons, every mouse and rat buck was now armed and ready, or as ready as they believed they were to be.

Azalar was patrolling around the walls of the fort, making sure that all was well and that there were no weak points that the enemy could exploit; and as far as his limited knowledge of construction saw, there were none. Azalar, nonetheless, made continuous routes along the walls, checking on and making sure that each watch group and patrol that he came across had what they needed. He even made sure to double check on Reemus and his friends, who had once again volunteered to take watch on the walls.

After the fourth round of inspecting, Azalar took one of the spare candles that had been set aside and made his way towards the back of the camp, which was a good few meters away from the camp. There, many rodents had been hard at work constructing a long platform that would hopefully take them across the gap of the bridge. No one knew how long the gap was, for it was nothing but gloom as far as they could see. Everyone was back at the camp now, and as Azalar wandered past, he inspected their little bridge. There were three long and thin platforms, each spanning two dozen or so mice long. The platforms had three layers of planks that overlapped one another, with long nails that had been hammered into the best of the rodents' abilities that stuck out through the tops halfway. They looked sturdy enough, at least according to Bogger and with what limited knowledge he had on the subject. All that was left was to place them together before they moved them to the bridge gap.

Azalar walked under the metal bars that hung horizontal above his head and wandered toward the edge of the bridge where it had collapsed. From there, he gazed out into the darkness that could possibly be their way out. Azalar peered over the edge, where the sound of roaring waters could be heard from below. From his perspective, he seemed to be staring into a deep endless abyss, where a terrible beast roared and raged below, waiting for him to fall in so that it may devour him whole. A shiver ran down Azalar's spine at the thought of falling down there and he slowly stepped away from the edge, where he then made his way back to camp.

As soon as Azalar crossed the huge archway, he doused his candle and placed it to the side with the rest of the spare candles. He then went back to the campfire next to the newly replaced lit candle in the center of the camp, where Amara, Bark, Frella, Brim, Della, Bogger, Nikamius, Borith and Mith were waiting, along with their two new guests as well. Once at the fire, Azalar sat down next to his beloved, who nuzzled up next to Azalar and rested her head on his shoulder.

Azalar returned the embrace and let out an exhausted sigh. He still had not gotten the proper rest he needed.

"Everything alright, my love?" asked Amara.

"Yes, I believe so," Azalar answered with a tired sigh. "Just wanted to make sure that everything is in order."

"I told you that you have nothing to worry about," Bogger said while poking the fire beneath the can with a thin nail. "I have gone through all the preparations. Once the last team comes back, we should have everything we need to complete our little bridge to cross the gap. Worse case we simply add more to the platform as we go. It shouldn't be too difficult."

"I know, Bogger. But I can't help it," said Azalar. "We've already made it so far. I just don't want anything bad to happen right when we're so close to freedom."

"I understand your troubles, my friend," said Nikamius. "But we must take heart. Like you said: We've already made it this far. All we need to do now is have faith that everything will work out the way it's supposed to."

"Easier said than done, Nikamius," said Bark. "Just sitting here waiting. I don't like it. Why don't we just cross over now?"

"Because we don't actually know that it will even hold us once we begin the crossing," answered Bogger. "We haven't had the chance or opportunity to test that part. For all we know, it could collapse under all our weight if we all pile on it at once. And not only that, we don't even know how large the gap is anyway. A lot needs to be taken into account first before we even attempt such a dangerous crossing. And everyone is already weary. No one has gotten a proper sleep in a while. So, it's best that we take a short break, gather our strength and form a proper plan."

"As much as I hate to say it, Bark," said Azalar. "But Bogger is right about this. Trust me, I hate waiting here as much as you do. But if we do things while not thinking things through, rodents could get hurt or worse." Bark thought about this for a moment and nodded in agreement, though he was still both impatient and anxious. Azalar smiled at his oldest friend, understanding exactly how the dark brown mouse was feeling. He then looked to his new guests, who were huddled up together on the other side of the fire. He thought they must be tired and hungry after the journey they've had.

"How are you two holding up?" Azalar asked gently. Elia glanced up and gave a small weary smile.

"We're doing alright," she answered. "Thank you." Kilma remained silent.

"You two must be hungry," said Della, noticing that they haven't eaten anything since they arrived.

"Oh no! We're fine, thank you!" However, at that moment, the poor chipmunks stomach growled, indicating that the young one was indeed hungry. The young chipmunk covered her face in embarrassment as everyone chuckled and giggled in merriment around the fire. Kilma remained silent, though he did have a small smirk at how uncomfortable Elia looked. Nikamius stood up, picked up one of the bugs, a decent sized cockroach, from the fire and gently offered it to Elia.

"Here you are, young one," Nikamius said with a warm smile. "Eat as much as you can. Though I must warn you, it has a rather unique taste to it." Elia glanced from Nikamius to the bug in his paws before slowly taking it in her own. She gave the dead insect a sniff, then winced from the fetid that entered her nostrils. She was very hesitant to eat it, but the rumbling that echoed in her stomach left her with little choice. She shut her eyes tightly and bit down on the lifeless, slightly roasted insect. The taste nearly caused her to gag, but she did her best to keep it in her mouth. After a few tedious moments of chewing, she finally swallowed. She stuck out her tongue in disgust. Everyone let out a hearty laugh.

"It's alright, young one," said Nikamius while chuckling. "It's not our idea of a good meal either. But your growing body needs all the nutrients that you can get. So, try to get at least a few more bites in." Elia looked down at the cockroach in her paws and grimaced. She really didn't want to put it back in her mouth again. Still, when she looked up into the encouraging eyes of Nikamius, she relented and took another bite of the foul cockroach. Kilma watched on with a smile as the young chipmunk, happy that the young one was finally getting something in her stomach.

"What about you?" asked Frella, gaining the gray mole's attention. "You haven't had anything to eat, have you? A stout mole like yourself must be hungry for…" she picked up a long bug with many legs on both sides, giving it a distasteful look, "whatever this thing is." For a moment, Kilma looked at the long insect, a centipede from what it looked like. He then gave a shrug and took the bug and bit down with no hesitation. The rodents all watched on in amazement as the mole gave no expression of disgust or discomfort. In fact, after Kilma had swallowed the insect with ease, he took another, much larger bite. All eyes were wide as they stared at Kilma. After he was finished, he looked up at the surrounding rodents with a smirk.

"Dwimor anûl niní bógmúku," Kilma said in his own language. The others looked at one another confused. Elia covered her mouth and let out a small giggle at their confusion. This earned a questioning look from Bark

"What did he say?" asked the dark brown mouse.

"He said that moles are natural bug eaters." Elia said with a smile. "So, they are more accustomed to eating this kind of food."

"So, you two can understand each other?" asked Azalar. "How is that?" Elia had just swallowed another small bite from the cockroach, though not without a great deal of reluctancy, before she turned back to Azalar.

"Well, our cages were right next to each other back at Helgan's lab," she said. "All my life I have known Kilma. He has been a dear friend to me; almost like a second father. And he has looked out for me. My parents were around of course, not saying that they weren't, but they were always so weak from the tortures that the humans put them through. So, most of the time, my siblings and I had to fend for ourselves."

"Where is your family now?" asked Della.

"My parents are probably with the others." Elia's face fell further to a mournful look. "We got separated in the chaos. My siblings, however, are no longer alive."

"Oh Háth!" cried Amara. "I am so sorry."

"How did they die?" asked Borith aloud, though he instantly regretted asking as Elia shifted uncomfortably where she sat. Noticing this, Nikamius placed a paw on the young chipmunk's shoulder, causing her to look up at the elder mouse.

"You don't have to say anything if you don't want to," Nikamius said. Elia stared at him for a moment before she gave him a soft smile.

"No, it's fine," she said before turning back to the rest of the rodents. "One of the humans stuck us with this strange liquid that caused our bodies to change. The process was terrible, and my body hurt so much. I don't remember how long I was in pain for. But at the end of it all, I woke up and found that my body had changed, and all of my siblings were dead."

"That's exactly what happened to us," said Frella. She then gestured to her right side just above her hip. "They took these big needles and jabbed them into our sides. The next thing we all knew was excruciating pain, then waking up to find our bodies had changed." Borith looked down towards the floor, his face full of sorrow and anguish.

"We've lost dear loved ones, as well," Borith said as he glanced over to Mith, who was also looking down in sadness, and placed a paw on his dear friend's shoulder.

"So, we know a thing or two about the pain you've gone through," said Nikamius. Elia glanced at all the rodents around her, and her heart ached. Even Kilma, who had given no sign of expression throughout the conversation, had a deep frown of sympathy. Elia then looked to the elder mouse and placed a gentle paw upon his arm.

"I'm so sorry," Elia said. She then glanced around at the other rodents. "I'm so sorry for all of you."

"It's quite alright, my dear," said Nikamius as he patted Elia's paw. "We've faced many hardships before. At least we can be at peace knowing that all of our loved ones are in the arms of the Great One, and that they do not need to suffer anymore." Elia smiled at Nikamius. There was a moment of silence that followed, that soon became quite awkward after a while.

"So how did you guys escape anyway?" asked Bark. Elia responded by gesturing to Kilma.

"Kilma was able to reach over the cage and open it with his claws while the humans weren't looking."

"Is that how he broke his claw?" asked Azalar, pointing to the broken tip on Kilma's finger. Elia looked towards Kilma, who instinctively looked down at his broken claw before closing his paw into a fist in an attempt to hide it, slightly wincing from the pain.

"Yes," Elia answered. "After that, we were able to free everyone, when everything suddenly went loud, and a red light started shining on and off. That's when we started hearing screaming from outside. That's when we saw all the chaos happening."

"But how did you two get separated from the rest of your people?" asked Brim.

"As our people traveled through the halls, a giant beast appeared out of nowhere and attacked us."

"What was it?" Azalar asked with interest. "Did it stand on two legs and have huge tusks and reddish skin?" Elia shook her head vigorously.

"No. It was a terrifying beast. Its body was massive with a long tail. It must have been nearly a human high just standing on all four of its legs. And it had huge horns all along the back of its body and all the way down to its tail. It had long and sharp claws on all paws. And its teeth were so sharp that it tore us apart with every bite. It killed so many of our people. We tried to fight back, but our teeth couldn't break its hard, scaly skin. And its eyes stared at us with nothing but hunger and malice. It was a monster!"

"What kind of beast is that?" asked Bark to no one in particular.

"I don't know, but it's definitely not anything we've seen," said Nikamius.

"Or anything that I've read about," said Bogger. "But no doubt it was another one of Helgan's experiments."

"But how did you both get away?" asked Frella.

"Our people were hiding in this great chamber when that beast attacked. It chased us out until we came to this hall that split three different ways. The beast drove down different paths; Kilma's people fleeing down one hall, my people down another. I was separated from my parents and was trapped by the beast. But then Kilma came and grabbed me just as the beast tried to snatch me in its teeth. We ran down so many twists and turns to avoid the beast. Eventually it must have taken interest in something else and left us alone."

"Oh, you poor things!" cried Della. "Separated from your families like that. How terrible!" Elia glanced downward sadly.

"Yes," she said solemnly. "I just hope that they are all okay."

"I'm sure they're fine," said Nikamius. "Afterall, you've made it this far with just the two of you. So, I wouldn't be too worried, my dear. If they are as courageous as you are, I have no doubt in my mind that they'll be safe."

"I suppose," said Elia, not entirely convinced. "I just miss them terribly."

"We will do all we can to help you find your family, dear one," said Amara. "Won't we, my love?" Azalar was a little caught off guard by his fréfil's statement and glanced over at her with surprise.

"Uh…" Azalar said with hesitation. Amara looked back at her mate with a warm smile, but her eyes were pleading with him to help this poor creature. However, Azalar wasn't too sure about it, as he was far more focused on keeping his own people safe; and running about trying to find a large band of chipmunks didn't seem like a safe and logical venture. But as hard as he could, Azalar could not find it in his heart to say no.

"Yes, of course," Azalar said with a smile, earning a grateful and loving nuzzle from his beloved fréfil.

"I agree wholeheartedly!" Frella chimed in excitedly. Truth be told, she was rather enjoying this whole adventure, despite the threat of the Fornóc looming over them. Being trapped in a cage at the lab all her life, this was the most excited she had ever felt in her life. And the prospect of going off on an expedition into the unknown to find a whole other group of rodents was more than she could hope for. "This will be exciting! An adventure out into the world to find new people to befriend. I think it's a fantastic idea. Don't you, Bark?" Bark, who had seemingly been paying more attention to the insect he was eating than to what was going on, looked up at the group around him at the mention of his name.

"Huh?" he asked, confused. This earned him a small smack from Frella's tail to the back of his head. Though it wasn't hard, it still left a slight sting. "Ow!" he cried. This caused everyone to laugh at the dark brown mouse's slight misfortune, even Elia couldn't help herself and let out a small giggle. Although Bark too, let out a small chuckle himself. After everyone had calmed down a bit, Nikamius spoke.

"But don't you worry, young one," he said gently to Elia, "we will do all we can to help you find your loved ones." Elia smiled at the elder mouse, almost as if she believed in their words. Elia turned to look at the fire in front of her when she then noticed something in Amara's paws.

"Excuse me, Miss Amara" she said gently, but still loud enough to gain Amara's attention.

"Yes, dear?" Amara asked with a gentle smile.

"I was just wondering what that was in your paws?" Amara looked down at the blue gem she held.

"Oh this?" she asked. "This belonged to a good friend of ours. It was one of the last things she gave to us before she left. She was very dear to us. She was human, but she was a good human. She actually cared for us and taught us so much. She even helped us escape from Helgan's lab." Amara smiled down at the blue earring, gently caressing it. "I've held on to this so that we can remember her for what she did for us." Azalar then held up his needle.

"She even gave me this needle," he said with pride. "It has been of great use to us. Without this needle, or her, we would never have had the chance to be free. And it is another reason for us to remember her. She was our friend. We will never forget what she did for us.”

Elia turned her head to one side and looked curiously at the pair of mice.

“And did this human have long, bright colored fur on her head?” Elia asked. “And did she have another blue gem in her other ear just like that?” Both Azalar and Amara glanced back at the young chipmunk.

“Yes, she did!” said Azalar. “You saw her?” Elia nodded her head.

“Where? When?” asked Nikamius earnestly.

“Back at the lab,” Elia answered.

“Is she alright?” asked Della. It was at this moment that the young chipmunk's face fell to a slight frown.

“I’m sorry, but I don’t know,” she answered honestly. “Just after we had all escaped from our cages, a human female entered the room. Our cages were all empty, but I don’t think she noticed. In fact, I don’t think she was even looking for us. But she was looking around the room frantically. And she looked panicked for some reason, as if she was looking for something important; but she looked like she was afraid. But we didn't pay her much mind and quietly made our way to the small passage in the wall. It was covered by a metal cover that a few of Kilma’s people had managed to open slightly. Most of our people were able to get out before she could notice us. Only Kilma, my mother and father, and I were the last ones behind. But just before Kilma and I were able to make our way across the room without being spotted, she stepped in front of us.

“We thought we were caught, but when the human looked down at us, she looked at us with soft eyes and a smile. She then stepped aside. ‘*Go!*’ she told us. It was at that moment that the doors to the lab slam open. I only managed to glance at the door to see Helgan standing there, and the fear in her face, before Kilma picked me up and carried me across the room and threw me inside. But then the metal cover snapped shut, and Kilma was trapped in the room. We tried to get it opened again, but he told us to just run and get out and that he would find a way out himself."

"Well, I suppose that worked out in the end," said Borith, gesturing to the mole sitting beside the chipmunk. Elia turned to Kilma and gave a soft smile.

"Yes, it did," Elia said. "After we escaped through the passage, we climbed up this tall shaft. My mother had to carry me, but the walls were so slick that she nearly fell, as many unfortunately had. But once we reached the top and traveled through seemingly end-less paths, we found another way out through another metal covered hole like the one we came in through, and we found ourselves in this giant hallway. Kilma eventually found us as we were trying to find a place to hide, and… well… you know the rest of the story from there."

"But what about Alice?" asked Azalar earnestly. "What happened to her?" Elia shook her head.

"I'm truly sorry, but I really don't know. Kilma never mentioned what happened after we separated, and I never thought to bring it up. I only remembered just now when I saw that blue stone in your paws and remembered seeing a similar stone that this '*Alice*' was wearing in one of her ears."

"And what does he say now?" asked Bogger. "Can he tell us what happened to her?" Everyone turned to the mole, who was seemingly not paying them much attention until he noticed everyone's eyes on him. Hesitantly, Elia conversed with Kilma in his language. They talked for what seemed like an eternity, though in reality it was only about a minute. Finally, Elia seemed to ask the question they had been waiting for, as there was a long pause. Kilma looked at the rodents around and a small frown formed on his lips as he slowly shook his head.

"Suíl atzem," Kilma said. Elia lowered her head for a moment before turning to the others.

"He says he's sorry," she said wistfully. But there was no need for translation. Though they could not understand him, the band of rodents knew from the tone of his voice confirmed their fears as each rodent lowered their heads towards the floor.

"Does he know how she died, at least?" asked Bark. Elia translated the question to Kilma, and he responded in short, brief sentences. Elia translated his words.

"He says that there was a fight. He said that Helgan shoved Alice into some sort of machine. Helgan then pulled a switch. Then there was a bright light. That's all he knows. I'm sorry." The silence that followed was deafening, save only by the crackling of the fire and the occasional chatting from the surrounding rodents.

"I can't believe it," said Brim. Della nuzzled closer to her mate, tears forming in her eyes. Amara held Alice's earring close to her chest while Azalar wrapped an arm around her shoulders.

"Such a terrible fate," said Nikamius. He then stood up and addressed the whole group. "She was such a kind human. Though we have not truly known her for very long, she has shown us tremendous kindness. More than any human that we have known all our lives. She did her best to shield us from those awful, torturous experiments when she could. She taught so much, and in turn we taught her more about ourselves. And through this, something grew into something none of us ever thought possible, a friendship between humans and rodents. She will always be a friend to us all. We will always remember her. We will never forget all that she has done for us. May she rest in peace and may Hath watch over her soul."

"Hear, hear," everyone said in unison. Just then, Azalar noticed movement to his right. He turned to see Ragath walking through the camp and heading towards the bridge. Azalar's eyes followed the largest of the rats until he walked through the archway. Curious, Azalar stood up and was about to follow the black rat until Amara spoke up.

"Where are you going, Azalar?" his fréfil asked. Azalar smiled down at his beloved as he gently placed a paw on her cheek.

"I'll be right back, my love," he said, then turned around and headed back towards the bridge. There, he found Ragath standing at the edge of the collapsed bridge, staring out into the darkness beyond. Slowly, Azalar made his way towards the black rat until he was around a foot away. He spoke gently so as to not spook him.

"Ragath?" Azalar asked. Ragath didn't respond right away, nor look his way. He stared out into the gloom of the cavern that was formerly the bridge for a moment or so before he finally spoke.

"What do you want, little mouse?" Ragath said. Azalar hesitated, but then decided to risk taking a couple steps towards the black rat.

"I just thought I would let you know that we just got some news from our two new guests," Azalar said. Ragath took a quick side glance his way.

"And what would that be?" he asked. Azalar let out a heavy sigh.

"Alice is dead," he said after a long pause. "Elia told us that Kilma witnessed it." There was no reaction from Ragath, but Azalar noticed that there was a change in the air.

"I see," was all Ragath said. Azalar almost missed it, but he could hear the slight change in Ragath's tone. Nothing more was spoken on the topic as they both just stood in silence by the edge of the crumbled bridge.

Azalar thought that this was as good of an opportunity as ever to question Ragath.

"Ragath, are you alright?" Azalar asked. "You're not acting like your usual self. Is something wrong?" Ragath gave a sharp snort as his face deepened into a frown.

"Nothing is wrong!" the black rat snapped, glaring back at the smaller mouse. "And I don't need your concern!" But Azalar was unfazed and stood next to Ragath nonetheless, staring out into the darkness as well.

"I know you don't need it," Azalar said. "But you are an important member of this group, Ragath. So, if something is bothering you, I can't help but be concerned. Whether you like it or not, Ragath, we are all in this together. We have to look out for one another; and help each other." Ragath's features softened slightly at Azalar's words. He then turned back towards the great hall, letting out a heavy sigh.

"It's nothing you need to trouble yourself with, little mouse," Ragath said, his voice still low, but not in the same threatening tone as before. "You just focus on the task of protecting your people, and I'll focus on mine. My troubles are my own; not yours. So, there's no need to press further on the matter."

"Ragath, I know that we have never been exactly friends in all that time that our cages have been next to one another. And I know that talking about things that trouble you isn't easy; but there is no reason why we can't work together to help each other, especially during these times of hardship. So, if there is something bothering you, please, let me help you." Ragath stared at the little mouse for a long while, listening to his words. He then turned his head towards the darkness ahead. Though he was still silent, his face remained hard, yet not angry or threatening; but as if he was pondering with something. Finally, after a long while, Ragath relented.

"Very well. If you must know so badly, I will tell you. But let us return to camp first. The others may need to know this as well." Azalar furrowed his eyebrows slightly at this, wondering what it could be that the others might need to know about this. However, Azalar didn't question it further and nodded his head, nonetheless. With that, the two rodents made their way back to the camp where the others were waiting. When Azalar and Ragath arrived, the group of mice all turned to the two, some with looks of concern upon seeing the giant black rat standing next to Azalar. They could tell something was amiss.

"Is everything alright?" Nikamius asked. Azalar sat down next to Amara with Ragath taking a seat in the open space next to Azalar.

"Yes, Nikamius," he said. "Everything is fine. But Ragath has something that he would like to share with us." Ragath looked to see that all eyes were now on him. He felt slightly uneasy and a large part of him wanted to drop the whole thing and walk away.

"Ragath?" Amara asked. "Is everything alright?" Ragath's first instinct was to glare and lash out at them, and to storm off to his fellow rats, where he knew they wouldn't press him on any matter. But her voice was so soft and sweet, that even if Ragath wanted to glare and bark at the white mouse, he could not find it in his heart to do so. So Ragath held back this urge, taking in a deep breath to calm himself down before beginning.

"Do you all remember that story that Reemus told before? That tale about the Fornóc?" Ragath asked. Azalar did not answer but nodded his head. "It is a tale that all rats know. At least a great number of them do. It's just another story of the humans and their tortures, and what they can do to us." Ragath shut his eyes and lowered his head.

"But I know this story better than most. For it bears closer to my heart than you might think."

"What do you mean?" asked Bark. Ragath glanced at the brown mouse with a deep frown.

"That tale about the Fornóc was about my great grandfather. He was one of those Fornóc. And what happened to him was over sixty years ago." Many faces went aghast at this new astonishing revelation.

"But that's not possible!" said Bogger. "There must be some mistake or miscommunication. There's no way that could be your great grandfather. Even at your age, that would have only been seven to nine years ago." Ragath shot Bogger a hard look before turning to the rest of the group.

"Let me ask you all something," he said in a low voice. "Just by looking at me, how old do you think I look to all of you?" Everyone was silent as they stared at Ragath, but all looked rather confused by his question. Then it was Bogger who spoke up again.

"If I had to make a logical guess, even if we account for the genetic experiments that you've endured increasing your lifespan; and for how long Nikamius has known you, I'd say you couldn't be more than three years old." Everyone seemed to be in agreement as many nodded their heads. Ragath, however, suddenly burst into laughter, as if he had just heard a very humorous joke. He couldn't stop laughing. Everyone was confused more than ever.

"What's so funny?" asked Brim. It was a moment before Ragath spoke again.

"You couldn't be more wrong," Ragath said after finally calming down. He then turned to elder mouse. "How old did you think I was when Helgan brought me in? Do you have any idea?" Nikamius placed a paw under his chin and thought back to the time when he first saw Ragath enter the room.

"Well, I would have assumed that you were only one year old," Nikamius answered. Ragath let out another roar of laughter.

"Would you just tell us what's so funny?" asked Frella with growing annoyance. "And why is any of this relevant?" Ragath took a moment to calm down for the second time.

"It's relevant because when I first came to that lab, I was just twelve years old." Everyone stared in awe at the large black rat, their eyes wide and their mouths agape.

"Twelve years?!" exclaimed Nikamius. "How? How is that even possible?" Ragath's face grew hard as he turned back to the fire.

"That liquid that the humans placed into my great grandfather had other effects as well. It gave them longevity. Yes, I do know what that word means. And it also twisted their bodies and made them appear less like rats and more like monsters. But just before the Fornóc escaped, my great grandparents were still able to mate. But after their pups were born, they nearly ripped them all to shreds, save for only one pup: my grandfather. The humans took the pup away so that the Fornóc couldn't kill him, as well as experiment on him, no doubt. I don't know the details, but he lived for a long time, much longer than any rat before."

"How do you know this?" asked Azalar. Ragath gave a low snort.

"Humans love to talk when they make new *discoveries*. Remember how long they talked after you learned how to walk on your two feet?" Ragath made a gesture with his fingers to indicate a walking motion. "The humans are all about their gossip. My mother overheard them all and told me all of this. My grandfather lived to the age of twenty-five, constantly breeding and multiplying. But as he grew old, my grandfather's mind slowly went away and he became more *forn*, and so did all of his children. But the humans weren't satisfied just yet, so just before his mind was completely gone, they had him mate with another rat and a litter of pups was born. One of them was my mother.

"These genes must have passed on to them because they all lived to be around twenty-two to twenty-six years. Most of them went *forn* before they died. But before they did, they ripped apart all those that weren't *forn*. My mother was one of the last to survive from her litter. She was twenty-three when she had me and my siblings, but she was the only one who never went *forn*. She must have grown too old to bear anymore pups, because after we were born, she turned twenty-four and she was unable to have another litter again. And like the disgusting humans that they are, they forced my mother to breed over and over again. My mother must have had dozens of different litters through the years by the time she had me. I suppose they wanted to see how many litters she could bear before she could no longer."

"But if there were so many of you, how come we never saw any of them on our way out? And why did you come to us alone?" asked Bark. Ragath let in a deep breath before continuing.

"Not long after I was born, a disease spread throughout the lab and killed almost everyone. Only my mother and I survived."

"Oh no!" exclaimed Amara as she placed a paw over her chest. "That's horrible! I'm so sorry, Ragath." Ragath waved a paw dismissively.

"I barely knew any of them. But since only my mother and I survived the disease, the humans ran terrible experiments on us. They tried to bring in more rats for my mother to breed with, but she was never able to conceive again. She died no more than a year later. And because I was the last line from my great grandfather, I alone was subjected to all kinds of cruel torture for the next twelve years before Helgan brought me to where you all were." The surrounding company gave the black rat sympathetic looks.

"I'm so sorry," said Azalar. "You've suffered more than any of us here. You didn't deserve any of that." Ragath frowned and shrugged his shoulders.

"I'm not looking for sympathy," Ragath said. "I'm just letting you know what truly happened."

"Even so. It's still a fate no one deserves. You've suffered through more than any of us for so much longer."

"It's no wonder you've been such a grouch," said Bark in a half joking manner, earning a look from the giant black rat. "Anyone would be if they've been through what you did." Ragath furrowed his brows at the dark brown mouse.

"Yes, I have had a lot to be *grouchy* about," he said. "That *hréka* Helgan has tortured me all my life. But I don't want any of your pity. I've been doing just fine until now. But if I ever get the chance, I'm going to drive this blade through his skull. And anyone that gets in my way!" Ragath took his sword in both of his paws and stared at the blade with a menacing glare, imagining the blade red with Helgan's blood.

"Don't you worry. Helgan will get what's coming to him," said Brim with a confident smirk. "That we can all be sure of."

"He already did," said Kilma. Everyone immediately turned and stared wide eyed at the mole, who was simply looking down while munching on what was left of the cockroach in his paw. They were all silent as they watched Kilma eating his food as if nothing had happened.

"You can talk?" asked Bark. Kilma raised an eyebrow at the dark brown mouse and frowned.

"Aye, of course I can talk," he said. "You clearly heard me talking not too long ago, did you not?"

"No, no, we heard you," said Bogger. "We were all just under the impression that you couldn't speak our language." Kilma turned to the dark red mouse with a frown.

"Yes, I can speak your language," he said firmly. "I taught Elia to speak my language when she was just a pup and in return, she taught me to speak the rodent language. It wouldn't do too well for us to spend our lives in cages next to one another and not be able to speak each other's tongue, now, would it?" Bogger paused as he glanced away with a sigh.

"No, I suppose not," Bogger replied. Kilma let out a soft grunt.

"Now that I have spoken your tongue to you," he said with a huff, "I have been meaning to tell you something about your walls. They are very insecure." The mice all turned to the dark mole curiously.

"What do you mean?" asked Brim. Kilma pointed to the walls with his broken claw.

"Your walls are unstable. They have no proper structure and will be easily toppled over should a great enough force press upon them. I would highly recommend placing planks vertical against the walls to increase their stability." Bogger frowned at the mole.

"Wait a moment," he said, almost sounding offended. "How would you know what is unstable? Or even how to build a proper fortification? Have you read about it in the humans' books about this subject?" Kilma turned to the red mouse with a frown of his own.

"I'm a mole," he said simply. "We have a natural instinct when it comes to constructing ourselves proper dwellings. And though I may have never built such *fortifications*, even I can tell that your walls are very lacking." Bogger furrowed his brows at the mole questioningly.

"I'm sorry," Bogger said, feeling rather insulted, "but I find it very difficult to believe that someone could know how to build a proper structure or even know what was wrong with said structure without ever having the experience before." Kilma gave a shrug.

"Guess you're not as smart as you think you are," he retorted. This got a small snicker from Bark as he tried to cover his mouth, earning a hard glare from Bogger.

"Kilma! Don't be rude!" said Elia, frowning at her companion. Kilma gave another shrug.

"Excuse me," said Azalar, stopping the arguing before it could escalate further, "but what did you mean by '*he already did*'?" Kilma glanced over to Azalar.

"I mean just what I said," he answered. "Helgan got what was coming to him."

"But what does that mean?" asked Bark.

"It means that Helgan is dead." The air was silent the moment those words left Kilma's mouth. The rodents all stared dumbfounded, almost unsure if they even heard him correct. But none dared to speak up, for fear that if they did, then what they thought they heard would be nothing more than a hoax. But after a long silence, someone finally spoke up.

"Could… could you say that again?" asked Azalar, still not entirely believing it.

"Helgan is dead," Kilma repeated. He then looked over to Elia. "Am I not saying it correctly?" Nearly every mouse looked at one another, with a few of them having smiles beaming on their faces.

"How?" asked Borith, smiling ear to ear. Kilma pointed to the blue gem in Amara's paws.

"She did it," he said. The company turned their gaze to the gem.

"Alice?" asked Azalar and Amara in unison. Kilma nodded.

"Just before Helgan threw her into the machine, your friend Alice grabbed something from behind her and stabbed it into his chest. But the strange thing was, Helgan didn't seem to react to it at all. He just looked down at the thing in his chest before just pulling it out. And even stranger, there was no blood, but a black mist slowly poured from the wound. But Helgan remained unfazed. That's when Helgan grabbed hold of your friend Alice and threw her in the machine. The poor girl tried to fight him off, but it was futile. Then the bright light happened, and I couldn't see anything for a moment. But when my vision came back, I saw Helgan lying on the floor motionless. That's when I took the opportunity to escape." After Kilma had finished his tale, the company of rodents sat in amazement, staring at the mole. No one moved a muscle, as they were unsure that if they did they would wake up and find that this tale was nothing more than a dream. Then, Bark stood up and glared at the mole.

"Why didn't you say that from the beginning?" he said. Kilma simply shrugged his shoulders.

"You didn't ask," Kilma replied nonchalantly. Bark wanted to respond, but too many things were running through his head that he had nothing significant to retort with and just sat back down.

Then Azalar turned and noticed Ragath, who was sitting there with wide eyes and his mouth agape.

"Ragath? Are you okay?" Azalar asked. Ragath didn't answer. He just stared bewildered at the fire in front of him for what seemed like forever before a gleam entered his eyes and a smile, the first genuine smile that Azalar had ever seen the black rat give, slowly spread across his lips.

"Helgan is dead," Ragath said, his voice softer than anyone had ever heard before. It was a clear contrast to the harsh and low tone that he always held. Ragath then closed his eyes and turned his head upwards and took in a deep breath. He held it for just a moment before letting it all out in a great sigh of relief, as if a huge burden had been lifted off his chest. Then, he did something that Azalar would never have expected; Ragath laughed. This wasn't just some chuckle, or a snort. This was a genuine, heartfelt, wholesome laugh. Something that he had not done in his whole life.

Seeing this, Azalar couldn't help but join in the laughter. He was then joined by Amara, then Bark, then Frella. Soon every rodent was now laughing with such joy in their hearts. It was then that Bark let out a loud cheer, which caught the attention of the whole camp.

"Everyone!" Bark called out. "Fantastic news! Our guests have just informed us that Helgan, the terrible human who subjected us the most horrible torture; the human who had taken the lives of countless loved one; is dead!" The entire camp was in shock at the sudden revelation, unsure of what to make of it. But then Reemus, Ramy and Litha, who were on watch duty on the wall close to the barricade, looked at each other with wide smiles and cried out in joy. Suddenly the entire camp was in an uproar, all cheering and celebrating the news of Helgan's death, with many rodents dancing and singing around the campfires.

There wasn't a soul within the camp that wasn't happy with the news. Even Razor couldn't contain the joy within him and let out a hearty yell as he danced with his fellow rats. Never before had the rodents of Helgan's lab had felt such joy and delight in all their lives.

Azalar had taken Amara in his paws and was dancing around the campfire alongside Bark and Frella. The four mice were dancing with such merriment that Azalar and Amara even took Elia by the paw, who in turn grabbed hold of Kilma's paw, and danced away with the rest of the camp. It was then that both Azalar and Bark noticed that Bogger was still sitting down, his arms crossed with one paw under his chin, seemingly in deep thought. Both Azalar and Bark glanced at one another before approaching the dark red mouse.

"What's wrong, Bogger?" asked Bark. "We just got the greatest news of our lives. Why aren't you celebrating with us?" Bogger didn't respond right away and continued to ponder where he sat.

"There's just something that's not making any sense in all this," Bogger finally said.

"What do you mean?" said Azalar. Bogger looked up at the two mice.

"Just everything that we have been told so far. And everything that we have learned. If everything that Ragath said happened sixty years ago. And everything else we learned…" Bogger paused as he placed a paw under his chin again. "Then that would make Helgan well over one hundred years old." Both Azalar's and Bark stood aghast at the dark red mouse's statement.

"What do you mean?" Azalar asked earnestly. Bogger glanced up with a frown.

"Think about it," Bogger said. "Ragath said that everything that happened with his family started over sixty years ago. And from what this journal says, it had been twelve years since the humans left Earth. And another thirty-seven years since they had arrived on this planet. That's at least one hundred and nine years give or take. And the average human only lives to be around to be just over seventy years old. Rarely do they live to be one hundred years old. And they never look as young as this journal has stated Helgan to look. And Helgan looked rather young to me." Azalar's eyes widened in realization.

"But how?" Azalar asked. "How can a human live for so long and still remain so young."

"I don't know," Bogger answered. "I don't understand it any more than you do. But somehow, Helgan has managed to live all these years and preserve his youth. For what purpose, I can't say for certain. But something is telling me that it wasn't for anything good. And the black mist. What was that all about? If I remember correctly, humans bleed the color red. So why would Kilma say that Helgan was bleeding some black mist?"

"Well, there's no need to think about it anymore," said Bark with a smile, though his tone indicated that he was very uncomfortable and wanted to end this conversation. "Helgan is dead now, right? There's Nothing to worry about anymore. I say we just put it in the past and forget about him." Bogger crossed his arms in front of him and looked down at the floor with a deep frown.

"I don't know," Bogger said softly. "Something just doesn't feel right." However, there was no time to ponder further as suddenly a blood curdling scream rang out, causing everyone to stop dancing and look towards the front of the camp where the scream came from. On top of the walls, on the left-handed side of the barricade towards the midsection, there was a spot where a mouse named Nor was supposed to be on watch, but was now empty. The entire camp was silent as they all wondered what had just happened and who caused that scream. But then, from the same spot on the wall, something with a dark gray paw slowly reached over and pulled itself up. What emerged was not a mouse, but a horribly deformed creature with great patchy fur and bright red eyes. The rodents of the camp watched in horror at what they were seeing as the creature snarled and growled before letting out a horrible deep cry, ringing out into the hall. It was at

that moment that they all knew what it was they were
looking at.

"Fornóc!" cried Nikamius.

Chapter XV

The rodents watched in horror as the Fornóc climbed onto the walkway, snarling and hissing, its red eyes gleaming with anger and hunger. It then turned to the pair of rats on its right side. Suddenly it lunged at them, pouncing on a dark brown rat, knocking him to the floor of the walls, only to be saved by a light gray rat who pierced the Fornóc's chest with his sharp nail and kicked it off. Five more Fornóc quickly climbed the same section of the wall, two pouncing on the two rats, pushing them off the wall. The Fornóc bit and clawed at them, but several rats close by dashed to their aid, quickly striking the Fornóc dead.

A loud outcry of snarling and screeches rang out and a rush of pattering paws rumbled in the darkness. An auburn colored mouse from atop the wall on the other side of the barricade saw dozens of Fornóc beginning to emerge from the surrounding darkness. Black shapes were scattered about from every point that could be seen. A great host of the Fornóc had gathered, and they were beginning their assault.

"They're coming!" cried the mouse as the Fornóc began to swarm towards the walls from all sides. Seemingly endless hordes of these creatures streamed from the gloom beyond. Azalar took his needle in his paws and turned to Amara.

"Get to the Archway!" he ordered. "Gather as many of the does as you can and get them to the bridge." He then turned towards the front of the camp.

"To the walls!" Azalar cried and rushed to the walls as many of those stationed there were already fending off the oncoming Fornóc. He was quickly followed by Bark, Brim, Borith and Mith. Ragath took his sword and called out to Razor and gathered as many rats as he could to his side and followed Azalar towards the walls. Nikamius looked around for anything to use as a weapon. He decided upon a long stick that was in a pile of firewood not too far away. It was a little taller than him, however it wasn't sharp, nor did it even come to a point, he took it in his paw it was sturdy enough to be an efficient enough weapon. Satisfied, Nikamius turned and headed towards the raging battle.

"Where do you think you're going?" asked Bogger in earnest.

"Towards the fight!" Nikamius answered. "I may not be of much use, but I will do my part to defend our people. You must gather whoever you can and complete the bridge. We may need it sooner than we expected. And take Elia with you! She's already seen too much as it is." With that, Nikamius turned and headed for the front. Bogger stood where he was for a moment, unsure of what to do. He wanted to help his friends fight off the Fornóc, but he was not a fighter, and he knew that Nikamius was right and that his uses would be better served by completing the bridge and getting everyone across.

"Alright!" he said to himself, then turned to all the remaining mice who had not joined the fight. "You all heard Nikamius! Azalar and the others will handle the Fornóc! Come help me get the bridge together! We must cross the gap as soon as possible. We don't know how long they can hold them off." He then turned to Kilma. Though normally he would be reluctant to ask for any help, this was not the time to wallow in self pride, and the mole seemed to know what he was talking about, and they were going to need all the help they could get. "Will you help us?" the dark red mouse asked. Kilma looked from Bogger to the chaos happening at the walls of the camp. He wanted more than anything to fight, but then he looked to Elia, and with a heavy sigh he nodded.

"Very well," he said. "But we need to gather as much wood and planks as we can to support the bridge so that it won't bend too much. If it bends, then it won't reach the other side." Bogger nodded and turned back to the mice around him.

"Gather as much spare wood as you can!" he cried. "We need to support the bridge and make sure it's sturdy enough to cross. And you four over there! Each of you grab a candle and light it up. We're going to need them for light. Let's go!"

Azalar had gathered many rodents and had managed to reinforce the walls just in time as the Fornóc were throwing themselves at the wall. He and many other rodents climbed up the ramparts, him taking the right-hand side with Bark and the Brim, Mith and Borith taking the left, filling whatever gaps there were on the walls. Azalar and Bark made their way towards the midsection of the wall, where the fighting first started and way at its most fierce. Azalar took his needle and jabbed it into any Fornóc that came too close to the top. Bark was right next to him, wielding a long nail tied to a stick for extra reach, swinging and stabbing at the Fornóc below. Brim had taken Mith and Borith, and a few other mice and rushed to the other side of the walls where the Fornóc were aggressive fiercely.

Brim, Mith and Borith were holding their own on the other side of the wall. Brim swung his scalpel at every Fornóc that climbed the walls, cutting and slashing at them, keeping them at bay. He was caught by surprise when a Fornóc jumped on top of another and launched itself upward. Brim barely managed to block the Fornóc by bracing his scalpel in front of himself just as the Fornóc pounced upon him. The force from Fornóc, as well as it snapping its jaws at him, caused Brim to stumble back, but he held firm and pushed the Fornóc back off the wall. Just in time to catch another Fornóc was climbing up the wall.

Chaos raged all along the walls of the camp, with every mouse and rat fighting for their very lives as they held off the advancing Fornóc hosts as they climbed on the walls. They nipped and clawed at the feet of the rodents as they poked and stabbed at the Fornóc as they climbed, desperately trying to keep them from climbing any further. They continued to hold them off, slaying dozens as they scaled the walls, but the Fornóc were relentless, and their numbers seemed to be endless. The rodents fought as hard as they could, not all were successful. Mith and Borith were fighting a few Fornóc that had managed to climb on top of the walkway and had managed to cut them down quickly with their tools. However, just as they did, a larger Fornóc, slightly larger than the others, jumped onto the wall and charged at them. Borith saw it coming and pushed Mith out of the way, but the Fornóc clamped its jaws onto the leg of another mouse, a younger mouse named Tam, and pulled him off the wall. Tam frantically dug his claws into the wood as the Fornóc pulled him further off the wall, crying out in terror. Mith and Borith leaped forward, each grabbing hold of the Tam's arms and pulling with all their might.

"Help me!" cried Tam. Mith and Borith tried desperately to pull him up, but more Fornóc bit and clawed at the Tam's, pulling him further down. Tam screamed in agony and fear, and Borith and Mith were slowly losing their grip. But they couldn't hold on any longer as they finally lost their grip and watched in horror as the poor mouse was dragged down and disappeared into the sea of the Fornóc, his screams being overshadowed by the screeches and snarls. Mith and Borith were horrified by what they saw, but they had no time to process what had just happened as they were soon beset upon by more Fornóc climbing the walls.

The battle raged on, and the rodents fought furiously. The sound of angry cries, horrid screams and terrible shrills echoed through the hall. Azalar and the rodents continued to beat, stab, and cut through them, but the attacks from the Fornóc kept coming, and were just as ruthless as the last. As they fought, the rodents struck down more Fornóc than could ever be counted. This did not come without a cost as many other poor rodents, both mice and rats, were pulled from the walls and devoured by the Fornóc below. Though they fought with all their might, they could not keep all the Fornóc from getting inside. Many of them had managed to slip past the rodents on the wall and jumped down to the camp below. Fortunately, Ragath had stationed plenty of rats below the walls waiting for them. Soon the entire length of the walls, and even below them, was engulfed in battle.

The worst of the attack came when a huge group of Fornóc had gathered and swarmed the barricade like a wave upon a rock. Dozens of Fornóc pushed against the heap of stone and wood, some climbing over top of one another, others impaling themselves on the sharp stakes and barbs protruding from the pile to get over to the other side. But fortunately, Ragath and Razor had gathered a large contingent of rats and placed them just behind the barricade.

"Don't let any of them through! Kill them all!" cried Ragath to his rats and they readied themselves. Several Fornóc had managed to climb over the barricade and dashed towards the group of rats, five of them charging right at Ragath. However, Ragath was ready for them. He held his sword up high and quickly brought it down on the first Fornóc that descended down the barricade. As quickly as he did, he raised his sword back up and struck down each Fornóc that came within reach. He swung his sword this way and that, each blow hitting its mark. Razor, for his part, was cutting down the Fornóc just as easily with his long scalpel spear; thrusting his blade into the heads and chest of any that came his way. With this extra reach, Razor was able to dispatch the Fornóc before they could ever get too close.

More Fornóc began pouring over the barricade and descended upon the thirty or so rats below. And just like both Ragath and Razor, the rats behind them were doing just as well. They held the line firmly, not letting any Fornóc break through.

Ragath had hued the head off a larger Fornóc and in a feeling of rushing adrenaline he let out a victorious roar, and there was a brief pause in the attack as the Fornóc hesitated. Feeling a vigorous fire in his chest, Ragath took the opportunity to climb to the top of the barricade, where he let out another loud battle cry. The Fornóc hesitated for another brief moment before continuing the assault. Ragath swung his sword at every Fornóc that climbed the barricade. Left, right, left, right, his sword went. Shrill cries rang out with every Fornóc that was cut down. The Fornóc began to overwhelm him as two of the dreaded creatures leaped up and pounced on Ragath, pushing him back down the barricade. Razor and the other rats killed the two Fornóc while Ragath was able to quickly pick himself back up, just as a host of Fornóc descended down the barricade.

Ragath and Razor held firm with the other rats, but as more Fornóc ascended over the barricade, their numbers grew, and the rats were beginning to be overwhelming. Even Ragath and Razor were forced to step back until they were within the lines of their fellow rats, and even then, they were beginning to be pushed back. Soon their numbers were too many and the line broke, and where there were two distinct battle lines quickly became a chaotic brawl, with nearly every rodent in the camp fighting for their lives.

Ragath and Razor were fighting back to back, with Ragath passing his sword with a thrust through the chest of a rather large Fornóc. Razor sliced through the neck of another, but they were quickly becoming surrounded. Two Fornóc pounced and pushed Ragath to the ground. Ragath had just barely managed to recover by blocking one Fornóc with the flat end of his sword, but the other had bit down on his leg, causing the large black rat to let out a painful cry. Another Fornóc leaped forward from Ragath's right side and was about to sink its sharp teeth into his neck when it was suddenly bashed aside by a wooden stick. A second blow came, knocking the Fornóc from Ragath's leg, allowing the black rat to throw the Fornóc that was on top of his and piercing it in its chest. Ragath then turned to see that it was Nikamius that had come to his aid.

"What are you doing here, old mouse?" shouted Ragath.

"The same as you!" retorted Nikamius, striking down another Fornóc. "I'm doing my part to protect our people!" Just then, a Fornóc appeared from within the chaos of the brawl and charged at Nikamius. The elder mouse was not caught off guard, however, and with a quick motion, struck the Fornóc across the head. Several more Fornóc came from every direction, and one after another, with a twist of his wrists and a twirl of his stick, using it as a quarterstaff, Nikamius battered each one of them over the head. One Fornóc even tried to attack him from behind by pouncing in the air. But once again, Nikamius quickly spun around and brought his staff down upon the Fornóc's head midair. Nikamius then turned to see Ragath staring at the elder mouse, his eyes wide and one eyebrow raised.

"Impressive, old mouse," Ragath admitted. Nikamius gave an uncharacteristically smirk towards the large black rat.

"Just because I'm old, doesn't mean that this old mouse doesn't know a trick or two. Now come! We have to reform the line, or we will lose more rodents! We must hold them off while Bogger finishes the bridge!"

Back up on the walls, the rodents continued to fight off the Fornóc. Azalar and Bark stood firm in their positions; Azalar at the front and Bark continuing to cover him from behind. Reemus, Ramy and Litha were fairing as well as they could, with the three of them working together as they kicked, beat and stabbed at the Fornóc beneath them. They had adopted the same strategy as Azalar and Bar. Reemus and Ramy stood side by side while Litha guarded the rear, making sure that no Fornóc got past her. This was the strategy that many of the rodents used along the wall, and so far, it was all going well.

Azalar had just stabbed a Fornóc in the neck when he suddenly felt the wall shake beneath his bottom paws, nearly causing both him and Bark, along with many other rodents, to stumble backwards. Azalar looked down the wall and saw that the pressure from the Fornóc continuously throwing themselves at the walls were causing the walls to give way. Azalar quickly looked around and saw the same thing happening on the other end of the walls.

Another large group of Fornóc crashed against the wall, causing it to lean back from the impact. Azalar thought about Kilma's words before, and his eyes went wide as he realized what was about to happen.

"Get off the walls!" he cried out. "Everyone off the walls now! They're about to collapse! Go now!" All the rodents within earshot all did as he said, and those that were not saw what the other rodents were doing and immediately followed suit, some even jumping down from the top of the walls. Once on ground level, they aided the rodents on the floor as best as they could in dispatching all the Fornóc. But it did little to stem the tide as more and more Fornóc streamed over the walls, jumping down into the chaotic brawl below.

Just then, one of the Fornóc that had climbed over pushed over one of the candles near the barricade, causing it to fall onto the barricade with. It fell upside down, with the stick laying downward and its flame brushing against the wood and sticks around it. Slowly the barricade became engulfed in flames, the fire slowly spreading from the barricade to the walls, which caused most of the Fornóc to hesitate a little, though they still scaled the walls on either side. This gave the rodents the brief time they needed to regroup. The rodents cut down as many as they could, and they seemed to be gaining the upper hand for the time being.

Ragath and Razor remained closest to the barricade, killing many. Brim, Mith and Borith, along with several other mice, tried to form a battle line, but this proved difficult with the Fornóc coming from every direction. Azalar and Bark got separated from one another. Bark had jumped down from the wall and had rolled into the chaos below. He managed to pick himself up just in time before he was immediately beset upon by three Fornóc. He struggled to fight them off, but fortunately Reemus, Ramy and Litha came to his aid. Reemus struck down one while Ramy and Litha fought off the other two. Bark was incredibly grateful for their help. Suddenly the tide seemed to be turning back in the Fornóc's favor as they avoided the fire on the barricade and focused on scaling the surroundings walls and were now pushing the rodents further back into the camp.

Amara, Frella, Della and Elia watched the horrific battle from the archway with the rest of the does while Bogger, Kilma and a few other mice worked on completing the bridge. They had placed the three platforms together and Bogger and several others were now attempting to hammer the nails in, each one of them holding a large rock. However, they were struggling greatly, especially Bogger.

Bogger silently cursed himself for not being as strong as the other rodents, but he wasn't going to let that stop him. With a few more strikes, the nails were firmly in place. Now they needed to do the same with the other sections. Kilma shook his head at the slow progress.

"This is taking too long," he muttered to himself before quickly turning and dashed away to find something more efficient.

While they were hard at work on the bridge, Amara, for her part, was feeling just as she did back at the chamber where they escaped from Helgan's lab. She wanted to help, but this situation was entirely different from then. She had no experience in fighting, nor was there any way to stop the Fornóc from getting through. She felt useless. Frella, on the other hand, was not so keen on just sitting back and watching as her friends and beloved fréfil were fighting for their lives. She took a rusty, bent nail from off the floor and dashed towards the battle, surprising both Amara and Della.

"Frella, what are you doing?!" cried Della. Frella stopped and turned back.

"I'm not going to just sit back and watch as our loved ones fight and die for us. I don't know about you all, but if I'm going to die, then I'm going to die fighting. Besides, someone needs to watch over Bark, and Azalar can't do it all the time." With that, Frella turned and headed for the battle. The others watched as she left to fight, but many of the other female mice and rats were inspired by her courage, grabbing whatever weapons they could find and following Frella to battle. Amara, Della and Elia, along with a few others, remained behind.

Azalar had just struck down a Fornóc when he heard shouting from behind. He looked back to see Frella leading her fellow does of both mice and rats to reinforce their fréfils. Azalar was greatly surprised by this, but a small smile couldn't help forming on his lips before he was once again drawn back to the battle. The reinforcing rodents clashed with the Fornóc within the crowd, giving them the leeway that they needed to cut down the remaining Fornóc and form a proper battle line once again. However, there were still too many of them. Although the fire from the barricade deterred them, the Fornóc merely refocused their efforts on climbing the walls. The weight from the added pressure of the Fornóc was causing the walls to give way.

"Everyone, get back from the walls!" cried Azalar, looking up and seeing the walls about to collapse.

"We must fall back and form a defensive line by the archway!" cried Nikamius "We need to buy more time for Bogger and the others to finish building the bridge!"

The rodents had gathered together and ran back to the archway as quickly as they could as more Fornóc poured over the walls. No sooner than they did, the walls finally tipped over from the weight of the Fornóc pressing against them. As they collapsed, the candles that lined the walls tipped over as well, with one in particular rolling away until the flame was touching the wood of another section of the wall. Due to how dry the planks were, the wood quickly caught fire, which slowly began to spread all along the walls. On top of this, the Fornóc were rushing through the camp, and many campfires were pushed over, sending sparks and smoldering ash across the camp, spreading the fire even more. Within moments, the whole camp was alight with fires spread all over. This seemed to have startled the Fornóc as they held back from the flames. This gave the rodents a brief moment of respite as they were able to form a defensive line under the archway.

"The fire is keeping them back," said Nikamius. "But how long that will be, only Háth knows."

"We need to give Bogger more time to complete the bridge."

"I don't know what's taking him so long, but Bogger needs to finish that bridge now!" cried Bark. Just as Bark had said this, Bogger had just finished hammering the last nail that connected two sections of the bridge together. However, there was still a whole other section that needed to be nailed together. Bogger was panting and his muscles were aching. He didn't know how much strength he had left in him. He saw that the other mice were feeling much the same. They had been hard at work hammering away at the nails, but many of them were exhausted and some of their rocks had cracked and shattered.

"We have to keep going," muttered Bogger with a heavy breath. "We cannot give up!" Though his muscles protested, Bogger headed for the last section of the bridge. He then took the rock in his paws and lifted it above his head. Just then Kilma stepped forwards and took the rock from Bogger. Bogger was about to protest but then he saw Kilma tying the large rock to another nail with a few sets of string that he found, creating a makeshift hammer. Kilma then struck the hammer against the nail repeatedly, which proved to be far more efficient as the nail went deeper into the wood with every strike until it was firmly in place. Kilma then moved to the next nail and did the same thing. Bogger watched in amazement at the mole's ingenuity and gave an impressed smile. He realized he could indeed learn a lot from this little critter. But that would have to wait. There was still work to be done. They still had to build the counterweight for the end of the bridge.

The rodents under the archway stood defensively as they faced off with the Fornóc as they hung back from the fires. As of now, there was a thin strip of fire blocking the Fornóc's path but, the shrill cries and deep snarling persisted. For a few moments, the two sides simply stared at one another. Azalar and the others thought that this would give Bogger and the others the time they needed to complete the bridge. Then a much larger Fornóc, the biggest one they've seen thus far, appeared from the crowd and stood at the front. It stood there for a moment, staring venomously at the rodents, before letting out a deep roar. Ragath glared at the large Fornóc, feeling as though it was trying to intimidate them. Not one to feel intimidated, Ragath took a step from the crowd and let out his own deep roar, much louder and stronger than the large Fornóc's. When he was done, Ragath gave a satisfied and victorious smile.

"What was that?" asked Borith with a raised eyebrow.

"These *mûk tuwahs* think they can intimidate us," answered Ragath, the smug smile never leaving his face. "I'm just showing them that they can't. "

There was silence from the Fornóc as they seemed to hesitate; all but the large Fornóc, whose red eyes glared dangerously at Ragath. It then did something that none of the rodents expected: it slowly stood up on its hind legs. The rodents stared in bewilderment at the huge Fornóc, who stood even taller than Ragath, and through the patches of fur that were missing, they could see that its muscles were massive. Even the confident smile that Ragath had fell. A moment later, many other Fornóc began standing on the back legs as well.

"Feeling intimidated, yet?" asked Brim nervously. Though He was a little surprised, the shock quickly wore off and he gave a serious frown.

"No," Ragath answered with a scowl. "Not in the slightest." He then took his sword in both his paws and pointed the tip of the blade at the large Fornóc. The large Fornóc hissed at the black rat before turning to the others behind him and giving out grunts and snarls at them.

"What is it doing?" asked Bark. Azalar watched on as the huge Fornóc continued barking at the other Fornóc.

"I think it's communicating with them," Azalar answered.

"They can do that?" Borith asked.

"It wouldn't be a surprise," said Nikamius. "Though they've lost their minds, they are still rodents. They've been down here for so long that it would only make sense for them to have their own language. As broken as it may be. And that big one right there seems to be their Alpha, or leader."

"I wonder what he's saying," muttered Reemus. He seemed to have gotten his answer when the Fornóc began gathering together in a large group by the Fornóc Alpha. Once they had all gathered, the large Fornóc gave out a deep shrill cry before quickly turning around and wiping his tail at the fire, sending hot sparks, and burning embers at the rodents. Azalar covered his eyes to avoid being blinded, and when he looked back, he saw that a patch had been cleared. The Fornóc Alpha then gave a loud roar as he and his host began to pour through the gap. The rodents braced themselves just as the Fornóc crashed into their lines.

The Fornóc Alpha charged straight for Ragath. Ragath swung his sword at the Alpha's head, but he ducked under the blade and scratched at Ragath's side. The black rat winced at the pain, but he did not falter and held firm. The rest of the rodents were doing their best to hold the line against the enemy. Azalar cut, stabbed and slashed with the sharp tip of his needle. He must have slain at least half a dozen within the span of a minute.

Bark, Brim, Borith and Mith had slain many of their own, but the Fornóc just kept coming. Bodies began to pile up and the rodents were beginning to be pushed back. Nikamius was then struck on the head when a Fornóc headbutted him, sending the elder mouse into a daze. Reemus, who was right next to the elder mouse, quickly pulled Nikamius back and stabbed the Fornóc in the chest and pushed it back, causing a group of them to stumble and fall back.

"Get him back!" Reemus called to his companions. Ramy and Litha then pulled Nikamius to the back of the crowd, where the others who had not partaken in the battle tended to him and many rodents who had been injured in the fight. Amara looked up and saw Ramy and Litha carrying Nikamius, and she and Della quickly rushed to aid them, taking Nikamius so that the two young rats could get back to the fight.

"We can't hold them off much longer!" said Ramy to the female white mouse. "There's too many of them. Is that bridge finished yet?"

"They're doing the best that he can," said Amara. She then looked to where Bogger and Kilma were hard at work completing the bridge. "Let us hope that it will be soon," she muttered to herself.

The battle was becoming more desperate as both sides fought ferociously. The Fornóc were slowly pushing the rodents back until they were almost past the archway. Azalar realized that if the Fornóc were to push them any further, they would be able to push past their flanks and completely surround them.

"We must hold them here!" cried Azalar. "Don't take another step back! If they get past us, our chance of a home, our chance for a future is gone. Is that what you want?"

"No!" cried the rodents.

"Then by all the strength that Háth has given us, kill these *mûk tuwahs* and let us see the sunlight!"

With newfound courage and spirit, the rodents let out a boisterous cry and began to push back against the Fornóc. They hacked, slashed and stabbed at the Fornóc, slaying many at their feet with such ferocity. The fear they had was now gone and replaced by anger and rage. They were not going to die in this dark hole. They were going to see the sun. And Azalar was going to show them the way.

Ragath was still battling against the Alpha, he had been on the defensive for the entire fight, but hearing Azalar words, even coming from a mouse, lit a new fire into his heart. He had never been defeated before, and he was not going to be defeated by this abomination.

The Alpha lunged forward once again, but Ragath was prepared for this. He used the flat side of his sword to block the Alpha's attack, then once his full weight was on his blade, Ragath pushed the Alpha off and slammed the butt of his sword against the Alpha's head. This stunned the Alpha and caused him to stagger back. Ragath pressed his advantage and swung his sword at the Alpha's neck. The Alpha was quick to recover and ducked under the blade. Ragath was expecting this, however, and kicked the Alpha under his chin. Ragath then brought his blade down and cleaved the Alpha's head open. The Alpha's body fell lifeless on the ground. The surrounding Fornóc, seeing their Alpha cut down in front of them, all began to turn and run back through the fire. Razor, who had been standing close to Ragath and watched the whole fight take place, raised his weapon and gave a victorious cry.

"Ragath has defeated the Fornóc Alpha!" Razor shouted. "Hail to Chief Ragath! Hail to the Chief!"

"Hail Chief Ragath!" cried the surrounding rats. Cheers of joy and relief rang out from the rodents, many of whom nearly collapsed from exhaustion, Bark included.

"Finally," he said, dropping to his knees and giving a huge sigh in relief. "It's finally over."

"No," said Ragath, staring out where the Fornóc disappeared behind the flames. "They'll be back. If they're like the rats that they once were, they'll be back to avenge their Alpha."

"Then we need to finish that bridge now," said Azalar. "We need to use this time wisely. We don't know when they'll be back." Shrill cries and screeches were then heard out beyond the camp, giving the rodents an eerie sense of dread.

"Let's hope it's not too soon," muttered Mith.

"Azalar!" cried a voice from behind. Azalar turned to see Elia running towards him. "Kilma and Bogger just finished," she said upon arrival. Azalar and the others quickly ran back towards the bridge where Bogger and Kilma, along with the other mice who aided, were waiting. The bridge was indeed completed and looked study and strong. They had even finished building the counterweight, which consisted of two long planks extended to either side and weighted down by several larger rocks on each side.

"It's finished?" Azalar asked. Bogger, though he was breathing heavily, smiled and leaned against the bridge exhausted.

"Yes," he said with a heavy breath. "It's finally ready. And with Kilma's help and ingenuity, we were able to finish much sooner than expected." Kilma glanced over at the dark red mouse with a raised eyebrow, not expecting to receive a compliment from a mouse he just recently offended. In fact, it was the first time he had ever received praise from anyone who wasn't Elia, so he wasn't entirely sure how to feel or react to this. But he remained silent.

"This news couldn't have come at a better time," said Nikamius, walking over while holding his head and balancing himself on his staff.

"Nikamius, are you alright?" asked Elia in earnest. Nikamius smiled at the younger chipmunk as she rushed to his side.

"I'm fine, young one," he said. "But there will be time for concern later. Right now, we need to focus our efforts on crossing the bridge."

"Look!" cried a mouse pointing out beyond the gap. Everyone turned to where the mouse was pointing to, and what the saw made their hearts sink. The fire from the camp had grown significantly and was now illuminating much of the empty chasm, allowing the rodents to see much further out. There at the far end of the gloom of the abyss, was the other side of the destroyed bridge; and the gap between the two sides was far greater than their bridge could reach.

"Oh no!" cried Della.

"The bridge won't make it!" cried Bark.

"What are we going to do?" cried Mith. Many rodents began to panic upon realizing that they were trapped, all asking what they were going to do, or if they were going to die. Even Azalar felt defeated upon seeing this and was at a complete loss. How were they going to get past this? With an empty abyss in front of them and the Fornóc to their rear, it all seemed impossible.

Azalar looked back at his people, seeing their frightened and anxious faces all looking to him. He then looked to his beloved Amara, who clung to the blue stone earring in her paws as she looked up at her fréfil, her brows furrowed in terror. Seeing this brought a fire in his heart. No! He was not about to give up. This was not how his people were going to die. There had to be a way out. They just needed to find it.

"Everyone, remain calm!" barked Azalar, his voice echoing against the walls. "We will find a way across. But we must not panic. There is always a way. Right, Bogger? Bogger?" When he didn't receive an answer, Azalar turned to the dark red mouse, only to find him sitting on his knees with an uncertain expression, staring out at the other end of the bridge.

"Bogger?" Azalar repeated softly, his voice full of concern.

"I… I don't know," Bogger muttered. "I don't know what to do. I didn't take into account how far the gap truly was. The platform isn't long enough, and we do have enough materials to expand it. And even if we did, the platform would be too heavy to support itself. It would break apart before it would ever reach the end. There's no way out. We can't do it. We're trapped!"

"Bogger!" cried Azalar, grabbing both of Bogger's shoulders to stop him from rambling on. "Bogger, pull yourself together. There's always a way out. We just have to find it. And we will find it. But we can't let ourselves succumb to panic."

A loud cry of shrieks and snarls rose from behind them. The rodents all turned and saw black shapes within the fires. The Fornóc were returning. Fearful cries came from the rodents, and they began to back away, slowly moving towards the edge of the broken bridge. The Fornóc quickly emerged from the fires and began to gather in the open space just beyond the archway, growling and snarling at the rodents. They slowly began to approach, seemingly knowing that they had them trapped with nowhere else to go, almost savoring the moments before the final blow. The rodents began to panic more, with many pushing against each other to get as far away from the Fornóc as possible. Ragath quickly took action and rushed to the front of the crowd.

"Everyone, stand together!" he called out. "Those that can fight move to the front. Those that are injured remain behind and protect the does." Bark, Frella, Brim, Mith, Borith, Nikamius, Reemus, Ramy and Litha all followed without question. Though they were still fearful and hesitant, many mice did as he ordered, though the rats were far more reluctant. That is until a booming voice echoed through the crowd.

"Rats with me!" roared Ragath in a commanding voice.

"To the Chief!" cried Razor. The rats immediately followed close behind and the rodents all formed a semi-circle to defend against the Fornóc. Ragath and Razor made their way to the front and stood next to Azalar.

"We make our stand here! If this is to be our last moments, then let us make them something that even the Fornóc will never forget! But do not give them the satisfaction of showing them your fear! Give them nothing but your anger. And should we fall, let us take as many of those *fûktas* with us as possible! Show Háth that his children will not be defeated so easily!" With renewed vigor and fire in their hearts, the rodents gave a cry of fury and readied themselves for a new fight. The Fornóc had gathered in a much larger throng and continued to slowly move towards the battle ready rodents, their shrill cries and sickly snarls and hisses echoing along with the roaring fire behind them. Azalar held his needle tightly in his paws, ready to fight until his last breath.

Suddenly there was a great *Boom* that seemed to come from far above. It sounded a great distance away, but it shook the halls like a huge drum and caused the cold stone beneath their paws to tremble. Both the rodents and the Fornóc braised themselves on the ground. A moment later there came another *Boom*, shaking the chamber some more.

There was a deep crackling sound from above and the rodents sprang their heads upward towards the ceiling. The cracking grew louder and louder. Then from the gloom from above, several large rocks and boulders fell from the ceiling and came crashing down all around them, most landing safely around the rodents, while the much larger ones fell into the gap. There was a loud splash, and a huge wave of water sprang up from below and rained down upon the rodents and the Fornóc, who had retreated in panic back towards the archway.

After the noise had settled, and when it seemed like no more boulders would be falling, the rodents stood up and looked towards the chasm where the ceiling had fallen. And to their great surprise, the huge boulders had formed a land bridge across the chasm to the other side, with only a small gap between them and the boulders; a gap just wide enough for them to place their bridge upon.

"There is our path!" said Nikamius to Azalar. "Háth has provided us with a safe passage. We must go now!" Azalar nodded and quickly turned Bogger and Kilma.

"Get that bridge over there now!" he ordered. "Take as many rodents as you can. We will cover you until then. But make haste! I don't know how long we can hold them off." He then pointed to a group of a dozen mice, then a dozen rats close by and ordered them to aid Bogger and Kilma in moving the bridge. The mice ran off without hesitation, but the rats weren't so quick to act and turned to Ragath for orders. Ragath narrowed his eyes.

"What are you waiting for?!" Ragath barked. "Do as he says!" The rats were startled and quickly did as he said, dashing off towards the bridge. The rodents took the bridge from both sides and dragged it across the stone floor until they reached the edge. From there, a group of six of the tallest rats lifted the platform above their heads while the remaining rodents pushed it from behind. Slowly they bridge hovered over the dark abyss below and made its way toward the closet boulder. However, just before it could reach the boulder, the bridge started to bend downwards. The rats tried to lift the bridge higher, but it wasn't enough to reach the ledge and their arms were growing tired from the weight. Bogger and Kilma tried to keep the bridge stable and not from tipping over.

"It's not going to reach!" cried Elia. Nikamius, who had been near the back of the crowd closest to the bridge, pushed his way through the others until he was at the front.

"Azalar!" the elder mouse called out. "Azalar, the bridge won't make it. It is bending down and it won't be able to reach the other side." Azalar looked back to the rodents struggling with the bridge, but he was at a loss on what to do. There had fortunately been no sign of the Fornóc's movements, but they could still hear their ghastly cries and horrible snarls and growls. They knew that they would be back soon as the fires were slowly dying down. Soon the entire might of the Fornóc would be upon them.

That was when Ragath, who had heard everything, turned to see the rodents struggling with the bridge as it was just barely touching the boulder. Impatient, Ragath quickly ran back towards the bridge, pushing aside a few rats before taking the platform in his paws himself. He then lifted the bridge high above his head and pulled the bridge forward until he was almost at the very edge.

Just as his bottom paws were about half a foot from the edge, Ragath lifted the platform as high as he could and tossed it over head, swiftly jumping out of the way before it slammed against the hard floor with a loud snap. However, the moment had caused him to stagger and nearly trip over the edge, only to be saved just in time by both Azalar and Razor, who each grabbed one of his arms and quickly pulled him back.

"They've made it!" shouted a mouse. "They did it!" The three rodents turned to see that they had indeed done it: the bridge had successfully landed on the ledge of the closet boulder, allowing them access to cross over.

"Great job!" Azalar said to the large black rat before calling to the others. "Everyone, get across the bridge now!" shouted Azalar. The rodents all began rushing towards the bridge, with Nikamius and Bogger doing their best to keep them from pushing and shoving each other.

"Don't push!" Nikamius called out. "Be mindful of each other!"

"Move in a single file line and try to keep calm," said Bogger. This seemed to work as the rodents were no longer rushing pushing past each other to cross the bridge. Those that were carrying the lit candles were the first to cross to light the way, with the rest following close behind. Kilma and Elia approached next, with the young chipmunk hesitatingly looking down at the bridge before glancing up at the elder mouse nervously. Nikamius smiled down at the young chipmunk before placing a paw on her shoulder.

"It will be alright, young one," Nikamius said softly. "Just take it one step at a time and don't look down." Elia's fears softened a little, but her heart was still beating terribly in her chest. She took in a deep breath before taking a step on the wooden platform. She took a few more steps before noticing that Kilma was no longer behind her. She turned back to the mole with a confused look.

"What are you doing?" she asked. Kilma was silent for a moment before looking back at the rodents who were guarding the rear of the group from the Fornóc. He then turned back and gave the young chipmunk a small frown.

"I'm going to help Azalar fend off the Fornóc," Kilma said. Elia's eyes widened in fear and panic.

"But why?" she asked in earnest. "Why can't you come with me?"

"Because I have to make sure that you are safe!" Kilma answered. "You are my top priority. I have to make sure that you return to your family safely. No matter the cost. Now go!" With that, Kilma took up his makeshift hammer and dashed for the back of the crowd. Elia tried to run after him but was immediately stopped by Nikamius.

"You heard him, young one," the elder mouse said. "You need to go with the others." But Elia was hesitant to move.

"But why can't he come with me to keep me safe?" Elia cried, tears streaming down her cheeks.

"Because the best way he can protect you is to see to it that those terrible creatures are not able to follow us. It is what Azalar and others are doing right now. Doing whatever it takes to keep all of us safe. And he will not be able to focus until he knows that you're safe." Elia, through teary eyes, looked back across the bridge as other rodents were crossing then back to Nikamius.

"But I don't want to go alone," the young chipmunk said.

"We'll take her," said Frella as she, Della and Amara approached the two. Nikamius smiled and nodded at the three female mice, then looked back down at Elia.

"Stay with these young does," he said. "They will keep you safe." Elia didn't say a word as Della and Frella each placed a paw on the young chipmunk's shoulders and slowly guided her across the bridge. It wasn't until a moment later that Frella noticed that Amara wasn't beside them. She turned to see Amara standing a ways back with her back to them.

"Are you coming, Amara?" Frella asked. Amara turned back to where she knew her beloved tan colored mouse was.

"No," she said. "I'm going to wait here for him."

"But, Amara," said Nikamius, "it's not safe here. The Fornóc are coming back and the cave is falling apart. We need to get you to safety."

"I don't care!" Amara said in a stern voice. "However long it takes, I will not move until *I* know that Azalar is safe." Nikamius looked into her eyes and he knew that no matter what he or anyone else said, no force on this planet would change her mind.

"Very well," Nikamius said with a sigh. "Let us hope that he doesn't take too long."

"Here they come!" cried Brim. Azalar and the others could see the dark shapes of the Fornóc returning within the fires. Azalar turned to Reemus, who was standing right behind along with Ramy and Litha.

"Reemus, you, Ramy and Litha must help the other safely cross the bridge. We will stay back and protect the rear."

"But I want to fight alongside you!" Reemus said. But Azalar was not having it.

"We don't have time to argue about this!" he shouted. "Do as I say and keep the others safe!" With that, Azalar turned and headed for the front with the few remaining mice guarding the rear. Reemus gave a disgruntled sigh before turning back towards the bridge to help Bogger and Nikamius; just as Kilma dashed past him and stood next to Azalar.

"What are you doing here?" asked Azalar.

"Making sure that Elia crosses safely," Kilma replied, holding his makeshift hammer in his paws. Azalar was about to protest, when the cries of the Fornóc echoed through the air and he turned to see the Fornóc gathering past the archway once more; their red eyes glowing angrily at the rodents.

"Be ready!" Azalar called out, holding his needle tightly in his paws, pointing the tip at the enemy. The dozen or so rodents that were guarding the rear readied themselves as well. Not a moment later, a terrible cry rang out in the hall and the Fornóc charged. Just as the Fornóc raced across the stone floor, a third *Boom* came from above, causing the cave to tremble once more. The rodents on the bridge braced themselves, clinging desperately to the wooden platform to keep themselves from falling into the darkness below. Fortunately, none had fallen.

Another shower of falling rocks and stones came crashing down from the ceiling, but this time they were falling right above the Fornóc. Large stones fell and crushed many Fornóc, sending most of them scurrying back where they came from. More rocks fell and trembled the cold stone beneath the rodent's paws. Once the last rock had fallen, Azalar looked up to see that a huge wall had been formed from the fallen debris, blocking the Fornóc's path.

"This is our chance!" cried Nikamius. "Everyone, cross the bridge now!" The rodents quickened their pace crossing the bridge, with the vast majority already across and were now climbing up the boulders that laid ahead of them. The boulders weren't that steep, nor were they difficult to climb, but they still had to be careful as to not slip off. And the ones carrying the candles had to be extra careful not to slip or drop the candles lighting their path. One such mouse, a young male brown mouse named Tilt, was the first to climb to the top of the boulder. Once there, he held his candle as high as he could and peered to the other side.

"I can see the other side!" he called out to the others. This seemed to motivate the rodents further, giving them the determination that they needed to push forward and the hope that they would make it out alive. The other side of the bridge was only a few boulders away, with the rest of the way being a much easier descent from one boulder to the next; almost like a stairway. The boulders were close enough together that there was no need to hop from one boulder to another, but they did need to watch their step as they descended down the slope, watching for any holes or large cracks and crevasses that they could stumble and trip over. Frella took it upon herself to take the candle from Tilt and led the way down.

Della was right next to her while holding Elia's paw. Frella watched as her sister and the young chipmunk made their descent for a moment before turning back towards their wooden bridge, watching the other rodents make their way across. She then looked to the few mice and rats guarding their escape, where her beloved fréfil was. Though she silently prayed for his safety, she knew that as long as Azalar was with him, Bark would be safe.

The few rodents that remained behind, Azalar, Bark, Brim, Borith, Mith, Ragath, Razor and Kilma, all watched the rock wall for the Fornóc to emerge. Though the wall was high, it would not be enough to keep the Fornóc at bay for long. They just needed a little bit more time, as there were still a few rodents that needed to cross. They could still hear their ravenous shrill cries just as Azalar could see the first of the Fornóc beginning to climb over the rock wall. Seeing this, Azalar quickly turned back to see how many rodents were left that needed to cross. Fortunately, there were very few left, including Bogger and Nikamius, as well as Amara, who were just now beginning their cross over the wooden bridge. Azalar looked forward once more to see the dozens of Fornóc climbing over the rock wall and were charging their way.

"Everyone! get back to the bridge now!" Azalar called. "We'll hold them off there." At his word, they all quickly dashed back towards the bridge. If they could make it there, the narrow point would help mitigate the Fornóc's numbers and give them an edge. Azalar was the last to move, however, still remaining behind to hold off the Fornóc a bit longer. wanting to buy his friends a little more time to get to safety.

"Azalar!" called Bark, who had noticed that his best friend did not move. "Get your sorry tail moving!" Hearing his name called caused Azalar to look back for a brief moment before turning back just as a Fornóc had quickly closed the distance and had just pounced at him. Yet, Azalar was too quick and thrusted his needle into its chest, killing it instantly. More Fornóc were fast approaching and Azalar was left with no choice but to flee back to the bridge with the others. Just as he was over halfway, he felt a great force on his back push him to the floor. Azalar instantly rolled to his back just in time to place his needle in front of him as a Fornóc attempted to bite at his neck. Azalar struggled with the Fornóc, trying desperately to kick it off of him. But its grip on his weapon was great and refused to let go as it tried to dig its sharp claws into Azalar's fur. Azalar had to do something quick, or he was going to be torn apart by the other Fornóc.

However, just at that moment, a piece of metal with a blue gemstone was jammed into the Fornóc's eye, causing it to scream in pain and release its bite on Azalar's needle. Azalar quickly kicked it off of him and looked up to see Amara standing above him, holding Alice's blue gemstone earring, now covered in Fornóc blood. Azalar quickly picked himself up and looked at his fréfil, whose eyes were wide and was breathing heavily.

"It seems that Alice is still watching out for us," Azalar said with a smile before taking Amara by the paw and running towards the bridge. They could hear the hundreds of paws pattering on the stone floor behind them. The rest of the rodents were now halfway across the bridge. Bark, Brim, Bogger and Nikamius were among the last on the bridge, and they looked back just as Azalar and Amara had arrived and saw that the Fornóc were quickly gaining ground.

"Azalar! Amara! Hurry!" cried Bark. The two mice practically jumped onto the bridge and continued running. They were a quarter of the way before Azalar pulled Amara past him and urged her forward before turning back to face the Fornóc.

"Azalar, what are you doing?" called Brim.

"Just go!" cried Azalar. He then held his needle forward and prepared for the coming fight. Amara was hesitant to leave her mate, but there was little she could do, and she was already getting weary. She followed her fréfil's command and ran across the bridge towards the rest of the rodents. Bark noticed that Azalar had remained behind on the bridge.

"What is he doing?" muttered Bark in annoyance.

"He's trying to buy us more time?" said Nikamius. Bark glanced at the elder mouse with a frown.

"No! He's being an idiot!" Bark retorted, taking his makeshift spear and ready to rush across the bridge to aid his best friend. Before he could do so, however, another figure dashed past them. "What the?" he muttered. The figure ran across the bridge and past Amara.

"Reemus?" asked Amara as the young rat ran past her.

"Please get to the others, Miss Amara!" Reemus called back to her and continued forward. Amara hesitated at first, but reluctantly did as she was told and rushed back to the other rodents. Once he was beside Azalar, he held his weapon ready in paw ready to defend. Azalar turned back and frowned at him.

"Reemus, what are you doing?"

"I'm doing my part to protect our people," Reemus retorted. "With all due respect, you know that you can't handle them by yourself. Please allow me to aid you as much as I can."

"We don't have time for this!" Azalar said, feeling a strange sense of Déjà vu. "Get back to the others now!" Just then, the first of the Fornóc jumped onto the bridge. They piled against each other, some pushing and shoving others off into the darkness below, trying to get to the pair on the bridge. Three Fornóc at the front rushed the mouse and rat, with the first one pouncing at Azalar. The tan mouse was quick though and stabbed the Fornóc in the chest and used its body to block the other two from getting close. Reemus then took his nail weapon and stabbed the Fornóc on the right and pushed, knocking the two Fornóc behind it off the bridge. Azalar tossed the dead Fornóc aside and stabbed another in the neck. The two rodents continued to fend off the dreaded creatures, and due to the narrowness of the bridge, their numbers were nullified. However, the Fornóc were relentless, and pressed forwards, swelling their numbers on the bridge, forcing Azalar and Reemus to step back quite a few steps.

"Get back there now!" cried Azalar again as he stuck down a Fornóc.

"Forgive me, sir, but I can't do that," Reemus replied. "You may have led us this far, but that doesn't mean you have to do things yourself." However, that was where he was wrong; that's where they were all wrong. He did lead them there. He led them out of that hellish prison. So, it was his responsibility to keep them all safe. He had to be the one to protect his people. This was what Azalar told himself the moment they escaped from their cages. Azalar felt that since he was the one who got them out, it was his responsibility to see to it that his people, both mice and rats, were safe and to find them a home, no matter the cost.

The Fornóc continued to push the two rodents further and further back, forcing them past the halfway point of the bridge. And with the additional weight from the Fornóc relentlessly pressing themselves against one another, the bridge was slowly starting to bend downward. Azalar felt the bridge trembling and sinking beneath his feet.

"We have to go now!" he shouted. The two rodents tried their best to turn and run off the bridge, but with the endless horde at their feet it was nearly impossible. If they were to turn and run now, they would surely be caught. The others watched on as Azalar and Reemus fought their way to get back to them. Suddenly Brim heard a new sound over the shrill cries and fighting. A deep crackling from overhead caused him to turn upward. The cracking and rumbling continued and his eyes widened in horror.

"Azalar! Reemus!" he cried out. "Get off the bridge now! This place is caving in!"

Hearing this both Azalar and Reemus gave a quick, horrified glance at one another before Azalar stabbed another Fornóc in the head and kicked it off, while Reemus picked up the dead body of another and tossed it at the crowd. This gave the two rodents the time and space they needed to take off across the bridge. Azalar was ahead of Reemus, who kept looking back at the Fornóc behind them. The cracking and rumbling grew louder, with a few large stones falling from the ceiling and crashing on either side of the bridge, some almost hitting the bridge itself.

The others on the other side all call out to them, encouraging and beckoning them onward. Amara held Alice's earring close to her chest, her heart pounding so loud and so fast she could hear it in her ears. She was squeezing the metal so tightly she almost thought she could bend it in her paws as she watched her beloved fréfil run for his life.

Azalar and Reemus were almost at the end of the bridge when it suddenly gave out from under their paws. As it turned out, the wood had been more rotted away than the rodents had originally thought, and the extra weight became too much for the bridge to bear. The bridge had finally snapped in the center from the weight of the hundreds of Fornóc piling on top of the wooden planks. Azalar and Reemus dropped to their knees, digging their claws and weapons into the wood to keep themselves from falling. Many Fornóc fell into the darkness.

"Azalar! Reemus!" the crowd of rodents cried out. Bark, Brim, Bogger, Mith, Borith, Nikamius and Amara all rushed to the edge of the bridge. The bridge was beginning to slip from the edge of the boulder and was slowly descending into the dark pit below. The ceiling continued to crumble above them as more stones and large rocks fell around them. The others tried to stretch their arms down to Azalar, however, they could not reach him. Bark then took his makeshift spear, which was much longer than Brim's scalpel, and stretched it down towards Azalar. Even if Azalar were to just, he wouldn't be able to grab it.

"Get out of my way!" shouted a deep voice. Ragath pushed his way past Brim, Bogger and Borith and grabbed the spear from Bark. "Grab hold, little mouse!"

Azalar tried to reach for the tip of the spear, yet he still could not reach. Azalar pressed his claws into the wood, then with as much strength as he could muster, he pushed himself upward, grabbing hold of the spear with one paw. With a smile he looked back at Reemus.

"Grab my tail, Reemus!" he shouted. Reemus reached his arm up, trying desperately to grab hold of Azalar's tail. Just then Reemus felt a bite on his rear paw and let out a scream of pain. He looked back to see a Fornóc sinking its teeth into his right rear foot. He tried to kick the Fornóc off, but its teeth were too deep into his leg. With no other choice, Reemus dug his nails into the wood and pulled his nail weapon out, using it to beat the side of the Fornóc's head. After four or five hits, Reemus stabbed the Fornóc in the center of its head, killing the horrid creature and finally got it to release into hold on his paw.

Suddenly the bridge slipped from the ledge and suddenly dropped; but was then caught by a much smaller ledge. However, it was barely hanging on the edge by a centimeter. The fall caused the majority of the remaining Fornóc to be sent flying, their horrid cries disappearing into the abyss. Azalar was now hanging a few inches above the bridge, his tail barely touching the wooden planks. The fall almost caused him to lose his grip on the spear, with his paw sliding down until it was barely a centimeter from the tip.

"Pull him up!" Bark shouted, reaching over and grabbing the spear shaft, trying to pull Azalar up. Ragath glared at the dark brown mouse.

"Reemus is still down there!" the black rat hissed.

"If you don't pull him up, we'll lose them both!" Bark retorted. Ragath's glare deepened before looking back down at Azalar. The tan colored mouse's grip on the nail of the spear was slipping. If he were to fall, it would cause the bridge to fall as well, and both Azalar and Reemus would be lost. With a deep growl of seething anger, he reluctantly pulled Azalar up and over the edge.

"No!" Azalar cried, seeing Ragath pulling him upwards. Once he was over, Azalar immediately rushed back and peered over the edge where Ragath once again lowered the spear to Reemus, but the young rat was too far away. "Climb Reemus! Climb!"

Reemus was petrified where he was. The bridge falling had caused him to slip nearly a foot down and he dropped his weapon and he clung to the plank of the bridge for dear life. His eyes were shut, and his body refused to move. Then, the sound of Azalar's voice calling out to him broke him from his petrified state and the young rat looked up, where he could see Azalar and Ragath above him, with the rat chief holding a spear down to him.

"Climb Reemus!" Azalar cried again. Through fear and pain, the young rat managed to regain control of his body and began to climb up the bridge. He dug his claws so deep into the wood that they grew numb, but he refused to stop. The spear was closer now, he could almost reach it. With a giant leap, Reemus pushed himself forward a good distance and was almost underneath Ragath. The young rat reached one paw up towards the tip of the spear. Then a large stone broke from the ceiling and crashed onto the bridge, destroying the plank that was underneath Reemus.

"Reemus!" Azalar cried, reaching out to the young rat. Reemus squeaked in terror as he disappeared into the dark abyss and was gone. The remaining rodents stood staring into the gloom, with only Azalar lying down with his arm outstretched, as if he could still see the young brave rat and was trying to pull him up from the watery pit. He stared down into the seemingly bottomless void, and his mind thought of Juro; a poor young mouse who was taken from this world far too soon. It wasn't until Bark and Brim came and pulled him from the edge that he had moved at all.

"We have to go!" Brim shouted, pulling Azalar from the edge. Ragath stared into the darkness, his eyes wide and his mouth agape. He stayed like this for a moment longer before the sound of Nikamius' voice broke his trance.

"Ragath, we have to go!" Nikamius shouted. Ragath shook his head and quickly ran back and began the climb up the boulder with the others. The ceiling continued to crumble and tremble, with larger chunks falling and crashing down. The rodents had just reached the top of the boulder when one of the large stones crashed on the ledge where they once stood. The rodents rushed down the slope, hopping from one boulder to another until they finally reached the other side, where the rest of their people were waiting.

"Run!" Bogger shouted. The crowd of rodents didn't hesitate and quickly ran down the path. Frella and the other candle bearers led the way down the path until they could see another archway in the distance.

"Move it" Frella beckon. The host of rodents pushed onward, somehow avoiding every rock and debris that fell around them. They finally reached the archway, and Frella stopped and waited for the other. She searched through the crowd, until the faces that she knew eventually came into view. A smile formed on her lips until she saw the looks of dread upon their faces, with Azalar looking the worst out of them all. Once they had all passed, Frella rushed over to Bark and asked him what had happened. A sad frown was his only response before they fled down the tunnel. With the last of the rodents gone, the tunnel finally collapsed, sealing the archway forever.

Chapter XVI

Azalar and the others made their way to the front of the crowd. As they did so, they passed all sorts of terrified and somber faces. When Azalar caught sight of the familiar faces of Ramy and Litha, he cast his eyes downward mournfully and shamefully. Once they had reached the front of the crowd, Frella attempted to hand the candle over to Azalar. However, she hesitated after seeing the state of being he was in. She instead handed the candle over to Brim, who then led the throng of rodents down the hall.

The tunnels had not stopped rumbling as the host of rodents ran down the halls. Dull crashing sounded behind them, and the halls trembled. It wasn't until they were a good distance away that the rumbling finally stopped. However, they did not stop running. They continued down the halls for a long while, turning this way and that, with Brim continuing to lead the way. Though they were sure that the Fornóc behind them were trapped in that cave in, the fear that there were other packs down there lingered in their minds and drove them forward. After a few more minutes of running, they were all becoming very weary and were forced to stop.

Brim had led them into a small little alcove in the hallway with a large door in the center of the wall. It wasn't a large space, and the door was sealed shut, but

347

it was a secure enough place to rest for the time being. After about ten minutes of rest, the reality of the recent events finally began to take hold. Soft cries echoed throughout the hall. Many rodents were lost during the battle with the Fornóc, and a great feeling of dread and mourning weighed upon them.

Azalar, Amara, Bark, Frella, Della, Brim, Mith, Borith, Bogger, Nikamius, Kilma and Elia had gathered together on the other side of the alcove away from the rest of the rodents to discuss their next course of action. Or at least that was the idea. Yet, their hearts were still heavy with grief, especially with Azalar, who sat along the wall with his head down and eyes shut. Amara sat next to her fréfil and nuzzled him close. She rested her head on his shoulder, holding Alice's earring to her chest. The events on the bridge were still fresh in her mind. The Fornóc, the chaos, the death, all of it. She trembled and nuzzled closer to Azalar, though he seemed to not have noticed her. Bark, not able to take the silence any longer, decided to speak up.

"So, what's the plan now?" asked Bark, sitting with his back against the wall. His muscles were aching, and his breath was heavy.

"The plan is the same as it was before," said Brim. "We stay together and find a way out of here." Bark gave a small scoff.

"That's not a plan," he laughed. "That's a wish list." Brim furrowed his eyebrows at him.

"It's the best that we have right now," Brim retorted. But then his face fell, and he looked towards the floor. "And it is all we can really do at this point."

"But where are we going?" asked Mith. "We can't keep roaming around the darkness forever. The Fornóc are sure to be on our tails before long."

"Now, now, there's no need for that kind of thought," said Nikamius, trying to calm them. "The Fornóc are trapped in the cave-in behind us, and it will be a long time before they find us again.

"We don't know that for certain," said Borith. "For all we know, they could very well be right behind us, and we wouldn't know about it until they're right on top of us."

"Will you guys quit it before you start a panic?" Brim said in a low tone. "We're on edge enough as it is. Right now, we need to focus on finding a way out of here."

"Was there anything in that book that you were reading before?" asked Bark. Bogger gave a heavy sigh. He had lost the book during the Fornóc attack, and it was no doubt burnt to ashes by now.

"No," Bogger replied. "Unfortunately, not. What I read to you all was all I could decipher. There was still so much we could have learned from those pages. But now they are lost forever. However, if I had to make a guess, my best would be to keep down the main hall and stick to it. It may be our best chance at finding an exit. Or at the very least find a way back to the main tunnel. There we can be sure there will be some form of exit, one way or another."

"We had better find it soon," muttered Bark. "We are all out of food, and those candles are only going to last us for so long. We also have many injured rodents amongst us. I hate to be the one to say it, but if we don't find that exit soon, many more rodents are going to perish."

"How many did we lose already?" asked Borith somberly. There was a brief moment of silence.

"Quite a few," said Mith with a heavy heart. "Nor was the first. We lost Milz, Jun, Trel, Tam, Ano, Bin, Macki and Fern during the initial fighting on the walls. Then we lost Mentro, Jennip, Ritter, Lock and Rocko during our final stand by the archway."

"We also lost Meeka, Vorola, Tilla and Gelora as well," said Frella, referring to the few female mice who charged the Fornóc with her.

"There were also several rats who died during the fighting," said Borith. "Six I believe it was. Rammin, Rorvu, Ronnto, Rathos, Radnif and… Reemus." Borith said the last name with great hesitation and sadness. He then looked over to Azalar, who still sat against the wall with his head down.

"That makes twenty-four," said Bogger grimly. "No small number."

"So many lost souls," said Nikamius. "Needlessly taken before their time. May Háth watch over them and protect them in the afterlife. May he guide them to everlasting rest and peace."

"At least they will no longer be suffering in this world," said Bogger. "I suppose we can think of it in that perspective."

"But what about their loved one?" Kilma asked. "I'm sure their loved ones would disagree with that statement." Every mouse turned to the mole. Many of them wanted to say something, but remained silent, for they knew that he was right. Amara, who sat nuzzled next to Azalar, looked over to the rest of the rodents. So many faces of sorrow and heartbroken cries. Amara's heart ached at the sight of their people. She then looked over at Azalar, who had heard the mole's words and lowered his head even further.

Azalar's heart was heavy with guilt and anguish. At first glance, it seemed as though he had fallen asleep, but his mind was anything but restful. All he could think about was all those who died, especially Reemus. When he shut his eyes, he could still see the terrified look in Reemus' eyes as he fell into the darkness. It was a look that Azalar would never forget.

"Azalar?" said a voice. Azalar looked up to see the familiar faces of Ramy and Litha, both of whom looked down at Azalar with furrowed brows.

"Azalar," said Ramy, his voice small and trembling. "What happened to Reemus?" Azalar could not bear to answer the young rat. His chest tightened and he almost found it difficult to breathe. He stared up at the two young rats for what seemed like an eternity before he lowered his gaze to the floor once again.

"I'm so sorry," he said in a low and soft voice. He started to feel tears welling up in his eyes, but he blinked them away, refusing to let them fall. "I'm so sorry. It was all my fault." Ramy took a step forward.

"What do you mean?" the young rat asked. Azalar took in a deep breath.

"All I could think about was keeping the Fornóc back. I fought as hard as I could to give everyone else time to escape, even if it meant that I probably wouldn't make it back." When he said that last part, he glanced slightly over at his frefil, who had a sad look in her eyes, before turning his gaze back down to the floor. "But then Reemus came to help me fight them off. I told him to go back but he refused. Instead, he chose to fight at my side." Azalar mustered enough courage to look up at the pair of young rats.

"He was an honorable rat. He knew the risk and danger, but he still chose to fight for his people. He was a brave rat. You should be very proud of him." Azalar tried to swallow the lump in his throat, remembering the courage and bravery he showed as Reemus fought alongside him. Azalar turned his head downwards again and shut his eyes tightly, trying to keep the tears from pouring out. "Then everything was collapsing. I told him to run, and we tried to make it back. But then the bridge collapsed. It all happened so fast. I turned around and he was just below me. I tried to reach him, but I couldn't. I'm so sorry. There was a moment of silence after his words. Amara gently placed a paw on her beloved fréfil's back in an attempt to comfort him, but he once again made no move of acknowledgement.

"So, you let him fall?" said Ramy, his voice lower and more serious. Azalar refused to look up and Ramy was standing right above him, his eyes furrowed deeply and his eyes hard.

"What?" was all Azalar could say before Ramy picked up the tan mouse and slammed him against the wall, causing Azalar to squeak in pain.

"You let him fall!" Ramy screamed. "You killed him!" The other mice, along with Kilma, all rose and nearly pounced on the young rat, but Azalar held up his paw to stop them, to which they reluctantly did so. The air was tense as all eyes were now on the pair, watching a rat pinning a mouse against the wall.

"He trusted you! And you killed him!" Ramy cried. Tears were streaming down his cheeks, and he stared angrily at the tan mouse, but Azalar made no move against him.

"Ramy! Calm down!" cried Litha, stepping closer to the pair.

"Young rat, release him immediately!" shouted Nikamius. But Ramy did not listen to either of them and continued to glare dangerously at Azalar.

"How could you let this happen to him?!" Ramy howled. "He looked up to you! He saw you as some kind of savior. He was my best friend. And you just left him behind! You didn't even try to save him, did you? You just let him die because you thought of yourself instead of him! You're no savior. You're no leader! You're nothing more than a pile of *mûk* hré-" He Was suddenly cut off when a massive paw came from behind and grabbed hold of Ramy's left arm.

Ramy turned and glared at the newcomer until he saw who it was standing behind him.

Ragath stared down at the young rat until he let go of Azalar, who immediately dropped to his paws and knees. Ramy stared wide eyed at the great black rat, who held a firm grip on the young rat's arm.

"R-Ragath!" muttered Ramy to himself. Ragath gave no reply, instead he simply gave a deep frown at the young rat. The intense stare from Ragath and his immense size, who, in comparison, was over twice the size of the young rats, did cause Ramy to back down just a little. Yet, the burning anger in his heart was strong and gave Ramy the courage to stare back defiantly.

"Young rat, you cannot blame Azalar," said Nikamius. "There was nothing that anyone could have done. We were beset upon by the Fornóc. If Azalar had held them off, the Fornóc would have continued to pursue us, and who knows how many lives could have been taken? Reemus was a brave rat and held true to the very end. Azalar did everything he could to save Reemus. You must understand this."

"No. He's right," said Azalar, who was still kneeling on the floor; his voice gaining everyone's attention. "It was my responsibility to protect him. I should have done more to save him. I should have just sent him back to the others instead of letting him stay on the bridge with me. I should have stayed behind and let him run ahead of me. then maybe he would have had a chance. But I didn't. And because of that he was trapped on the bridge. I tried to reach out to him. I tried to grab him! I tried! But it wasn't enough. I let him die!" Azalar was becoming more frantic with every word he spoke. By the end of it all, he was practically sobbing. He knelt forward while grabbing his head with both paws, grabbing tufts of his fur. Everyone sat silent as they watched the tan color mouse crumble before them, frowning sadly at their poor friend. Even Bark was unsure on how to comfort him.

"It was all my fault!" Azalar sobbed.

"No, it wasn't!" Amara said. "You did everything that you could. It wasn't your fault."

"Yeah," said Bark. "If anything, it was the Fornóc. They're the ones that should be to blame. Not you." But their words fell on deaf ears as he continued to sob. The others around him watched silently, feeling almost as defeated as Azalar. Other rodents had gathered because of the commotion and were now witnessing as their leader broke down in front of them. The air was silent with only the sound of Azalar's cries echoing through the halls.

"I'm sorry!" Azalar said softly between sobs. "I failed you all. I've only led you all into darkness and death. I've done nothing but bring you all more misery."

"That's not true, my love!" said Amara in a stern voice. She then placed a paw beneath her fréfil's chin and lifted his head so that he would look her in the eye. "You freed us from Helgan's cages. You led us through the unknown and have remained determined. You've stood against great foes by yourself and have never faltered once. You have done more than any mouse or rat has done before."

"That is right, my friend," said Nikamius. "We knew the road ahead would be dangerous and we chose to follow you nonetheless."

"You have led us this far, Azalar," said Bogger. "I see no reason for us not to follow you now."

"We were all ready to risk everything for freedom," said Brim. "You have given us courage that we have never had before. You've shown us the way. And we will continue to follow you." Azalar sat silently as he listened to his friends' words. He looked at each of their faces, and they all had genuine smiles. Those that had not spoken nodded their heads in agreement. Azalar then looked to the rest of the crowd around. It was the same with them as well. Though there was sadness in many of their eyes, they all smiled and nodded in acknowledgement. He looked to Kilma and Elia, and they were smiling as well. Azalar then looked to Ragath. And though he was not smiling, his eyes also held the same conviction and determination as before, and he gave a nod. Azalar stared at each and every rodent around him, and his heart fluttered. The sadness and defeat that hung in his heart slowly disappeared, and joy, pride and hope began to kindle within him. As if lifting the heavy weight of sorrow anguish on his shoulders, Azalar slowly stood up to full height, smiling at every one of his dear friends.

"Thank you all," he said. "Forgive me and my moment of weakness. The weight of the pressure and loss of our friends had overcome me. Though the guilt is still heavy on my heart, you have all reminded me of why I do this: to find us a new home, and to ensure that all of you are free and safe. Though, I daresay that I was foolish to believe that I could get us all there without loss, for that was a pup's dream. I know now that the world is full of danger and that many of us may not make it, including myself. This is the risk we all took. And I cannot thank you all enough for taking it with me.

"And I say this with my full heart that I am sorry. Sorry for the loss that many of you bear. I wish I could take it all back. But let us remember those who have fallen and given their lives to ensure that we made it out safely; and let us honor their sacrifices. They will be remembered as the heroes who faced off against the Fornóc, whose sacrifice gave us the chance to find our home and our freedom." There were soft murmurs of agreement amongst the crowd, many shedding tears not of sadness, but of pride for their loved ones whom they lost. Even Litha smiled tearfully, her heart full of both sadness and pride. She would remember Reemus for all time.

Ramy however, was not among them, as he had left and angrily pushed his way through the crowd. Emerging from the crowd, he saw another large group of rodents gathered on the other side of the alcove, all of whom were rats, some twenty or so. One of these rats in particular was Razor, Ragath's second in command. Ramy made his way over to the rats, where Razor took notice of him. The larger black rat approached the young rat and placed an arm around his shoulders.

"There, there, young one," said Razor softly, seeing the anger burning in Ramy's eyes. "What is causing you such distress?"

"He killed my best friend," said Ramy, his fists balled at his sides and angry tears running down his cheeks. "That mouse killed my best friend! Just left him to die."

"Yes, I know," said Razor. "Azalar has gotten many of our kind killed. Many of our friends fell because of his failures and incompetence. That's a mouse for you. But do not dishearten, young one, for we rats are a strong race. We will recover from this tragedy. But we will not forget." Ramy looked up at the larger rat.

"What do you mean?" he asked earnestly.

"I mean that we must be patient, young rat," Razor whispered. "There will be a time for us, but it is not yet. We must bide our time. But there will be more talk of that later. For now, let us rest. There will be plenty of time to plan for the future, once we finally leave this forsaken darkness. So come and take heart, young Ramy. For you are among friends now. We will hear your sorrow. And we will heal your troubled heart." Razor then pulled Ramy towards the group of rats, and though his heart was still full of grief, Ramy gave a warm smile to his new friends.

After an hour's rest, the large group of rodents set out again. Though they were still weary from the terrible events that occurred, they were very eager to get out of these dreaded halls as quickly as possible. Azalar took one of the candles and led the others onward, holding the lit wax stick, which by this point had melted a third of the way, and had a long wooden stick at the bottom as a handle, as were the other candles. Azalar held the candle high to light their way, and he was closely followed by his Amara. To his right Bark and Frella traveled closely, while Brim and Della walked to Azalar's left. Behind them was Bogger and Nikamius, followed by Borith and Mith. Kilma and Elia were close behind, who were then followed by the rest of the great throng of rodents. Ragath and Razor took up the rear guard, escorted by several other rats, in case of any surprise attacks from the Fornóc. Ramy was by Razor's side while carrying one of the candles, much to Ragath's curiosity. Razor noticed Ragath looking their way and told the giant black rat a story that Ramy wanted to learn how to be a fighter, and that he asked Razor to teach him how. Ragath raised an eyebrow at the two but said nothing else on the matter.

They traveled for over half an hour, turning this way and that around each corner. They were cautious as they turned every corner, checking to make sure the way was clear of any enemies. Though the light from their candles gave them some relief, the gloom of the halls ahead gave them much dread and anxiety, for at any moment they might see the terrible red eyes of the Fornóc. Azalar kept his courage and led his people onward, holding his candle high above as if it were their beacon of hope and bravery. They came across several intersections, forcing them to stop and plan for which way to go. At the first intersection, they made a right turn. After ten minutes, they came to a dead end: a collapsed hallway and were forced to turn back and take the right side. This led to another intersection, where Azalar led them down the straight hall, where their path came to several more twists and turns. They passed many great doors along their travels, some of which were opened or broken. But they were very cautious as they passed by, careful not to get too close for fear of ambush.

The rodents once again came to another intersection, but one path on the right was blocked by rubble, while the other two led left and straight. They decided to take the straight path, which then led to a sharp turn to the left. However, as soon as they turned the corner, they were met with another cave-in blocking their path. Left with no other choice, the rodents turned back and took the only remaining path left to them. Following down the hall for several minutes and taking a right turn, they came to the end of a hall, where a pair of black doors, both brokens of their hinges and hanging open.

The rodents passed through the doors, with Azalar holding up the candle higher to give them more light. The rodents found themselves in a great empty hall, with large tables and chairs thrown haphazardly about. Large pieces of rubble from the ceiling were scattered all over the hall, with some having fallen on many tables, shattering them, or breaking them in half. But what truly caught their attention and filled them with dread, were the remains of a human in front of them, whose bones were crushed under a large piece of rubble.

Azalar led his people slowly through the hall, avoiding the skeletal remains of the human as they passed. Though their flesh was gone, the smell of death seemed to linger in the air. The rodents huddled closer together, some of the female mice nuzzling their mates close to avoid the sight. Amara stood close to Azalar, but she made no attempt to avoid her eyes from the human remains. In fact, she stared intently at the bones, her brows furrowed in a somber frown, as if she were mourning their passing. Once they had passed, Amara turned back forward, but closed her eyes and raised the gemstone to her nose and began muttering to herself. Azalar wasn't certain, but he was sure that she was saying a small prayer for the deceased human. Though he didn't quite see the point it, he still appreciated how kindhearted Amara was.

The rodents passed through the hall without incident until they came to the other side, where another set of doors in front of them. A chair was wedged between them, so the doors were wide open, and the rodents could pass under the chair with no effort. They entered a long hallway, where to the left stretched far into the gloom, while the right was the same cave-in that they had blocked their path previously.

Turning to the left, the rodents walked for another half hour until they came to what appeared to be a dead end, a pair of great black doors, much larger than the ones they passed through before, barring their way. At first the doors appeared shut, and just as the doors they came across before, there was no handle on its black surface. But upon closer inspection, one the doors were slightly ajar, held open by a small stone. This allowed Azalar and several other rodents to pry the door open, allowing them to pass through, where before them they found themselves surrounded by darkness in a vast cavernous hall.

The hall was wide, long, and empty. Not even the light from their candles could illuminate the whole chamber. However, from what they could see, it was a hall similar to the one they had set up camp in before they were attacked; a stone floor with tall stone pillars lined along the hall. Only this time it was completely empty; no large piles of wooden pallets or fallen rock and debris. The hall looked as if it had just been untouched by time. Yet, it was that very emptiness that gave an eerie feeling. Nevertheless, they continued on their journey. As they traveled to the far end of the hall, Azalar caught sight of something strange up ahead. From what little light they had, he could see on the far wall four huge squares. It was strange because they were evenly spaced apart and looked different to the rest of the wall.

However, the closer they came to these huge squares, they could see that they were not of the stone that made the walls, but large, rippled sheets of metal, each with a long chain hanging from one side.

"What are these things?" asked Bark. Bogger stepped closer to get a better observation. He studied the steel walls silently for a long moment before he spoke up.

"I could be wrong," he said, "but it seems that these sheets of rippled metal were placed here to reinforce the walls. But for what purpose that might be, I wonder. But whatever the case, it seems that we have reached another dead end."

"What's that over there?" said Elia, pointing off to the far left side of the hall. Everyone turned their gazes to where the young chipmunk was pointing to, and there they could see faint flicker coming from underneath the far metal wall. Curious, Azalar led the crowd over to where the flickering was. There they could see that there was an opening along the entire bottom of the metal wall, just large enough for them to crawl underneath.

"I'll go first," said Azalar, holding the candle in his left paw and wielding his needle weapon in the other. He knelt down and crawled under the metal wall. There he found himself on a huge platform, where he was now in a massive tunnel just like the ones when he and his fellow rodents first entered. The flickering was from the light that hung from the ceiling above. Seeing the familiar sight of these tunnels almost made Azalar smile. If anything else, it possibly meant that they were that much closer to finding a way out. Azalar took a moment to check his surroundings.

"It's safe!" Azalar called back to the others. Slowly the rest of the rodents crawled under the metal wall and gathered next to Azalar.

"I stand corrected," muttered Bogger to himself, staring up at the metal sheets. "It appears that these are actually some sort of doors. How strange."

"So where do we go now?" asked Mith. Nikamius stepped from the crowd to the edge of the platform. He then lifted his head up as high as he could and sniffed the air. He turned his head to the left, then to the right, then back again. He did this several times before he finally lowered his head.

"That way," he said, pointing his staff to the left. "There is a very faint breeze and the air smells slightly fresher in that direction."

"Okay then," said Azalar as walked over to the edge and peered downward. The platform itself was several mice high, probably around shoulder length of a human. A jump from that would no doubt cause some serious injury, especially to those who were already injured. "Now we just need to find a way down."

"That won't be too hard!" cried Bark, gaining everyone's attention, The dark brown mouse was on the far right side of the platform pointing down. "We can just get down from here." Azalar and the others rushed over to where Bark was to see a set of stairs leading down to the floor below.

"Good job, Bark," said Bogger with a smirk. "Seems that you're not entirely useless after all." Bogger finished the statement with a wink. Bark glared at the dark red mouse and was about to retort when Azalar spoke up.

"Alright," he called out to everyone. "Let's get down gently! And be sure to help the injured down. Let's go!" With that, the large band of rodents began the climb down from the platform until they were all safe at the bottom floor. Once everyone was safely down and gathered together, Azalar led the way down the left side tunnel, with Nikamius right beside him.

The host of rodents travels in the center of the tunnel, between the tracks as they had before in the previous tunnel. They must have been walking for a good while because their candles were now halfway burnt out. However, unlike the tunnels that they traveled through before, these tunnels were far less damaged.

Every now and then they would come across a large boulder that had fallen from the ceiling, or a wide crack that they would have to traverse over. Those obstacles were few and far between, though, making the journey much easier on the rodents. However, after two hours of walking, the host of rodents were growing wearier by the minute. Their candles were slowly burning out and their pace was slowing, especially those that were injured. There were almost no lights within the tunnels, and they had only a couple hours left of their candles. Nonetheless, they had to keep going. They had to find the exit.

As Azalar and Amara were walking side by side at the front of the crowd, they heard a voice call out to them.

"Azalar!" called the voice from behind. Azalar and Amara turned to see Litha walking quickly through the crowd towards him. "I was hoping I could have a word with you, if that is alright?" Azalar smiled at the young female rat.

"Of course, you may," he said with a nod. Litha grinned and quickened her pace to catch up to the pair until she was between the two of them.

"I just wanted to apologize for Ramy's behavior," she said. "It was unbecoming and undeserving. I'm sorry and I ask you to please forgive him." Azalar gave a slight chuckle and placed a paw on the young female rat's shoulder.

"You have nothing to apologize for and there is nothing to forgive," Azalar said. "Losing a friend is a difficult thing to handle. His outburst is more than understandable. You can rest assured that I hold no ill will towards your friend." Litha's smile grew wider.

"Thank you, Azalar. That means so much to me." Litha's smile then fell into a frown, and she cast her eyes towards the floor. "Reemus was our best friend. He helped us a lot during the trials and experiments of Helgan's lab. He was what kept us together, and he was what kept us moving. If it wasn't for him, I don't think Ramy or I would have made it." Azalar glanced at Amara, who had a small smile on her face as she watched the young female rat, before returning his attention to Litha.

"He must have admired him a lot," Azalar stated. Litha smiled and nodded her head.

"Yes," she said with a sad chuckle, tears beginning to weld in her eyes. "He was very important to me. He gave me so much courage. He inspired me to follow you. He said that you were the savior." Azalar raised an eyebrow at this statement.

"Savior?" Azalar asked. "I remember Ramy saying something like that. What does Reemus mean that I was the savior?" Litha looked up at Azalar with a smile, tears now streaming down her furry cheeks.

"It was about a few weeks before Helgan changed our bodies, Reemus told Ramy and I about this dream that he had. He told us that a mouse would come and lead us out of that hell and deliver us to a better future. Where we would no longer be tortured by Helgan or any other human ever again. At first, we didn't believe him. I mean, a mouse of all things. I mean no disrespect, mind you. But if Ragath couldn't escape from the cages, how could a mouse accomplish this?" Azalar gave a chuckle in response.

"I don't blame you for thinking that," he said. "If I had heard that back a month ago, I probably would have thought the same thing." Litha gave a chuckle in return.

"But Reemus was so sure that a mouse would be the one to lead us. For weeks he would tell us about the same dream every day. It drove Ramy crazy. Then, on the day that our bodies were changed, Reemus saw you lifting those weights. No matter how many weights the humans placed on you, you refused to give up. That's when Reemus knew that it would be you. You would be our savior."

"It seems that Reemus had more faith in me than even I did," Azalar said.

"I never had any doubt," said Amara, glancing up with a loving smile at her fréfil. "I knew that if anyone could do it, it would be you, my love." Azalar returned the smile before turning back to Litha.

"So, what was Reemus like?" he asked. "Besides being courageous and stubborn." Azalar finished the last sentence with a laugh, which Litha returned wholeheartedly.

"Yes, he was very stubborn," she retorted. "He was also very brave. No matter what the humans put him through, he faced it head on and without hesitation. He was the bravest rat that I knew, I mean, besides Ragath of course. But he was also the sweetest. He always made sure that Ramy and I were alright at the end of every day. He didn't care how much pain he was in, he always put others before himself.

"Sounds like someone I know," said Amara in a teasing voice as she looked up at a certain tan mouse, who gave a sheepish grin in response. "Judging by how you speak, you sound like a rodent in love." Litha glanced away with a sheepish grin.

"Yes," she said. "I was indeed in love with him. No point in denying it. For a very long time I was in love with him. We actually shared a cage together. He was such an amazing rat. I will always remember the night I finally confessed my feelings for him." Amara placed both paws to her lips to hide the giddy smile she was having.

"Oh, how wonderful!" she squeaked. "How did it go?" Litha looked down at the floor with a loving smile.

"It was wonderful. It was the very night that we escaped, just before you got us out of our cages, Azalar. After the humans had left for the night, I told Reemus how I felt about him and he accepted me. It was then that we shared the nest and finally became fréfils."

"Oh, that's wonderful!" Amara cried, reaching over and nuzzling the young female rat. "I'm so happy for you!" Litha happily accepted as she smiled at the snow white mouse.

"It was wonderful," she spoke softly. "Our bodies joined together as we gave our hearts to each other and to Háth. Never have I had a more blissful night that ended too soon." As Litha spoke, Azalar's face fell into a frown, and he cast his eyes downward shamefully.

"I am so sorry, Litha," he said just above a whisper, his voice full of sorrow and remorse. "I wish I could have done more to save him. He didn't deserve such a fate." There was a brief silence, save for the echoing patter of the hundreds of paws tapping against the tile floors as they walked. Then Azalar felt a paw softy placed upon his right arm, and he turned to see Litha smiling sadly at him.

"You have nothing to apologize for, Azalar," Litha said. "I do not blame you for his death. You did all that you could. And you should not feel any shame for yourself. He greatly admired you. And I know that he would have gladly given his life if it meant for the rest of us to live. That's just the kind of rat that he was. An honorable rat. Just as you are an honorable mouse, Azalar. So please do not blame yourself anymore. I know he would not want that. Just as you said before: we should remember and honor him for his sacrifice. All of their sacrifices." Azalar stared at the young female rat for a moment before a smile traced his lips. He then gently placed a paw upon hers.

"You're right, Litha," he said. "I will not carry the weight of the dead, but I will carry their memories in my heart. And may we find and build a home that Reemus would be proud of." Litha smiled wider as Amara placed a paw upon Litha's shoulder, and the three shared a moment of silence with one another.

"It's getting brighter up ahead!" called Borith from behind. And it was true. Further down the tunnel, around the bend, a dim light shining on the wall. A small glimmer of hope kindled in their hearts and motivated them forward. Hopeful that this was the deliverance that they were searching for, the entire band quickened their pace towards the light.

Once they rounded the bend, there they could see it. Far up ahead, there was the wall opened up into a large platform on the right hand side and there was a dim light shining through. Next to the platform was a large metal cart parked a little further aways.

"There it is!" cried Bark! "We found it!" Cheers rang out from every rodent, and their hearts soared. Many rodents hugged each other while others hopped and cheered. Even Kilma and Elia couldn't contain their excitement as the young chipmunk began hopping in place with Kilma giving a soft chuckle. Azalar and Amara embraced one another tightly before the same embrace with Litha, who smiled and giggled happily. Azalar then took Amara by the paw and led her down the tunnel towards the platform. Towards their freedom.

Even Ragath and Razor couldn't stop themselves from joining in the celebration. The two black rats wrapped an arm around each other, laughing victoriously. Never before had they been so thrilled, not even when they finally escaped their cages. However, just at that moment, Ragath stopped where he was, his face falling to a frown. Something wasn't right, he could feel it. But what was it?

He searched left and right, and up and down, but he could not find anything wrong. He then looked back into the gloom behind him. He stared into the darkness for a few moments, then a chill ran up his spine. Ragath quickly knelt down and placed a hand on the floor and felt the stone beneath his paws beginning to tremble. Something was coming.

Ragath looked back up into the darkness of the tunnel. He pursed his ears up and listened carefully, trying to hear past the celebrating rodents. For a moment he couldn't hear anything out of the ordinary, but then he heard it. The faint shrilling cries deep in the gloom, and they were getting louder. Ragath's eyes widened at the sound and quickly turned around.

"Fornóc!" Ragath cried out, his voice carrying louder and cutting through the cheering rodents, enough for those at the back to hear him and quiet themselves, with some turning back behind them, including Azalar and the others.

"Fornoc!" Ragath cried again as he rushed back towards the throng, his voice more clear as it echoed through the tunnels. Hearing that single word caused the rest of the rodents to panic and run towards the platform. Azalar immediately took both Amara and

Litha by the paws and pulled them ahead. Bark did the same with Frella, as Brim did with Della. Bogger and Nikamius were right behind them, with Borith and Mith following soon after. Kilma picked up Elia and carried her on his back as he dashed forward, trying his best to avoid getting knocked to the floor.

The rest of the rodents were screaming and panicking as they all ran for the platform. They all ran as fast as they could, with some tripping and falling to the floor, while others getting pushed and shoved. Fortunately, they had all spread themselves apart as they ran, so no one was trampled or injured too seriously. Razor and Ramy came up from the rear, helping up any rat that had fallen, while leaving the mice to fend for themselves. Ramy tried to help an injured mouse up, but Razor quickly pulled him away.

"We help our own," Razor whispered sternly to the young rat. Ramy looked back at the injured mouse as he struggled to pick himself up before turning back and following Razor down the tunnel, a small part of him feeling guilty for leaving other rodents behind. Just then, Ragath came from behind and helped the poor mouse on his feet, along with any who had stumbled or had been shoved to the floor, both mice and rats. Unfortunately, Ragath had been too preoccupied to notice Razor and Ramy's actions, as he would frequently look back to see how far the Fornóc were. So far, he could not see them, but he knew they were getting closer as the rumbling beneath his paws slowly grew with every second.

Azalar, Amara and Litha had just reached the bottom of the platform, but the platform itself was far too high to reach. More and more rodents followed close behind, with some attempting to climb the walls, others trying to climb over their fellow rodents. Azalar witnessed the chaos before him and was unsure of what to do next. His mind was racing but he couldn't focus or think of what to do. The Fornóc were coming, and they were trapped down here waiting to be slaughtered.

Azalar looked over to Amara, who was holding Litha tightly in her arms as if trying to protect her. The moment he looked at his fréfil, he suddenly remembered how he was able to free her from the slab back on the lab table.

"Form a tower!" Azalar shouted. But they couldn't hear him over the sound of their own shouting. "Form a tower!" he called again. Bark and Brim, who were close by, heard what Azalar had said and called out to the other. "Form a tower!" they cried in unison. Some of the rodents heard what they were saying and quickly began forming a tower. But it was still not enough to get their attention.

"Shut it!" bellowed a deep voice. This was finally enough to get the crowd silent enough to listen as they turned to the source of the powerful voice.

"Everyone, shut your mouths!" Ragath shouted. "Stop panicking and start forming a tower. Now!" The booming roar of Ragath's voice was the push that they needed to cooperate with one another. The strongest amongst the rodents were down at the bottom, mostly made up of the largest and strongest of the rats; this included Ragath and Razor. They slowly began to climb on top of one another in a united manner, working together to help each other build and stabilize the tower. They were almost there, just a few more rodents needed to reach the platform.

Azalar, who was still at the bottom, told Bark and Brim to climb up next. They were hesitant at first, but they gave each other a brief glance before nodding their heads and climbing up the rodent ladder. They were able to reach the top quickly, with Brim climbing to the very top and Bark climbing on top of him. Bark stretched up to grab the platform above his head, but he could not reach it. They were just one rodent short and the tower was beginning to wobble from the wight.

Azalar was about to make the climb himself, until a small figure raced past him and began climbing the tower. Azalar watched as Elia climbed up the rodents with amazing speed, quickly placing herself on top of Bark's shoulders. She reached up to the platform and grabbed hold of the edge. Azalar couldn't help but smile at the young chipmunk's initiative before he turned to Amara, Della, Frella and Litha.

"As soon as I get to the top," he said, "get up there as soon as you can." The moment those words left his mouth, Azalar sprang for the tower, jumping up and climbing the other rodents as quickly as he could. He then reached the top, but the moment he did, he tossed his needle over the platform, scooped Elia up and tossed her on the platform above. Elia rolled along the stone floor before picking herself up and rushing back to aid Azalar, grabbing hold of his paws. Azalar smiled up at the young chipmunk, who returned the smile with a nod. Azalar then looked over his shoulders and called down to the others.

"Climb now!" he cried. Without hesitation, those that remained on the floor quickly climbed up the rodent tower and onto the platform, some turning back to help the others up. Soon over half the rodents were up on the platform. Ragath, who was at the bottom of the tower, could hear the sound of glass breaking in his ears.

Ragath turned his head slightly back down the tunnel and, from the far end of the tunnel around the bend, a light had fallen from the ceiling and was now flickering rapidly, shining a beam against the wall. It flickered three times before going dark. A moment it flickered once more, and dozens of large, black shadows shone on the wall.

"Get a move on!" Ragath bellowed, urging them to move faster. The last of the rodents had already begun to climb, with only those that made up the tower remaining below. Once the last of the rodents had climbed onto the platform, Kilma, who was the very last one to reach the top, turned around, grabbed Azalar's paws and began to pull.

Amara, Litha, Della, Frella and Elia quickly joined, each grabbing onto each other's waists and pulled. Others quickly joined them and together they slowly pulled the rodents up from the track floor. Those that had already been pulled onto the platform quickly lent their aid as well.

Ragath and Razor, as well as the several other rats that formed the bottom of the tower, were now, at this time, being lifted from the floor. As they climbed higher, Ragath turned his head back down the tunnel and dozens of Fornóc began to emerge from the darkness, their cries were deafening to the ears, piercing their ears like sharp knives. And for the first time, in his life, he felt fear.

"Pull us up already!" cried Ragath. Azalar, hearing Ragath's voice, instinctively looked up and turned down the tunnel. His eyes widened with horror at the sight of the Fornóc fast approaching.

"Pull harder!" he cried. Everyone together at once pulled as hard as they could, lifting the rodents below higher and higher. The first swarm of Fornóc rushed forward across the tracks, closing in on Ragath and the others. Once they were close enough, first of the Fornóc leaped forward and attempted to pounce on the vulnerable rodents.

Fortunately, Azalar and the others managed to pull them up just as the Fornóc jumped up and bit at their feet, just missing by an inch. Ragath, wanting to give them one last blow, used his tail that was currently gripping his sword and swung it downward, striking a

Fornóc in the head. Ragath and Razor gave a mocking laugh before they were lifted up onto the platform floor.

Once everyone was safely up, Azalar took one last over the edge, where there was an endless sea of red eyes glaring up at him going as far back into the gloom as he could see. For a moment, Azalar thought they were safe. That is until they began climbing over each other, slowly getting closer to the platform's edge. Azalar's eyes widened, and he quickly turned back to the others.

"Let's go!" he cried. "Follow me!" He then picked up his needle from the floor and dashed forward through the crowd, taking Amara's paw as he ran by. Bark and Frella followed close behind, with Brim, Della, Blogger, Nikamius, Borith and Mith right at their tails. Kilma also took Elia by the paw and pulled her with the rest of them. The rest of the rodents quickly followed suit, all running as fast as their legs could carry them across the floor.

The platform extended into another cavernous hall, much wider than any they had been to so far. But instead of a stone surface, the floor was a smooth tile pattern, much like the floors of the Helgan's laboratory. The hall itself wasn't as long, nor was it as lofty, yet there were still several rows of tall pillars stretching from one side of the room to the other. The pillars were much smoother and more neatly carved, giving them a more elegant look. They were also round in shape instead of the square they had seen before and were not as thick or as spaced out as they were in the other halls. There were dozens of large pieces of furniture shaped like wide chairs all throughout the hall. Many of them were tipped over, while others shattered into pieces, but most stood upright and facing towards the back of the hall. The floors were littered with trash and debris, and the rodents had to be careful not to trip or stumble over them.

When they emerged, Azalar and the other rodents were on the rightmost side of the hall. At the far end, Azalar could see two great archways by each corner of the hall. They made their way for the nearest to them. Within the archway, there was a staircase going upwards that reached a little over the halfway mark of the arches, before sharply turning to the left. On the wall just up the stairs there was a dim light casting upon it.

"Hurry!" Azalar cried.

They were halfway across the hall, but the cries and shrieks of the Fornóc did not falter, nor did they grow faint. Ragath took a quick glance behind, and due to his great height, he was able to see over the heads of most of the rodents. There he could see the Fornóc were climbing over onto the platform.

"Get moving!" Ragath barked, beckoning the others forward.

The horrid cries of the Fornóc grew louder as dozens of them climbed onto the platform and chased after the rodents and were slowly gaining ground. Before long they would be upon them, and out in the open hall they would be overwhelmed. The rodents quickened their pace, pushing their aching muscles as hard as they might, desperate to reach the exit. They had finally reached the bottom of the stairs and Azalar stepped to the side and urged the others on.

"Climb!" Azalar barked. "Climb!" The stairs were not that tall, and each rodent barely had to struggle to climb, save for those most injured. He then looked to his beloved fréfil.

"Go on ahead," he said. "I'll be right behind you." Amara was hesitant for a moment, thinking that Azalar was going to do the same thing he did on the bridge. However, once she looked into his eyes, she could see a different look in them. She then nodded her head and did what he asked and began climbing the stairs. Azalar then looked to Bark, Nikamius and Bogger.

"Lead them out of here!" he said. Bark frowned at his friend.

"What are you going to do?" he asked sternly. Azalar smiled and placed a paw on his best friend's shoulder.

"Don't worry," Azalar said softly, "I'm not going to do anything stupid this time. I promise." Bark stared into Azalar's eyes for a brief moment before sighing and turning up the stairs. Nikamius and Bogger gave the tan colored mouse a nod before ascending the stairs as well. Just then Azalar noticed Kilma and Elia fast approaching. Azalar aided the chipmunk and the mole up the first step and went on to help others. He then took notice that Ragath in the center of the crowd was doing the same thing as well. Azalar smiled at the giant rat before returning to his task. As soon as the vast majority of the Rodents had already begun the climb, Azalar and Ragath quickly began their own climb up the steps. Azalar could hear the shrill cries of the Fornóc behind him and dared to take a quick glance. He almost regretted it.

Down below, the entirety of the hall was covered by thousands of Fornóc, far more than he ever thought possible. Their red eyes gleaming with rage and anger in the dim light.

"What are you doing?!" Ragath shouted, startling the mouse out of his shock. "Get your sorry tail moving!" Azalar followed the great black rat up the stairs, practically hopping over each step. They reached the topmost step and followed the path to the right, just as they rounded the corner, Azalar saw from the corner of his eye the Fornóc reaching the bottom steps. The throng of rodents pushed onward down the long hall, where in the center of the left hand side wall opened up to another set of stairs. Azalar and Ragath hurried with the crowd, glancing back every now and then just as the Fornóc rounded the corner. By that time the rodents at the front had already begun climbing the next set of stairs. Once Ragath and Azalar had reached the bottom steps, Azalar looked up to see a dark blue and bright orange ceiling at the top. Something was off about it, the ceiling looked bright for some reason. He had no time to dwell on this as he quickly hopped over the first step.

The rodents' pace was slowing down as their muscles were growing weary with the climb. Yet, they had to keep going or else they would be at the mercy of the Fornóc, and they didn't seem merciful. Around halfway up the stairs, Both Ragath and Azalar took a chance to glance back down the steps, expecting to see the Fornóc pursuing them. However, upon glancing back, Azalar noticed that the Fornóc were no longer chasing them; they had all gathered at the bottom of the stair, hissing, and screeching at them, but refusing to move any a step further. Azalar and Ragath briefly looked at one another, greatly confused by their actions and wondered what had caused them to halt. He quickly pushed the thought aside, not wanting to stick around for the Fornóc to change their minds.

They had finally reached the top of the steps, where Azalar and Ragath saw that the rest of the rodents had gathered some distance away. They were all looking at their surroundings in wonder and awe. Azalar, seeing as the Fornóc were no longer pursuing them, took a moment to look up to survey their new environment. What he saw greatly astonished him.

Before them was a whole new world entirely. Tall and imposing structures surrounded them, taller than anything they had ever seen before. Great green trees were scattered about, their branches softly dancing in the cool and fresh breeze that gently caressed their fur.

Far off in the distance, past the tall structures, they could see huge peaks stretched up towards the great ceiling. It was then that Azalar realized that that wasn't a ceiling at all. It was the sky.

The sky was a dark blue, and the closer it got to the great peaks there was a beautiful pink and orange rim on the horizon, where a great golden sphere slowly began to rise up from behind the peaks. Azalar looked up at the sky and there, just a little towards the south, or at least that's what he thought to be south, a single star gleamed above their heads. Azalar stared at that star for what seemed like forever. He let out a long sigh, as if he had been holding his breath for his whole life. He closed his eyes and felt the fresh air circle around him.

They were free.